# The
# Kilhellion

Cover art by Roslyn Lindquist
Interior book design by Kamila Miller
http://kzmiller.com

Also available as an ebook.

ISBN: 978-1-952110-01-6
First edition, November 2025

Thank you for your patronage.

# The Kilhellion

Book One of the True Dawn Series

# E.M. PRAZEMAN

Wyrd goat PRESS

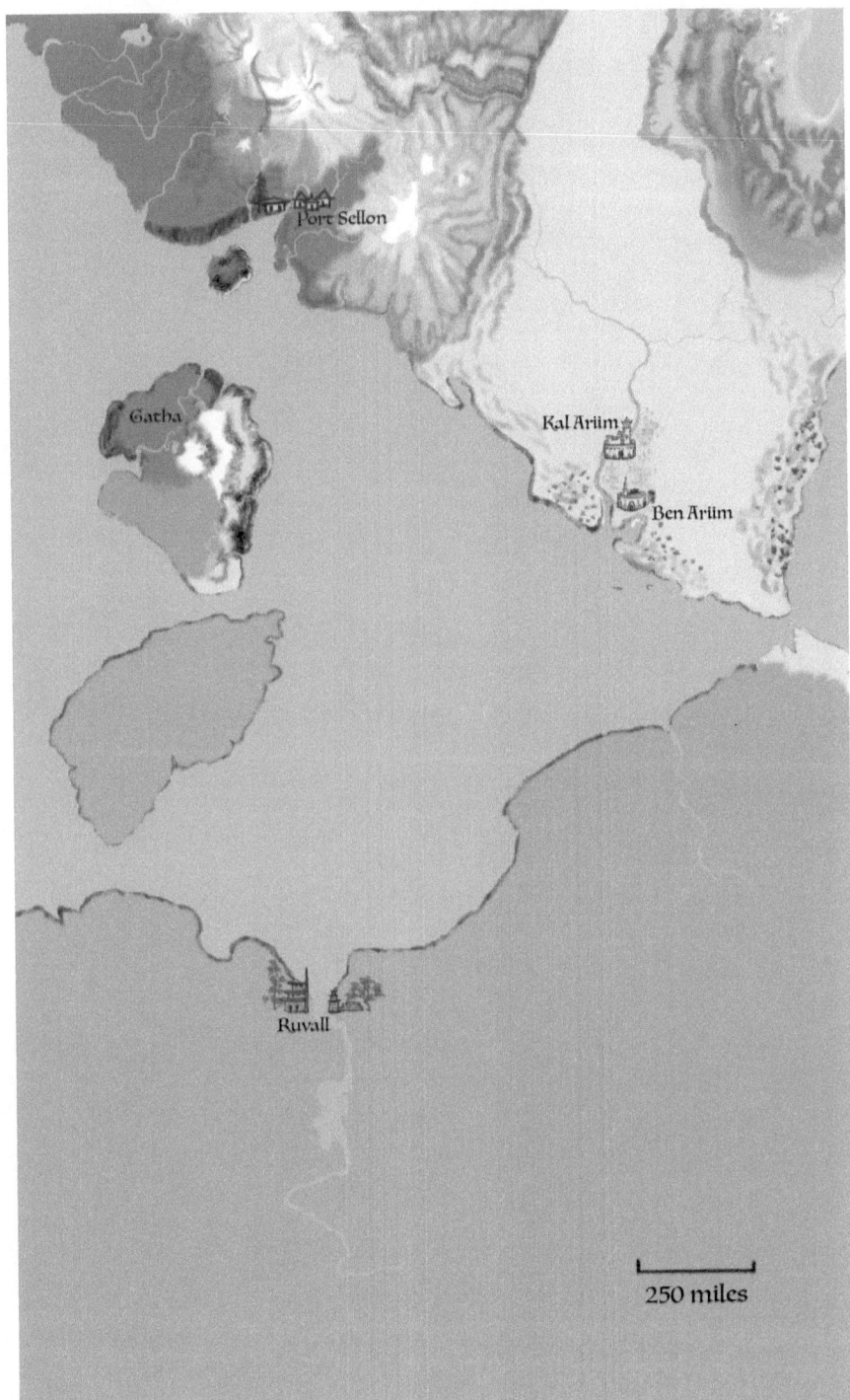

# Days and Nights of the Week

| Meet Day | Bless Night | Labor Day | Rest Night | Trade Day | Gift Night | Somber Day |
|---|---|---|---|---|---|---|
| True Night | Fear Day | Dark Night | Lost Day | Blind Night | Dread Day | Watch Night |

There are four of each day and night every month
Good Days: Four Days and Three Nights (Meet-Somber)
True Night: Four Nights and Three Days (True-Watch)
Every month has 28 days and nights

# Months of the Year
## and Common Festival Days

**Fangs**
Timeless Watch (continued): 1st Meet Day

**Fast**
Elders Day: 1st Labor Day

**Storms**
Life Equinox: 4rth Somber Day

**Rains**

**Bloom**
Solace: 2nd Rest Night

**Sun**
Festival of Flowers: 2nd Labor Day

**Flame**
Sun Festival: 1st Somber Day–2nd Somber Day
Games Day: 4rth Labor Day
Honors Day: 4rth Somber Day

**Harvest**
Offerings: 3rd Gift Night

**Wandering**
Star Gazing: 2nd Gift Night

**Fall**
Feast Equinox: Second Somber Day

**Frost**
Cellar Festival: 4rth Labor Day

**Keep**
Builders Day: 1st Meet Day
Forge Night: 1st Bless Night

**Night**
Death's Night: 3rd True Night

## Chapter One

◇◇◇◇◇◇◇◇◇◇◇◇◇◇◇◇◇◇◇◇◇◇◇◇◇◇◇◇◇◇◇◇◇◇◇◇◇◇◇◇◇◇◇◇◇◇◇◇◇◇◇◇◇◇◇◇◇◇◇◇◇◇◇◇◇◇◇◇◇◇◇◇◇◇◇

# The Message

◇◇◇◇◇◇◇◇◇◇◇◇◇◇◇◇◇◇◇◇◇◇◇◇◇◇◇◇◇◇◇◇◇◇◇◇◇◇◇◇◇◇◇◇◇◇◇◇◇◇◇◇◇◇◇◇◇◇◇◇◇◇◇◇◇◇◇◇◇◇◇◇◇◇◇

*Nuvar College in Ruvall, Sothron Empire*
*The Two Hundred and Seventy Eighth Year after the First True Night*
*1ˢᵗ Trade Day of Sun Month*

Gods it was hot. Sweat trickled down Billie's face and soaked her woolen clothes, making her skin sticky and a little itchy as she walked in booted feet on a soft earth path from her basic surgery class toward the building where her anatomy class would soon begin.

The lush foliage that grew around the college's worn, vine-covered stone buildings looked deceptively cool and inviting. The thick leaves of bananas, the fierce blades of palms, and gigantic tree ferns dripped from a recent rain. Trees with leaves big enough to wear as a shawl cast a deep shade. But the shade was a lie. There was no relief from the heat and humidity except within the college's stone buildings, and even there the damp warmth got to her.

The path led to a brick-paved square. A fountain exposed to the full glare of tropical sunlight burbled and sparkled in the center. Water flowed over and through tiers of stone serpents and lacy copper leaves into a large, round pool where a pack of students had gathered.

She hesitated, partly sheltered from view by a weird, thick-leaved plant with purple thorns as big as lion teeth and tiny flowers that smelled like antiseptic.

Today the pool was packed with people mostly her own age, though there were a few in the throes of adolescence, and a handful with wrinkles alongside their eyes. Most of her fellow students had flawless rich brown skin, some as tender as a fawn's, a few as deep as a panther's coat with everyone else's somewhere in-between. Bright, perfect teeth flashed as they smiled and laughed and splashed.

Most of them thought of her as a joke, a crass and uneducated 'bumpkin', whatever that was. They mostly left her alone. But not the tall, handsome one, seated knee-to-knee with a pretty, giggling young woman preening under his attention. Kamesh actively hated her. She considered doubling back and taking a different route, but that might make her late to class.

*Just ignore them.*

Billie walked across the square.

Some of the students had stripped off all their clothes to swim in the pool, heedless of the danger that came from the sun, but they weren't as vulnerable as Billie. The rest wore small vests and airy, knee-length trousers woven from the seed pods of green wool trees, dyed in bold colors with a subtle gloss. Floor length overcoats, light and diaphanous, were draped carelessly over benches and random shrubs. Satiny head scarves covered the hair and sometimes the faces of the students. The fabric was so fine that she wasn't sure her mother could weave anything like it. Many were painted with gold or sparkled with tiny glass beads.

It seemed like everyone here had an endless supply of expensive clothes that they changed frequently and discarded as rags on a whim.

Billie's woolens were the lightest and best her tribe could afford to give her. Her delicate shawl with its diamond pattern in green and gray, protected her scalp and face from the worst of the sun. Her green, knee-length tunic, edged in an elaborate black and gray trim, a calf-length summer skirt embroidered with irises, and close-fitted hose were things she'd have worn with nervous pride for a special occasion back home, if she'd been allowed such luxuries at all. She'd been surprised when presented with not one but two complete sets of clothes and a new cloak before she left. They were delivered with a stern admonition—keep them clean and tidy, and dress like a proper Kilhellion woman.

She'd known the Sothron Empire would be much warmer than her mountain home, where every winter felt colder than the last. This endless, oppressive heat, though, was beyond any Kilhellion's imagination. Here her clothes were too heavy. She often thought about going bare-legged, but if anyone back home found out about it, they'd be ashamed of her.

She'd only bothered to unpack her full-length vests and cloak because her roommate had warned her that if she didn't, they might mold.

At least she could be proud of her blade. Though this place was safer than anywhere on Mount Cross, safer even than inside the songhouse within her home village of Torath, everyone here kept swords close at hand. That practice, at least, was familiar to her. Her lone blade was shorter and thicker than theirs. Most of the Sothron majority wore matched pairs of blades, long and lean with an elegant curve. But as fine as those blades looked, hers was Kilhellion steel, which was much prized here, and everywhere.

The only partner for her sword was a fighting dagger so old and pocked that its edge wobbled, making it hard to hone. She used it more as a working blade than a fighting blade; always had since she'd been old enough to use any kind of sharp. She'd been so small when her father had given the old dagger to her, she'd fancied it a sword at the time. Remembering that day still brought her joy. Brian, her baby brother, had been as excited as she'd been, if not more.

What she coveted now was far more precious.

She wanted to be welcomed among the students. But they saw her and treated her like a pale maggot. They sneered at her lack of wealth and the accented way that she spoke Sothron. But she knew in her heart that she had every right to be proud of her people. Kilhellions thrived in a mountainous wilderness without the benefit of markets to shop for needed goods, without vast farms that could grow food all days of the year, or powerful temples to protect the people from hellions during true night.

Once she'd completed her training here, she would be her tribe's first healer since before the days of her mother's birth, while the people of Ruvall had a healer on every street of their vast city.

She couldn't think of a single person at the college who would survive a week in the Kilhells.

She'd looked forward so much to coming to a place of learning, of power, of endless fascination and delight, that she'd wrestled with a guilty suspicion that she might never want to go home again. She'd expected that they would be as eager at the college to teach her as she was to learn the healing arts, and not just because her tribe was paying a fortune for it. To shepherd the sick safely through a serious illness, to properly knit together an open wound using the healer's gift and skilled use of thread, to ease pain and lessen fever—healers saved lives. In a way, it was just as sacred a gift as the power to commune with the Gods and channel faerus, the power that emanated from the Gods.

So it frustrated her that most of the instructors at the college treated her like a burden, or ignored her as best they could.

In a place this plush, they probably didn't understand how the survival of an entire tribe might rely on one person's ability to fight, or make cheese, or weave … or heal.

At least she would be happy to return home. She'd begun to learn not just healing, but the fact that she belonged on Mount Cross as she never would anywhere else. Life was hard in the village, but there wasn't a person there who wouldn't die to protect her.

The other students started to mutter and giggle. She forced herself to believe that they were not talking about her as she passed the fountain. But then Kamesh stood up, and the other students noticed him. They noticed how his eyes narrowed as he watched her walk by.

She'd flirted with him when she'd first met him. She hadn't realized at the time how much he hated her. Gods, what a fool she'd made of herself.

His books were damp from the fountain, books that Torath's scribes would have handled only while wearing gloves because they were so precious. Books that she and most of her tribe could not read, though they could speak the languages written in them.

He had skin as dark as the silt-laden river that carried a never-ending feast into the desolate clarity of the Cerulean Sea, beautiful and dark enough to protect him from the glare of tropical sun. His chin, lifted proudly, was level with the tip of her nose, about as tall as Gareth, her chieftain back home. As he gazed down at her with a subtle sneer, she met the challenge in his eyes. It wasn't hard. Back home there were men as tall as him, thicker men, and she'd stood up to them many times.

His gaze measured her with disdain. The Thedran he'd been flirting with stood up beside him, and an older Arrak moved in behind Kamesh. Like most Thedrans and Arrak, they were shorter than Billie, the Thedran far more so. Like Kamesh they were finely dressed and well-armed. They each carried a lone, light blade rather than the pair of heavier, single-edged long blades that Kamesh had girded to a sturdy, many-layered silk belt around his waist.

The Thedran was Pomei, another who Billie had ill-fatedly imagined kissing until Pomei had insulted her that first, painful time Billie had dared to say hello to her. Pomei's perfect coils of black hair spiraled past flawless dusky skin and over silken clothing with patterns of gold leaves on green. The irritation that tightened her expression was not so pretty.

The delicate way her nose wrinkled implied that Billie was as welcome as a mosquito. The Arrak had never spoken to her, but he stood back with a guarded expression just behind Kamesh and Pomei, observing with his thick brows furrowed and his arms crossed. He was an older student, nearly her father's age, and mostly kept to himself. It was unusual to see him involve himself in anything, never mind gang up on Billie.

"Where are your books?" Kamesh asked, feigning curiosity.

Pomei was scowling fiercely now, her dark eyes staring at Billie with open hostility. "Why are you even here?" Pomei's voice was soft but harsh.

Warmth rushed to Billie's cheeks. In the Kilhells their words would be an invitation to a fight. But she wasn't there, and she had been reprimanded for fighting several times already.

Maybe Kamesh and Pomei wanted her to be banished from the college. Billie's father would never forgive her if she let that happen.

But the heat inside her refused to let their challenge go unanswered. People like Kamesh took pride for granted without knowing how fragile it could be. Did Kamesh think his family would be filled with pride for what he was doing now? "Where are your manners?" she asked, and marched past them.

"Disgusting cannibal," Pomei muttered.

Billie's head jerked back and her face burned like she'd been slapped. "What did you say to me?"

Pomei blanched. Either she hadn't meant for Billie to hear her, or she realized she'd gone too far. But Kamesh stepped protectively closer to Pomei and lifted his chin even higher, like a horse preparing to strike. "You heard her, cannibal."

Billie's body moved without her thinking about it. Every muscle rippled with power into a wave that crashed with her fist into his face. The impact shocked through her and filled her with power and joy.

He fell back, not so proud now. The look of hurt surprise in his eyes seemed to wonder, how did she hit me?

*That's right. I can't make you respect me, but I can defend myself just fine.*

But then she was surrounded by a mob that rushed in to defend him. They hit and kicked her, thankfully following the familiar rules of a Kilhellion brawl. The Arrak was the only one who tried to stop the fight, and he got shoved down for his trouble.

Fortunately, they didn't know how to hit. Her attackers were young adults, masters of swords that they had fenced with since they could walk, but infantile with the hands they'd been born with. With every little bruise they gave her, she gave back a bruise that they would feel for a month.

She was only one person, but this pack of weaklings flinched away from her. That almost-respect felt like justice. When they backed off, she eased off on them. This was, after all, a squabble, not a fight to the death.

Maybe now they'd leave her alone for a while.

The thick, hot air made it hard to catch her breath. She did her best to deepen her breathing, too winded to offer a truce just yet.

The distinctive rub of leather on steel and the faint ring as the tip of a fine sword cleared its sheath changed everything.

Everyone but Kamesh scattered like sheep chased by a badly trained sheepdog. They huddled into small groups, clutching at each other dramatically, acting scared but unwilling to leave and miss the fight, as if this wasn't a very real and very deadly situation.

Kamesh's eyes were wild, his face bloody from a broken nose. "How dare you touch me?" he raged. Despite his anger, he drew his smaller, second sword with perfect, practiced control.

While he'd drawn his second blade she'd drawn her own sword. She sucked in a deep breath and screamed with defiance as a rush of fear liquor flooded her body. The God of Death would not take her soul today. Not alone, anyway.

That scream interrupted his attack. Doubt, visible in how his eyes twitched side to side, held him back. He was older than her, but he was acting like a child, quick to tantrum, and terrified of real consequences.

Unfortunately, he held deadly weapons in his hands and had a lot more reach than a child. Her arm-length double-edged sword felt inadequate against his longer, single-edged blades. Her fighting dagger betrayed a tremble in her off hand when she brought it to bear as well. Its point quivered in the air, a consequence of the fear liquor building inside her. Death stood near both of them, but Kamesh looked at her as if he didn't know it, like he believed the worst thing that could happen was that she'd make him look foolish.

And oh, how he stupidly looked away from her to the onlookers before his gaze returned to her. She could have killed him in that moment, but he didn't seem to know that either. Kamesh, his handsome face distorted by anger, hot and dark with blood, bared his teeth, clearly trying to work himself up to making the next move. "You think you're a Champion or something?" Though he should have been used to the heat and humidity, he too was gasping for air. It couldn't just be that he was winded. His rage had him by the throat. "You're nothing but a filthy savage!"

The last of her heat bled from her and a terrible cold took its place. His words echoed her father's voice from long ago. *You fancy yourself mighty as a Champion? Well, you're nothing but a child with a gift that's of no use to anyone but yourself.*

From behind her a man shouted with the voice of a warrior and then the onlookers scattered. They grabbed their books and clothes and ran. Kamesh looked toward the shout, away from her again, as if she couldn't attack while he was distracted. When their gazes met again, the hate was gone, replaced by wide-eyed fear. He sheathed his blades, grabbed his books, and ran.

She was alone by the fountain as an instructor, his red and gold robes billowing like the wings of a strange butterfly, charged toward her. The Arrak that had tried to help her trailed behind. The Arrak stopped, then turned and hurried toward the dormitories.

She stood there, momentarily transfixed by the sight of the person who would decide her fate. Belatedly, Billie sheathed her weapons.

*I will not run.*

It was hard to decide that, harder still to hold herself to that decision as the instructor, Doctor Val, closed the distance between them.

She'd been fooled by Kamesh and his snobby friends again. She should have learned the first time, when she'd thrown away her bone flute because of them. She'd hoped they would see that it was more important to her to behave by this civilization's rules than to keep that priceless token of her adulthood.

They hadn't cared one bit. If anything, her sacrifice and denial of her heritage had made them bolder.

And now she would be judged, no doubt harshly, by someone with the power to tell her to leave and never come back.

Hopefully he would see that the cowards that ran were in the wrong and that she, who stayed, had done the right thing.

Or at least she believed she'd done the right thing.

Mostly.

Doctor Val, a trace taller than Kamesh, his hair silvered by age, confronted Billie with such a look that she thought he might draw his long blade. "What did you do?" he demanded.

Billie braced for a slap.

The slap didn't come. Only then did she remember that it would never come. This wasn't the Kilhells. Here, instead of a blissfully quick if painful physical punishment, instructors assigned unpleasant duties like cleaning up after patients that had soiled a bed, or vomited all over a room.

Or they banished anyone who had broken too many important rules.

She'd recovered her wind from the fight, but now her heart thundered in her ears, and she felt faint. She focused on her nodes, most of them fist-sized pools placed at spiritually significant locations along her spine, and used the vinus that flowed from them to steady her heart. It didn't help much. The fear liquor in her blood was powerful stuff, and she didn't have the skill to manipulate the gland near the top of her spine that insisted that she needed even more fear liquor.

"Did you cut anyone?" the doctor asked sharply.

"No." Would he believe her?

Doctor Val's expression softened, but not by much. He looked at Billie's hands, then at the state of the rest of her. Billie could only guess what she looked like. The blood from her nose and a split lip tasted salty-sweet and familiar. Warmth bloomed across her skin, both from embarrassment and from the fever that came with her healing gift. It made the heat in the air almost unbearable. Fresh sweat trickled over her body and made the wool feel scratchy. She tried to think of something to say to excuse her behavior, but what else could she have done?

In the Kilhells she would have ranted freely to her friends, but he wasn't her friend, and the rules were different here.

She suspected that social missteps early on had a lot to do with how she was treated now.

Why did all of this have to be so hard?

He frowned. "Who started it?"

In the Kilhells, if she complained to the chieftain and named names, she'd be forever known as a coward. She had no idea if the doctor held the same cultural position as a chieftain, but she had learned that complaining about a student to a teacher had similar social consequences.

"Did you start it?" he asked.

She assumed that she could safely answer that question, but it could mean the end of everything if she said yes. Gods. But she *had* hit him first. "I struck the first blow. But they called me a cannibal!" *Please*, she pleaded with Gods that she knew couldn't hear her. *Please, give me the strength to bear the consequences of my actions.*

He let out a sigh. Was that forgiveness in his expression? "I'm sure they said more than that. You would have been within your rights to demand a duel." Relief rushed through her. "I'd say that whoever dared say such a thing got off lightly," he continued. "Now, who was it?"

She suspected that his persistence meant that he didn't care that she would be hated even more for giving the names away.

*Can I be hated even more than I am now?*

Whatever the answer to that depressing question, she didn't want to say it was Pomei who had called her a cannibal. She didn't even want to say it was Kamesh that she'd punched, though she verged on hating him now.

"In my tribe," she began, then faltered at the warning look in his eyes. Billie bit her lip and pressed on, hopeful that she wouldn't make him regret his earlier words. "It would be shameful to admit it." She fervently hoped that he wouldn't make her tell him. "I was raised to fight my own battles against my equals. But, if it's the way of things, if I have to …"

His expression softened even more. He raised a hand toward her face. "May I?"

Billie nodded, her heart quickening. It was a huge honor.

He set a thumb gently on the split in Billie's lip. His vinus tingled as it entered through the wound. Immediately her own vinus resisted, despite her attempts to draw her gift back into her nodes, and her lip throbbed in reaction. The localized fever bloomed hotter, making his fingers burn like a dark stone heated by the sun. His vinus neatly slipped into the nearest, tiniest of her channels, swept around under the skin of her face, slid between the muscles, passed through a small channel that traveled through her eye socket into her brain, and then slipped back out. Her body tingled all over, but especially her head, as if he'd filled it with fireflies. "Nothing serious," he said gently, and stepped back. "I imagine I'll find the culprits by their bruises." He took one of Billie's hands and felt over it. Her knuckles were skinned, and tender. They were already starting to bruise and form sticky scabs, her skin pink and hot from her healing gift. "No broken bones," he said, looking over Billie's other hand. "Do you sense a serious injury?"

Billie shook her head. "I'm sorry I brawled." Billie had learned to say such words because they were expected in this culture, but they tasted like bitter dust. "It's just the worst thing they could have said." Her arms stiffened along her sides, and she balled her hands into fists, but she managed to keep her expression neutral and, hopefully, respectful.

They'd said it because of the flute she'd shown off to her roommate, Bora. With her father's help, Billie had made it from the thighbone of the first man she'd killed.

*That was part of a human being, and you carved it into a flute? That's horrible!* Bora had said.

*I never should have brought it with me.*

She wished even more that she hadn't thrown it into the bay.

But of course, the real problem had stayed with Billie, like the tattoos around her forearms that everyone here looked askance at, as if her arms were dirty. To hide them, she'd trained herself to resist pushing up the long sleeves of her tunic up to her elbows except when washing her hands, even when the heat drove her to the verge of madness.

There were many people from faraway lands that came to learn healing at Nuvar College in Ruvall, one of the most famous cities on the Cerulean Sea, pride of the Sothron Empire. But she was the only Kilhellion at the college, one of a very few in Ruvall. She'd learned the hard way that Kilhellions weren't welcome because they had a reputation that she'd been completely unaware of, a reputation for savagery and ignorance, and of course …

"I'm not a cannibal," she told Val. *But to you it doesn't matter, does it, because you still think I'm horrible.*

*Maybe I am.*

Such thoughts had been in her mind more and more of late. She had no idea what to do with them except to remind herself that when she returned to Torath, none of this would matter.

"I know." Val crossed his arms. He ran the fingers of his right hand along his bicep, as if soothing a cramp, before he spoke again. "I'm familiar with certain Kilhellion traditions that might make it seem that way." His voice was too smooth and calm, probably trying to hide his disapproval. He must have heard about the flute. Maybe everyone in Ruvall knew by now. "I will say this—it's never difficult to find you. If there's a fight, you'll be in it."

That almost sounded like a compliment. A smile made the split in Billie's lip sting.

Was that a hint of an answering smile in his eyes? But then he shook his head and set his hands on his hips. The sleeves made his willowy body seem much larger. "What are you doing here, Billie Maiyem?"

She wasn't sure what he meant. "I was on my way to anatomy."

"That's not what I meant." He sighed and looked past her. She glanced that way, but there was nothing there. "You're brave. Strong. You have a quick mind." Her cheeks burned from the compliments; words she assumed were meant to soothe the sting of what he really wanted to say. "Your gift … it's not your best quality."

Now she blushed for a completely different reason. "It's what my tribe needs."

His head twitched in what might have been negation. "Actually, that's why I was looking for you. I just received your tuition from your family."

It seemed too soon. Had so much time passed already? Maybe not, because the doctor seemed mildly confused as well. "Yon brought an envelope with the money. I suspect it's a letter," he added.

"A letter?" That was highly unlikely.

"Judging by the weight of the pouch, they sent more than the college requires for the next term. Perhaps it's for something else." He scowled. "I know you're homesick. Maybe they sent passage money so you can be with them during the Sun Festival."

Whether her family missed her or not, they wouldn't do that. It was too expensive. Besides, they didn't have a big Sun Festival like the one in Ruvall. It was more of a feast, and it only lasted a day.

"I would advise against it," he went on, as if that had to be the answer. "The danger of such a journey is great, and you would be away at least a month. It's more important for you to continue your education. Have you made progress on learning how to read?"

She was too distracted to answer. More money than the college expected? A letter?

"I know it isn't easy, but it's important. You understand that, don't you?"

*Of course I know!* But the last thing she wanted to do was to express her frustration, especially when he was trying to help. Maybe if she spent more time at it, she'd have a chance, but she had to spend every spare moment practicing using her gift. "May I see what my parents sent?" she asked, instead of admitting that she'd never learn.

Billie tried not to fidget while Val reached into his pocket. As was tradition for formal wear in Ruvall, his pocket was a stiff, padded pouch tied behind his back over a broad, elaborate belt of quilted silk. He felt about with both hands for a moment, then drew out a well-waxed leather packet. It did look like a letter, but maybe it was something else.

The thing was laced very tightly, and Val wasn't having an easy time prying at the rawhide knot that bound the lacing. It spoke of his patience, sense of economy, and respect for even simple objects that he worked to untie the knot. Someone like Kamesh would have cut the knot and the lacing too, which would mean the packet's lacing would have to be replaced.

If it was a letter, they would have had something very important to say to justify the expense.

Maybe her brother Brian was coming to Ruvall! She thrilled at the thought, even if he'd be cloistered in some temple, probably at the other end of the vast city. Gods, she hoped his life at the temple wouldn't be as miserable as hers had been at the college.

But the plan, as she'd understood it when she'd left home, was that as soon as Billie returned, they would send Brian to Ruvall where he'd be tested for affinity and learn to commune with a God in the appropriate temple. That way, both of them wouldn't be away from home at the same time.

Maybe her tribe had come into some wealth, and the extra they'd sent was meant for something else.

Maybe her sister was getting married, and they wanted Billie to come home for the house raising and ceremony!

She could see Stayce quickly saying yes to a proposal from Tris, especially since it would mean Stayce would finally be able to leave Torath. Stayce had always wanted more than a life of raising and training ponies, and she and Tris had been making eyes at each other for the last several grand harvest festivals.

Billie could imagine little nieces and nephews to dote on. That would be so amazing. It would almost be as good as having children of her own. And she'd have an excuse to visit Ribbonton, the beautiful town not too far from Torath where Tris worked as a carpenter.

Such thoughts made her life here at the college seem all the more grim.

Val painstakingly unlaced the packet flap. As her nodes warmed, releasing more vinus to help her body heal from the fight, the oppressive heat and humidity in the air made her want to jump into the fountain's pool, clothes and all. Sweat flowed over her like rain, soaking through the wool. She felt a little shaky from the lingering fear liquor in her blood as he pulled out an embroidered pouch made of fine lambswool, a smaller oilskin envelope sealed with amber wax, and a leather purse with a wax-sealed buckle.

The long, narrow knot that hung from the envelope's top corners was her father's signature knot. It didn't actually hold the envelope closed—the wax did that—but it was a sign that he was the one who'd sealed the envelope and had dictated the contents. It seemed out-of-place here, like Billie herself. Val offered the envelope, the pouch, and the purse to Billie. Billie tucked the pouch and purse under her arm, then held the envelope to her face, relishing the contact with her tribe. It still smelled like home, mostly wood smoke and pine, with a hint of fine wool. For a moment Billie felt like she held her entire village in her hands.

She broke the seal and opened the envelope. A fine piece of parchment was inside, about the size of her palm, with writing on it. She recognized

Andrea's—the scribe's apprentice's—lettering. Although Billie hadn't been taught to count, she could measure in her mind how expensive it would be to hire Andrea to write so much. Billie's mother had probably made Andrea a pair of her coveted socks that she turned the heel on so perfectly every time.

There were more knots inside. Her father's knot had been tied in dark green yarn. Her mother's had been knotted in bright red yarn. Stayce had chosen pale blue. Most precious of all, her brother's knot was there, tied a bit clumsily in white ribbon. The last one was Andrea's knot, done in thin strips of suede.

Billie's joy was short-lived as she stared at the writing. It was done in Sothron writing—that much she could tell. Though she tried hard to figure them out, most of the sounds represented by the clusters of dots and brush strokes remained a mystery.

The idea of reading and writing had seemed obscure and tedious back home, but at the college she felt her lack of literacy keenly. She'd had no idea how much reading was expected of healing students, and it embarrassed her to have to ask Bora read to her. And now she faced the airing of a potentially personal letter. She wished she could read the words herself.

She handed the letter to Val. "Can you read this for me please?"

His brow furrowed. "It's in Sothron Fulill lettering, but I think this is Kilhellion. Should I try to sound it out?"

*Cleverly done, Andrea.* "Please."

"Tiha beratrur hovis fouella." Even with the awkward pronunciation, Billie pieced together the meaning, which made her heart pound. *Your brother needs you.* "Resh Sellon." *Hurry to Sellon.*

All the air in her lungs rushed out of her. For a moment she choked on her fear.

In the next breath she seized on her courage. She knew what she had to do.

"I have to go to Sellon Port." She grabbed the pouch and purse from under her arm. The purse had a good weight of coins, and the pouch most likely held sapphires. This wasn't for tuition. This was to pay and bribe as needed to get her home as quickly as possible. "Something is wrong with my brother." She stuffed the pouch inside the purse. The world around her seemed to vanish as she remembered his blue eyes and rusty red hair and the smile he reserved only for her.

"What happened?" Val asked, his posture suddenly tight with concern.

"I don't know. They say he needs me. Maybe he's sick." Her family wouldn't send for her unless they thought he might die without a healer. Gods, Brian ... "Is there more written?"

"No." Val scowled at the parchment. "You'd think if they were going to send a letter that far and at such expense, they'd at least tell you his symptoms."

The whole tribe had probably sold everything they could to buy Billie fast passage and food on the way. Andrea had probably written the letter on behalf of the tribe, for the sake of the tribe, as part of her contribution. For Brian.

Maybe Melissa hadn't written the letter because she was sick too. Maybe the whole tribe had been stricken by some terrible illness. It could be that they had been deliberately vague to avoid showing weakness, in case the letter was intercepted.

She couldn't think fast enough. "I need to find passage." Maybe the ship that had brought the message was waiting for her. "I have to go to the docks."

"You should pack. Take your medicines with you."

He was right, but ... "I can't afford to pay for them."

"You made them yourself, and your tuition paid for the cost of the ingredients. They belong to you, and they may help."

"They're not in my room." They were scattered in various classrooms where she'd made them during her classes. "I don't know that I have time to run around the campus to gather them all before—" Then she realized that her family might not have arranged for passage on a ship heading for Sellon Port in advance on her behalf. "I should go to the docks. I can't imagine that there are many ships leaving the port so close to true night, and tomorrow there may be none at all. If all I have are my sword, my dagger, and this money, that will be better than preparing better and arriving too late." *My gift may be better than medicine anyway, depending on what is happening. Please, please let it be something I can fix.*

It was already Trade Day. True night would fall at sunset tomorrow, at the end of Somber Day. She hadn't spent time outside of a blessed building during true night since she'd sailed to Ruvall to study at Nuvar College.

The dread of facing that again dried out her mouth and made it hard to breathe, but the thought of losing her brother was worse.

*I'd sail through true night over and over again to save him.*

"I'm sending Tilla with you," Val told her.

That made no sense. "What?"

"You've only been here just over a year. You'll need someone with more experience to help."

"I …" She clutched the purse harder. She couldn't count the worth of the coins and gems her tribe had sent her, but she knew how expensive healers could be, and how expensive ship travel could be. She had to be as thrifty as possible to make it home. "I can't. What if it takes everything I have to get home?"

"I will convince her family to pay her way."

Billie's gut clenched. "We … no. We don't take charity." Her parents would be appalled at the idea.

Val let out an exasperated sigh. "Tilla could stand to see the world outside Ruvall. I would consider it a favor if you showed her. Maybe you don't need her help, in which case no one owes anyone anything. But if you do need her to save your brother's life, I think your parents will find a way to keep their honor. Don't you?"

Tilla, in the Kilhells? She doubted the jungle flower could survive, though the rumor, and the way Tilla bore her ever-present three blades suggested that Tilla had been raised to be a warrior before she came to the healer's college.

The thought of Brian in pain, asking for her, wishing that she was there at least to hold his hand, refocused her. If he needed someone with healing stronger than Billie's, she'd be an idiot to refuse. "The ship may not wait."

"I understand. Give me the key to your room," Val said. Billie slipped the silk cord off her neck and gave it over. "I'll find Tilla. It may be possible to send your possessions and medicines with her, so wait for her if you can."

"Thank you." His kindness threatened to overwhelm her. She bowed her head to hide the threat of tears that contorted her face.

Val set his hand gently on Billie's arm. "Billie. I'm on your side. You're not alone."

The contact startled her with its tenderness. Her breath still came hard, and her heart still hammered against her ribs, but the touch reminded her that she wasn't entirely surrounded by enemies. "Thank you," she said again, this time looking into his dark eyes.

Val nodded. "Try to stay calm. This message took time to reach you, a week or even more. It will take more time than that for you to return home. It's almost always better to act wisely than swiftly."

"It's my brother." She couldn't stand there anymore. Billie ran toward the docks.

Chapter Two

---

# Port Ruvall

---

*Ruvall, Sothron Empire*
*1<sup>st</sup> Trade Day of Sun Month*

Vines covered many of the buildings she hurried past, giving the impression of a city being devoured by the rainforest. Her boots pressed deep into soft earth alleys and carried her with sharper strides on cobblestone past walls covered with ferns and mosses. Some streets were thick with people in airy clothing, and the humid air was heavy with their sweat and perfumes. Billie skirted a crowded seating area shaded by a deep awning, narrowly avoiding getting raked by an annoyed leopard on a gold chain. She noticed a familiar obelisk covered in scarlet flowers and dashed through a weedy alley to reach it. A bustling marketplace on the other side forced her to slow. It seemed full of nightmarish beauty, a blur of color and noise as she squeezed by busy shoppers.

Her heart still pounded in her throat, despite the respite from her run. Back home she could have run on and on. Here, in the heat, with the air as thick as steam, she struggled for air, and her legs felt unnaturally heavy.

At last she won through and passed the obelisk, through massive stone gates into a world of cool twilight. The underground city, though just as busy as the one above, had a central road meant only for rapid passage to the bay. Thin waterfalls and massive trees lit by dazzling light stones created the illusion of a garden among the stars. It was much easier to run here, moving with carts, runners, people riding horses—in one case a huge lizard—toward the pale glow of daylight on the far side. She followed the people on foot that traveled up the stairs rather than the carts up the ramp.

Suddenly the color bleached away to pastel sails, weathered wood, and the myriad colors of blue in the sea. The crowd dispersed in countless directions amid broadly spaced buildings or crossed the main square with its view of the bay in diverse angles. She put a hand on her shawl to keep it from blowing back from her face in the strong breeze coming off the water as she strode across dark brick paving toward the docks. Using her other hand to try to shield her eyes from the sun's glare off of sails and the water, she searched for signs of a Kilhellion ship. The ship would be low to the water, with square sails bundled under spars slung from thick masts. Long oars would serve as rails on the ship's sides until they were needed when the wind failed or to maneuver along rivers.

Sleek, sharp-nosed Sothron ships had a similar profile, but were far larger than any Kilhellion ship. Broad-bellied Thedran ships with their built-up cabins at both the bow and stern wallowed lazily among the Sothron ships. The rest she couldn't identify. There was such a tangle of masts, sails and ropes, she wasn't sure she could find a Kilhellion ship from her vantage.

She feared there wouldn't be time to dash up and down the docks for a closer look.

*It might not even be a Kilhellion ship,* she realized. *They would send the letter with the next outgoing ship, whatever it might be.*

Billie sprinted to the lighthouse with its huge tower and blindingly bright light stone at the pinnacle. The harbormaster's office was set up within red-and-white-striped open-sided tents at the lighthouse's base. By the time she got there, she felt dizzy and gut-sick. There were a few people ahead of her in line. She waited just inside the tent's main door and tried to catch her breath. She wouldn't get to Brian any faster if she fainted.

The harbormaster's small army of assistants managed most of his affairs, writing and filing endless pages of paper, while he himself sat in the center of all the bustle. At the moment he was discussing business with some noblewoman seated beside him. Like Tilla, the woman was a so-called black noble: black-skinned and black-blooded, rare and important. She was like a chieftain, or a monk, or a scribe in the Kilhells, though she was born to that status, rather than having to work or fight for it.

*Remember. Be especially, weirdly, stupidly polite. Be soft-spoken and calm.*

*Do it for Brian.*

When she finally reached the table, the harbormaster gave her no more than a glance. Instead, one of his assistants, a slender, gray-haired Sothron woman with a sharp face, her body draped with voluminous, bright orange silks, excused herself from conversation with a short, heavy-bellied Thedran man. She moved to stand before Billie. "I believe I remember you. You are …?"

Billie didn't remember her. "Billie Maiyem of Mount Cross." The woman continued to stare at her. "I came to study healing at Nuvar college?" She wouldn't have admitted that in public at home, but here, she trusted that it would be safe. She had no choice if she wanted this woman to take her seriously in a city where birthright and occupation meant so much.

Judging from the woman's expression, that wasn't enough.

"Someone delivered a message—" Billie began to offer.

"Do you remember my name?" the woman asked, interrupting her.

"No," Billie admitted with a defeated sigh.

"I am Zima, harbor master's second accountant. Now, how may I help you?"

"I received a message from my family," Billie began again. "I'm hoping that you can tell me if the ship that carried that message is going to bring me back home."

"Who delivered the message?" Zima looked irritated now.

Why did Sothroners have to insist on knowing all the details? Val had mentioned someone … "I don't remember. My instructor—" She took a breath and realized it would be faster to give the exact details. "Doctor Val. He received the message for me."

Zima frowned "I see. Perhaps Doctor Val hadn't realized that the name of the messenger might be useful to you. Go on."

It was Billie's turn to be exasperated, though she did her best not to let her emotions control her expression. She glanced at the harbormaster. Thankfully, neither he nor his important friend had taken any notice of Billie. "Is there a ship here to take me back home?"

"And where is home?"

"Anywhere in the Kilhells will do, but I'm trying to reach Sellon Port." It was the port closest to home. Unfortunately, it was a long way from her village, which sat high on the shoulder of Mount Cross.

She hoped Brian would survive the journey to Port Sellon, and that he would still be alive when Billie got there.

He had to be.

"No. There is no ship waiting to carry passengers to Sellon Port. There is no ship bound for the Kilhells at all today."

How could she be so sure without even asking anyone? "Well I need to get to Sellon Port. It's urgent." She had to fight to keep her words steady, and to keep from raising her voice.

"Few ships fight the currents to sail from here to the Kilhells, and even if there were, none would leave so soon before true night, so please, try to calm down. I'll find a way for you. It might not be today, but it will be soon."

*I am calm!* Billie wanted to shout, but of course that wasn't true.

*It's all right, Billie.* Her brother's voice whispered to her from the past. She could almost feel his small hands on her face as he did his best to wipe the blood away. *You did it. We're safe now.*

*He's younger than me, but he's always been wiser.*

She forced herself to take a breath, and slowed down her words even more. "I have to leave for the Kilhells today. It's very important."

Zima brought herself up to a greater height and looked down on Billie with clear disdain. "By who's decree?"

Billie felt the urge to vault over the table, blades bared, but she managed to hold her temper. Brian needed Billie to follow the Sothron rules of etiquette. Anything less and they wouldn't help her. They might even jail her if she released the screams building inside her. "I apologize." It wasn't entirely a lie. She shouldn't have expected any sympathy. Instead, she should have done her best to gain this woman's goodwill, and her help. "I would be grateful if you would help me find the fastest way to the Kilhells."

A thin smirk curved on Zima's sharp face. "So you do have manners after all, Billie Maiyem of Mount Cross."

The sting of that remark felt even worse because calling Kamesh out on his manners was what had spurred him to call her a disgusting cannibal. Gods, how they hated her, and Gods, how she was beginning to hate them. Etiquette was so fucking important here. They'd probably let someone bleed to death after their arm had been hacked off because they couldn't handle putting a tourniquet on someone to whom they hadn't been introduced.

*Billie!* Brian's voice, still that of a child, piped up in her mind. For a moment she wasn't in a sweltering bay surrounded by a city half-eaten by rainforests, but in the lower huckleberry fields, fingers stained purple. In that moment she'd realized she was the only one who could save him.

*I might be the only one who can save him now.*

"Your fastest return to the Kilhells is through Ben Ariim." Zima's voice brought her back, but not before she remembered how blood had mingled with the huckleberry juice on her hands that day. "There are two ships leaving for Ben Ariim today. If you're ready, one will be leaving in moments." Billie couldn't hold back her gasp of relief. "However, she may be full. I can make inquiries."

Inquiries? Seriously?

*Stay calm. Be polite.* "Perhaps I can go to the ship myself and ask if they'd be willing to take me." *Maybe Thedran sailors are more compassionate than Sothron administrators.*

"You may be disappointed," Zima pointed out. "It's a long way to the correct berth."

"Thank you for your consideration, but I think I would prefer to walk than wait."

"I'll send an escort with you."

*Blessed fucking Life ...* She had to remind herself that she might get lost on the docks. Better to wait than to run off in the wrong direction. "Thank you."

Her escort, a Sothron boy formally introduced as Kawa and puffed up with pride and pomp, took up a stately pace with his brilliant red and silver silks flowing around him. Billie followed behind him, doing her best to keep her impatience under control and to look inoffensive.

The bay was vast, and the docks long, a slightly more compact city floating alongside the immense, land-bound city it served. The docks were built of thick wood. Steel-clad light posts, etched with sacred symbols, helped ward off hellions. The fishing vessels tied in the berths had already finished their work and rocked empty while their owners sold their catch in the market or rested at home. Many canoes, longboats and rowboats floated just as idly, though some worked in the bay. Of those, a good measure ferried people and goods across the bay because sometimes that was easier and faster than navigating Ruvall's streets. Others rowed or sailed between the docks and the largest ships, most of which were anchored in deeper waters. The harbor was so busy she had no hint of which of the Thedran ships might be leaving soon, or which of the longboats might be ferrying the last of the passengers to that ship.

Suddenly, Kawa broke with decorum and took off at a run. Billie ran after him. "Wait!" he cried, his voice breaking. She remembered how proud Brian had been when his voice began to break, and it tugged at her heart. "Wait! Longboat for Silver Parrot, wait!"

One of the longboats, slipping out of its berth loaded with sacks and dragging a net full of water barrels, stalled as the rough-looking Thedran crew dipped their paddles deep into the water and held them there. The woman at the rudder, a soft-faced Thedran with tightly bound curls and sinewy arms, stood up. "What is it, Kawa?"

"Madame Jistra. This is Billie Maiyam of Mount Cross, in urgent need of passage to Ben Ariim!" he called out.

The woman's face tightened into a scowl. "We don't have time to negotiate passage for another passenger."

*No. No!* "I'll pay anything!" Billie cried.

Some of the people with paddles tensed, their postures like armor against the potential assault of a Kilhellion on their vessel.

Brian's fate rested with someone who probably hated him without ever having met him. Billie had to say something, anything, to sway her, but no words came.

The woman's gaze strayed down the docks. Kawa turned, following her gaze, and stared.

Billie turned to look.

It was Tilla, bearing a heavy load of bags suspended from straps that hung from her shoulders. Her exceptionally dark skin set her apart far more than her height, which was commonplace among Sothroners and Billie's own people, but stood out among the other people on the docks. The display of strength as she carried Billie's and her own bags, armed with the traditional weapons of a Sothron duelist, made her even more impressive. And then, like jewels on a crown, layers of dusky rose silk swathed her hair and covered her face with a translucent veil, declaring her a healer at the cusp of graduating from college. Unlike Billie's Kilhellion gray and green shawl, which protected her vulnerable fair skin from the sun's unceasing threat, Tilla's veil was more of a formality. Her skin's deep color was ample protection. But then everything about Tilla, even more than most Sothroners, was the epitome of formality.

Rumors held that a black noble's blood was so dark it was almost black, and that when impassioned they blushed deeper than the night sky. Whenever she saw Tilla, Billie believed those things to be true.

Kawa abandoned Billie and ran toward Tilla. "Lady, is there something I can help you with?"

"Passage to Port Sellon, with my companion, Billie Maiyem," Tilla answered.

Companion? No glance, no smile, no sign of recognition at all came with this surprising declaration.

All at once, everything became about getting the two of them onto the longboat.

In just about any other circumstance, Billie might have resented the disparity of treatment. But the way Tilla had spoken, and how she'd carried Billie's bags, heavy bags Tilla had by all signs carefully packed for her, said more than any verbal offer of aid or even friendship. For some reason, getting to Brian *mattered* to her.

"Thank you," Billie breathed as they settled unsteadily among the sacks and sailors in the longboat. The narrow vessel rocked and swayed even in the bay's calm waters. "Thank you," she said again, because once didn't seem like enough. No amount of gratitude felt like it would ever be enough.

"It is my honor," Tilla assured her, though she didn't meet Billie's gaze. "Say nothing more of it." Those last words sounded more like a command than modesty.

Tilla coming with her would complicate everything, but Billie trusted that Gareth, Torath's chieftain, would sort it out once she explained that Tilla, just by being with Billie at this moment, might have already saved Brian's life.

*Silver Parrot, A Thedran Sailing Vessel*
*1st Trade Day of Sun Month*

Captain Lily was a large-eyed beauty like so many Thedrans, and much more fastidious about his looks than most if his elaborate clothes and the long coils of lightly oiled black hair, held back neatly in a silver hair clasp, were any indication. Deep brown eyes swept over Billie, taking in her pale skin, red-brown hair escaping her shawl, and woolen clothes. Like many Thedrans, he was a head shorter than Billie, and the fact that he had to look up to meet her gaze seemed to annoy him. His skin was dusky and olive-toned, darker than many Thedrans, maybe because of all the time he spent in the sun. In typical Thedran fashion, his clothing had gores everywhere: on his sleeves both above and below the elbow, on his vest from the waist down so that it flared like a skirt, even on his trousers. Those colorful trousers bloused over his multi-colored leather boots. If she'd been wearing as much as him in Kilhellion wool, she would have fainted from the heat, but his clothes were made of tree wool, which tended to keep people cool.

His handsome frown eased as he nodded respectfully to Tilla. He kept his gaze lowered, and didn't seem to mind doing it. "Lady. I will arrange for proper accommodations for you in a private room." He glanced back at Billie before forcing a smile. "May I ask, who is this person to you?"

Tilla looked smoothly at Billie.

Billie had no idea how Tilla felt about her. She could be sure of only one thing: Tilla had never said anything unkind about anyone, nor did she treat anyone rudely. That, at least, was something.

"We don't know each other well, do we?" Tilla asked Billie in lightly accented Thedran.

"No, lady." She usually spoke this formally only to instructors. It felt awkward, especially in the Thedran language, which she'd only used informally until now.

"But it's important that she reach Sellon Port safely." Tilla looked back to the captain. "I'm here to help her in any way that I can."

Lily's eyebrows shot up. He took a breath and composed himself while Billie silently cheered. "I see. Well. Follow me. I'm sure I can find you appropriate quarters." He led them along a narrow walkway, the waist-high rails on the right guarding against falling into the sea. The rails on the left stretched between steps or ladders leading down to a deck where most of the sailors did their work. If the sailors below reached up, they could have just touched the underside of the walkway. The number of people, the relatively low ceiling under the walkway, and all the crates and casks and coils of rope everywhere, combined to make the ship feel cramped despite its overall imposing size.

The ship rose, fell and rocked slowly from the caresses of the bay's lazy waves as they walked. The movements were small, but they still made Billie feel unsteady despite her best efforts to match the captain's confident stride. The weight of her bags made it even harder. Some crew members carried Tilla's bags for her, so she had it easier, but she too walked with a less-than-confident stride along the gently shifting walkway.

The resinous fragrance of wood and the faintly fishy, salty scent of the bay mingled with the less pleasant odors of tar and sweat, things she remembered from her first and only other sea voyage. Her heart quickened. *This is happening. I'm on my way home!*

He led them toward what he called the folksul, or something like that. The building looked sturdy, but like the rest of the ship it was made of wood. A wide landing in front of the building allowed plenty of space for sailors to go by to the opposite walkway, or to the main deck below if they wanted to take one of a pair of steep stairs down. It was a relief to reach the building and put hands on it. It was made of a peculiar wood, run through with many colors: creams and golds, reds, browns, soft grays, silvery greens and even a slate that verged on blue. The grain was so striking it nearly obscured the blessings carved into it. It felt satiny, like good fabric.

"Paintwood," Lily told Tilla proudly, though she hadn't asked or, unlike Billie, even noticed it. "It's strong, resists fire, and can endure the strain of blessings longer than any other wood. As much of the ship as possible is covered in it. The rest of the ship is made of elephant wood, some as thick as the length of your arm. It's worth the expense. *Silver Parrot* has been in service for nearly twenty years, and we've never had a problem with worms or beetles." Lily's proud expression sobered. "Our mage reinforces the ship's blessings just before true night, but unfortunately they won't last long against a determined nefari attack. It's always a risk when sailing through true night. Our best protection is not this ship, but the vastness of the waters and the darkness. We will be like a tiny bird in Kal Ariim's grain fields. As long as we're quiet, we won't be noticed."

"Such attacks are rare, are they not?" Tilla asked, suddenly concerned.

He frowned. It seemed like he was put off by Tilla's worries, as if he expected more of her, and there was a subtle shift in the tone of his voice. "Yes. But if they see us, if they can get to us …." He looked to Billie this time. "No one would think less of you if you changed your mind and decided to stay in Ruvall."

Tilla lifted her chin, no doubt fully aware that his words weren't directed at Billie, but at her. "I won't turn back."

Naturally Billie wouldn't either. The true night she'd spent at sea on the way to Ruvall had been nerve-wracking during the first storm, but she'd ended up sleeping through most of the rest of true night. This journey would, most likely, be the same. It made no sense to dwell on the terrifying possibility that hellions would capture the ship and decide who to eat, who to rape and enslave, and whose souls to sacrifice to their cruel gods. Like she'd been taught since her first hunt, she forced those fears out with every exhalation, drawing calm in with every breath until her nerves settled.

The captain didn't look impressed by Tilla's show of courage, and he didn't seem to like Billie's silence either. "Should the worst happen, the only way out is to escape overboard. It's said that nefari can't abide the sea—that it burns their flesh, and sucks them down into the depths as if they were stone. If you dive in and swim down as fast as you can, you'll be out of their reach. Even if you drown, at least your soul can be reborn someday."

Judging by Tilla's expression, the noble was struggling to hold onto her courage. No doubt, like Billie, she'd been taught that if hellions broke into the place she sheltered over true night, or if she was caught outside of blessed shelter during true night, there was no hope, no way of fighting back without channeling power from the gods. Billie didn't like the idea of drowning—it went against her dedication to Life and seemed like a nasty way to die—but at least there was a chance she could protect her soul.

Captain Lily glanced up at the sky, then looked to a sailor standing nearby. "It's time." He faced Tilla and set his hand briefly over his heart. "If you'll excuse me, I should get us under way before we sort out your accommodations."

Tilla nodded, her dark eyes fixed on blank air. The sailors dropped her bags and followed the captain, who called out strange orders. It was in Thedran, but even the familiar words were used in ways she couldn't comprehend. What did a cat have to do with an anchor?

Even before every sail had filled with wind, the ship began to move with a steadier, more insistent rise and fall that made keeping her balance less complicated but more important. Billie went to the rail as, with each new sail hoisted, the ship picked up speed. She looked back over the bay to Ruvall, and the safety of stone buildings, as the ship cut over and through the smooth ocean swells. From here, as when she arrived, the city looked like a ruin overtaken by the forest, and yet it was a thriving city full of more people than there were stars in the sky. A person didn't have to be able to count to know it. The hot spices, the birds and butterflies, the busy streets and music and lights …

… so many lights …

And the tallest building of them all, the lighthouse, grew brighter and brighter as the sacred light stone within its peak rotated until it shone directly at them. She had to look away until its piercing beam swept past them.

There was no telling if the tribe could afford to send her back to Ruvall. Probably not.

This … this was very likely the end of her learning to become a proper healer.

She hated so many things about Nuvar College, but she loved the healing itself, and the learning. It gave meaning and purpose to what she'd always felt moving within her. And the most exciting part turned out not to be the use of her gift, though that made her feel as if she could fly every time she managed to heal someone.

She loved learning the physical medicine. There was so much more to it than she'd realized. Massage. Herbs. Manipulation of the muscles and skeleton. Cold treatments. Hot treatments. Drying treatments. Moist or sweating treatments. Surgery. And dentistry! She thought all that could be done for teeth was to pull them if they went too bad.

She'd just begun to understand a tiny portion of all the things she might do for her tribe, and her tribe had no idea what she could do to help mothers survive childbirth, to properly set bones, to return someone's strength quickly after an illness, and every day she wondered what new revelation would come.

As important as healing was to her tribe, her brother's abilities would change Torath's entire future for the better. If he learned how to build a sacred space and create sacred things, he would bring security and prosperity to their village for generations to come.

He just had to hold on long enough for her to get there.

Was it possible that Brian had made it safely down the mountain by now? When Billie had last made the journey, she and her father rode the ponies at a steady walk, and had to spend a true night in Caudron. Stephen probably trotted much of the way and changed ponies in Caudron to get the message and money to Sellon Port as quickly as possible. He was their best rider, and a good fighter, reliable, brave … he would have made the entire distance between Torath and Sellon Port in the days between true nights.

The message would have travelled over a true night and the days following until today to reach Billie.

If Brian was fit to ride, it was possible that they had just now reached Sellon Port. If not, if he had to be carted or carried on a stretcher, her family and any tribe members coming along to help might still be trying to get down off the mountain.

How long had Brian been suffering? As she imagined the measure of it, her gut tightened.

"Are you all right?" Tilla asked.

Billie's mind had been spinning with so many thoughts that Tilla's voice startled her. "Yes. I'm all right," Billie assured her.

Tilla accepted her word. It had to be politeness, or perhaps indifference, because Billie, within and without, especially her hands, trembled.

What if he had something like cancer, something that was beyond her and likely even Tilla's skills to heal?

Chieftain Gareth would chastise her for giving in to worry. She knew what he would say if he was with her now, because he'd said similar things to her mother when Billie's father had gone missing overnight in a snowstorm. Billie recited his wisdom silently to herself, trying to will her fears away. *I don't know what's happening, and even if I did know, there's nothing I can do until I get there. Breathe in the clear, breathe out the fear. Breathe in the clear, breathe out the fear ...*

## Chapter Three

<>‹›‹›‹›‹›‹›‹›‹›‹›‹›‹›‹›‹›‹›‹›‹›‹›‹›‹›‹›‹›‹›‹›‹›‹›‹›‹›‹›‹›‹›‹›‹›‹›‹›‹›‹›‹›‹>

# The Rill

<>‹›‹›‹›‹›‹›‹›‹›‹›‹›‹›‹›‹›‹›‹›‹›‹›‹›‹›‹›‹›‹›‹›‹›‹›‹›‹›‹›‹›‹›‹›‹›‹›‹›‹›‹›‹›‹>

*Silver Parrot, A Thedran Sailing Vessel*
*1ˢᵗ Trade Day of Sun Month*

The captain opened a door into the folksul. The wood surrounding the door and the door itself was as thick as the length of her arm from wrist to elbow, but it wasn't solid. The wood had been glued in layers, each run going a different way so that the edge was patterned. It seemed that only the outer layer was paintwood. The rest looked like it might be oak. What had the captain said? Elephantwood, whatever that was. "This hall leads to the passenger cabins. The sail master's cabin is at the end," Captain Lily told them as he led them in. He could simply step through the doorway, but both Tilla and Billie had to duck. The hall beyond was so narrow that Billie's bags dragged along the walls, helping her stay upright. Tilla kept her head tilted sideways a bit to avoid the ceiling. For Billie it was close, but she could walk without bowing her head.

In a display of casual wealth, several sacred light stones with the quality of bright sunlight were set in the ceiling. They showed off the satiny polish of the wood walls and the bright colors in a handful of small paintings of garden scenes. A number of closed doors stood on each side of the hall. A lone door stood at the end with its own light shining in the ceiling just above it. Each ceiling light had a cover that could be rotated over it should darkness be needed.

Ruvall had been much the same, with beautiful sacred lights everywhere, some with elaborate shades that could dim or conceal the light, some that blazed at all hours. In her home village of Torath, they had a single sacred light. It was half the size of these, and shone about as brightly as a campfire. They only needed that light, a few candles, and the light from the hearth to keep the darkness crowded back to the edges of the great songhouse where everyone stayed over true night. The warm glow of Torath's sacred light might seem dim in this part of the world, but it had brought comfort to her people since her grandparents' time. She missed it. She missed laughing, and drinking with friends, and being with people who loved her.

Depending on how ill Brian was, it might be a long time before she sheltered in the songhouse at Torath again. Had the chieftain traveled with her parents and Brian to Sellon? She hoped so. The chieftain rarely left Torath, but he was well-respected in Sellon. The influence and allies he had there might help. Billie had to wonder as she thought about that fact. What could be so wrong with Brian that they'd call her home, but not wrong enough to take the risk and hire a healer in Sellon Port? Of course there might not be a trained healer in Sellon Port willing to help outclansfolk. She didn't know. She couldn't remember a time, or even a story, when her tribe had asked for help from a healer.

She hadn't had much interest in politics, and now that lack of knowledge left her with important questions that wouldn't get answered until she got home.

It probably didn't matter. Her tribe had decided to summon her home, and her only concern was to answer that call. That was the logical conclusion, but it left her feeling confused and just as worried as before.

The captain looked in the first door on their right. "Protector Aliiren, we have an unexpected passenger in need of a private berth. I hope you won't mind if I ask you to share with Temric. He seems to be a quiet, studious sort. Hopefully he won't disturb your meditation."

A protector! Though not as powerful as a mage, never mind a sage, Billie had always been in awe of anyone that could not only channel faerus—the energy that came from the Gods—like her brother could, but shape it to their will. Until she'd traveled to Ruvall, she'd never even seen anyone that powerful. Since she'd been in Ruvall, she'd met a handful of protectors, but only in the context of learning how to use her gift on their unusual physiology. Protectors were a temple's soldiers and craftspeople, channeling faerus through their weapons with killing force, or imbuing objects, mostly made of stone or metal, with that sacred energy to repel hellions.

Light protectors were the ones that created light stones. Did this protector follow Light, or one of the other Gods, like Life or Darkness?

Tilla and the men carrying her bags blocked Billie's view of the doorway to the protector's room. She stood on her tiptoes.

Nothing.

Tilla went into the room, and the men dropped her bags off. Billie backed up against the door opposite Tilla's room as the men squeezed past her and her bags on the way back toward the deck. They gave her impatient, sour looks.

The door suddenly opened. She lost her balance, knocking her head on the top of the doorway as she fell.

A young man caught her. "Hi!" he said brightly. He helped Billie find her balance. "A Kilhellion!" His happy exclamation caught Billie off guard almost as much as falling into their room.

"Yes, thank you." Judging by their nearly identical, straight and narrow noses, the young woman sitting on the floor in the small room was close kin to the young man. Their crystalline blue eyes sparkled in the sacred light in the room, both pairs large and curved with mirth beneath expressive eyebrows. She relaxed and decided to introduce herself. "I'm Billie Maiyem."

"Wow! Welcome. I'm Edrion." His jaunty Sothron dialect had a colorful lilt with pleasant lifts and falls that made his words sound musical.

He did his best to make room for Billie and her bags. He was only a little shorter than Billie, but he was so thin that he seemed much smaller than her. Nonetheless he was quite strong. His narrow shoulders made his bloused sleeves seem especially large. Those sleeves were tied at his elbows with elaborate ribbons. His vest was short, probably to show off his trousers. They were a patchwork of small diamonds in bands of black, violet, sapphire, emerald, and then below the knee a buttery yellow, carrot, crimson, blood, a deep plum, and then back to black. Black scarves glittering with silver threads hemmed in the volumes of fabric at his knees. His bare feet had rings on each of his pinkie toes. His fine, glossy hair was tightly braided in a clever interwoven pattern around his skull, and then fell loose to his waist. He had some leather in his hand. He picked up a small leather knife that he must have dropped when he caught her.

They had dusky skin, a kind of grayish brown that darkened to a cool, almost metallic slate-and-bronze on the woman's exposed arms and on their cheeks, brows, and noses.

The young woman's more cautious smile revealed straight, white teeth with the two front lower ones crossed just enough to be cute. The young woman had dark, straight hair, not a true black but with red tones where the sun had bleached it a bit, especially at the ends. Her mouth was very full, and such a deep color it almost seemed stained with juice like a Kilhellion bard's. She wore a blouse with very short sleeves. The waist-length vest over the blouse was a patchwork of navy triangles and gold stars. Her pleated skirts were also patchwork and incredibly full. As she sat in the very small space available to her on the floor, it flowed around her in endless folds and waves. A bare foot peeked from under the skirts. She had a tiny, beautiful ring on her pinkie toe, sapphire maybe, set in gold. Her fingers were light and quick at their work, fixing a frayed edge on a Thedran blouse. "Your bag strap has broken threads," she said. Her words had throaty purr that wasn't present in Edrion's voice, most likely from vocal damage.

The young man sat on their bed and crossed his legs, looking at Billie askance with a shyness belied by a gleam of mischief in his eyes. "This is my sister, Larani."

Billie nodded to her. "I'm glad to meet you."

A hint of exotic incense wafted back to Billie from the hall, distracting her. She looked out and managed to get a glimpse of dark hair, a powerful hand, and a sky-blue sleeve before the protector closed the door to the neighboring room.

"I'll have a meal brought to you," the captain told Tilla through her open door. Then he looked to Billie with impatience. "We should be able to find you a hammock somewhere."

"You can stay with us!" the siblings said in not-quite-unison.

There was barely enough space for them without her, but Billie didn't want to decline, not in the face of those bright, welcoming smiles. "Thank you." Billie returned their smiles and put her hand over her heart to emphasize her gratitude.

"Fine," the captain said. "I have work to do."

The protector's lingering incense tantalized her as the captain walked past the door, dragging the scent with him. It was sharp, musky, but also full of cedar that reminded her of fires back home, and it had a floral edge, and something sweet, like vanilla. She wanted to chase that scent down and really drink it in. It took effort to focus back on her new living quarters.

Most of the room was taken by a bed built into the wall. It was barely large enough for the pair to sleep in comfortably. With Billie, it would be impossibly snug, so she resolved to sleep on the floor. Beneath the bed was a very large, single drawer. The cabinets above the bed would leave just enough space for someone of Billie's height to sit up, barely. To either side of the bed were more cabinets, and in the center of the ceiling, an amber-colored sacred light stone shone. It was larger than the ones in the hall, brighter, and had two different kinds of covers that could slide over it. One cover was blue glass. The other was silver that had tarnished to near black.

Billie closed the door. On its back was a mirror. Billie quickly looked away, but not before she got a glimpse of her face. There wasn't much swelling, thanks to her healing gift, but she was bruised and every shadow of those bruises showed on her pale skin. The scab from a cut on her lip had hardened already. By morning it would start to peel free. She resisted the urge to pick at it. She tucked the loose hair back under her shawl as best she could. It wasn't a copper red like her mother's, and most of the other people in her village, many of whom were related to her mother. Copper hair would have been lovely. No, hers was what was known romantically as blood red, but mainly it looked brown. The red tones sometimes showed in strong sunlight or when it was wet. Otherwise, it was extremely uninteresting.

Blood red showed more in beards. At times her father's beard seemed like it was soaked in blood, as it actually had been at times after a friendly, or sometimes not-so-friendly, brawl in the songhouse during true night.

Edrion gestured with his thumb toward his sister. "You can call us Edri and Rani."

"Just call me Billie. Thank you for taking me in." Awkwardly, she set down her bags, one atop the other because there wasn't space to set them side by side without crushing Rani's skirts.

"Have a seat on the bed," Rani said. Edri edged over to make room for her. "Make yourself comfortable. I prefer to sit on the floor most of the time. Are you hungry? Thirsty?"

She realized she was in fact thirsty. She doubted Tilla had filled her water canteen, but Billie sat on the bed and started looking through her things anyway. And thank the gods and Tilla too, there was her canteen from back home, and it still had some water in it from when she'd filled it last night. She guzzled what was left and sighed.

This was happening. She was going home.

With everything that had happened, and what she might face, all she wanted was to curl up on a bed in the songhouse, embraced in a soft wool blanket that smelled like her, and sleep with a depth she hadn't managed since she'd left home.

A gentle hand lightly touched her knee. It only startled her because most people in Ruvall avoided touching her. "Sorry," Rani said, pulling back. "I only meant—"

"It's fine," Billie assured her.

"I just wanted to say …" Rani exchanged a glance with her brother, then returned her blue-eyed gaze to Billie. "You're with us now. Whatever it is that's making you so upset? Rill luck is beside you."

They were Rill! A rare, nomadic people, she'd only heard intriguing bits about them in a few lines of an old song. She *had* heard of Rill luck, though, even in Torath.

From the few mentions she'd overheard, not many in the Sothron Empire believed in Rill luck. But Sothroners thought she was a cannibal, so, screw them. "Thank you."

"Of course," Rani said warmly.

She believed. How could she not, as the Rill gave each other knowing, confident looks?

What she wasn't sure she should also believe was that Rill only loved, trusted, and honored their promises exclusively to other Rill.

Obviously, not everything people believed about Kilhellions was true, and yet, those things weren't entirely lies, either.

She had a gut feeling that urged her to trust in their kindness and spoken intentions.

But what if she did? Even if they became friends, they'd soon part ways. *I'm not coming back. I probably won't see any of these people ever again.*

What did that mean? Should she stop bothering to try to get along?

Maybe all of this was like a dream from which she wouldn't wake until she got home.

The thought reminded her of a poem the chieftain used to recite at the sunset of the Star Festival, especially the first line.

*The dream is damned, and dreamers too, if dreaming is all that dreamers do.*

She couldn't remember most of it, but the bits and phrases she could remember lulled her, as did the slow, steady rocking of the ship. Her eyes drooped, and then her head. She jerked from near-sleep several times. Each time the Rill were still there, working on their mending in a comfortable silence, her presence apparently of no more notice than the bed she sat on. With a deep sigh, Billie forced herself to relax, leaned into the cabinet beside her, closed her eyes, and surrendered to sleep.

## Chapter Four

<><><><><><><><><><><><><><><><><><><><><><><><><><><><><><><><><><><><><><>

# The Historian

<><><><><><><><><><><><><><><><><><><><><><><><><><><><><><><><><><><><><><>

*Silver Parrot, A Thedran Sailing Vessel*
*1st Trade Day of Sun Month*

"I need free air," Edri suddenly declared, setting aside a sailor's trousers he'd been mending. "Would you like to go out with me?"

Billie pulled her attention from deep within her body where she'd been practicing linking her nodes. She'd only managed to chain her spiral and lantern nodes to her lotus node. The rest kept breaking away, like she was tugging on badly spun wool that parted at every weak spot. "Thank you, yes." Anything to get away from the feeling that she would fail not just Brian but the whole tribe. If only she'd had more time at the college, and if only she knew what was wrong so that she could prepare!

They got up and Billie followed Edri out. Even though their door had been open, the hall felt slightly cooler than their stuffy quarters. An even cooler breeze blew in from outside when he opened the door onto the broad walkway above the deck, chilling the sweat on her skin. Edri propped the door open with a little padded brass foot that hinged from the door's corner. It was still warm out, but the air moving around them helped immensely. Edri spotted his sister below on the deck and he flew down the stairs toward her, as confident and balanced as any of the sailors.

Billie's gaze stopped hard on the protector. He stood facing the main mast, sword in hand, the point of his blade turning small circles in the air.

Edri had told her that his name was Aliiren.

The name seemed apt. Aliiren, a desert healing shrub, opened its alluring, deep red and black speckled flowers after first light throughout the hottest part of summer. She remembered its qualities by a kind of rhyming scheme: aliiren for a fever's end, but fear for them. Too much could cause vomiting and internal bleeding.

He was so striking. His dark hair, nearly black and tinged by red like Larani's but thicker and less glossy, parted around his bare shoulders to coil over his chest and shade his shoulder blades. Also like the Rill, his skin was dusky, but darker than theirs, and the sun-kissed places were plum-toned. He had only a hint of very fine facial hair, and a thin line of equally fine chest hair, but he was clearly an adult, her same age or perhaps a trace younger, broad-shouldered and incredibly fit. She'd never seen such starkly outlined musculature. A few veins stood out along his powerful arms. The whole of him gave the impression that he was as strong against hellions as stone.

He was Arrak.

She'd thought, because his name was a flower, that he would be Thedran. That he was bled from a nomadic people known for their wild courage and legendary horsemanship made him seem more approachable than a Thedran. Thedrans seemed strange and complicated, and their urban culture had so far proved to be incomprehensible. Even Sothroners, with their strict rules and hierarchies, were easier to understand than Thedrans.

There were several Arrak at the college, but they had a softness to their bodies that belied their almost feral, stand-offish nature. She didn't know what had chiseled Aliiren's form into such harshly sculpted grace. Maybe it was his training. Maybe it was from channeling faerus. He was also tall compared to other Arrak she'd seen, perhaps her same height.

This was the first time she'd seen him out and about. Maybe that meant that he preferred to be left alone.

He wore pale blue trousers, and a matching headscarf kept his hair from blowing into his eyes, which were closed. His bare feet were thickly calloused. His hands were nearly as calloused, but not at all rough. He took good care of his skin.

Tilla surprised Billie by coming up alongside her, her gaze roving over him as well. In a subtle glance to Billie and a hint of a smile, she revealed that she found him handsome as well, but then she straightened with a breath and found an unoccupied place a few paces away on the walkway. There she leaned on the rail and looked out over the waves. Her face, framed by her rose-colored veil, looked smooth and calm, but the way her dark eyes stared at the sea suggested that dread consumed her.

There was someone else unusual on board. He sat in the shade cast by one of the walkways that ran between the front and back of the ship. He would have been as pale as Billie, but the sun had darkened his creamy skin to a burnt peach-pink color. He was as tall as a Sothroner, somewhat gangly, long-limbed and long of face, as if he'd been stretched. He had blue-gray eyes, small but keenly focused on the book he'd propped on his knees. He turned the pages of his book after giving each a swift, sweeping glance. He couldn't be reading that fast, could he? His hair was short, less than a finger-length, and curled this way and that like Brian's had before it had grown out into a shoulder-length mane. The man's clothes were strange in that they were very simple and economical—just a tunic and straight-legged trousers, made so that the clothing wasted very little fabric when it was cut out and sewn. They were garments common to many cultures, worn mostly by farmers and very poor laborers. But, having spent many true nights spinning, even without touching it she could tell it was a fine linen. His trousers were a deep green that verged on black. The dye was exceptionally even and hadn't faded anywhere, even at the hems. The tunic was a pale cream with no off-colored threads in it—

He'd caught her staring. She blushed and looked away.

Too late. He shut his book, stood up, and made his way up to her, skipping a stair with each step. He hadn't bothered to mark the page with the ribbon that peeked out from under the soft leather cover. His jaunty manner made her smile.

He smiled back. "Hello. You must be the Kilhellion everyone's talking about," he said in Sothron. He had a difficult accent, with many odd pronunciations and an off-beat cadence, but she didn't have too much trouble understanding him. "I'm the other one everyone's talking about. Temric. I'm an historian." He lifted his hand toward her, then looked apologetic and quickly lowered it to his side again. It was almost as if he expected her to take his hand for healing or an assessment or something.

No one had said anything about him to her, but then she had been either with the Rill or napping since they'd set sail from Ruvall. "Billie Maiyem of Mount Cross. Nice to meet you." She briefly touched the place over her heart as the Sothroners in the area usually did when they wanted to show friendliness, sincerity, or begged for forbearance.

"Mayhem?"

She'd never heard the similarity between her last name and the Markan word before. It made her chuckle. "No, Maiyem, as in one who makes a way," she said, switching to Markan. She hadn't practiced Markan since she'd left home, but it was close enough to Kilhellion that it was easier for her than Sothron or Thedran. "It's my family name."

"No, no," he laughed. "Sorry. I can't understand you."

"You don't speak Markan?" It took her a moment to realize that he'd just pronounced her family name badly. He hadn't meant the word mayhem.

"No, I don't. Or Thedran. I can read a little of each, though."

It seemed strange to be able to read something but not speak it. "I can teach you if you like," she said, switching back to Sothron. "Since you can read it, it should be easy enough for you to learn to speak it."

"I said a little! I shouldn't have admitted even that much." He laughed in a breezy way that made her smile even wider. "If you want to teach me a bit of language, make it Thedran, please," he said. "I won't need to learn to speak Markan. I don't intend to go nearly that far north. Just Ben Ariim, and then, if the Gods are gentle, I'll travel back home." He sobered and let out a sigh. "I've been away too long."

She heard the heartache and homesickness in his voice as clearly as she felt it in her own heart. "So, I'm guessing an historian is one who studies history."

"Yes. I'm studying the first true night, and I'm hoping to learn about what caused it."

"Settmin caused it," she said, using the Sothron word for hellion. She was surprised that an historian wouldn't know that. Or maybe they just didn't know that in the south.

"Maybe," he said evasively.

She didn't know what else would do it. The creation of true nights was the most devastating thing that had happened to humanity.

Actually, not just humanity. The whole world had staggered.

The humans that had escaped death or enslavement those first true nights were driven into hiding. The darkness that lasted half of every week had not only given hellions free reign with the full use of the power given to them by their gods, it had weakened or outright killed countless plants and the living things that depended on them. If it hadn't been for Light and the other Gods sacred to humanity, things would have been a lot worse. "Who, or what else would gain by it?" she asked. "Who would even have the power to do it? Angry senti? A Sage?" What a horrible thought.

In the Kilhells senti were known as godlings, and in Thedran, ascended. Not Gods, but no longer human, stronger than any sage, they were enlightened beings.

*A truly enlightened being wouldn't unleash that kind of destruction, no matter how angry, or bitter, no matter the injustice they might have witnessed.*

The thought, so true-seeming and sure at first, wilted as she considered that she had no direct experience or assurance from anyone who had contact with the Gods or godlings. All she had were hearth stories.

Temric's brows stormed over. "Maybe a group of sages would have enough power. I hadn't thought about senti."

*Maybe there are hellion godlings out there.*

It was a disturbing thought, especially the idea that a malignant being might ascend based on a paradigm very different from humanity's virtues. She didn't voice her idea, though. She didn't know enough about religious matters to suggest such a potentially ridiculous thing.

"I've shocked you," he said, ducking his head and blushing. "Sorry. I tend to do that."

"I know humans are capable of evil," she assured him. She had to admit that it was interesting to think about what might drive a person, evil or good, to cause such devastation. "You know," she mused, "if a human did it, that could be a good thing. It might mean a human could undo it." The last words faded in her throat as she caught Aliiren staring at them. His eyes were gold, looking all the brighter against his dark skin. His nose was long and narrow, his cheeks high and sharply cut, and he had a deep dimple in his chin. His expression remained serene, if she could call that cold stillness serene. He appeared, despite the warm color of his skin, utterly glacial.

When she looked back at Temric, he looked as if she'd slapped him. But before she could ask if she'd offended him, he shrugged the look off and turned his attention toward Aliiren, who had sheathed his sword and carefully manipulated his hands and wrists to stretch the joints. "He's an interesting bed fellow. I'm glad your friend pushed him out of his room, though I'm not sure he's equally grateful." He blushed again and chuckled. "We had a nice, long conversation about Light and knowledge. I'm eager to pick up where we left off, but I thought I'd let him start the conversation this time if he wants. I don't want to annoy him."

She was curious to know what a protector thought of Temric's idea. "Did you tell him that you thought something other than settmin created true nights?"

"That and more." Temric's mouth puckered into a peculiar expression, like he was thinking and trying to stop himself from blurting out those thoughts at the same time. He relaxed and chuckled. "We'll be up talking most of the night again if I have anything to say about it. He has the closest relationship to Light I've ever seen in a protector. His mind is quick, inquisitive, and full of insight, ideal for a Light protector. I'd be surprised if he doesn't become a mage soon."

*Beautiful, intelligent, skilled ...*

She'd have to be careful. He was just the sort of person she'd turn into a fool over.

*And I'm going home.*

Her feelings had shifted now that she'd had a nap and time to think. She'd suspected that she was never going back to Ruvall as the ship first sailed away, but now she felt it in her gut. In fact, she figured that the farthest she'd get from Torath ever again would be to go to Sellon for the summer horse fair.

As sweet as being home would be, returning so soon, having accomplished next to nothing, tasted bitter in her mouth. She had not become a talented healer, nor learned any important lessons, hadn't done any great deeds, nor found a lifelong love.

It felt like failure.

"Would you mind if ..." Temric's cheeks pinked. It seemed he blushed at anything and everything. "Do you have Kilhellion tattoos?"

"Of course." To him, though, it probably wasn't a natural, obvious thing. She hadn't met anyone else with tattoos outside the Kilhells. "They're an important custom. It would be unusual for a Kilhellion to have no tattoos."

"I'd love to see them." His smile faded, and his brows furrowed. "If it's private, I understand. I only ask because I'm curious. I've never seen them before. Well, drawings of them, but never on a person."

"Would you like to draw mine?" she offered.

"Yes please! But maybe later. I'd like to see them in daylight before we sit down in my room for that. The light is better here, but I want to sit at a desk to draw. I'll have a good look now and then hopefully I'll be able to do them justice when it's time to depict them on paper." His brows furrowed again. "You don't mind showing them to me over several sessions, do you?"

"Not at all." Billie pulled up her sleeves, conscious of the fact that Aliiren was watching them. But then Temric edged so close that their shoulders touched, blocking her view.

"Good Gods, you're not just tall, are you! You have arms like a blacksmith." Though he sounded startled, his tone was clearly complimentary.

Billie grinned. "Thanks!" He was taller than her, as were most Sothroners, so it was odd that he'd comment on her height. Maybe he'd spent most of his time around shorter people, like the Thedrans and the Arrak. She did, after all, stand a lot taller than most of them.

Temric leaned closer, fascinated. "What … the color … that's a beautiful blue. It's almost has a sheen, like silk."

"It comes from tube scorpions."

"Tube scorpions? What are—" He stopped himself. "First, let's talk about the tattoos. So, these describe you, I take it?"

"So far. Some are part of my birthright. Some, I earn. I'm young, so there's room for more." She started with her left arm. "This is Mount Cross," she told him, tracing the triangle. The mountain's base wrapped around her arm below her elbow, while the double point ended at the bracelet tattooed around her wrist. Her mother had left a droplet-shaped bit of bare skin, about to drip free of that point, for the symbol that would represent Billie's gift. Someday, eventually, the Kilhellions of Mount Cross would learn that she was a healer. Hopefully, unless she had some bad luck, her brother would come fully into his powers before that happened. "These are blades coming from a forge. The flames are the heat of the forge and the heart of the mountain. These ponies on either side represent my parents. My father is a mining pick on my sister's arm. He was already training ponies by the time Stayce got that part of her tattoo, but he wanted that part of his life to be remembered, and she liked the design of it, so …." Their family—the whole village really—had been more prosperous before the highest quality iron ore petered out.

Maybe by the time she got home someone would have found another good pocket of it. In the meantime, their main trade items were horses, goats, sapphires, textiles, and herbs.

He wouldn't care about that.

"These designs represent our village. It's still within the tree line, but only just. These designs here are rock and snow. That's an avalanche. And this is—" She wondered how much she ought to say. It wasn't a secret, but it was private. Temric continued to stare at the tattoo. He was so fascinated that she didn't want to cheat him of any of it just because she was nervous. "It's where we build the altars to honor our dead." She turned her arm over. "These are my mother's parents, and this is Beela, my name-mother." When Temric looked confused, she added, "The name Billie is the ... derivative ... of Beela." She couldn't think of a better word to explain the relationship between their names. It wasn't quite right, but Temric seemed to understand. "Her family will be my guardians should something happen to my village, if I manage to survive." Beela was a chieftain's wife in a village similar in size to Torath, but lower on the mountain. Billie had spent a whole summer with her. Though she'd missed her family, especially Brian, she'd had so much fun and had learned so much, she was sad to leave. She still wanted to go back someday. *Maybe, when they need a healer, I will.* "This knot on my bracelet is the top view of my father's knot. This one is my mother's knot, and this is our chieftain's knot." She offered him her right arm. "I don't have as much on this arm because I haven't done much. But here is my brother, shown as a fox, and my sister, a silver tree." She traced her fingers over the scar around which her mother had tattooed forked lightning. "This is from my first real fight. My mother told me that if I go on being fierce and brave, she'll tattoo the lightning all the way around here, and here, so that it makes a mountain, protecting my brother and sister inside. And this is me." She showed him the stylized badger on the back of her arm. It wasn't flat and heavy like a real one. It was more like a person, lithe and rather pretty she thought. She'd been thrilled when her mother showed her the design sketched on a stone. When her mother had tattooed it on Billie's arm, using pine soot to deepen the blue to a near black to stripe the badger, making it even more striking and beautiful. Best of all, the charcoal outlines of Billie's badger was still on the stone by the river where Billie had been born. Not everyone had their tattoo drawn on the very stone of Mount Cross like that.

Their chieftain, Gareth, did. His spear-bearing bear was etched on a big stone that had fallen to rest beside the pool at the base of Curry's Veil. That high, sometimes entirely frozen waterfall was their village's main landmark. Its roar could be heard a long distance down the trail that led to the road to Sellon. The cliff and surrounding rocks were adorned with petroglyphs of chieftains that went back generations.

She'd been born not far from there, though her parents didn't like to talk about that.

"And on this bracelet is my knot, my sister's knot, and ... and my brother's."

"Are you all right?" Temric asked.

"Yes." She spoke more sharply than she'd intended. "Yes," she said more calmly after a breath. It made no sense to fret when there was nothing to be done. Even so, her gut kept twisting into knots whenever she thought of him.

*There's no faster way to reach you, Bri. You have to be strong. I'll be there soon.*

"Well, thank you for showing me these." Temric said, and went back to reading his book, just standing there alongside her, as if it was the most natural thing to do. After a moment she realized the conversation was over, and so she decided to join Tilla at the rail, feeling a bit shy about it, but unable to resist. Tilla might not be the friendliest person on the ship, but the kindness she'd shown Billie encouraged her to try being nice back.

Tilla's hands were tight on the rail. Though the tropical water was incredibly beautiful with its constantly shifting shades of deep blue, mysterious green, and violet reflections, she didn't appear to see anything at all.

Billie started to ask if something had scared her, but that might sting Tilla's pride. "Is something bothering you?" Billie asked instead.

Tilla closed her eyes and lowered her shoulders deliberately, as if she could force herself to relax. "True night is soon upon us."

"Tomorrow." The thought of the storm that came with the beginning of true night made Billie's skin prickle and the hairs rise on her neck. Unfortunately, the passengers and crew weren't the only ones in danger from storms and hellion attack. If they died, Brian might well die too.

There was nothing she could do about it. "We just have to see it through," Billie said, as much to herself as to Tilla. "Our chances are good. This ship has made this journey many times. And we have Rill on board."

Tilla nodded and they watched while the sun deepened and descended toward the horizon.

Tomorrow was Somber Day, the last good day of the week.

Tomorrow the sunset would look quite different.

Tomorrow true night would come.

## Chapter Five

◇◇◇◇◇◇◇◇◇◇◇◇◇◇◇◇◇◇◇◇◇◇◇◇◇◇◇◇◇◇◇◇◇◇◇◇◇◇◇◇◇◇◇◇◇◇◇◇◇◇◇◇◇◇

# Before the Storm

◇◇◇◇◇◇◇◇◇◇◇◇◇◇◇◇◇◇◇◇◇◇◇◇◇◇◇◇◇◇◇◇◇◇◇◇◇◇◇◇◇◇◇◇◇◇◇◇◇◇◇◇◇◇

*Silver Parrot, A Thedran Sailing Vessel*
*1ˢᵗ Gift Night of Sun Month*

**B**illie hadn't realized how tired she was until she curled up in bed—a bed that turned out to be a comfortable mattress within the big drawer beneath the main bed—beside and slightly below the Rill.

But Gods, the dreams.

In the worst of them, she walked with Brian through dark, thick woods on a steep slope on Mount Cross. He got too close to the edge of a cliff, and he fell into a frothy, riotous river. She'd leapt in after him. No matter how hard she tried to catch him, the milky green water carried him farther and farther away. Bille fell down larger and larger waterfalls until she woke, heart-pounding, to darkness.

After that one she snuck out of the room and settled beside a set of stairs where she could watch the stars. The fresh, warm breezes and quiet talk among the sailors on night watch chased the dream away. There she dozed, leaning against a rail post. Her body moved with the rise, roll and fall as the wind carried them over the waves, the ship's creaking serving as a lullaby.

She woke to morning light as a sailor trundled noisily down the steps by her head. Tilla was talking to Temric nearby, referring to Billie and her as *we*. But the smile that inspired quickly cooled as Tilla went on. "…

been studying at Nuvar College for some eighteen months but we don't know each other. I noticed her immediately, of course, but I didn't want to interfere. Being a black noble … it can be complicated. Show too much favor, and it can create jealousies that can make life even more difficult for someone like Billie."

"Someone like Billie?" Temric sounded uneasy. Billie held her breath, dreading the likelihood that Tilla's true feelings about Billie's people would embarrass them both.

Just then Tilla looked Billie's way and noticed that Billie was watching her. Her already dark cheeks deepened in color.

Billie gathered her thoughts, which had scattered like sheep running from a wolf pack when their gazes had met.

Whatever Tilla meant to say about Billie didn't matter. What did matter was that they were getting closer to the Kilhells, and there were things that Tilla needed to know, especially when it came to talking to people about things like the healer's college. This moment, while Tilla seemed to want to extricate herself from the turn in conversation, could be a good time to discuss that. Billie heaved herself up and strode over to them.

This whole situation with Tilla coming to Sellon Port was a matter for chieftains, not daughters of pony breeders.

*But I'm the one who's here.*

"May I speak with you privately?" Billie asked.

Tilla's eyes were wary, but she nodded, led the way to her room, and shut the door. She gazed down at Billie from a height that seemed to have grown. Her head scarf brushed the ceiling, and her cool, imperious posture emphasized the sharp look in her dark eyes. It was hard to tell if Tilla was offended, if she was being cold because that was her natural state when she was uncertain about something, or if Billie was simply misunderstanding her.

Up until now Billie had tried to fit in with Sothron culture. Soon it would be Tilla's turn to try to adapt to Kilhellion culture.

"I hope you're not regretting coming with me to the Kilhells," Billie began awkwardly, offering a smile.

Tilla shook her head and sat on her bed, still imperious, but more introspective.

"Good." Nothing for it but to say what Billie needed to say. "The Kilhells are dangerous," she began, because it seemed like the best place to start. "Life is difficult there, and the people—not my tribe exactly, not—" She realized that she couldn't honestly make excuses for her tribe, because they could be just as brutal as any other if they had to be. But did Tilla need to know that? Not really, she decided. Not yet, anyway. "Let's say that a tribe is in desperate need of a healer. Maybe a serious illness is spreading through their village. If they know of a healer nearby, and that healer is unwilling or unable to go help them? They'll raid that village to get her. They might even enslave her, to keep her forever. If they have to destroy the other village to do it, they will."

Tilla's large eyes widened. Her pupils were fully open, making her deep brown irises seem almost night-black.

*I've started too hard,* Billie realized. She bowed her head and tried to think, then settled on looking at the reflection of Tilla's head in the mirror instead of directly at her. Hopefully it would take the pressure off of them both. "My village will let our closest allies know about me if they feel it's safe and the time is right. But the last thing they'd want, and I'd want, is for everyone on the mountain to know." She didn't even want to think about the people of Kings Valley. To mention them would be to claim them as Kilhellion. Which they were … but at the same time, they were as different from the mountain Kilhellions as Ruvall was to Sellon Port.

Tilla's expression hollowed out, and her gaze lowered, emphasizing her long, dark lashes. "I apologize. If I had known, I—" She winced. "I am very ashamed of the indiscrete way in which I've spoken about you."

Billie stopped herself from assuring her that no harm had been done, because there was a small chance that a sailor might talk about Billie as a healer to someone in Sellon Port who would recognize her by name or description. But she didn't want Tilla to think that she was angry, either. She knelt and tried to meet Tilla's downturned gaze. "You couldn't have known. We don't usually admit to outsiders that things like that happen sometimes." It was an ugly thing her parents had taught her at a young age. As far as she knew no one on Mount Cross had slaves, but her father frequently reminded her that desperation might drive a nearby tribe to do the same awful things that the valley people did so casually.

He knew exactly what people were capable of. He'd been a slave in the Valley of Kings.

He'd taught her that keeping someone against their will was a thing that valley people did with impudence, but true Kilhellions—he considered the mountain and coastal people 'true' Kilhellions—survived by trusting each other and working together. Enslavement was not only cruel, but it carried serious risks, and of course it diminished a person's honor and integrity.

Not that the valley people would see it that way. For them, slavery was part of the natural way of things. It seemed impossible that anyone could believe that, but all she had to do was remember the father and sons who'd attacked her, her mother and her brother. They'd seen her as nothing more than a resource to use as they pleased.

"Sothroners don't usually admit their faults." Tilla's gaze stayed focused inward. "We're too proud, Billie. We're too proud and we think we're better than everyone else, but you only have to watch someone like Kamesh for a day and you realize we are not superior. We only think we are, like children who are told they're smart and then treat everyone else as if they're stupid. I will be more guarded on the ship, and I will be on guard in Ben Ariim and of course in Sellon Port."

Billie nodded, though her thoughts were still back on Mount Cross. "When we reach Sellon, maybe we should let it be known that you're a noble. I want them to believe that if something happened to you, the entire Sothron Empire would sail in to get you back."

"Not the whole empire, but they would come, and they would deal harshly with Sellon Port."

Billie shouldn't have been surprised, but it still startled her to know that Tilla was that important.

"I would not wish that," Tilla added quietly.

She was a good person. A feeling of trust softened a tension in Billie's shoulders that she hadn't noticed until it eased. "If you wouldn't mind … it might be best to let the people in Sellon believe that you're the one who heals Brian, even if I'm the one who does it. That will help keep me and my village safe." Her father would like that. Then Tilla would have a clear purpose, something better than to make up for Billie's failings as a healer.

"The ones who will need to know the truth already do," Tilla replied, unbothered.

That reminded her. If she did need Tilla's help to heal Brian, Tilla would sense that he could channel faerus. If it came to that, Billie would have to coach her to not say anything about it, in case someone was spying. Who in Sellon wouldn't want to spy? She had no doubt that her brother would be accompanied by the chieftain, their best fighters, and Billie's entire family. It would seem strange, and anything strange was always interesting.

Once Brian found his affinity and learned to shape faerus into a weapon, he'd be able to protect not just himself but everyone in Torath from raids. Until then, he was vulnerable.

Even now, so far away from helping Brian, she could see him build Torath into a place with a future beyond ponies and mining and praying to godlings. Torath had survived without a healer for generations, and after she died Torath would go on just the same. But her brother ... he would bring wealth and safety. Everyone on Mount Cross would trade their best goods and services for his blessings. No one would dare attack Torath for fear of his powers. Perhaps best of all, he would leave behind a legacy of blessings that would last for generations.

Tilla was tense. Was she afraid of the Kilhells? Tilla needed to be careful, but maybe Billie had gone too far in her warnings. "You'll be all right. We both will. My family and I will make sure of it," Billie assured her.

Tilla looked even more tense than before. "Thank you, Billie."

That made no sense. The debt belonged to Billie, not to Tilla. "I don't think you understand. I owe you a great deal for helping me, and for the help you're offering my brother." Much as she'd resented it when Doctor Val had foisted Tilla upon her, Billie now realized how critical it was to take on this debt for Brian's sake, and for the sake of everyone in Torath, potentially for generations to come.

"I think I do understand," Tilla said gently, crossing her arms. "But I know that my coming was not entirely your choice. It was mine, and it's a great honor to do what I can. I neither want nor need anything material in return." Billie started to argue, sure that despite her words Tilla in fact did not understand, but Tilla raised a hand to ask for patience. Billie had to admit that maybe *she* was the one who didn't understand, and made herself listen. "You are fierce and strong," Tilla said. "You've been tested in many ways, and you've survived. I have *never* been tested." A quiet anger simmered behind those words. What for, Billie couldn't say, but judging by how Tilla's gaze remained downward and inward, and the tension in her jaw, it wasn't for anything Billie had done. "I have trained my whole life not just for healing, but for combat. And yet, because of my status, I have never had even one duel. I've never even been in a fistfight."

That shocked Billie to her core. She realized, retrospectively, that maybe she shouldn't have been. Who would have dared? Another black noble? Tilla, ever polite, ever patient, being part of the same caste as the royal family ...

"I want to be tested," Tilla continued, though now she gazed straight into Billie's eyes, full of strength and pride. "Not necessarily to fight, though I'm curious if I have the courage and skill to win. But I have to know if I'm truly brave and wise, or if the accident of my exalted birth has made it seem so to others." A smile that didn't touch her eyes also tucked her brows together with subtle pain. "I've already learned so much. How much more will I learn of my true qualities when I reach the Kilhells?"

"I think you'll prove yourself," Billie assured her. Tilla's attitude reminded Billie of Gareth, Torath's chieftain. She wondered if Tilla had the same sense of justice and desire for worthiness that Gareth did. He was strict but kind, as solid and comfortingly immovable as granite. "I've seen your strength, and courage. It was you that have brought us this far. And, so, again, on behalf of my tribe, thank you." It was the first time she'd declared anything on behalf of all of Torath. Her father would bristle at her impertinence.

There was no one else here to speak for the tribe.

Tilla nodded. The circumstances and agreement hadn't changed, but now Billie felt this was a good thing. Tilla's brows furrowed, and she gave Billie a long look. "Does this mean that you will not wear a red scarf after you graduate?"

"I won't wear the red," Billie confirmed, not just because it wouldn't be safe, but because she wouldn't graduate to full healer's status.

"I want to become a doctor." Tilla stood up, as if this admission had given her fresh strength. She looked at herself in the mirror.

Billie stood up with her. "I think you'll make an excellent doctor." It wasn't false praise. Everyone knew she was one of the most talented healers attending the college. In fact Billie would have been surprised if she didn't become a doctor.

Tilla wasn't one to fidget, at least not that Billie had noticed before, but now she fussed with her silks, smoothing them nervously with long-fingered hands. It would be a long, difficult path to achieve that status. Her willingness to go to the Kilhells and practice healing outside of the supportive embrace of the college now made even more sense. "What about you? Have you dreams beyond being a healer?"

Maybe she'd misunderstood some nuance in Sothron. "Dreams?"

"Hopes. Desires." She raised a hand and drew it toward her mouth, touching her lips briefly with her fingers. Her gaze withdrew, and a private smile curved on her lips. "When I was very young, I turned a small shed into a doctor's office." She let out a laugh. "I would put my hands on my friends and declare various ailments, and then we would imagine that I healed them. I'm fortunate that I had no control over my gift, or someone might have been seriously hurt. As it was, I gave us all belly aches making tea from jasmine leaves." She shook her head, and then turned her full attention to Billie, clearly seeking a similar story.

Billie blushed. She and Brian had always played a game where she was a champion, and he was a mage. Together they'd defeated countless demons and devils that came in the form of stumps or older children willing to play the part of the terrifying, clever monsters they all feared. "Just silly ones. My true hope has and always will be to become useful to my tribe. I always wanted to go on hunts, and once I stood behind the chieftain during a meeting and pretended ..." The heat on her face was almost unbearable, and she placed her hands on her cheeks to cool them. "... that I was one of his personal guards."

"You ...." Tilla pressed her lips into a thin line for a moment, then looked away. A rueful smile erased some of the tension in her expression. "I don't know why I'm so awkward around you. Doctor Val is right. I need more experience outside of Ruvall."

Billie was grateful for the change of subject. "I'd better stow away my things. The storm at the start of true night is rough. At least, it was the last time I sailed through true night."

Tilla looked back into the mirror. "Four nights, three days. It seems like a very long time outside of blessed shelter; almost forever. It's going to be all right, though. Yes?"

"Most likely, yes. We have the Rill with us. I think we'll be fine." When Tilla didn't say anything, Billie let herself out.

*1ˢᵗ Somber Day of Sun Month, on the eve of True Night*

THE LAST LIGHT OF SUNSET SILHOUETTED CAPTAIN LILY AS HE STOOD IN the doorway of the hall that led to their rooms. The color of the sky seemed wrong, as if it was hidden behind a thin, brownish-red fog. "Bar this door, and don't open it until the storm passes," he told Aliiren. He spoke in Sothron, presumably for Temric's benefit, as Temric's grasp of Thedran was poor at best.

Billie watched from the Rill's doorway, with Rani and Edri tucked tightly against her on either side. She'd instinctively put her arms protectively around them. Temric wasn't far, watching from his and Aliiren's doorway. Tilla's door was already closed, and, judging by a scraping noise that came from it earlier, barred.

"The storm that comes with true night only lasts an hour, but it's dangerous," the captain continued. "If the ship starts to sink, jump overboard and swim away from the ship as fast as you can or you'll be sucked down with it. Once it's under, find something to hold onto until one of the longboats finds you."

Billie wondered if he spoke from experience, or if he was just repeating something he'd learned. If she'd been forced to guess, judging by the lack of emotion in his expression, it was the latter.

His heart's fire might simply have gone cold, she supposed.

The captain seemed to hear her doubts, though he appeared to misinterpret her skepticism. "It's not a pointless effort. Men have been found after many days at sea clinging to a scrap of wreckage." He glanced behind him and edged back from the door. "Certainly the chances that you'll survive at sea in the water during the storm are small. But if you stay in here when the ship sinks, you'll have no chance at all."

"I understand." Aliiren's voice gave Billie a pleasant shiver. It was very soft, just barely over a whisper. She wondered if he'd always had a soft voice, or if he practiced it as part of his observance as a Light protector. Softening the voice seemed more like something a Darkness protector would do, but she didn't actually know. Her knowledge of gods other than Life, like her knowledge of Rill, came to her through poems and songs rather than serious study.

"What if settimin find us?" Larani asked, slightly mispronouncing the Sothron word for hellion. "Do you have a plan?"

"We have a Darkness mage on board." Finally there was some emotion there; his eyes unfocused, remembering something. "And we're lucky to have Protector Aliiren," the captain added, the memory vanishing from his expression. His gaze focused into Larani's eyes for a moment. He took another partial step back. "If it looks as if the settmin will win, cut your own throat, or drown yourself. Believe me, you will not find a better option." The way he said it, as if it was nothing he cared about one way or another, gave her a chill. "Make sure your rooms are in good order and the drawers are latched. I wouldn't want you to get hurt by your own possessions." With that the captain shut the door.

"If we're attacked, I will protect everyone in this hall for as long as I can," Aliiren promised softly.

Alone? "I'll fight." She'd probably last only a moment, but maybe that moment would help. Sometimes a moment made all the difference.

His gaze didn't move to her but remained with his own hands, which rested on the door. "There's little you could do."

Something about his tone, a kind of question with a hint of fear, made her more determined than ever. "Little isn't nothing." She realized how silly that had to sound to him. "Unless I'll just be in the way."

"No." That simple word communicated so much. There was a promise, and a silent pact. "You won't be in the way."

Edri and Rani exchanged a glance. "We'll fight too," Rani said, her eyes bright and proud. "We'll fight, and luck will fight with us."

"May the vastness of the sea keep them from finding us." Aliiren lowered the steel bars at the top, center and bottom of the door. As he closed each bar, he latched them with the clasps on their cradles into place. And then he set a hand briefly on each clasp and muttered something under his breath, his voice so low that she couldn't make out the words.

The bars lit briefly with a beautiful, silver-blue light that chased along the existing blessings on the steel, and then flickered over the door itself. Though the blessings carved into the door were only on the outside, the light following the grooves glowed through to the inside.

It made her sad to see that beautiful light fade. She wondered if he could make it permanent. But that probably wouldn't be smart. It was taught in the Kilhells that hellions, or nefari as Thedrans called them, could see even the smallest light in the darkness of true night.

Aliiren lingered by the door, his powerful hands resting on the center bar. He had girded on his sword over his tunic. If she held her arm out to the side, the Thedran-style weapon would, point to pommel, span from the tips of her fingers to her opposite shoulder. The sheath was steel, and etched with blessings sacred to Light, protecting a perfectly straight two-edged blade. The blessings on the sheath gleamed and twinkled like starlight. The cross guard was straight and flat, engraved with six-flamed suns on both sides at each end, joined to an ornate hand guard made of elegant interlocking rings. Within some of the rings were medallions, six-flamed suns, beveled to catch the light. The globe pommel was covered in engraved blessings filled with a metallic blue gemstone. She didn't know if the weapon contained faerus or if it only served as a channel to that power that came from the Gods, but it looked impressive.

She'd heard stories about sages that had killed more than one hellion during true night. If those legends were true, wouldn't Aliiren at least have a chance to do the same? He'd have a good chance if it wasn't true night—of that she had no doubt. Though he wasn't yet a mage, it seemed to her that he might one day become something even greater than a sage, something more physical than a God, but beyond flesh and bone and blood.

She wondered if he'd become something like Valent. Valent had been a Light sage for a village on Mount Cross so long gone its name was forgotten. Somehow, he became a being of golden white light with coppery, flame-like wings: a godling.

She'd captured a glimpse of Valent once as a child. A flame-like light distracted her from some deer tracks she was following, so bright and alive that she'd thought a branch had somehow caught fire. Her terror quickly blossomed into wonder, but faster than a falcon, Valent had slipped away through the thick trees out of sight.

Her aunt died soon after that.

Those memories connected with the present, inspiring her to wonder what Aliiren might be like if he ascended, and if he would still care about humanity after it happened. It was strangely wonderful to think about, but it made her a little sad, too.

"Billie," Temric called from the doorway just as Aliiren finally turned away from the door. Suddenly she was pinned by Aliiren's golden gaze, made all the more striking against his dark skin. She'd been told at the college that the gold eye color was common among the Arrak people, but there was nothing common in that cat-like hue flecked with copper and pale blue, ringed in bronze. "Do you have time to teach me better Thedran? I'll teach you to read in trade," Temric continued.

She knew she'd never learn to read, but with Aliiren staring at her like that, she didn't want to admit it. It was hard to say anything at all as his incense-laden scent teased her senses.

He looked away and went to his and Temric's room. She drew in a breath and blew it out. She hadn't realized she'd been holding it. "Yes, please."

She was being ridiculous. Yes, he could channel faerus and communicate with a God, but he was just a man. *At least for now.*

By the time she'd corralled her wits, Aliiren had already moved past her.

Edri grinned at her. "Good luck." He winked at her.

Rani made a scoffing noise and lightly slapped his arm. "Don't tease." But then she grinned at Billie. "You don't need any luck. I think he likes you."

"Temric?"

Rani pushed her down the hall. "No, silly! Now go on and make friends."

It was just the sort of thing her friends back in Torath would have pushed her to do. "Easy for you to say," she grumbled in Kilhellion. Rani's laugh suggested that she understood. Blushing, Billie walked sheepishly down the hall and let herself in to Temric and Aliiren's room.

## Chapter Six

<><><><><><><><><><><><><><><><><><><><><><><><><><><><><><><><><><><><><>

# Learning

<><><><><><><><><><><><><><><><><><><><><><><><><><><><><><><><><><><><><>

*Silver Parrot, A Thedran Sailing Vessel*
*1ˢᵗ True Night of Sun Month*

Aliiren had settled onto the bed, which was covered with a buttoned-on oilskin cover to protect their bedding during the storm. He sat cross-legged. His gaze focused on a small shelf where a candle glowed within a stone box. He hadn't lit any incense. Despite this, the whole room was scented with that sharp, woodland sweetness, along with a hint of Temric's sweat mixed with a honey-like perfume that reminded her of witch hazel blossoms. Billie surreptitiously sniffed at her shoulder and winced. She was used to taking two baths a day, but on the ship all she could do was rag off the worst of the sweat and grime.

A beautiful spear leaned against the bed the men shared. The leaf-shaped blade was as long as her forearm. Faceted designs, or maybe they were letters, followed the blade's thick spine. A small cross-guard had diamond points honed so sharp it made her skin tingle. The shaft reminded her of the pale ash they preferred in the Kilhells.

Temric had girded an axe, and it wasn't the kind for chopping wood. It was stouter than a Kilhellion war axe, and the head was shorter, but the blade was longer and deeply curved. The head was counter-balanced with a diamond-shaped spike. Killing purpose gleamed clearly in its heavy edges.

Temric started to tear paper, incredibly precious in the Kilhells but apparently of little worth to him, into small squares. Then he sat at the edge of the bed and started writing on them on top of a narrow shelf at the foot of the bed. The men, back-to-back on the same bed, looked like a very unlikely pair, and yet something about them fit together. *Sword and spear, Arrak and Sothroner.*

Just as Billie settled on the floor, the candle flickered and then faded to an unsteady bead of light. The sacred light stones in the room dimmed until they cast barely more light than the last coals of a fire.

Aliiren's breath hitched, like he was in pain, but his expression remained smooth. The color drained from his face as he concentrated on the candle flame. After a moment, he ungirded his sword and rested it across his lap. His skin stretched tight and pale across his knuckles as he gripped the sheath.

True nightfall bothered Brian, too. He complained about feeling like his ears were plugged and colors not being as bright. At the college she'd learned that true night didn't do any damage, though the initial onset stressed the bodies of those who could channel faerus. "Is there anything I can do to help?" she asked.

Aliiren didn't answer. Maybe he didn't hear her. Or maybe he thought she'd been talking to Temric.

"Aliiren?" Temric asked gently.

Aliiren slowly opened his hands, and then closed them again, this time keeping his grip loose. "No. Thank you. There's nothing anyone can do." His whispery voice tingled over her skin. "True night affects me more here than when I'm inside a temple, but it's not painful. I'll be fine."

The ship groaned restlessly, and the soft sounds of waves against the hull began to bang and drum with greater and greater violence. She thought she heard a shout, but it sounded far away. She started to get up to see if anyone needed help, but sat back as she realized that the door leading to the deck was barred, blessed, and meant to remain closed during the storm.

*They know Tilla and I are here if they need us,* she reminded herself.

The ship leaned over. The banging on the hull grew louder, vibrating through her body as well as the hull. The ship creaked and then squealed and screamed.

Something lifted the whole ship up. The ship began to right itself.

They plummeted, her body momentarily weightless, and slammed down hard. The impact jarred through her like she'd fallen off a pony.

Billie had been through this before on the way to Ruvall. She knew it would probably turn out all right. But her heart still hammered in her chest. She gripped the edge of the bed frame in case the ship fell between waves again.

The ship leaned and rose up once more.

"Shall we?" Temric asked in Thedran, his voice a higher pitch than usual, a nervous smile on his face.

And so they set to it, as the storm tossed the massive ship up and down the waves. The wind kept pushing them, sometimes leaning the ship hard over when a howling, prolonged gust caught the storm sails, sometimes allowing it to level off again when the wind switched, only to return with renewed force. Billie taught Temric rhymes in Thedran that would challenge his vocabulary. Rhymes, songs, stories and poems were how Thedran and Sothron were taught in her village, and it seemed to work well for him.

For his part, Temric made her memorize the sounds that went with shape after shape that he drew with swift ease on pieces of paper. There were so many letters, many of which she'd never seen before, and so many that were similar to each other, that she soon grew confused. If it weren't for Aliiren sitting there, listening, she would have given up in frustration.

Not that she was likely to impress him. If anything, he probably thought she'd have a better chance of learning how to breathe water than how to read.

Anyway, it was a welcome distraction. The longer the storm toyed with the ship, the more unpredictable it became. None of them could brace for when and which direction the floor would lean, rise or drop. Each time the ship shivered, bucked, crashed and banged into what sounded and felt more like solid rock than water, she expected the ship to splinter to pieces around her. Water seeped in from above them, and trickled down the wall across from the door.

So she tried to focus on this awful reading thing to keep herself from thinking too much about drowning.

But then she realized suddenly that of course, *of course* Temric's Sothron child's 'game'—one that combined shapes he made her draw and the sounds she made while drawing them—had nothing to do with language.

It was a trick to try to teach her how to count.

*No wonder I don't recognize most of these.*

"Why are you teaching me this?" she protested. "I can memorize the words, but they don't mean anything to me. Why didn't you start with teaching me words that matter?"

"But numbers are words too, and they *do* matter," he insisted. "Look. You have ten fingers. One, two—" He went on, but he also touched on her thumbs.

"This is not a finger," she said, holding up her thumb.

"Yes, but—"

"No but! I had the same trouble at the college with recipes." Even the word recipe made her angry. "It's easier to remember the reasons for the ingredients and their strengths, and mix accordingly. Not everyone is going to have the same fever or the same toothache or the same infection, and one person may need less of something while another person needs more to heal them. So why bother with all those stupid numbers when they have to change anyway?"

Temric opened his mouth to argue, but then shook his head. "I suppose that could work. But then there's money. You really ought to learn how to count money."

"Money will never make sense to me."

He leaned forward and spread the papers at the edge of the bed with one hand while the other gripped the bed's shelf for balance, the picture of patience. She did her best to cool her temper. He was, after all, trying to teach her. "Let's say that someone says that a sweet bun costs four dinn. How are you going to count that out for them?"

"I'll just show them the dinn I have, and they can take what I owe." She wanted to keep her words soft so she wouldn't bother Aliiren's meditation, but her irritation made them hard and sharp.

"But how do you know they won't cheat you?" he asked before she could apologize.

"You don't understand." It was the only explanation for why he kept pressing his point. "I hate money. I use it because I have to. It's not like I can eat the money, or cut with it, or spin with it."

"But you *do* have to use it now," he pointed out.

She made herself take a breath to keep from snapping her next words. "I didn't grow up with it, just like I didn't grow up with reading. I don't have time to learn how to do everything there is to know in the world." He opened his mouth to argue, but she cut him off as she realized something. "Anyway, Tilla is with me. She can help me with it until I get home, and then I'll never have to look at it ever again." Those last words left her with a feeling of defeat.

"Do you really want to be dependent on her?"

That got to her. The feeling of helplessness and embarrassment burned in her chest and face. "I'm never going back to any of this. I don't even know why I'm trying to learn to read."

"Wait." Temric touched his mouth briefly, and then lowered his hand to the page where all of his marks seemed to dance and blur. "You haven't completed your education yet. Have you?"

She squeezed her head between her hands, wishing she could squeeze the knowledge of how she felt out of her head. "No. The tribe is going to have to get by on what I've learned so far. There's no way they'll send me back." It hurt her to think so. "Even if everything turns out all right, obviously they need me at home." It would be Brian's turn next. She looked Aliiren's way, thinking that maybe it would be better for Brian to go to Ben Ariim so that he could be safely guided by someone she'd at least met before.

Aliiren snuffed out the candle and now held the back of a hand to his forehead, breathing deeply through his nose. Clearly, it wasn't a good time to bother him with questions.

"I see." Temric gently wiped away a drop of water that had landed on one of the papers. "I know you trust Tilla, but I hope that you'll keep trying anyway. With this skill you'll be of more value to your tribe, just like you can help your tribe by knowing how to fight well, and heal well." He made sense, but all she had to do was think about being back home to realize it wouldn't work. "And who knows? They may send you back to finish your education after all. Unless there's some reason they wouldn't."

She knew she was a fool to hold onto any hope for that very thing. *We can't afford it.*

When she didn't say anything, he added, "will you at least try to count? I promise it won't be that bad."

"It would never be my responsibility to work with money. That's for the chieftain and the scribe." And then she realized that in fact she had been entrusted with money. She'd lied. Her cheeks burned, and she wished she hadn't said it. Even so, she'd never learn to count in time to help with the money she had. "Everything you're talking about learning takes time. No one has time enough to study to be a scribe, and a healer, and a fighter, and to spin wool, and do all their work …." She forced herself to take a breath. "Please. I didn't ask you to teach me how to *calculate*." The word had always sounded like a nasty curse to her. "You said you'd teach me to read." Even that seemed like an impossible task at the moment. She thought it wouldn't be so bad, but this … this was awful.

"And write. You can learn basic math at the same time." Temric had an odd expression on his face, as if he was offering her a treat and couldn't figure out why she wouldn't take it. "I'm not expecting you to do geometry."

That was going too far. She wasn't stupid! "But I *can* do geometry."
*Temric is just trying to help,* she reminded herself.

"I can do geometry," she assured Temric more gently. He was a good person. He didn't deserve her snarling at him.

"Without numbers?" he asked skeptically.

"You don't have to use mathematics for geometry. You measure. With string, or with time, or with your body."

"With a string," Temric said skeptically. And then he quirked his head. "And how do you keep time without counting?"

"The way everyone keeps time," she told him. "With hourglasses, and music, and the sun and moon and stars and clocks and calendars."

"But clocks and calendars have numbers," he protested.

"No they don't," she argued, but then realized his were probably different. "Well, ours don't."

"Clocks are complicated and delicate instruments. I'm impressed your tribe has them," Temric mused, mostly to himself, his gaze turned inward.

The heat of her blush slowly faded, though the humiliation stayed tight in her gut. There had to be a miscommunication if he thought clocks were complicated. "It's a ..." She couldn't think of a different Sothron word than clock. She realized she'd probably used the wrong word. "Sundial," she said in Thedran. "It's a globe made of steel wire and arrows on a carved dais. And we have a calendar made of stone columns."

"Oh." Temric looked away and worked his jaw back and forth for a moment before he looked back at her. "I think if you used numbers, all the things you're talking about would be easier and more accurate."

*Enough of this.* "If you have a string, I can show you."

Temric straightened up, then nodded. He pulled a leather lace out from a cabinet drawer. Just as he tried to latch the drawer the ship heaved up and rolled sideways. The drawer slammed open into him and Temric fell forward toward her. Billie managed to catch him before he crashed onto the floor on top of her. "Thank you," he gasped. He pushed the drawer shut, managed to latch it and settled back down, this time on the floor with her.

"You're welcome." She was glad he wasn't hurt. Aliiren hadn't been caught off-guard enough to shift at all. He'd simply spread his arms to brace between the wall beside him and the cabinet overhead.

Temric offered her a much larger piece of paper than she expected, and a fresh piece of charcoal. He must have notice the expression on her face, because he said, "we needed a new piece of paper for more of your writing anyway. It's all right. Draw on it as much as you like."

The man had no sense of economy. On the other hand, the paper was damp like everything else was by now, including their clothes, so it was probably ruined anyway.

She glanced at Aliiren. The sweat didn't surprise her. The air was so heavy with moisture that the very walls might sweat. But he was pale and his skin was mottled. His body heaved with the strength of his breaths. "Aliiren—if you need help …"

He shook his head. "Save your healing." His voice was even softer than usual. He swallowed hard and closed his eyes a moment. "In case someone is hurt."

"If you feel worse, please ask." She trusted he knew his own body, and yet … "But don't wait too long. If you start throwing up, there won't be much I can do until after the storm."

"I understand."

Billie worked with the charcoal and the string, tracing a line and a curve at each end of the line. She folded the measured piece of string she'd been using in half, and used that to mark the middle between the two ends of the line, checking from the other side to make sure she had it right. "Do you have a straight edge?"

"I do." Temric went back into his drawers, a different one this time, and found a beautiful folding instrument that had two straight edges connected by an arc. One straight edge rotated along the arc's curve. Both straight edges had lines marking perfectly even intervals along their lengths. If she'd known he had it, it would have been more precise to use the instrument, but never mind. She drew a line from the halfway point on the line to the point where the curves met. "There."

Temric glanced at it. "What's your message?"

Aliiren made a pained sound in his throat. "She drew a right angle without using the three four five rule," he said.

Billie had no idea what that rule was with its pointless numbers but yes. "I didn't need numbers to make it accurate."

Temric looked over at Aliiren. "You're not helping."

Aliiren smiled—he had a gentle, subtle smile that won past his nausea—and closed his eyes. His expression eased.

Temric lifted his hands in surrender. But then he laughed, and Billie chuckled along with him. The ship lurched, and this time everyone caught themselves in time.

"Has it been a long time? Since you left the Kilhells," Aliiren asked. The question surprised her, not because it was anything other than ordinary, but because Aliiren had made the effort to ask it.

Temric probably wanted to point out that if she'd learned, she might have been able to give Aliiren an answer in months or years. But would that have been accurate, even if she knew? "It feels like a long time. I feel older, and different, like I'm barely the same person. Unfortunately, it wasn't long enough to learn everything I needed to."

"Were you very young when they sent you to Ruvall?" Temric asked politely.

"No." The children taking classes at the college would certainly have an advantage, but she wouldn't have wanted to spend her childhood there. "My family wanted me to be fluent in Sothron speech, and strong enough to defend myself. Every summer my father would sit us among traders in Sellon so we could practice our languages. By the time I became fluent in Sothron, Thedran and Markan, I was strong and tall enough to brawl with the toughest of our women." Brian, by then, had surpassed her in height, and he was devilishly quick, but he still struggled with Sothron, and his Thedran was terrible.

They wouldn't have let him go ahead of her anyway. The chieftain first wanted to make sure that if they sent a valuable tribe member out into the world, that the tribe member would return safely. "How about you?" she asked Temric. "Have you been away from your people for long?"

His blue-eyed gaze lowered. "Years. I was sixteen when I left. I'm nearly twenty now." His arms crossed and he braced harder between the wall and cabinet than necessary to keep his balance. "Um … without using numbers … I was barely a man, though I thought I was a man at the time because I'd started to grow whiskers." He quirked a quick smile with a hint of sneer, as if he felt some disdain for who he'd been then. "I've seen a lot of seasons since then. I'm taller than I was, stronger." He shook his head, and his gaze dropped. "I've been scared for my life so many times I've lost count. It's made me miss home more than ever, now that I really understand that, by accident or by mistake or even chance, I might never see the people I love again." He shook his head again, then looked up. "How about you, Aliiren? I know that Ben Ariim is home, but I don't know how long you've been in Ruvall."

"A little over a month," he said softly. "But it seems like a year. It was still spring when I left. Now, I suppose there will be butterflies in the gardens. And there's The Sun Festival in a month. Our temple will have already begun to prepare for it." His sickness seemed to fade, replaced by sorrow. "It won't be the same without my teacher. She's dying, and I've been called back to sit with her."

Billie knew all too well how horrible he felt. At least, unlike when her aunt had died, she would be able to do something for her brother. Or so she hoped.

If there was no chance to save Brian, they wouldn't have called her home, not even for his funeral. There had to be hope.

"I'm sorry. I hope you each find comfort in the other, and that her passing is easy." The words, taught to her at Nuvar College, held even more meaning now that she spoke them to someone who was actually in the throes of impending loss.

"Thank you."

Nothing she could say would be good enough.

*I wonder if he regrets leaving home.*

Home. *Soon now,* she promised herself. She closed her eyes, and tried to imagine that she was already there. She thought of the cliff drums, how they'd played as she'd left for Sellon Port. Drumming and rhythm permeated Kilhellion life—sound and silence, light and darkness, meal to meal, task to task.

Life at Nuvar College had been so chaotic and disordered by comparison, with people up at all hours, eating at different times, never gathering as a whole. How could they? There were so many, with so many different paths of study, so many different lives.

She could almost hear the cliff drums now, calling her home. And yet, as difficult as it had been, she wished she could have finished her education. It wasn't just because she would have been more useful to the tribe. She felt as if she'd been on the cusp of something important, something more than learning how to assist in a birthing or the best way to set a broken bone.

Temric sighed. "I think we're all tired."

Billie nodded. "My mind is full." Besides, Aliiren looked like he could use some quiet. "Maybe we can do some more of this after everyone's slept, after the storm." The storm was already calming, though the ship still pitched and rocked severely. She could tell by the noise of the water on the hull, which now drummed and banged with less force. The water coming into the room dripped slowly, like drops falling from fir trees after a rainstorm.

"I'd like that," Temric said.

That was reassuring. She was starting to worry that she'd annoyed him by arguing with him. Billie grinned, but Aliiren didn't notice, and Temric seemed distracted. She sobered and reverted to politeness, which seemed to be the best thing to do in Ruvall. Or at least, politeness never made things worse. "You know where to find me when you're ready." She slipped into the dark hall and shut the door quickly behind her before the lean in the ship changed. Just in time, too, because the ship suddenly rose up and then slammed down. For a moment she felt suspended in the air, and then crashed sideways. The force smashed her hip and shoulder against the wall. She picked herself up and staggered toward the room she shared with the Rill.

Now that she was up and walking, the motion made her nauseated. It wouldn't take long before the vague ache in her head and the tension in her belly grew to full blown seasickness. She hadn't been seasick on the way to Ruvall, but it had been a near thing, and she'd had to spend quite a lot of time on the deck in the fresh air before she felt right again.

She'd probably do the same again this time, if the captain deemed it safe. The rules would probably be the same as they'd been on the other ship. No lights, and no talking on the deck. Even within the rooms, lights and voices were supposed to remain subdued over true night.

She hadn't done a very good job with that, but then the storm had been going on the whole time they'd been talking, so she doubted anything hellish would have heard her. Still, she wasn't used to minding her voice. She'd have to be more careful.

It had been a very strange feeling that first true night on a ship on the way to Ruvall, sitting in the quiet, total darkness after the storm, listening to the water and the ship being played by the wind and sea like a huge instrument. Before then, she'd never been outside of a stone building during true night. It was much as she'd imagined, except that in her imagination a huge, spider-like hellion snatched her up and started eating her alive.

She opened their door. It was dark within the room she shared with the Rill siblings. It smelled like sleep, and the increasingly stale, fishy scent of the sea that had worked its way through the ship's tiniest cracks in the storm. As the lean in the ship changed yet again, a puddle on the floor traveled out the door. She shut it.

Rani groaned in her sleep. It was a distinctive sound, strangled, like she was trying to scream and couldn't. Billie's father made those kind of sounds in his sleep sometimes. As harsh as Mount Cross could be, he'd come from a much crueler place: the lands of the valley kings. He always told her and her siblings how soft they had it in Torath, and how everyone in the lands of the valley kings was a slave to someone or something. He had lash scars on his back and the backs of his legs, and blade scars on his arms and shoulders and even one on his forehead. He didn't talk about coming to Mount Cross to find a bride, though that's what he'd done. He'd called it an escape.

He'd escaped.

She wondered what it must have been like to run away, to be hunted for days upon days, to try to find shelter during true nights without getting caught. Her father could be harsh at times, but she was proud of how clever and brave and tough her father was. When she became a mother, she hoped to be strong like him.

Well, she probably wouldn't beat her children so hard. She knew from watching others with their children, and knew in her own heart, that it wasn't needed.

Anyway, because of her father, she knew somewhat what to do for Rani.

Billie sat on the edge of the bed where she guessed Rani's head was so she was less likely to get kicked if Rani woke up in a panic. "Hey," she said softly, and set a hand on Rani's body. She'd found Rani's back, just beneath her shoulder. "It's all right. It's just a dream. You're dreaming. Wake up."

Rani moaned, and then she curled up and started to shiver, her breath coming in gasps.

Billie rubbed her back. "It was just a dream," she soothed.

Rani sobbed. "I dreamt … I dreamt we were in the desert." Her voice was hushed, but Edri stirred and woke nonetheless. "I dreamt we took shelter during true night in a building made of wood, like this ship but it was full of gaps and holes. I hoped that it would be all right if I left raw meat and milk outside the door for the nefari."

Billie shuddered. She'd been taught that any communication with hellions, even non-verbal exchanges, was a big mistake.

"I had the raw meat, but I didn't have any milk, and suddenly I was by myself, and there was light coming through the cracks. I was trying to fill a glass with my own blood to put outside instead of milk. But it was too late, and the nefarin was there, in the room with me."

Billie's heart quickened with fear, though it wasn't even her nightmare.

"He sunk his claws into my gut and gripped." She squeezed her belly with both hands. "He said, give it to me. I wanted … I knew he would kill me while he did it and I didn't care. I wanted him, and I wanted it to be over."

"Come here." Billie took Rani into her arms and rocked her. "That's not going to happen."

"Shh," Edri soothed. "I'm here too. You're all right."

Rani shuddered and drew in a sharp breath. "Tell me a story."

Billie's mother used to tell her stories when she'd wake up from nightmares. It felt natural to do the same for Rani. "How about a story about a hummingbird?" It was the first one she could think of where nothing died.

"Tell me about where you were born."

She considered, then decided there wasn't any harm in admitting her less-than-auspicious beginning. Besides, it was one of her favorite stories. "My mother was stubborn when she was pregnant with me. She went for a long ride when she shouldn't have, and ended up giving birth to me all by herself on the shores of our tribal river." When she needed to think or just be away from everyone for a while, she'd sit on the white rock near where she was born, where her mother sketched her badger with lead. She'd watch the milky green water rush by until she knew she'd have to get back to work. She hesitated when she realized she really didn't want to talk about being born by the river. "But we survived, though the chieftainess insisted that my mother and I stay at the songhouse for a month. It was partly to make sure we were both okay, and partly as a reprimand."

"What's a songhouse?"

That wasn't a question Billie had expected. She had to think about how to describe it. She supposed that talking about the differences between Torath's songhouse and what people in Ruvall called lodges or common houses would just confuse things. "Ours is built into the cliff. It used to be the main cavern at the start of the first and largest mine begun by our ancestors. The back is sealed off with a thick wall with very tight seams, and a huge hearth is built in front of that. The smoke vents into the mine shaft before it goes out the mountainside so that anything that might come through the chimney won't be able to breathe, not even nefari. The mantle for the great fire is made from the incense trees that grow all around us, and when the great fire burns, the whole lodge smells sacred." She closed her eyes as her memory filled her senses with the phantom of that powerful scent. "It's safe there."

Rani let out a sigh, and Billie felt her relax.

"When you first go in, there's a small stone door that protects the tunnel that goes through the front wall. At the far end there's another door that leads into the songhouse. There's an even smaller door barring the tunnel that leads to the barn cave. That's where we keep our most precious animals over true night." She'd always felt safe in the songhouse over true night.

The big doors on the buildings in Ruvall were made of stone reinforced by powerful blessings that repelled hellions and their god power, but the idea of leaving an opening in a building large enough for a sizable hellion to go through had terrified her. She couldn't sleep well in Ruvall in part because of that. The heat didn't help.

It would be good to sleep in the songhouse again, knowing that it had never been breached by hellions.

"It sounds damp and cold," Edri said with a shiver.

That made her smile. "Not at all. And when people start dancing and drumming and drinking and eating, it can get almost as hot as it does in Ruvall." She chuckled, and then she shrugged. "You might find the main hall a bit dark, but it's homey, and so beautiful. The walls are carved with blessings and painted with bright designs and art, some new, some from ages long gone. Part of the wall is painted with the essence figures of chieftains and important heroes. The timbers that support the roof of the songhouse are stained red from tura flower dye, and the floors and roof are washed white. All the furnishings are very fine, ancient oak and incense cedar with steel and gold and copper fittings and designs. The chairs are covered with soft wool, embroidered well with flowers and trees and animals …" She let out a sigh, her own body relaxing at the thought of being there.

"If it's a cave, why do you need support beams?" Edri asked.

It was a smart question. "It's survived earthquakes since ancient times, but it might develop faults in the rock that we can't see. The village engineers are responsible for checking them often and making sure everything is in good repair, especially after an earthquake."

"Do you have cliff drums in your village?" Rani sounded like she was feeling a bit better. Her low, musical voice, almost as rough as a cat's purr, held hints of thoughts and memories of her own.

"Yes." She could almost hear Torath's cliff drums, and feel their voices vibrate through her body. "They aren't as big or famous as the ones in Sellon Port. But ours are still powerful, deep-voiced, and we play them until our bones shiver with the sound. We dance and sing and scream with joy, and defiance, before every true night and after every festival feast."

"What do you defy?" she whispered.

Billie had to think about it. She'd never had to explain what she felt when she screamed at the world from the cliffs. "There's so much in the world that can crush us. I guess it's in defiance of that. That we survive, come storms, earthquakes, volcanoes … even nefari."

Rani shivered. "But what if they hear you?"

"Let them hear us. They'll come for us anyway, right?" But that wasn't helping Rani. Billie gentled her voice. "Let them hear us, and maybe they'll decide it's not worth it." That probably sounded insane to the Rill. She felt a need to explain. "It's an ancient tradition of my people, and we're still alive. We're strong. All of humanity is stronger than you think." Billie closed her eyes. In her mind she leapt and hammered the drum that was taller than her grandfather, and howled with joy at being alive and strong and proud to be Kilhellion.

Rani shivered. "Let's talk about something else."

"What about that story about the hummingbird?" Edri suggested.

Rani nodded and snuggled into Billie's arms with a sigh. Billie held her, a surge of protectiveness rushing through her. She spoke slowly and softly until Rani and Edri were safely asleep. After a moment, she shifted to get more comfortable, closed her eyes, and joined them in dreamless darkness.

## Chapter Seven

◇◇◇◇◇◇◇◇◇◇◇◇◇◇◇◇◇◇◇◇◇◇◇◇◇◇◇◇◇◇◇◇◇◇◇◇◇◇◇◇◇◇◇◇◇◇◇◇◇◇◇◇◇◇◇◇◇◇◇◇

# Edrion the Mender

◇◇◇◇◇◇◇◇◇◇◇◇◇◇◇◇◇◇◇◇◇◇◇◇◇◇◇◇◇◇◇◇◇◇◇◇◇◇◇◇◇◇◇◇◇◇◇◇◇◇◇◇◇◇◇◇◇◇◇◇

*Silver Parrot, A Thedran Sailing Vessel*
*1ˢᵗ Lost Day of Sun Month*

**B**illie sat on the deck and closed her eyes, though it made no difference if her eyes were open or not.

The ship sailed swiftly through the darkness. She knew this only because of the movement of the ship, and of the air, and the rushing sound as the ship cut, rose and dipped among the waves. Her fear that she might not reach her brother in time had grown worse than her fear of hellions. She sweated in anxious misery, each moment dragging on longer than the last. She'd never known a true night this long, though in truth it would last the same as any other.

She heaved herself up onto her knees, crawled up the stairs, and found the door to the forecastle. She let herself in to more darkness, and found the door leading to the Rill siblings' room. She knocked softly.

The door opened, letting out a blue-colored light. It seemed bright only by comparison to the darkness everywhere else. Edri peered up at her from where he sat on the floor. "You don't have to knock. You can just come in whenever you want." The place smelled pleasantly of food and wine with a hint of fresh seawater. The air was a little stagnant compared to the deck, but she didn't mind.

Rani was asleep, or trying to sleep. "I'm sorry," Billie whispered. "I can —" He was fixing the frayed strap on her bag. Her cheeks warmed. She needed to save her tribe's money for the journey home, but was she supposed to pay him for his work? "I—uh—How much do I owe you?"

Edrion worked swiftly with his awl and thick, waxed thread. "Nothing. I'm bored," he whispered back. "The sailors keep bringing us work but it's stuff they can fix themselves. They just pay us to do it because they think it'll bring them luck."

That sounded reasonable, but … "I can pay," she assured him.

"I know you have this thing about charity," he said, continuing to punch strong threads through the leather strap. He'd cut away the frayed end and was re-attaching the strap in a place where the rough canvas hadn't stretched and become threadbare. "But you're not in the Kilhells anymore. It's rude to argue when a friend is trying to do something nice for you. The correct response is, 'thank you.'"

Chastened, she forced herself to smile for him. "Thank you."

"You're welcome."

Now she felt like she needed to apologize. "I guess … I don't know what friendship means outside of the Kilhells. I thought the word friend meant the same thing everywhere, but …" She didn't want to say it, because she didn't want to think about the fact that once she left the ship, she wouldn't see Edri or Rani again. "There are a lot of words that I thought I knew what they meant, but I was wrong."

"Like what?"

Though they were still mostly strangers to each other, when she sat, Edri shifted to tangle his legs comfortably with Billie as if they'd been friends all of their lives. "Like … alone."

He smiled. "Now I'm curious. What do you think it means?"

"That you don't have anyone in your life," she said. "But a native speaker used it to say that they were by themselves. Which is a different thing."

He looked to one side and nodded. "I think I understand." He nodded again, seeming to agree with himself. "I think if someone meant it the way you understood it, they would say that they're *all* alone."

She wasn't sure she would remember that, but she hoped so. She also hoped she wouldn't have to use the word in that context. "Thank you."

"Any time." He got back to work. "I'm nervous about Ben Ariim," he admitted. "We don't know anyone. There are Rill there, of course, but it'll be different than it would have been if we went to Ben Ariim with our tribe. In a way, Rani and I will be all alone." He looked into her eyes, his eyes tinted a more intense blue by the light, his body moving easily with the ship's sway as he worked.

He kept treating her like a close friend, and that added to her confusion about what friendship meant in the world. It hadn't come up in Ruvall, like she'd hoped it would. She hadn't earned a single friend there, though she'd tried.

She hadn't even had to try with Edrion. He trusted her even though she hadn't earned that right. And he made the feeling of closeness that she felt for him feel safe. He made her want to offer to stay with him and Larani in Ben Ariim, so that she could protect them, so that they could all take care of each other.

*I wish I could.*

There was something special about Edrion, something natural, and animal that felt familiar. Edri's sister was the same way, though she wasn't as relaxed. If Edrion was a cat stretched out with its belly bared to a fire, Larani was a cat napping in the shadows nearby.

Edri was a lot like Brian, she realized. A friendly sort of wild, she thought with humor. She was part of the same litter of wild babies, but she was the more awkward and nippy one.

Edrion smiled a very boyish smile edged in mischief. "What?"

She grinned. "You remind me of my brother."

"Because I ask annoying questions and follow you everywhere?"

She shook her head and laughed under her breath. "When he was too small to keep up, I would carry him on my hip. I wasn't that much bigger, but I wanted him with me." She didn't have much memory of that, but her sister Stayce told stories about the two of them. "He called me Horsie back then." He still did sometimes, when he wanted to tease her.

Edri did his best to muffle his laugh with his fist. "Well, you certainly don't remind me of my sister," he said. "But I feel it too. Like we've known each other a long time. Maybe we did, in a previous life."

"Could be," she admitted, though it was hard to imagine.

"You don't sound convinced," he teased.

She realized that it was just prejudice. There wasn't any reason, really, to doubt. "We're taught that Kilhellions are reborn as Kilhellions. I can recite the names of my former lives and everything. And ..." It was hard to put into words. "Part of me believes that, but ... Now I've been outside the Kilhells. Humanity is so vast. And it makes me wonder, why would that be true? I mean, we're House of Life, very nearly all of us on and around Mount Cross. When there's been a recent death, it isn't unreasonable to believe that a Kilhellion born right after on the mountain is the same soul. But I've come to realize, there's no way to know for sure."

"We're House of Life too, but our tradition is exactly the opposite," Edrion told her. "We believe that you're only born Rill once. We have the duty and privilege to make the most of it."

It was an intriguing idea. "And how do Rill make the most of being born Rill?"

"We travel. Try to see as much of the world as we can. Take risks, because we're lucky and so why not take a chance? When the tribe decides we're ready, we're sent out on our own or in pairs, sometimes in small groups, so that we can learn to be more independent. That's what my sister and I are doing. And then, eventually, when the time seems right, we find our way back to our home tribe. Or not. A lot of Rill end up marrying into other tribes when they wander."

That tradition made all kinds of sense to her. "Sounds like fun. Learning new things all the time, meeting people …."

"Mostly it's fun." He ducked his head, maybe to better watch what he was doing, or maybe he wanted to hide his expression from her. She worried that she'd pinched an old wound similar to the isolation and humiliations she'd endured at the college. "But there are limits. We're expected to love and have children only with other Rill. If you fall in love with someone who isn't Rill, well … the tribes take it really seriously. Even if your family is willing to accept it, they'll do anything they can to prevent a heart match. But it happens."

"We're strict in the Kilhells too," Billie said gently. He was a bit young for something as serious as a life bond, but maybe not. It just seemed like there was a sad story behind his words. "Because most of the villages on the mountain are small, you can't just fall in love with anyone. Except that, of course, it happens. Cousins." She winced. "And then they tell you that although you can dally with whomever you want outside the clan, it's shameful to take a relationship with a foreigner seriously. I could bed you all I wanted, even have children with you, but if I brought you home and told my parents that you were my one and only?" She shook her head.

"They'd cast you out?"

"No. They'd cast *you* out before winter, unless you could prove you were worthy. Which you might, but if you don't … people who love each other separated like that … it's not easy to find a partner in life. To find someone and then lose them? That's hard."

"What if there are children?" he asked softly.

"Oh, they'd stay. They'd be Kilhellion, bled of my body." Saying it out loud to a stranger, though it seemed natural and normal in the moment, in retrospect made her feel uncomfortable. The fleeting expression of shock on Edrion's face made it worse.

"And if the mother was the foreigner?"

Billie cringed to think of it. "If she was lucky, she'd never know she was pregnant before she was forced to leave. Because a child bled in the village with at least one Kilhellion parent ... they'd be tribe and clan. The child would stay. The mother would have to prove herself worthy." She couldn't bear to think of any parent being forcefully separated from a child, but a mother from a nursing babe would make a horrific situation even worse.

Edrion sucked a sharp breath in through his teeth.

She'd been taught beautiful poems and songs and sad stories about it. She doubted Edri would consider them as romantic or as heroic as she'd once thought them. She especially used to love the stories where the mother proved herself worthy. But could an outsider prove themselves to someone like Billie's father? And even if they could, would they want to live and raise their child in a place like Torath, when everywhere else seemed so much safer, richer, and grander?

*Father warned me not to be lured by the false promises of wealth and leisure. Have I begun to lose my way? Maybe Brian, by falling ill or whatever else might have happened to him, has saved me from forgetting what really matters. Family. Service. Integrity.*

Edrion worked slowly and quietly with his awl. She must have offended him. She started to gather herself to leave when he spoke. "In our way, the lovers can stay together, as a family, with children even. The Rill, though, is disowned."

"Disowned." She whispered the word. It seemed like a comparatively small crime for a disownment.

He cocked his head and his eyes narrowed. "I'm not sure you mean it the way I mean it."

"How do you mean it?" she asked. "What happens?"

"They're treated like anyone who isn't a Rill. And their children are treated as if they aren't Rill. It's said you lose your luck, too. That you're stained, and you'll never wash clean again."

That sounded awful, but given a choice, she would prefer a traditional Rill disownment to a Kilhellion one.

He stopped working to look into her eyes. "What happens in the Kilhells?"

She felt bound to tell him the truth, even if it horrified him. "You have to leave forever. It's like you're dead. They even set up a shrine for you and keep it like you were lost forever on the mountain. Depending on why you were disowned, other villages might join in. And if you try to stay, or try to come back? They'll kill you."

"That's …" Apparently he couldn't think of anything polite to say.

"You have to do something really awful to deserve it," she assured him. "Like murdering someone in the tribe."

He frowned and his brows puzzled together. "Why don't they just kill that person if they did something like that?"

The thought appalled her. She wasn't sure she could explain, but she needed to try. "We all depend on each other to survive. Even when you drive each other crazy, or feud over something serious, you need one another." She wasn't explaining very well. "It's more than dependence, though. There's no one in my village that I wouldn't die to save, if that's what it took. And they'd do the same for me. Do you think I could kill someone from my village, no matter what they'd done? But there are things that happen, things we can't forgive. Disownment … in a lot of ways, it's worse than death. If you die, at least you can live a new life, hopefully with more honor. But disownment isn't meant to be merciful to the one disowned. It's a mercy to the family and friends, so that they don't have to execute someone they love. It's a symbolic death, only made actual if the person refuses to accept it."

Edri nodded. "I think I understand."

She smiled with relief before she realized that understanding didn't mean that he thought it was right.

"Why do you do that?" he asked.

"What?"

He let out a sigh. "It's like you're trying to hide how you really feel."

"It's not that," she assured him. "It seems like whenever I talk about my tribe, I horrify people."

"It might not be what you tell them, necessarily," he offered. "A lot of people are afraid of Kilhellions. They *expect* to be horrified." He sighed again. "I wish I could say I don't know why, but I've heard the stories."

"What stories?" She dreaded his answer.

"The ones where Kilhellions are heartless brutes who'll do anything for money."

*What?*

"I guess I can see how people could get that impression," he continued, "but I lived with a Kilhellion tribe when I was young, in Gatha. I liked them a lot. They were fun to hang around, and I knew I was safe with them." He grinned and set aside his work to gesture with his hands as he spoke. "They'd put together some cliff drums on the rocks above the Shellush River for festivals. They let me play a few times. It was one of the happiest years of my life." He closed his eyes for a moment, then got back to work again. "You must be really homesick."

Billie nodded. She didn't trust herself to explain how much.

"Me too." For a moment she could see past his affable manners into eyes weary and too bright. He probably hadn't been sleeping well either. Had he trusted her to see the truth behind the easy smiles and ready laughs, or had exhaustion broken his armor? "I especially miss the storytelling after dinner, and the circle dances."

"I miss my family, and the quiet, and my mother's apple cobbler. And I'm loved there." She took in a deep breath of the room's warm, damp air and blew it out, then forced herself to smile. "I'm glad I was able to go to Ruvall. I understand better what I have in Torath. Maybe people outside of the Kilhells see us as brutes, but you know what? We don't treat other people like shit, because we know people are precious, and life is short and hard enough without making each other miserable. I've experienced more cruelty in one day in Ruvall than I had my whole life on Mount Cross. People in Ruvall ... they treat each other like they don't matter unless they're bled of the right family or know the right people."

"I think that's true."

His words made her dare to say something that had bothered her about Ruvall, something deeper than the disdain she'd been subjected to. "I think that in cities there are so many people, and so many blessings, that they no longer appreciate them. Honestly, I don't know what they appreciate."

Edri nodded. "I've traveled with my tribe to quite a few places, but they've all been large cities. I think it's time I visit a place like your home, so that I can learn to appreciate all the things I take for granted."

She wanted him to, very much. She was a little afraid of how he might be treated. Not badly. No. He'd be welcomed, respected, an honored guest come from far away. But ... "You know they'll test your courage and skill and mettle."

Edri smiled shyly. "I remember a little of it from Gatha. Mostly the brawls. I was too young to be a part of that. But I wanted to fight. I still want my courage tested. I want to know."

She squeezed his foot and waggled his leg with it. "I already know you're brave."

"Because I'm talking to you?" he said with a little laugh, kicking back a bit.

She chuckled and let go. "No. Because you talk to everyone. Because you open your heart to everyone. You're right. I've been hiding, not my feelings, but my heart. It feels safer to expect to be hurt, like I have control." She sniffed at her own ridiculousness. "When I say it aloud it's obvious that's not true. I should be more like you."

"No. *You* should be more like you." He nudged her with his foot. "I bet you're not like this at home."

"No, I'm not. But I have my family." It wasn't her whole family, though, that made her feel like she always had someone beside her, no matter what. "I have my brother."

He cocked his head to one side and glanced up at her with a slight smile that carried up into his bright blue eyes. "Sounds like you and he are a lot like me and Rani."

"There's something about him—" She couldn't wait to hug him, and then punch his shoulder for making her worry. "My parents like to say that my sister and I were promises from Life that something amazing would come of their love, and that Brian fulfilled that promise."

His brows bunched up and he pressed his lips into a brief frown. "I don't know why you're smiling. That would make me feel like I mattered less than Rani."

She'd never cared about that. "If you meet him, you'll understand. It would be silly to be jealous of him. It would be like the moon being jealous of the sun."

He shrugged, smiling again. "Maybe the moon *is* jealous of the sun. But I'm convinced he's amazing, and I want to meet him."

*Come with me,* she wanted to say. But she'd have to ask permission from the chieftain and her parents before she invited the sibs.

"Can I practice some healing on you?" she asked instead.

He tossed aside his work and eagerly held out his hands. "I thought you'd never ask! My neck is so sore. Can you fix it?"

"I'll try." She took his warm, calloused hands in hers, closed her eyes, and carefully, slowly, gently, began her work.

## Silver Parrot, A Thedran Sailing Vessel
### 1st Watch Night of Sun Month

"WHAT SOUND DOES THIS MAKE?" TEMRIC ASKED IN THEDRAN, HOLDING up a card he'd made. It was one of a thick stack. The symbol, thankfully drawn large so it was easier for her to make out the details, made her think of a cup with a few loops on one side and a tail that might have been a stem if it were a glass.

"Tur?"

"Correct."

She grinned, thrilled that the sounds the shapes made were finally working their way into her head. For his part, Temric had made a lot of progress with Thedran as well. Speaking to him in Thedran using simple, common words helped. "Your turn. What's the Thedran word for wool?" She used the Sothron word for wool, but she spoke the rest in Thedran.

"Wool?" Temric cupped his hands over his nose and looked up, then swept them down onto his lap and rubbed his thighs as if he could massage the answer out of his long legs. "I don't think you taught me that yet."

"I did," she promised. "I can start the rhyme to help you."

His fingers dug into his legs. "No. I want to try no help."

"Try *with* no help," she corrected.

"Hmm. I want to try with no help." She nodded when Temric looked to her for approval. "Why do I need for to learn the word anyway? It maybe not useful." Though he struggled at times, she could tell he'd already learned a lot from trying to read Thedran before they'd met. He just needed more confidence, and a bigger vocabulary, was all. The rough grammar would work itself out with practice.

"It's valuable." That was a hint, but she refrained from taking it further.

Aliiren slept nearby. Exhaustion had finally won out over the ship's noisy complaints and wild bucking during the storm before true dawn. He'd curled up adorably within a pile of cushions and blankets, head pillowed on his elbow, a half-closed hand tucked up against his mouth. His hair shaded his eyes from the light. She carefully drew an extra blanket over him.

He let out a soft sigh that might have been contentment.

If he dreamed, she hoped that they were sweet, calm dreams.

True night would be over in moments. She could feel it in her body, a kind of anticipation like early morning on a clear spring day. Above them, rain drummed against the thick roof boards. It had been going on and on, even before the dawn's eve storm winds began to push the ship around. Everything was damp: clothes, bedding, even her hair.

It had also cooled off enough that she felt an occasional chill. The Rill, and many of the sailors, had bundled up into heavier clothes and some even swathed themselves in blankets to stay warm. Apparently living for long periods in the heat made a person's skin thinner, or something.

"Ah!" Temric's eyes lit with inspiration. "It sounds like the Sothron word for coin. Wool!" His accent would probably remain with him always, but that wasn't a bad thing. Sothron accents always sounded smart, controlled, and dignified in Thedran. But then he frowned again. "I asked you with no help." He drew from the pile of cards.

The symbol looked like dying snakes wriggling through rings. "Moo?" She knew it was wrong immediately after she said it. "No. Ren."

"More trying."

Her hands clenched at her sides and she gritted her teeth. "Gun."

"Do you want help?"

"Yes," she relented.

"Two together they mean more than one."

Which, if she remembered right, meant the sound would land at the end of a word, and only when the same letters were paired.

Gods, there were so many ways to think of the number two! Why weren't people who counted more specific? Because a pair was different than mates was different than twins …

She was letting herself get distracted.

Anyway, his hint wasn't much of a hint. "Fey?"

He stared at her as if he could send the sound from his eyes into her brain.

A familiar sense of frustration filled her chest with pressure and clouded her head. She hadn't learned to read any words yet. And she wasn't even close to learning all the letters. There were more letters than stars, or so it seemed. "I think I would remember these better if I knew what whole words looked like."

"You need to learn the core block letters before you can learn even simple words," Temric told her, switching to Sothron.

"Why?"

He sighed. "All right, maybe it's better if I do teach you some words." He turned the previous card around and wrote on it, then showed her two symbols together. "What does this sound like?"

"I have no idea. What's the word?"

"You're supposed to sound it out. That's how Sothron writing works.

All these letters are symbols to represent the sounds we make. You just told me the sound for the first letter," he said. "This letter," he amended, pointing to Tur.

Aliiren rolled over in his sleep. His shoulders relaxed, and his breathing slowed.

True dawn had probably come. The storm did seem less ferocious. Maybe.

She turned her attention back to the card.

All at once she remembered the sounds the letters made. "Tur-fah?" she tried.

"Turfah," he said. "Yes."

Turfah, which meant foot in Sothron. A thrill passed through her. She laughed, and then her chest felt heavy. Tears threatened to well up. It was overwhelming, this thing, a tangle of shame that she could do so little when everyone else found it so easy, mixed up with a feeling like she'd fought past a tough enemy and won, only to realize that a whole army awaited her. She looked at the thick stack of cards and knew she'd never succeed.

"You did it." Temric smiled as he sorted through his stack of papers, clearly pleased. "Excellent." He looked up as he started to offer her a square, then lowered his hand. "You've made great progress," he said gently, like he was soothing a colt separated from the herd for the first time.

"Small children all over the Sothron Empire do better," she reminded him, and herself.

"Not when they begin. You have to—"

"No!" The woman's voice—was that Rani? —was muffled by the walls around them but its desperation made Billie lurch to her feet.

It felt like a god yanked the deck out from under them. She slammed into the wall. Temric fell into her with bruising force. The ship moaned, and then groaned and creaked, the sound growing louder and louder. A finer, splintering sound focused above them and then spread along the large beam in the center of the ceiling. Water pounded against the ship, like it was trying to get in. Aliiren had surged up from his bed, wild-eyed. They were all on their feet now, bodies close in the tight quarters. They were all quiet, straining to hear past the ship's agonies for any sound that might tell them if they were about to die.

"What is that?" Temric breathed.

She didn't know. Hellion attack? A sea monster?

She looked to Aliiren. "Is it a hellion attack?"

His golden gaze darted back and forth, then fixed on his sword. He picked it up from the shelf at the head of the bed. "I don't know. I don't think so. It's already true dawn."

"Isn't this the storm?" Temric asked. "I thought the storm would end at true dawn."

Aliiren nodded. "That storm has passed."

"Are you sure?" Temric clung to the bed, clearly unconvinced.

Running footsteps thumped in a fast line above them.

"I'm going to check on Rani and Edri." Billie checked her sword and dagger to make certain of their place, then went into the hall. Aliiren followed close behind. Tilla had opened her door, and thank the Gods, so had the Rill. They all looked all right, if wide-eyed and a little tousled. Billie went to the door leading out onto the walkway and cracked it open.

A blustery wind drove rain against her through the crack. A faint light glowed near what she guessed was the horizon. Was that the sunrise? Instinctively she touched her hair, aware that she didn't have her shawl, though the dim glow couldn't possibly pose a threat.

It didn't seem like sunlight. More like moonlight.

The sailors rushed to take down the sails. Nearly all the multitude of sails had already come down. The seas sounded strange against the hull of the ship, almost like the storm waves, but not as tall. It made a racket, as did the protests from the ship's body.

She realized that they weren't moving.

They'd stopped.

She stepped out fully into the weather. It was then that she finally saw the source of the light.

It stood out against the darkness like a distant lantern in fog, but it revealed little of their surroundings. Curtains of rain fell through a dark mist made ragged by the capricious wind, and something dark loomed beneath the light—a hill? The diffuse light faded and grew in a slow rhythm.

*What is that?* The hairs prickled up on her arms, and not just from the cold rain that soaked through her clothes and clung to her skin. Her hand closed on the hilt of her sword, but that gave her no comfort. She let go. "Can I help?" she asked a passing sailor.

It was the one from the longboat that had taken them in. "You?" It was hard to see her expression beyond a gash of a mouth downturned by fear, but her voice was hard with frightened anger. "No."

"What is that?" Billie asked, pointing to the light.

"It's the Embrer Light Tower," she said.

A light tower? Did that mean they'd reached Ben Ariim? But if they had, where were the rest of the city lights, and … "Why aren't we moving?"

"We've run aground."

Billie went to the rail and looked over. All she could see was water alive with glowing froth. Whatever had stopped them was beneath the waves, which rolled and crested like they were running up a beach, but there was no land to be seen.

"It's high tide, too," the sailor told her. "We're in shit."

Chapter Eight

<><><><><><><><><><><><><><><><><><><><><><><><><><><><><><><><><><><><><><><>

# Go Right a Ship

<><><><><><><><><><><><><><><><><><><><><><><><><><><><><><><><><><><><><><><>

*Silver Parrot, A Thedran Sailing Vessel*
*2nd Meet Day of Sun Month*

Though clearly overwhelmed, and though it seemed that they had more work than sailors that could do it, the captain told Billie and the other passengers to stay in their quarters. Before he shut them in, he quickly explained their predicament. The heavy rain had tricked the watch into thinking that the hints of light they'd seen had heralded the first light of dawn, when in fact it was the Embrer Light Tower. They'd realized their mistake too late to change course. Now the sailors were going to try to get the ship unstuck from the sand bar, and it was best if everyone stayed out of their way.

When she'd asked if someone could row for help, the captain had explained that Embrer Tower was on an island too far from the mainland to risk sending a boat, especially on the wild, choppy waters following true night.

Apparently they were lucky to hit sand and not rock. The captain believed that they owed their good fortune to the presence of the Rill siblings.

Nothing about the situation seemed lucky to Billie.

She wanted to rage and shove and howl. Instead, she sat in the doorway to the room she and the Rill used, and tried to take slow, even breaths while her heart raced.

Rani settled beside her but facing into the room, her back braced against the narrow width of wall beside the door, the great volumes of her skirts a splash of color in the damp, dimly lit room. "It's going to be all right," she said gently.

Billie didn't dare speak. There was a danger that she'd say something she'd regret. She attempted to squeeze some of the damp out of her sleeves, but it was no use. Just a few drops trickled out from between her fingers. If she wanted her clothes to dry, she'd have to change out of them and properly wring them.

The ship suddenly shrieked. A faint cry penetrated their room from outside. Billie started to lurch up to go see if someone needed help, but Rani grabbed the fabric at Billie's shoulder to check her. "They'll come get you if they need you."

*She's right. They won't want me unless they need a healer.* The ship's shriek deepened and softened to a groan, then faded into the cacophony of the waves against the hull.

Rani took Billie's hand and squeezed. It felt sisterly, though Billie's sister was never this good to her. "We're with you. Nothing bad is going to happen to you."

"I don't care what happens to me. I have to help my brother."

"Worrying isn't going to help him." Rani offered Billie a canteen decorated with symbols of Sea, one of the lost Gods. "At least have some water."

Billie dutifully took a sip. The metal mouth on the canteen gave the water a tinny flavor. "Thank you," she said, offering it back.

"Drink the whole thing. You need it."

Rani was right, and not just about the uselessness of worrying. The moment Billie thought of her own body, her gift came into her awareness, as sensitive as skin but all around inside her, telling her that not only was she parched, but hungry. A moment later her stomach growled in agreement with her gift.

Was the wind dying down? The ship moaned, but with a sound that reminded her of relief, like someone who was no longer in excruciating pain.

Billie got up—this time Rani didn't try to stop her—walked to the end of the hall and opened the door.

There was light out there, and it definitely wasn't the lighthouse this time. Pale, silvery light glowed through the clouds and soft rain. It was daylight, but the storm kept them shrouded in twilight.

Obviously, they were still stuck.

The majority of the sailors had loosely encircled the captain on the deck below, conferring in a mixture of Thedran and the language of sailing. Billie couldn't follow the arcane conversation, even if she'd been able to catch every word over the noise.

Edrion and Larani moved up behind her. "This is not good," Edrion whispered.

Billie pressed the canteen into Rani's hands and trotted down the stairs. "I have to get out of here." She didn't know how, but she had to find a way to Ben Ariim.

At least the rain had softened to a drizzle. The crew looked wrecked, soaked, every one of them exhausted.

Captain Lily lifted a finger in her general direction while he muttered something to one of his people. She forced herself to be patient.

Temric stepped up alongside her, a book in hand. "Billie, why don't we practice some more? There's nothing you can do."

"Actually," the captain said, turning to them, "there are a lot of things we have to do. Gather up the other passengers and bring them back here."

Maybe the water had calmed enough that someone could risk rowing to Ben Ariim for help.

*They have to take me with them.*

Moments later everyone, including all the sailors, stood at the edges of the deck. The captain took the center of their glum assembly.

"The tide is already turning against us," the captain told everyone. "The ship will not move as she is. The plan now is to unload everything we can—including all the passengers, all the gear, everything not fastened hard to the ship—to Embrer Island. The idea is that when high tide comes again, she'll be lighter. We'll try again to shift her, this time using the anchors and assistance from the long boats. With some luck …" He looked at the Rill siblings with significance, "we'll be free of the sandbar by this afternoon. We'll need all hands, passengers too, to make this happen. Let's get to work."

That sounded far better than what Billie had in mind. She eagerly joined a group of sailors tasked with getting the long boats and row boats in the water. Then she helped roll huge water barrels to the side where the rail had been removed and pushed them into the sea. A pair of sailors roped the barrels together to tow to the island. She helped row the barrels to the shore, and then returned for more.

She hadn't done much rowing except on a little rowboat that her friends had on a lake near Torath, and that had been a long time ago. The lake didn't have anything like the waves that complicated every stroke, either. At least the lee on the island was close, and it had a small, gravel beach, so the waves weren't pushing them into dangerous rocks. Her drumming came in handy too. She quickly learned to move in rhythm with the other sailors, who worked as if the sea was a great shared drum for them to beat with their oars. As long as they moved in time, her weary body moved almost on its own with them. As soon as anyone stopped for a rest or faltered, though, it bled the strength right out of her.

A thin mist hung in the air. Everyone and everything was damp. Many of the sailors shivered, even while they worked. Waves bucked and peaked in a confusion against the hull, sending spray up all around the ship. To the east, silhouetted against the brightening sky, stood a small, rocky island shrouded in ragged fog. A tower stood at its flat-topped peak. A large sacred light's glare forced her to look away as its beam slowly passed over them. Now it shone clear, but it was too late to warn them.

As the day wore on, she had to stop for longer and longer spells to rest, and her throat tasted of blood.

The island was little more than a pile of rocks soaked by sea spray. Razor-edged grass grew from tiny patches of gravel and pebbly sand. Olive-toned seaweed and pale green anemones sulked near the shore, abandoned by the retreating tide. The dark, cracked rocks beyond the loose gravel shore formed steep slopes and broken walls, which made moving the barrels up above the high tide line extremely hard work. Gulls screamed and pelicans flapped nearby, hunting in the shallow waves in the island's lee while she sweated in her sea-soaked clothes. As much as they'd taken from the ship, there always seemed to be more to move from ship to shore.

By the time the work finally ended, the ship had, with the force of water and tides, leaned over. According to the captain, the rising tide would help right her.

*This will work. It has to,* Billie told herself.

Though all she wanted to do was drink a whole canteen of water and collapse somewhere quiet until her body stopped aching, she nodded when the captain asked if she wanted to help paddle on one of the longboats. Aliiren also agreed to paddle. The Rill siblings had to remain on the ship in hopes that their luck would help. Tilla and Temric had already agreed to some other work needed on the ship.

Captain Lily tried to hide it, but she noticed the tight line his mouth made when he thought no one was looking. He was anxious about his ship. *He's not sure this will work.*

*Shit.*

Temric and Tilla were dropped off on the ship, while Billie and Aliiren were placed at the rear of a large longboat. They waited by *Silver Parrot's* massive hull, paddling only as needed to keep the longboat close without smashing into the ship's side, while some sort of work went on aboard.

The rowing had been exhausting but felt natural. Paddling, on the other hand, felt awkward. The shaft was a little shorter than a broom handle, with a T grip at the top. The blade was almost as long as her arm from shoulder to wrist. Leather wrapped around the shaft just above the paddle formed another grip. To use her paddle with full force she had to twist her body and lean over the side of the boat. Quite often she dipped the hand that gripped near the paddle's blade into the water itself when a wave caught the stroke.

At least she had time to practice before they began any serious work. The sailor on the bench ahead of her coached her and Aliiren, having them each go through the proper motions very slowly while everyone else kept the boat from moving astray. He wanted them to keep their 'dry' hands on the T grip relaxed, and to make sure the paddle entered and left the water with as little splash as possible. He taught them to brace their legs so they could use most of the strength in their bodies rather than just their backs or arms. "Never move the water hand past your hip," he told them, "and your dry hand never goes lower than your heart. Straight arms—maybe with a little bend on the dry arm—back straight, and don't lean too far forward when it's time to dip into the water. The twisting of your body does most of the work when you pull. Move in time with everyone ahead of you. You're in the back so you can watch, and learn, and not make too much of a mess if you have to stop to rest or you'll backsplash. Oh, and keep that dry hand above the water when you dip in, not inside the boat. The shaft should move straight along the side of the boat, not at an angle."

The waves weren't much compared to what they had been right after true dawn, but as each swell lifted the longboat up and plunged them back down near the ship, Billie still got an alarming view of the ship's hull. Little spiny sea creatures and tiny shells promised to catch and drag under anything that brushed up against them.

The captain leaned over the rail high above them. "I'm sending down the anchor!"

"Ready!" their foreman answered.

The anchor descended toward them. They wouldn't be doing this if anyone thought the anchor would sink the boat, would they?

"You two," the foreman told Billie and Aliiren. They stood as he guided the anchor into the water and then allowed the massive links of the anchor chain to slide along his hands. There was a ball of some sort, huge, made of stiff leather. Billie and Aliiren helped push it out so the ball wouldn't hit the boat. Once the ball floated on the water, together they gripped the thick, painted iron chain links and made sure the longboat stayed close as everything moved with the waves. Meanwhile the foreman set a hook in a metal hole at the rear of the boat. When the anchor dragged the ball just beneath the surface of the waves, he looped a chain link through the hook.

Slowly their boat took on the anchor's weight, offset by the air-filled ball. The crew on the ship played out more anchor chain, and then thick rope. The longboat's nose came up a bit and the waves threatened to wash into their end of the longboat, but somehow they didn't sink.

The foreman returned to the front of the boat. He took up a small drum, then whistled sharply. "Paddles up!" Everyone extended their paddles over the boat's sides into the water. They set their paddles as far forward as they could comfortably reach without leaning forward over their legs or hunching their backs. "Pull!" he called as he rapped the drum. Billie pulled hard alongside the boat, the blade deep in the water. "Chop, chop, chop, chop," the foreman called in quick succession as he rapped the drum, timing their paddling so that they could get their boat moving with swift, short pulls. "And pull! Pull!" He stretched the drum's rhythm, giving them time to use all the power in their bodies. She heard similar calls from a boat on *Silver Parrot's* other side.

The anchor's weight dragged at the normally nimble boat. Billie pulled hard with each stroke, body twisting to keep her dry hand over the water while the blade traveled beneath the surface. Her breath began to labor but she was determined to keep up with the sailors.

At last they began to make some progress. The thick rope attached to the anchor chain snaked behind them on the water as they paddled away from the ship.

They finally ran out of anchor rope a long way away. The other longboat had gone the same distance, but at an angle from the ship's stern, as if to pull her back the way she'd come as much as drag her upright.

The foreman returned to the longboat's stern. Billie, sweating and still panting hard, shifted on the bench to make way for him. She looked at

Aliiren and their gazes met. For a moment she felt a sharp connection, like he'd taken her into his arms. Then he frowned and looked away.

What was that about?

The foreman did something to cause the hook to drop down, but the chain was still hung up on its end. He did something deep in the water, then took a tool and forced the chain off the hook.

The ball bobbed up to the surface while the anchor plunged out of sight. He nodded at the water grimly. "Well, that's our part done." The foreman had them settle in and then they paddled back to the ship. They took up a slow pace that was probably meant to let them rest, but Billie was already exhausted. She had to stop several times to catch her breath. At least she wasn't the only one. Aliiren and several of the sailors had to do the same.

The sailors on *Silver Parrot* tossed a heavy line to the foreman, which he tied to the longboat's hook while everyone took a proper rest, the shafts of their paddles across their legs. Then they had to get back to work. The other longboat moved parallel and slightly behind them as they paddled away.

Finally they reached the end of the rope. And waited.

And waited. She rested the paddle's shaft across her legs and took deep, slow breaths. Her gift gently woke and slid vinus into overworked muscles. She didn't try to stop it. The heat from the healing was negligible, and her body would be better prepared to work hard again.

Sails began to go up on the ship, but not very many and they weren't raised all the way. Much of the sailcloth luffed and billowed unevenly in the wind. She wasn't used to seeing the sails like that. Before, if there was so much as a flutter on a sail edge, the captain would command his sailors to play with ropes until the problem was fixed.

"Why don't they just sail the ship off the mud?" Aliiren asked.

"She's stuck hard," the sailor that had coached them explained. "Sails won't be enough. Even if they were, the masts might snap before she broke free."

The anchor lines the two longboats had set in the water began to tighten.

"It'll be the tide, the work on the capstans, the sails, and us together that'll free the ship," the sailor added. "We want her righted before the twelfth hour. That's high tide."

"Almost halfway between noon and midnight," Aliiren told her helpfully.

"And the Rill will help," the sailor across from him told them.

"Yes, the Rill too," their coach said, unmoved.

Billie had the same doubts. If Rani and Edri were actually lucky, why did they get stuck in the first place?

"Ready," the foreman warned them. Billie got her paddle in the water, the fist gripping just above the paddle washed over by waves, and prepared herself with a series of deep breaths. The weather had warmed, and the clouds had broken apart, exposing them to frequent glares from the sacred sun. Her woolens were soaked down one side from paddling. The wool felt unpleasantly sticky and scratchy with seawater and sweat even through her linen undergarments. "Together now, let's tighten the line. Pull," he said gently, and Billie tenderly stroked the water. "Pull …"

"Pull! Pull! Pull!" The foreman suddenly screamed the words, pounding the poor little drum with his thick drumstick. Billie paddled with all her might, her body in concert with the drum and the sailor ahead of her as if they were lovers. The foreman didn't let up. His voice fired her soul. She felt like she was swimming up a powerful current, her body straining for freedom, for purchase, for motion.

They weren't going anywhere, not that she could tell. The rope strained as they hacked at the water. The motion of the waves sometimes made her miss the water with the paddle. Sometimes she'd cut into a wave near the surface, the paddle only half-buried, and sometimes she plunged elbow deep. The water swelling in the wool weighed at her arms. Her breath came in gasps, and her ribs felt as if they would shatter. Gods, this was as hard as she'd ever worked in her life, and for nothing!

"Pull! Pull! Pull!" the foreman continued to cry. Every moment her body wanted to give up and rest. But each time he called she had to answer.

She had to get home. She drove herself hard until her heart felt like it would burst.

Meanwhile, the rope with the anchor began to sing. She thought the anchor would slacken as they pulled on their longboat's rope, but then she realized what they were doing on the ship.

The people on the ship were hauling on the anchor lines with the big wheel … the capstans.

All at once it felt possible that they could do this. Sails, anchors, and them. She was so exhausted she couldn't see anymore, but she surrendered to the rhythm.

"She's righting!" the foreman cried. "Put your legs into it! Pull! Pull!"

Hope seized her and kept her from giving up just when she thought she'd fail. She shifted her feet and legs to better brace herself, to lend even more power to her strokes.

"Don't let that Kilhellion shit out-stroke you," the foreman jeered.

She gritted her teeth and powered into it, though she was starting to see spots.

"And hold!" the foreman called. "Paddles to rest."

She felt really, really ill. Her head throbbed and she couldn't catch her breath. Someone ahead of her retched. Billie closed her eyes and focused on her nodes. Just taking her consciousness there helped steady her. Her body was starved for air. Nothing for it but to stretch her back and fill her lungs over and over.

Was the ship free? She opened her eyes and looked over her shoulder. For an ecstatic moment she thought the ship was floating free, but then her gut sank. The ship was upright, but still stuck. She could tell by the way the waves struck the hull, and how the ship didn't rock in the water.

The foreman let them rest for a long stretch, and then they paddled slowly to a new position directly behind the ship's stern. The other longboat moved their anchor. While they did that Billie wrung out her clothes as best she could. Most of the sailors had stripped to the waist, as had Aliiren.

She was too tired to truly appreciate his body, but she briefly admired the ridges and clefts of it, and the breadth of his shoulders, before she closed her eyes and retreated once more to her nodes. A skilled healer could have recovered more quickly by manipulating vinus, but her clumsy efforts would likely do more harm than good. She did divert a little vinus to her hands and back to patch up numerous tiny tears and clear some of the waste that had built up in her muscles. Then she opened her eyes again.

The foreman came down the line with a bucket of water. They each got two scoops of a wooden ladle. It seemed that the sailors could take as much time drinking it as they wanted; the foreman didn't do anything to hurry them. Billie and Aliiren were last, but she didn't care. She needed time for her stomach to settle.

The first sip was bliss. She gulped the rest down, careful to spill as little as possible. Aliiren accepted the water with a formal poise that reminded her of Tilla's trained grace. He drank with care as to not spill even a drop.

When they were done the foreman covered the bucket and returned to the front of the boat. The ship signaled, and they set to paddling again.

Her body fell into the work with a desperation barely caged by the punishing rhythm the foreman demanded. With the waves swelling around and beneath them, she couldn't tell for certain if they were going anywhere, and she didn't have a moment or the strength to spare to look back. But the longer they paddled the more it felt as if they were going nowhere at all.

"Don't you give up!" the foreman snarled. "You want to be stuck on the island over true night? Think you're tired now? Think you'd do anything to stop? Well think what you'd be willing to do if a nefarin had you by the throat! You'd beg to be here again, giving everything you had with no thought to pain. Think this hurts? There are worse things. Pull! Pull! Pull!"

They hadn't been working long but her body began to fail. Her throat burned, her lungs burned, her arms and back burned and her heart thundered in her head. But the foreman's words kept her going. This was what she'd do for a second chance to avoid the horror of being claimed by a hellion over true night.

And this was what she'd do, and more, to see Brian again.

In her mind Brian reached out to her. Fresh strength surged through her body. *I'm almost there, Bri. Hold on. I'm almost there.*

"And hold! Rest!" the foreman called.

Billie looked back over her shoulder.

Still stuck.

She took a breath to scream in impotent rage and frustration, but spots gathered in from the edges of her vision. She had to focus to keep from throwing up or passing out, her desperation unvoiced.

"Good work," the foreman told them. "Good work, all." He walked to the back of the boat and untied them from the ship. With care, he tied the balloon to keep the end of the line afloat.

"What are you doing?" Billie's voice growled with exhaustion and challenge.

"The tide has peaked," he said. "I got the signal from the ship. We'll head back to the island, get decent rest, food, water, maybe some sleep. We'll try again at the next high tide."

"When will that be?"

He looked at her as if she was an idiot. "Just before dawn, at the zero hour. We'll likely start sooner, depending. Probably the twentieth hour."

That meant nothing to her.

"Late tonight," Aliiren told her. "Considering how long it took to arrange everything, some time before first light." He looked to the foreman. "Depending on what?"

"Not every high tide is the same," the foreman told him. "And they're not exactly twelve hours apart. The captain will know more. If the high tide at first light isn't as high as this one? As long as the ship doesn't heel over again, he may decide to let us rest and try tomorrow before dinner instead. Or maybe the tide will be high enough we won't have to do hardly any work at all. Wouldn't that be nice?"

It would, but she couldn't help but think about her brother waiting for her.

The foreman took up his drum. "All right, let's head to the island."

She wasn't the only one who felt defeated as they paddled toward the gravel shore. Aliiren's back, normally held straight, now bowed.

She didn't know what else could be done, but she had to find something. She would talk to the captain. Maybe together they would find another way to get her home, and Aliiren to Ben Ariim.

## Chapter Nine

<><><><><><><><><><><><><><><><><><><><><><><><><><><><><><><><><><><><>

# Negotiations

<><><><><><><><><><><><><><><><><><><><><><><><><><><><><><><><><><><><>

*Embrer Island, Cerulean Sea*
*2nd Meet Day of Sun Month*

The cook set up a crude kitchen among the rocks well above the tide line. A group of sailors went off together with fishing poles to try their luck. They tried to convince Larani and Edrion to go with them, but the siblings chose instead to teach a small group of sailors a game of chance that involved dice and cards.

Despite their predicament, the general feeling among the sailors appeared to be festive. The captain seemed pleased with the condition of his ship and with the progress they'd made, and his pleasure infected just about everyone with the same disease.

Billie sat on a cold, flat rock, her body bedeviled with a sour stomach and spikes of pain that traveled through her back. She made herself keep her breathing smooth, rather than release a scream of frustrated fear. If she'd been among Kilhellions, she would have let it out without hesitation, but here, with these people …

She didn't know how they'd react. She just knew it would be awkward for them at best, and she wouldn't feel any better with everyone staring at her as if she'd lost her mind.

Nearby, Aliiren stared at the waves breaking on the shore, standing with uncharacteristic rigidity. Temric sat with his back to the steady breeze among his crates of belongings. He was attempting, and judging how rarely he turned the pages, failing to read, his body protectively hunched over his book in a vain attempt to protect it from the damp air. Tilla sat apart from everyone on a large piece of bleached driftwood, watching everyone as if she stood guard over prized ponies grazing in the field.

The captain finally finished giving orders to his people, and Billie felt the time was right to approach him. His smile, as he stood near the cook and chatted, faded as Billie approached. The wind switched and the smoke swept over both men into Billie's face. It stung her eyes, but she hardly cared. "I need your help," Billie told him.

Apparently he hadn't expected her to say that, because his eyes narrowed and he leaned toward her attentively. All signs of annoyance fell away. "I'm listening."

"My brother needs me," she told him. "I think …." She didn't want to say it out loud, as if speaking it would make it true. "He might be dying."

The air of annoyance returned. She wanted to shout into his face: *What is wrong with you?* That wouldn't get her any closer to home, so she kept her mouth shut. "You're not the only passenger who's in a hurry to get to Ben Ariim." He looked in Aliiren's direction. Aliiren might have sensed something, because he looked back their way. His golden gaze fixed on Billie, lending her, to her surprise, fresh strength. She reluctantly turned her attention back to the captain. "You were out there, helping right the ship," the captain continued, gesturing to her with an expression that he probably thought was magnanimous. "I was told you worked as hard as any of my people. It's fair to say that you earned the right to ask for more from me. But …." He shrugged his shoulders, and his pressed his lips tightly together for a moment, perhaps to bite back something he didn't want to say. "I have nothing to give. The tide is low. We're all stuck until high tide comes again. And, unfortunately, we're not likely to succeed then, either. Our next best chance will come tomorrow morning. But—" he said quickly as Billie took a breath to interrupt him, "with each passing day our chances improve. The tides increase and decrease in cycles. The highest tide of the week will happen on the morning two days hence. I'm sure we'll be free by that morning. And—" he cut in when she once again tried to speak her mind, "between now and then it's possible that another ship will come upon us. If that happens, the power such a ship can apply to my little vessel should be enough to free us. If the tides were fading in height, I'd be less optimistic. But the hull is undamaged and likely to withstand the strain. We have the Rill to thank—them and the current and the weather so far—for the fact that our situation isn't hopeless. We *will* reach Ben Ariim, at the very latest Labor Day after the next true night." He crossed his arms and looked to the cook, who stirred a big pot of soup with intense concentration, before he offered Billie a smile. "So, catch some sleep. We'll need your help the third hour after midnight."

At least he'd given her an idea of how she might better convince him other than begging for compassion. "Why wait? Send one of the longboats to Ben Ariim for help. Then you'll be sure that a ship will come to free yours, maybe even before true night. I know you don't want to spend a true night on this island."

"My mage told me that the lighthouse is well-blessed and secure," he assured her. "And the light no doubt makes the island unpleasant for nefari." He didn't sound like he entirely believed it, which make her feel a different sort of fear than she felt when she thought of Brian. "But it would be better to be underway before the next true night. We'll need everyone to make sure that happens."

"Why take the chance?" She was ready to start begging. "Everyone benefits."

Aliiren crossed his arms as he walked over to join them. "I'm willing to take the risk. Perhaps she and I can take one of the rowboats. You didn't use them to try to free the ship, meaning, perhaps, that you don't really need them here."

The captain worked his jaw, a half-smile that had no humor in it tightening his expression. "Please don't take my next words as a sign of disrespect, Protector, but neither of you have any idea how far we are from Ben Ariim. Getting there in a rowboat would be tricky, and if the winds aren't favorable, a shit house full of work."

"How far is it?" Aliiren asked.

"If everything goes well? A solid two days and two nights. Trust me, it's much faster going in my ship, and much safer."

Though Billie had struggled with much of what Temric had tried to teach her when it came to numbers, she could figure out what two days and two nights meant. She just had to count on her knuckles and the spaces between. It was a method of tracking the days and nights of the week ingrained in her from early childhood. Her pinkie knuckle on her right hand was Meet Day, the space Bless Night, ring knuckle Labor Day, the space Rest Night, Trade Day, Gift Night, and Somber Day.

It meant sailing and rowing through what remained of this day and Bless Night, then Labor Day and Rest Night. She would have to account for the time they'd wasted today—the sun was quite high in the tropical blue sky—onto Trade Day. With no land in sight to aim for .... Gods.

Because at the end of Somber Day, at sunset, True Night would come. If they didn't find a blessed shelter by then, they would be vulnerable to hellion hunting parties. And no one would open their doors during the left hand that represented the entirety of true night.

The names of those days and nights marched through her mind. True Night. Fear Day. Dark Night. Lost Day. Blind Night. Dread Day. And lastly, Watch Night.

That was a long time to run, to hide, to be found and be tortured and suffer whatever else hellions liked to do with humans.

What if the captain was wrong about freeing his ship? Naturally she didn't want to spend true night here, but much more intensely, she dreaded the thought of Brian waiting an extra day, never mind through to the other side of the next true night, while the captain did his best to free his ship.

She tapped her finger joints over and again, gauging the time again. Meet Day was half gone. Bless Night, Labor Day, Rest Night, Trade Day—that would leave the other half of Trade Day, all of Gift Night, and all of Somber Day to reach blessed shelter.

At least they would be closer to Sellon Port than they were now.

*Can the distance from Ben Ariim to Sellon Port be made over part of Trade Day, all Gift Night, and Somber Day?*

She didn't know. If not, a ship's captain would set sail either at a time when the ship would be at sea during all of true night, aiming to land at Sellon Port sometime after true dawn on Meet Day, or he wouldn't leave Ben Ariim at all until sometime on Meet Day.

*Silver Parrot*, if they had to spend true night here, would still be on the way to Ben Ariim during that same time.

Aliiren bowed his head and put his hands on his hips. She thought he'd walk away, but instead he looked back into the captain's eyes. Though Aliiren spoke softly, his words had a steady power to them. "Two days and nights. That sounds like enough time for us to send help. Help might even reach you and free you before the next true night."

"It sounds very well, doesn't it?" the captain said. "But I suggest that both of you practice patience. The tide is getting higher with each passing day, improving our chances of getting back under way and to Ben Ariim before true night."

Why was he being so stubborn? "My brother can't wait. *Please.* You're not using the rowboats anyway."

He laughed, and her face warmed to a temperature somewhere between anger and embarrassment. "There's a reason why I'm not.

They're not made for serious work. Do you know what an ocean current is? It's like a river, and the one that follows the coastline is faster than you can imagine. You'll be swept far west of Ben Ariim. There's a lot of wilderness between Ben Ariim and Port Sellon. That means there are no shelters. There's nowhere to hide in those mountains. A morchaintatha might survive, but not you. Assuming you aren't swamped by heavy seas, or eaten by a sea monster even before you reach shore."

Her thoughts were briefly distracted by the idea that he believed that morchaintatha, little green people that lived in the forest, actually existed.

It didn't matter if they did or didn't. "You're right. It's risky. But everyone here will benefit if I succeed."

The captain scoffed. "You'll need someone to navigate, unless you have the skill to find Ben Ariim on your own."

Her heart tapped fast and light. She respected the captain. If he said this would be hard, she believed him. But she had to try. "It doesn't matter if I end up in the wilderness," Billie told him rashly, telling herself that her father had survived in the wilderness on his way to Mt. Cross and therefore so could she, somehow. "If I have to, I can stay on the boat over true night. Maybe this current will carry me home, and—"

"You don't understand the least little thing," he said, clearly exasperated with her. "A skilled sailor might survive true night in a rowboat. But not you. If you're still at sea during true night, you're dead, or lost, which leads to death soon enough. As for the sea itself, the current will not simply carry you to shore. You'll be out of sight of land, with no way to know if you're rowing farther or closer to your goal."

"I can help her navigate." Temric stood up. A breath rushed out of Billie from the shock of it. Why would he take the chance?

"There's our proof," the captain said loudly to everyone nearby. "Madness is infectious." He spoke those words in Sothron, rather than the Thedran they'd been speaking until now. Was he being rude by insulting Temric in a language he'd more easily understand, or did he want to include Temric in a fair debate?

It seemed unlikely the captain would want to insult Temric. What was happening?

Although she'd come to know Temric, and enjoyed teaching and being taught by him in turn, he was a stranger. Why was he offering to take this considerable risk to help her? Maybe, like Aliiren, he had urgent business in Ben Ariim. And yet, he hadn't seemed worried, then or now.

"Billie needs to get to her brother," Temric said. "And I'm willing to help her." He gave Billie an apologetic look. "It might be faster for you to get to Port Sellon from here, and we wouldn't have to fight the current, but the captain is right. We could easily become disoriented, and we won't know where we are. At least, not without someone experienced enough to navigate in proper detail. We'd also need the right instruments and maps. I think heading for Ben Ariim is our best chance. It's close, and it's big."

The captain clapped his hands three times in sarcastic applause. "All true. You'll have no way to know your direction or speed," he said. "I have to add that big as Ben Ariim is, there's a good chance you'll miss it rowing from here if you try navigating by starlight and guesswork. Assuming you'll even have stars to guide you. Clouds and fog come and go on a whim this time of year."

"I have a compass," Temric told them. "And I have a map, but it doesn't have the sea currents on it."

"I'm not giving you a single one of my charts," the captain informed him.

"I wouldn't expect you to. But I hope that you'll allow me to copy the most important of the currents and their speed."

"I can tie a measure for them," a sailor offered.

"They won't be going fast enough to bother with it," the captain snapped. Something had changed, though. His expression wasn't as set as before. He seemed to be thinking about it.

Finally, he ran a hand over his face, glanced over at his cook who cocked his head in a 'why not' gesture, and finally looked Temric in the eyes. "You'll die horribly, and that will be on my conscience until Death relieves me of the memory."

"Or we might live," Temric countered, "and you and your crew will have help before true night if you need it."

"I'm not going to refund your fare." The captain gazed at Aliiren and Billie with a look in his eyes that suggested he was sure his words would dissuade them. "Any of you. You," he added, focusing on Billie, "still owe me for that fare. Black noble as a friend or no, I expect to be paid in full before you leave my protection. And I will want compensation for my lifeboat." His smile warmed, and she realized that he expected her to balk at the price.

She swallowed hard on a dry throat. "Shall I measure it out for you?" She fetched her pouch from within her bag.

His expression slid into a frown. "You have a long journey ahead of you. Will you have enough to reach Sellon Port if you spend your wealth so foolishly?" It almost sounded as if he honestly cared.

"I'll throw in," Temric told her.

"I will pay you one hundred wulla for the rowboat," Aliiren said, pointing sharply toward a rowboat for emphasis.

Temric and the captain turned to stare at Aliiren, and the Rill siblings with their patrons paused in their game to watch. The Rill siblings began whispering between each other. Their secret words soon sharpened into a hushed squabble.

Aliiren shifted uncomfortably beneath the scrutiny of so many. "It's urgent that I reach Ben Ariim as soon as possible," he explained in his soft voice, "But more importantly, from the beginning she's told you that her brother's life depends on her. A life, Captain. What is a life worth?"

He looked at each of them in turn, then looked to his cook. The cook shrugged and said, "You'll still have your fares."

The captain's gaze settled on Billie. He tucked his upper lip against his lower teeth and scraped, plumping his lips. "I don't know what to make of you. You do understand that if you die, you won't be able to help your brother."

Tilla had been watching them from a distance. She now made her way over. The captain noticed, and they all waited respectfully until she was among them. Billie fidgeted, aware that if Tilla went against her, the captain would refuse to help.

"I hope you don't mind if I join in this discussion." As she had been in every encounter Billie had had with her, Tilla proved herself the perfect example of Sothron manners. Nothing in her tone gave away her thoughts.

"Please." The captain looked certain she would bring a welcome voice of sanity.

"Your objection revolves around their welfare and the welfare of your ship," Tilla told him. "Is this correct?"

"Yes," he said cautiously.

"Your ship will not be in harm's way if they leave," she explained in a way that would have sounded condescending coming from anyone else. From her it verged on a question, as if she wanted to know if she had the right of things.

"Yes," he agreed even more cautiously. Billie's heart thundered with hope, and fear. Would this happen?

"They are neither prisoners, children, nor your wards. They are willing to compensate you for your boat. Your final objection is valid, in that you think that their chances of survival are poor, and you mean to advocate for Billie's brother, who will be no better off if she perishes. I have a solution." She looked to Billie. "I will remain here and make my own way to Port Sellon. That way your brother will have me to tend to him, even if you don't survive." She then turned her attention to Temric and Aliiren. She gazed into their eyes each in turn. Whatever she saw there apparently satisfied her.

Billie wanted to whoop and hug her, but she managed to restrain herself.

The captain frowned and stared at Tilla's back as she left to watch the Rill, who had returned to their game. He let out a sigh. "You'll need provisions." Billie wanted to hug him now too. She clasped her hands together and held them tightly to her chest to keep her joy from exploding out of her. "I will supply some, for a price. I can't be overly generous. We always carry more than we'll strictly need, but I don't know how long we'll be stuck here, so ..." He shook his head. "I'll have my people set you up."

She couldn't help herself. She let out a whoop and laughed. "Thank you! Gods, thank you." Rather than hug him she hugged Temric, who let out a little grunt of surprise and then laughed with her and hugged her back. Billie calmed down, slipped free of his arms and faced the captain again. "I'd like to leave today. Now. Right now. Please."

He shook his head and let out a short laugh. "Oh, you'll leave today," he assured her. "I want you to get a good start. But it's going to take two or three hours to arrange everything." He put his hands on his hips and chewed on his lip for a moment, then shook his head. "Sleep if you can. You're going to have a long night." With that, he picked his way among the rocks to the gravel shore where some of the sailors had gathered around a small campfire. He got them up and started ordering them about.

She trusted his wisdom, but Billie had work to do first. She got a small bit of rope from a sailor, unwound it, and then tied her signature knot using the smaller, more flexible strands. She presented it to Tilla. Without it, Billie's family wouldn't trust her. Billie explained how to best find them in case Billie didn't make it to Sellon Port before her, and told her to deal as much as possible with her mother. Tilla would have to treat Billie's father as the head of household, but he would likely be angry that Billie had asked a stranger to take on the work in her stead. Her mother was good at tempering him, though, so Tilla's best chance was to appeal to him through her.

She also warned Tilla not to draw a blade of any kind unless she thought she was in mortal peril. Arguments that led to a fight were always handled without weapons and weren't intended to be lethal. If anyone drew a blade on her … though Billie dreaded who might be lost, she advised Tilla that it would be wisest to kill that person if she could. If they drew first, no one would expect her to show mercy, nor should she show mercy unless a chieftain intervened. No one would respect her, or thank her, if she hesitated to kill such a blatant coward.

The more they talked, the more advice Billie wanted to give. Tilla made it easier by asking good questions. Yes, most Kilhellions, especially those living in Sellon, would know how to speak Sothron. The best way to win over Kilhellions was to tell them stories, to drum, to dance, chant poetry, or sing, in that order. Never refuse an offer of soup and bread, even if it wasn't to her liking. She wouldn't have to finish it, but she had to at least make a show of eating some. Refusing alcohol was acceptable unless offered by a chieftain, in which case she would be expected to slowly nurse that drink over an evening. She could offer her cup to anyone who seemed willing and thirsty if she didn't want to finish the drink. A place like Sellon would have a pack of chieftains, with the youngest and the eldest holding temporary reign over the others if there was a dispute. Tilla couldn't refuse a command from any chieftain except by leaving the port entirely, which they would freely allow unless there was a special circumstance.

Tilla blushed when Billie explained that she shouldn't dally with anyone with braided hair. Another Kilhellion might get away with it, but outsiders would be dealt with harshly. Also, as an outsider, she shouldn't speak to children unless they asked her a direct question, to which she could give a simple answer.

By the time Billie had finished explaining everything, the sky had cleared, the sun was low in the sky and the boat was packed up. Her body hummed with anxiety. She couldn't have slept if she'd tried. She sat braced against a rock and rested, carefully swathed in her shawl, her healing making her feel slightly feverish. She drank water from her canteen and watched the waves curl and crash on the shore, too tired to worry anymore.

Temric walked over. "I've figured out how much your share is."

It took her a moment to realize what he was talking about. "My fare too?" she asked as she pulled her money pouch free from her belt. It was damp, like the rest of her.

"Your fare too," he assured her.

She handed it up to him.

"I don't suppose you'd want to practice counting."

Billie shook her head.

When he got a look inside, he made a small noise of surprise. "What are these?" He drew out a dark, uneven crystal with bits of gray stone still attached.

"That's a sapphire," she told him.

"A sapphire? How much is it—" He made another noise, this time in his throat, and let out a sigh. "Well, you have some coins in here too. I'll talk to the quartermaster."

"Thank you." As she watched him walk away, she realized that she trusted him not just with helping her get home, but with her tribe's wealth. She wasn't sure when she'd started to do that.

Aliiren joined Temric, and after some haggling, together they paid the quartermaster. The deal was done.

The captain met her, Aliiren and Temric at the little boat, which was now ringed by sailors and passengers curious enough to want to see them off. "This is your last chance to see reason," the captain told them. "Do any of you even know how to sail?"

"I do," Edrion said, stepping out from among the others. "I can sail." He flashed a rakish grin at the three of them. "Besides, you'll need the luck." He glanced at his sister, who stood beside him, proud as any chieftain, her hands clasped neatly behind her and her chin held high. "Rani and I talked it over. Actually, we rolled dice to see who got to go. I won." He wagged his chin in her direction, and she told him off with a hand gesture Billie didn't recognize. Maybe it was meant to convey ram's horns, or legs in an obscene position. Billie laughed along with Edrion and won a bright smile from Rani in answer.

The captain's face darkened with an angry blush. "I can't afford to lose half our luck." Was that a warning she heard beneath his words? Her body tensed. Her hands tingled as she lowered them to rest on the hilts of her sword and fighting dagger.

But Edrion gazed at the captain with a serene, wide-eyed lack of concern. "Luck must be free, or it doesn't work. You can't stop me."

She expected the captain to argue further with Edrion, but strangely, he turned to her. Did she give him some false sign that she might change her mind? She was the least likely of all of them to do that. He had to know it.

And yet, the captain gazed up into her eyes. She stared back down at him, daring him to try. "Maybe you don't care about your life. Maybe you'd rather drown than face the possibility that your brother is already dead."

Those words slapped her hard, but she refused to flinch.

The captain worked his jaw and his head twitched sideways in a sharp negation. "Fine. There will be one less Kilhellion in the world. Only your family will miss you." He spoke quietly, like her father did when he was especially angry. She felt a chill, but she refused to avert her gaze. "But what about them?" he asked under his breath. "Hmm? They'll die with you."

"It's their choice." She spoke the words, and she even believed them, but part of her wavered.

No. Together, they could do this. They had to do this.

Temric cleared his throat, startling Billie into stepping backward. The captain slowly looked away from her and gave Temric his attention.

"Captain. I, for one, am determined." Temric's blue eyes had a strangely calm clarity to them that showed no sign of fear. "Thank you for all you've done, and for what you will do. We all appreciate that this is difficult for you. If it's what you want, I absolve you of whatever might happen to us. What happens to us is our own doing, not yours."

The captain growled softly under his breath. He reluctantly stepped away from Edrion and Billie with a nod to Temric. "You can count on my quartermaster to manage those of your possessions you've chosen to leave behind, and your affairs in the likely event that something will go badly wrong."

"Don't worry. I'll take good care of everyone," Edrion said cheerfully.

That made the captain grunt. "Sail swiftly. Sail true." The captain turned quickly and walked away. His crew, after each of them touched their hands to their hearts, followed him back to their makeshift camp on the shore.

Rani hugged her brother. "I love you," she said, squeezing him tightly. "Keep them safe." It hurt Billie's heart to watch them hold each other tightly, as close as twins. Rani kissed him on the cheek, and reluctantly they let each other go.

And then Rani surprised Billie by hugging her too. "Watch out for my little brother."

"I will," Billie promised. Rani's arms were strong and held her close, as close as Billie's closest friends in Torath. It felt so good she never wanted to let go. But she had to. Rani hugged Temric as well, telling him to watch out for Edrion too. Temric murmured something to her, and she smiled and let go. And then Rani faced Aliiren. There was a hesitation that stretched, and then Aliiren opened his arms. They held each other delicately, as if he might break. It lasted just a breath, but it was full of respect and care, wordless and honest. When Rani let him go, Aliiren backed up a step and bowed his head.

His reaction was more than shyness. It made her curious, but she also worried for him.

Billie and her cohort of fellow idiots grabbed onto the sides of the little boat and pushed it into the water. The waves weren't very big on the lee side of the island, but they weren't nothing either. They got soaked just getting the boat far out enough that they wouldn't be driven back to shore again. They clambered in awkwardly between waves. Billie and Aliiren each took up a set of oars as quickly as they could. Billie struggled but managed to get the rowboat's nose pointed toward the incoming waves before anything bad happened.

Thank goodness they had a rowboat instead of a longboat. Paddling was much harder on her back than rowing. But clearly Aliiren had never rowed before, and his awkward struggles with the oars didn't keep time with her, even when she slowed down to help him learn how to match her rhythm. The unruly ocean waves didn't help. They had to battle a long time to make any progress.

It made her realize just how slowly this would go. But she couldn't stop.

Meanwhile Edrion went to the mast that the sailors had kindly stepped into a thick collar close to the front of the rowboat. He asked Billie and Aliiren to put away the oars and move to opposite sides, then lowered the boom that nestled against the mast. Once he'd arranged and tensioned the ropes at the end of the boom, he raised the single triangular sail and then sat and took up the rudder at the stern. The wind seized the sail and pushed them with surprising speed over the water.

Billie looked back. The island wasn't all that far off. That had been a lot of work for little gain.

Maybe the captain was right.

But even if he was right, Tilla would see to Brian's care.

Now it was a race, and it was a race Billie intended to win.

Billie wrung out the hem of her tunic, but it was useless. She stripped it off so her under-tunic could cool her off and dry at the same time, and did the same with her trousers, leaving on her hose. The white linen clung to her body, translucent, revealing more of her body than she was used to exposing to anyone outside her tribe that wasn't a lover.

There was nothing for it. She couldn't sit around in soaking wet wool for hours, especially if she had to row again. Her skin was already tender from her labors on the longboat. At least the tail ends of her shawl provided some modesty for her chest.

None of them seemed to care. Edrion kept his attention on the rudder and sail, while Temric held the map in his lap with his compass in hand. Aliiren watched the waves, his mind clearly working hard on something.

Billie got up to give her clothes a far more serious wringing. The water that dripped out was cloudy. She hadn't realized how filthy living on the ship had made them.

"I can see the sun through the clouds now," Edrion pointed out to Temric. "I just have to keep it on my left shoulder and we should find our way there."

Temric didn't look up from his studying. "I think we'll be better off if I use the compass and chart our bearing on the map from the beginning. That way we can try to take the speed of the current into account, once we reach it."

"Fair enough," Edrion said with a smile. "But try not to worry. Once we spot land we'll be fine, and that part is inevitable. The Cerulean Sea isn't all that big, and *Silver Parrot* took us most of the way. We don't have that much farther to go."

His confidence leant Billie a few more threads of hope. The captain had made it sound hard to find their way, and she expected that he would know better than any of them, but Edrion's words made sense. One way or another, they would find land. And once they did, they'd know what to do to get to Ben Ariim, or Port Sellon, whichever was closer.

She might have managed on her own, but she was grateful that she didn't have to. "I'm glad you're with us, Edrion. Thank you."

"I wouldn't want to be anywhere else," he said with a grin. "For the first time in my life, I'm doing something important." But then he sobered. "I just hope I don't let you all down." He looked so fragile in that moment, she was afraid that even a reassurance would break him, and so she let her thanks stand within the following silence.

BILLIE HADN'T REALIZED HOW VULNERABLE SHE'D FEEL ONCE THEY lost sight of the island.

She remembered, when she first left the Kilhells, how the big ship seemed to shrink in size once they were on open waters. Maybe it was because she was surrounded by seasoned sailors, but at the time she'd enjoyed the sense of fear. It had felt like sledding down a steep, snowy slope at the start of the winter season, not knowing if she'd stop where she'd planned or if she would end up in the lake.

This was entirely different. The same waves that had bumped and splashed off the big ship's bow now rose and fell around them, in turn cupping them as if they were a pearl within a pair of massive hands, then lifting them up to rest like a seed on a molehill. When they were up, they could see the horizon. There was nothing but the hazy evening light of Meet Day and the sea, a deep blue verging on black that hinted at places where sea monsters lived, unseen and unknown.

Temric steadfastly kept track of their progress on his map. He seemed calm and focused. Rather than keep correcting Edrion, he'd taken over the rudder himself while Edrion pulled on various ropes to keep their single sail full of the changeable wind. Aliiren alternated between stretching and sketching symbols in a small book, completely in tune with his body and mind.

She hated having nothing important to do. Fortunately, Edri helped keep Billie's mind steady once the sail was set. He told her stories of his travels with his sister, and taught her a game that, thank the gods, needed no counting. She just had to learn about a set of simple pieces that moved, each in their own way, on a grid that he drew on the center bench. While they played, she taught him a traditional Kilhellion drum chant in case he and his sister met up with Kilhellions again. It was a game in its own way, a call-and-answer where they could pass the lead role back and forth.

But the game ended, and their voices tired out. The sun blushed beautifully as it neared the horizon. The wind switched again, hassling the sail. She settled on the bench just behind the mast near the rowboat's prow, sitting askew so that she had her back more or less toward the sunset. There she could stay out of Edri and Temric's way while they did the serious work of getting them to Ben Ariim.

Aliiren sat beside her on the same bench, but he straddled it to face full-on toward the sun, setting a bare foot on a bag of his possessions nestled beside the seat along with her bags. Like his hands, his feet were sinewy and strong, with veins branching starkly under the skin.

"You seem tired," Billie observed. She wondered if he'd managed to take a nap before they left.

He nodded. "So do you."

"Mostly I feel useless." She gripped the seat, then set a hand on an oar and wished she could use it to get them there faster.

He made a soft, warm noise in his throat that might have been the beginning of a word. "You're doing more than most would in your same circumstance."

"Hmm." She wasn't sure she agreed. Anyone would go as far, or farther, to help a sibling. Wouldn't they? Even though she and Stayce didn't get along, she'd fight just as hard to help her sister.

But it wouldn't feel the same, she realized. Brian had always been the center of her happiest moments. He'd been there for her when things were at their worst, too. She could trust him like no one else. Life without him … no. She refused to imagine it.

"Your parents will hire a healer in Sellon Port if he starts to fail," Aliiren said with innocent ignorance of the Kilhells. He watched the sun's fading light apparently without fear of going blind, its light casting the shadow of the rowboat's little mast perfectly parallel to their seat. His golden eyes changed with the sunset and the light glittering across the waves, full of quiet emotions she couldn't read.

She didn't know Aliiren well, but she knew that he sought knowledge in a deeper way than she did. It was part of his devotion to Light. Something else stirred in her too, something more than wanting to offer him the complete truth in honor of his faith. She wanted him to know why she was so scared for Brian. "You know something of Sothron culture," she told him. "And how people don't like to deal with you unless you're known to them, or you've been introduced by someone they trust?"

He nodded, clearly unsure of why she brought it up.

"My tribe isn't related to anyone in Sellon, and the Kilhellions they know the best are traders and ranchers, who don't have much influence. My chieftain will try, and maybe he'll find someone. But Kilhellions ask family first, because family is safest. Family can be trusted. If you can't rely on your own family, you're vulnerable. That's part of the reason why it's my responsibility to save him."

While she'd spoken, his expression tightened until at the end he winced.

"Did I say something wrong?" She'd meant to confess even more to him, but now that didn't matter nearly as much as apologizing for pinching his feelings.

"It's nothing," he said, but then he shook his head. He crossed his arms and briefly bowed his head. "No, that's not entirely true. But it's nothing to do with what you said. I think what you say makes sense." He glanced away from her. "My situation is very different," he added even more softly than usual.

Without knowing anything about his circumstances, she'd stupidly blathered on about how people with no family had nothing. Obviously she'd poked a tender spot.

He sat in his tight way, his gaze turned inward. Was he an orphan? Or maybe something even worse had happened to him.

But he did have people that he cared about in Ben Ariim. Or maybe just an exceptional teacher, or friend … a parent figure? "Your teacher … you care for her a great deal, I think. And she for you."

"Yes." He sighed and rubbed his hands over his knees. "Unfortunately, there's little hope I'll reach her before Death draws her soul from her body. I have to try, though. I owe her that at the very least."

"I'm sorry."

"Thank you." His composure slipped, just a bit. The corners of his mouth barely twitched downward, but she felt it as if something had broken within him.

"I hope you're in time." The words were so inadequate.

"Thank you." His gaze remained with the sea around them. "I pray I have the strength for this journey. Until now, my life has been so easy. It's made me weak."

She scoffed. "You weren't weak on the longboat. If anyone's weak, it's me. Life at the college … I used to run everywhere, or ride, and I had so many chores every day. I've gotten soft and lazy." Besides, he could channel faerus. He didn't have the same limitations that she did. He wasn't restricted by the reach of his physical body like most human beings.

He shook his head. He shifted in his seat, and his hand came to rest near hers on the bench. "If you think you're weak now, you must have been terrifying." A quick smile suggested he meant that in a good way.

She remembered Light's energy dancing over the blessings on the door. His eyes caught the colors of the sunset, seeming to glow from within with the power of his God. "Says the one whose prayers are answered by the sacred sun itself."

"Your faith surprises me." He spoke so softly she could barely hear him over the wind and water, his eyes downcast.

"Maybe that's because you don't see yourself as others do," she told him.

He looked into her eyes with his bright gold ones, startled out of his subtle frown. He looked very innocent with his eyes so wide. But that was silly. She was the innocent one. She had knowledge of one small place in the world. Not just small, but isolated. The things she knew, and had seen, and could do, could not compare well beside anyone bled and raised in Ben Ariim, the greatest trade port on the Cerulean Sea.

His gaze lowered to their hands, resting so near each other on the bench. She resisted the urge to take his hand in hers, remembering how he'd reacted to Larani hugging him. And that had been with his consent. She wanted to tell him things that would sound stupid if spoken aloud, about how he'd filled her heart, and how she'd think about him long after they parted, especially at sunrise, when the sunlight turned the snow on Mt. Cross into fields of gold and diamonds. Such things would sound even more ridiculous because they barely knew each other.

They sat so close, but they were still as far apart as Ben Ariim and Torath.

His eyes reflected a thin line of white as the last sliver of sun sank beneath the horizon. The darkening sky overhead glowed with a blue that seemed to cast its own light, turning the waves iridescent with violet and sapphire hues.

It kept bothering her, what she'd said about family and having nothing. But could she apologize without making it worse? "The thing I said about family," she began. He didn't seem irritated, so she went on. "I didn't mean ..." That was a bad way to start. "Things are different in the Kilhells. What matters there is what matters there and what matters somewhere else is what matters in that other place." He didn't seem upset, so she continued. "I can tell that you're part of something great, something more than family. I don't know what that's like, but I can imagine what it would be like to serve something greater than anything I've known. And I think that's something missing in our village, something I hope will come to us someday."

*Brian has to live.*

"I don't think Kilhellions are as different as I believed before I met you." Aliiren's gaze returned to her face. "I can imagine what it would be like to have a brother, and to want with all my being to protect and save him."

It pinched her heart to think of Brian's smile, and how they used to fight about silly things that made them burn with anger. Then, in a flash, Brian would turn it into a game where they both laughed until they were breathless.

At the same time, Aliiren's words soothed her. "Maybe family isn't the right word for what we have in the Kilhells," she decided. "Maybe it's love. Maybe it's sharing the burdens and joys of life without holding anything back. I think anyone has a chance to have that, regardless of blood."

Aliiren's chin lifted, and his expression smoothed. "I think that's very true," he whispered.

She gazed at him as the fading light played across the keen angles on his face.

She remembered this feeling.

She'd fallen in love once before. This felt like the first blush of that.

But she'd never see Aliiren again, once they reached Ben Ariim.

Just like Crellan.

Crellan was her first love, hot and wild and eager, and then his family went back down the mountain with the ponies her family had sold to them. She'd waited for what felt like forever, but he never returned.

Crellan. He could barely speak proper Kilhellion, and she knew nothing of his obscure dialect from the other side of Mount Cross. She'd learned a bit from Scribe Melissa in anticipation of Crellan's return, for nothing it turned out.

She'd just about forgotten about Crellan. She'd lost the memory of what he looked like beyond broad shoulders and an even bristle of pale hair and beard. He was short compared to the men of her tribe, but he wasn't that much shorter than she'd been at the time. Farming had made him strong and scrappy for his size. Their bodies …

*We were equals,* she thought wistfully. *Strength for strength, will for will. Even Father liked him.*

Yes, that had been long ago. But she still remembered the sting of his absence, and how it had gnawed at her the longer it stretched.

*I'm being ridiculous.* She and Aliiren hadn't even kissed. *So what if I like him? That's not love.*

*But I really, really like him.*

Aliiren gazed at her with an enigmatic expression. "What are you thinking about?" he asked.

She decided to take a chance. "I was lonely in Ruvall. It would have been different if you were there." When he tensed and withdrew his hand from beside hers, she realized she'd been too forward with him. "Or Temric, or Edrion, or Larani," she added, trying to make it sound more like an offer for a simple friendship. Which, honestly, was more than she expected from him. Her cheeks burned with embarrassment.

He clasped his hands together protectively across his belly. "You're the first friend I've made in a long time too." It wasn't quite a smile, but his eyes had a lift to them that hadn't been there before.

They agreed on one thing, then. They were friends. Her cheeks still felt warm, but she felt lighter, and more at ease.

The brightest of the stars had begun to glimmer. It would be a beautiful night.

## Chapter Ten

<><><><><><><><><><><><><><><><><><><><><><><><><><><><><><><><><><><><><>

# A Rowboat At Sea

<><><><><><><><><><><><><><><><><><><><><><><><><><><><><><><><><><><><><>

*Somewhere on the Cerulean Sea*
*2nd Trade Day of Sun Month*

**B**illie grunted in time with the drum rhythm she played in her mind. By listening to that beat within her, she forced her body to obey when all she wanted to do was to lean over the oars, close her eyes and sleep. She didn't think she could pry her hands off the oars anymore. They were locked in place like bands of hot, painful metal hammered around the handles.

She closed her eyes and started to doze off. The rhythm in her head played on, though, and her body moved with it. She felt unpleasantly drunk. Her head throbbed. Her shoulders burned. Heat spiked in a sharp line on one side of her neck. Sweat soaked her hair, her shawl, her underclothes. She'd packed the rest of her clothes away because in this heat she didn't want them. She wanted to strip her shawl and underthings off too, but she didn't dare. Her pale skin would burn and blister if she did. She'd protected it for too long, especially her face. She had no defenses.

Aliiren had the advantage of dark skin, but he suffered in the heat too. His sweat had been running so freely that it smelled as clean as the sea, though faintly spiced with incense.

Temric and Edrion had taken turns at the oars too, but they were exhausted. Edrion slept like a dead thing on the floor of the boat between her and Aliiren. The scant shade cast by the furled sail moved over him as the lazy waves undulated beneath them. Temric had draped himself over the rudder, which he'd tied in place to hold their course.

She suddenly realized that he was asleep too.

The compass dropped from his hand onto the chart spread over his knees. It slid off and rolled along the boat's floor to land near her foot.

He didn't even twitch at the sound.

He was definitely asleep.

If she kept going maybe Temric could get some real rest. Every stroke would help him recover more, which meant she might sleep a little bit longer once he took over.

Aliiren worked silently behind Billie. His oars moved with a smoothness that suggested that he could do this forever. She was supposed to keep the pace for him. She had to keep going. But her eyes ached and her body screamed for relief. Maybe if she rested her eyes for just a moment …

Her eyes closed of their own volition.

The oar hit water, jarring her awake. She wasn't sure entirely what happened, only that she'd mangled a stroke. One oar now trailed in the water while the other was cockeyed just above the surface.

The rowboat turned off course. "Sorry." Her voice rasped. Thirst grated along her throat. "I need to stop and have some water. Maybe you should too."

Aliiren let his oars drop. She turned around just in time to see him tuck his arms into his lap. It was then that she realized how much pain he was in. The whole time he hadn't let out a single whimper. His hands trembled. Bloody blisters had burst in several places on his hands, mostly on the left but the right hand was bad too.

Slowly the boat drifted to what appeared to be a full halt. If they were in motion, which she couldn't tell if they were, they were being carried by the vast current that the captain had warned them about.

According to Temric they'd been fighting that current since they got into it midday after their first night at sea. Which was expected, but then just after dusk, the wind had died away to nothing. They had to account for the current as it carried them west while making progress north, angling their way toward the direction in which they hoped they'd find Ben Ariim. That involved rowing all night, without any help from the sails.

When morning dawned, a terrible heat came with it, quickly sapping their strength.

The sun glared at them from directly overhead now. The water was flat, seemingly as exhausted as they were. They'd seen no sign of land, but none of them expected to see anything until later in the day, or maybe not until dusk.

They couldn't go on. Not like this. She knew they might end up a dangerous distance too far west of Ben Ariim in a wooded wilderness of steep hills and ravines, but she couldn't fight the relentless sea anymore.

Judging by Aliiren's swollen shoulders, neither could he.

She gave herself a moment to feel sorry for herself and then forced herself up. She unwound a rope from its cleat and lowered the boom with its rolled-up sail from where it was folded against the mast.

"What are you doing?" Aliiren asked while she tied off the rope again. "There's no wind."

In a series of painful tugs, she raised the sail, then moved the boom over. "It's for the shade." She tied off the rope, then took one of the oars and gave it a couple of light strokes so that the shade moved to cover Aliiren and Edrion. Once she'd stabilized the rowboat at that angle, she tucked herself at the edge of the shade by Temric's legs. She wished that she could find a way to shade him as well. She toyed with the idea of waking him long enough to help him move into the sail's shelter, but then decided it was better to let him sleep.

"If you want to rest, I can row on my own," Aliiren said.

He was so tired that he wasn't thinking straight. "For all we know we've been rowing in the wrong direction. Temric is asleep. I don't know how long he's been that way."

Aliiren looked up for the first time since they'd stopped. "You didn't see him fall asleep?"

While they were rowing, she'd been between him and Temric. If their positions had been reversed, Aliiren might have noticed what had happened sooner. "I'm sorry. I was half-asleep while I was rowing myself. I thought he was just staring at the compass. But then he dropped it." She cringed.

Aliiren scowled.

"I'm sorry," she said again, though she knew saying sorry wouldn't save her brother, nor help Aliiren reach his beloved teacher in time. Gods, what had she done?

The anger she expected didn't show in his eyes. It made her uneasy. Maybe he was too tired to be angry. Or maybe he was just that good at hiding his anger. "May I see the compass?" he asked.

She picked it up and passed it to Aliiren. The brief contact with his hand was gentle, but she kept her guard up.

Aliiren set the compass on the bench beside him and then turned it in place. "You're skilled at steering the boat using just the oars," he said. "What if I taught you how to use this? Then you could rest, using the oars to adjust our course, while I keep rowing."

She didn't expect such soft words from him. He should be angry, far angrier than she was at herself, and she was plenty mad. Maybe he was, but in a different way than the hot frustration building inside her.

"Billie?" he prompted gently.

She realized she'd been staring at him. She was far from sleepy now, but obviously she was still addled.

He wanted to teach her how to use the compass, and he wanted to keep rowing.

Rowing was better than screaming. She did her best to shrug off the feelings that had hardened in her gut before she spoke. "Let's do it, then." Except, he couldn't, not as he was. "But first, would you please let me do something for your hands and shoulders?"

He tensed like a shy pony that didn't want its hoof lifted for a trim. "There's nothing to be done."

Did he think she couldn't do even that little bit of healing? Or maybe he just didn't want her touching him.

If she couldn't convince him, he wouldn't be able to row much longer whether he wanted to or not. "I think you might be injured." Actually, it was pretty obvious that he was injured, but never mind that. "If I can't heal that, how much longer do you think you could row?"

He stared at the compass in his hands, one finger stroking it absent-mindedly. "Not much longer," he admitted.

She decided to take that as an invitation. Billie edged carefully around Edrion, stepped past Aliiren over his bench, and got behind him. Not only were his shoulders swollen, but he held his right shoulder higher than his left. "Can you put your hands behind your head?"

He winced—clearly it hurt—but he did as she asked. He was lean enough that every surface muscle was revealed in stark detail. Many of the muscles were bound up, lumping in awkward places, or so tight that they impeded the others as well as doing little good in and of themselves. And he could barely do what she'd asked him to do. "Are you a healer?" she asked.

"I channel god power," he reminded her.

"I still have to ask," she said. "It's not impossible. Just rare. You can have a stronger than usual healing gift and not be able to use it." She started to reach for those shoulders, but hesitated when she realized she was getting ahead of herself. "Would it be all right if I tried some massage on you?"

His breath caught, and he lowered his arms. The worse of his shoulder muscles twitched violently. She couldn't imagine what might make someone so reluctant, unless there was something about her that made him recoil?

*Or something in his past.*

He might accept it better if she used a tool instead of her hands. "I could—"

"It's all right." His shoulders shifted down, a forced movement that made her think he'd practiced relaxing but had never felt truly at ease. "I'm … honored."

It sounded more like resignation. She wanted to thank him for trusting her, but really, he obviously didn't trust her and saying something like that would be like prodding a bruise. "I'll go slowly. Tell me to stop if it's too much." Carefully, Billie put her hands on either side of his neck. He twitched again, and she pulled her hands away.

"No. It's … go ahead. I can tolerate it."

She settled her hands on his neck again, applying firm, steady pressure. The muscles felt hard and hot, like rounded stones that had baked in blazing sun all day. "Relax your arms and put your hands on your knees." She started with slow, gentle kneading, working down and out over his shoulders, down his upper arms, back up his arms, and then across to the base of the spine. His breath caught a few times. It shouldn't have hurt. She was just exploring. She worked her way up his back to make sure she knew which places needed the most attention. And of course it was his shoulders and neck. But it would be a mistake to work there first.

Billie put one hand under his left shoulder and made a fist of the other below his shoulder blade. "Are you all right?"

"Yes." That short, soft answer, free of fear, reassured her.

"Lean back into me and let me take your weight," she said.

He surrendered to her, honoring her with his trust. She braced her arm on the inside of her thigh so she could drive her fist up into a knotted muscle in his back as his weight came down. She helped him keep his balance with her other hand as his shoulders lowered down toward her knees. His face was tight with pain, but as the knot released, his expression smoothed. She shifted her hands to support him better and balanced his body for him.

Once she had his weight steady on her knees, she got both arms between her legs and worked the centerline along his back. Then she had him flip over with his hips resting on the bench, his arms stretched out on either side of her waist, his head between her knees looking down. It was an incredibly intimate position to put him in, but it was the best position she could come up with to work his shoulders and ribs and along his spine.

It hurt him, especially when she leaned forward and went in with her elbows. But she made a lot of progress, enough that he could sit up, put his back to her, and she could finally work those higher muscles around his shoulders and neck.

The work consumed her. Exhaustion fell away as she learned and manipulated his body in ways that gave her more insight into him than she'd had into either of her lovers.

Once his shoulder and neck muscles felt supple, she had him stretch his arms, and then move them as if he was rowing. His flexibility had nearly returned to normal.

"It feels ... better," he breathed.

"Good." She wasn't sure how much more contact he could tolerate, but the way he'd completely given himself to her made her bold. "Can I try using vinus?"

To her surprise he nodded. He turned to face her, and his golden eyes gazed into hers. The intensity of that color, the depth of his skin, the sharp angles of his face made her heart quicken. She lowered her gaze to her own hands. This was no time to behave like a silly two-year-old filly in heat. She spread out her fingers and turned her palms up. His palms settled onto hers without hesitation. The heat emanating from them didn't come from his God's power, but from blisters.

She closed her eyes and threaded her vinus from her nodes through the channels leading to her palms. It took a quick moment of concentration to push the vinus through her skin, past his skin and into the large channels at the center of each of his palms.

Her vinus quickly sailed through his smooth, broad channels. She'd begun with protectors and mages at the college for the very reason that they were so simple to move healing power through, and so Aliiren's physiology didn't catch her by surprise. But the health that glowed within him did. Lungs, liver, kidneys, stomach, intestines and brain all had a clarity to them as rare as perfectly clear glass. They were, however, pushed to the limit. His brain was working slowly and in a patchwork fashion. He was dehydrated, which strained his kidneys and upset his stomach and intestines. His muscles were swollen with fluid, less now that she'd massaged a lot of it out, but those waste-filled fluids were overloading his bloodstream, which further taxed his kidneys.

This wasn't anything that needed detailed work or a lot of control. He did have a trace of native healing, but not enough to interfere with her. She directed her gift to give his body extra strength to do what it naturally wanted. He began to sweat as she helped move even more of the toxins out of his overworked muscles into his blood stream. His bladder quickly filled as his kidneys, now better supported from within and without, worked swiftly to clean his blood. If he didn't already have a headache, he probably would get one soon.

She withdrew her vinus when she started to feel a bit feverish and nauseated. "I think that helped. Take a piss and then drink lots of water. You should feel better soon." She pulled down her underpants and eased out over the boat's side on the opposite side from where he stood so that his weight counterbalanced hers as she took a piss as well. They met in the middle again and both drank from their canteens.

He was definitely moving better. His natural grace had returned, and his shoulders weren't as swollen anymore.

He gazed back at her, an enigmatic expression on his face. "Thank you."

She smiled back at him before draining the last of her water. "You're welcome. Now, show me how to work the compass."

He crouched behind her and set the compass on her bench beside her left hip. It was a beautiful glass globe scored with very fine lines. The globe sat within a thick silver ring that kept it from rolling away on the bench. The globe was filled with a liquid and colorful workings. In the center of the liquid a loosely pinned arrow was able to rotate freely over a moveable platform. The platform had various lines and curves drawn onto it, and Markan lettering as well. "This arrow always points toward the Mark Star, even during the day when the sun shines so brightly that we can't see it." He demonstrated by tipping and rotating the compass. The panel tilted while the arrow rotated, remaining fixed in a consistent direction. He set it back down on the bench. "On the disk, you see there are lines and letters in Markan."

"Yes."

"When we're traveling in the correct direction, the arrow will point toward this letter here, which is the first letter in the word 'north' in Markan. The centerline of the rowboat should align with these lines on the platform, since I think we're trying to go a little east of north to beat the current. The NNE letters stand for north by northeast."

She was pretty sure that she didn't understand exactly how it worked, but the instructions were simple enough to follow. "All right."

"Don't move the compass so that the arrow points where we want to go. Change our course so that the arrow points toward north. Do you understand?"

She nodded. He looked into her eyes, perhaps searching for deception, but then he nodded back to her. He helped her take down the sail and fold up the boom. Perhaps unsurprisingly, neither Temric nor Edrion woke while they did all that work. Aliiren took his seat at the oars closer to the front while she carefully aligned the compass on the seat beside her. She sighted through the globe from both sides to make sure that the line that corresponded with north by northeast sat exactly over the centerline of the boat from front to back, using the prow and the rudder as guides.

Aliiren took up his oars. She grabbed onto her oars too—yikes her hands hurt! —and worked them independently until the arrow pointed toward north.

Suddenly it became clear to her how the compass, by being aligned with the boat's centerline in the direction they wanted to go, would guide them. She grinned and began to row. Her shoulders cried out in protest but then Aliiren joined in and she kept on until her muscles resigned themselves to the work.

"You can stop rowing and rest," he said.

"I'm all right." She hurt all over, but drinking the water and relieving her bladder, combined with her native healing and this fresh new knowledge in her mind, buoyed her.

And so they rowed.

The more she thought about it, the more she realized how important it was for Temric to guess where they were on the map in order to decide how to set the compass and travel along a given bearing. Although she hadn't used a compass before, she would take her bearings using large, familiar landmarks on the mountain for navigation, and watch the shadows cast by the trees if she had to travel through woods. It was true what Edrion had said—that eventually they would find land—but just like traveling over a long distance blindly through the forest without taking another bearing on a landmark, it would be easy to miss even a place as large as Ben Ariim, especially since they couldn't just row straight for it as the map showed. The current would push them off a straight course like crossing a river in a canoe. How far off that straight course to set the compass was pretty much a guess, unless Temric was using some form of mathematics—ugh—that accounted for it. But she had nothing. She had no idea if they were keeping even with the current, or if the current pushed them off course. If they'd succeeded in getting to the other side of the current, they might not even be on a course for Ben Ariim anymore.

Those thoughts kept her mind off of her pain until the sun began to wester.

This was the day they might see land. Well, Temric might if he woke up, but neither Billie nor Aliiren would because of the way the rowboat worked. Land would appear behind them.

She needed to wake either Edrion or Temric to help them navigate again, and to watch for signs of the coast.

She stopped rowing and her arms cramped in protest. Her palms were raw, and it felt as if spikes had been driven through every joint from her fingers down to her ankles. On top of it all, there was a hot spot in a deep muscle where the top of her shoulder met her neck that signaled a strain. If she didn't do something about it, by morning she might not be able to move either arm at all.

With a groan she locked the oars so that they'd stay out of the water. She shifted her weight forward to reach toward Temric. Her hip and ankle cramped in protest. With effort Billie set a hand on his shoulder. "Temric."

He muttered something in Sothron that might have been a name.

"Temric, wake up."

"Mmm." He sat up and hissed, blinking blearily at her. Then he looked around, eyes suddenly wide. "It's nearly sunset."

"Do you see land?" she asked.

He stood up and used her shoulder for balance against the surge that came with each pull of Aliiren's rowing. "I don't. There's nothing but water."

She didn't know what that meant, but she knew it wasn't good.

The captain had said that they might drift far past any civilization. He'd also warned that the current, if it caught the rowboat, would never guide her to land. Was that what had happened?

Temric looked at her hip.

No, he was looking at the compass. He stepped forward and picked it up. "Aliiren. Aliiren! Stop rowing. Take a rest. I … I have to work out where we might be."

Aliiren let his oars drop so that they dragged in the water until their rowboat halted. Billie turned to look at him, wincing as a sharp pain spiraled from her side up through her back into her shoulder.

Aliiren's head bowed so low that his hair, hanging in sweaty locks, veiled his face. He shone with sweat, and his shoulders were even more swollen than before. She doubted he could row any farther without wrecking himself.

"You shouldn't have let me sleep so long," Temric growled. "You're insane. Both of you."

The way he said it made her feel proud. "You needed the sleep."

"And so you both intend to kill yourselves so I can get it?" Temric snapped back. "You should have woken me hours ago."

"It's done," Aliiren croaked. His voice wasn't just soft anymore. It was weak, and it sounded as if it had taken the last of his strength to speak those words.

Edrion sat up. "Where are we?"

"I don't know," Billie told him as she turned around to face Aliiren.

Edrion got out of her way so that she could kneel in front of him. "Aliiren? You're hurt."

He didn't deny it.

"What can I do to help?" Edrion asked.

"Fill our canteens and add a pinch of salt to each of them."

Edrion rushed to obey.

"Can I have your hands?" Billie asked Aliiren.

He nodded, but he still gripped the oars. Maybe he couldn't let go.

She smoothed her fingers over the back of his left hand. The way the tendons stood out made it obvious that it was worse than his right. The muscles were locked in place. She carefully soothed the joints and the places between the bones, then worked her fingertips along his wrist on the underside up until she could almost touch the center of his palm. His hand began to relax. She worked her way deeper and all at once, he released his grip. She held his hand, her palm to his, and closed her eyes. Working quickly, she sent her vinus from her nodes into his body.

The sense of health was gone. His mind was more like someone in a coma than a conscious person. His organs felt hot and poisonous. She filled him with her healing energy until it suffused every part of him

He sucked in a sharp breath. His mind cleared a bit, and his body surrendered to the healing. It terrified her, knowing that her gift was keeping his body from failing everywhere all at once. It was worse knowing that the pain, which he'd become numb to, now consumed him.

He'd been dying. He wouldn't have died tonight, but he would have been dead by morning. It wasn't just dehydration anymore, or waste from overused muscles spilling into his blood, slowly poisoning him. He was starved and overheated. "He needs honey, jam, sugar, something." She couldn't see—her sight had retreated inward as her mind traveled with her vinus through Aliiren's body—but she sensed Edrion when he stepped close, and heard the tap of a canteen when he set it beside her. "Aliiren, you need to drink something." Fever flushed through her as her gift began cleansing him, lending strength to his body, easing pain and doing things his body was too exhausted to do on its own. This wasn't just light support work like she'd practiced at Nuvar College. Her gift became something like a fresh supply of rich, clean blood. Everywhere that she sensed lack, her vinus went there, and then she'd notice something else and her gift split into more streams that filled each need. He drank something—she could tell as soon as the liquid began to suffuse his body—and something sugary soon followed.

His organs woke to their work with fervor, and blood vessels returned to a state of balance, neither too open, nor too constricted, either of which could have spiraled him into shock. *Thank the Gods.*

"Billie." Aliiren's gentle voice penetrated her thoughts. "Enough. Billie. You're fevering."

Fever. She withdrew with a gasp as her awareness came back into her own body. She'd become as hot as if she'd been wrapped in a blanket left by a fire too long. It gave her a throbbing headache.

"You went too far," Aliiren said, his voice tight with worry.

"I'm fine." She wasn't sure of that, but she hoped she was. "I'll just get in the water. Hold onto me in case I faint." She climbed out of the boat, Edrion's and Temric's hands gripping her wrists, and lowered herself in.

She gasped as the water shocked like ice against her skin, and then a bliss eased the worst of the fever. She drew the fever down out of her head using her gift. Most of the heat she shunted to her skin, where it bled into the water. The rest she pushed into her lungs. With every breath she exhaled hot air, drawing in the cooler air near the water with each inhalation. Of course using her gift increased the fever, but as long as she used the water to her advantage it would get rid of more heat than she gained.

She had no choice. She was on the verge of a seizure.

Aliiren's dark skin flushed with fever too. His channels could carry much more power than her gift, but her vinus had gone deep into his muscles and organs. Even someone with Aliiren's capacity couldn't shed all the excess heat from such well-insulated, slow-draining places. And so she did the other thing that only healers could do.

She didn't have to have palm to palm contact. In fact it was better if she didn't. She wrapped a hand around his wrist and pulled his hand into the water. Her gift danced along the surface of him, like a breeze carrying away the heat of the day. At the same time, he used deep breathing to vent off as much as he could himself.

Bleeding his fever increased her own fever too, but the seawater was cool enough that it helped draw it out of her body. She still couldn't risk drawing out his fever for long. His body, trained to survive channeling god power, would have to cope on its own. Billie released him.

"Let me dunk under," she told Temric and Edrion. Temric let go while Edrion shifted his grip and lowered her down until the water closed over her head. Strange sounds worked their way past the pressure against her ear—ticks and hums, burbles and the lapping against the rowboat's hull.

After a moment he pulled her back up to the surface. She tipped her head back and reveled in how the water drew out the heat from her throbbing head. The headache eased. She sighed with relief and rested her head against the rowboat while the sky softened closer to sunset.

She knew she was safe when she began to worry about how far they'd drifted and why they hadn't seen the shoreline yet. "Get me back into the boat."

Edrion and Temric pulled her out enough that she could hook a leg over the side. She struggled the rest of the way in more or less on her own. Her soaked underclothes helped keep the remaining fever from worsening into something dangerous while Temric sat and stared at the map, lost in thought. "Water," she told Edrion. "Make sure Aliiren drinks a lot of water."

"You too," he said, handing her a canteen. Billie forced herself to sit up and drank in short sips. The headache was coming back, but it wasn't too bad. It would get a lot worse if she didn't drink faster. She trailed a hand in the sea water as she sipped, and concentrated on breathing deeply.

"We can't be far from shore," Temric said at last. "We just can't see it yet. According to the captain, we'll only be able to see about three miles from the boat. That means we might be less than an hour from shore right now, and still not be able to see the beach."

"You might be right," Edrion said, though he didn't look convinced. "But if we're close, where are the birds? Close to shore there are always more birds."

"It's getting dark," Billie pointed out. "Most birds don't like to fly when it's too dark."

Temric chewed on his lip nervously for a moment. "According to my calculations, we should be looking at the Arrak Thedran coast right now, but we're not. I guess that means we're off course." He met Billie's gaze while she silently hoped, selfishly, that they'd been carried far enough west of Ben Ariim to end up near Sellon Port. "The good news is that after dark it's likely we'll be helped by the lighthouses along the coast. Nearly every fishing village has one, and of course Ben Ariim has the largest of them all. It stands over a hundred feet tall. That means we'll be able to see it from farther away than three miles, as long as there's no fog. It can guide us to where we need to go far better than this map and compass."

"Then we should get back to rowing," Aliiren said.

"Not either of you," Temric informed them sternly. "Get some rest."

"I hurt too much to rest," Aliiren said. "And the healing worked very well. I can carry on."

Billie couldn't. "I'm sorry," she told Aliiren. "I'm done." The weaker she got, the more her healing would work to try to fix her, and then the fever would grow worse until she couldn't think, much less stop it from burning like wildfire through her channels in a desperate, misguided attempt to save her. It could send her into convulsions and possibly even kill her. "And you need to eat, and to drink more water than you want to, and yes, you need to rest. I won't be able to save you a second time."

"Save me?" Aliiren asked faintly.

Why did he look surprised? Didn't he know that Death had already begun to wait beside him?

Or maybe he drove himself this close to Death all the time, so much that he thought he could survive just about anything.

"It's my turn anyway," Edrion said. She realized she'd been staring at Aliiren, and he'd been staring back as if …

… as if she was a complete stranger.

She looked away, because she was in fact a stranger to him, and he to her.

Friends? In the Kilhells, friends would fight and die for each other.

*Would I die for him? Would I die for any of them?* It was a big question, too big for her think about right now. She turned her thoughts instead toward what to do next.

Convince Temric to keep them in whatever current might have them and try for Sellon Port?

But what about Aliiren's teacher?

"It's my turn too," Temric told them.

She felt a little shaky and light-headed as she took Temric's place at the stern. "I can at least steer the boat," she told them.

"No," Temric said. "You sleep. I can only guess where we are on the map anyway. I'm just going to keep us on a steady bearing like you did while I was asleep. Get some rest. Please."

Aliiren refilled everyone's canteens from a water cask at the foot of the mast, then got into their food. She noticed for the first time that the woodwork on the food boxes seemed unusually fine. As she watched he moved to reveal the Death blessings carved into stone tiles on the inside. Those blessings would keep their food safe from decay.

Such beautiful, useful things were made with love and pride, and would serve for generations if kept well. As such they were extremely valuable.

Did they belong to Temric? Did he have them all along, or had he bought them from the captain?

The captain wouldn't have parted with them cheaply.

The idea upset her, not because she thought it was a wasteful luxury, but that she couldn't afford to pay her fair share for them to have fresh, nutritious food.

Her purse was much lighter than when she'd started, and she still had a long way to go.

"You look angry," Edrion said just before he took a sip of water from his canteen. Temric started rowing awkwardly, and belatedly, Edrion joined in.

Edrion was obsessed with her moods. "It's nothing I can do anything about."

"You're with friends," Edrion reminded her. "Come on. Talk to me."

He'd lived with Kilhellions. Did he know what being friends meant to her? Did he mean it that way?

Anyway, she couldn't just talk to Edri, of course. They were in a boat, and everyone could see and hear everything. "It's not—" But it was important. "I'm worried about stupid money. And I hate it. I hate money and I hate worrying about money, but I have to because of my brother. And those boxes … I wish I'd known we were going to buy them. We're only going to be on the boat for a little while. I would have gotten by on bread, olive oil and vinegar if I was on my own. So I'm angry. And it's not at any one of you. I'm angry because my purse is light and I can't afford what's needed, is all."

"You didn't pay for them," Temric said. "I did. I can afford them. I'm happy to share as long as we're traveling together."

Gods, she felt awful for saying anything. Why did she let Edri talk her into revealing her feelings? "Then I'm sorry, and I thank you." She forced herself to breathe that in, and to exhale her anger and embarrassment along with her lingering fever.

"And I will continue to need them," Temric added. "I have a long way to go before I reach home. I'll take them with me. Think nothing on it."

She wondered what else he'd paid for. "But I paid my fair share for the boat, and the food and all, right?"

"I bought the boat," Aliiren reminded her. "I'll sell it when we reach Ben Ariim and return the money to my temple."

"But yes to the food, and to the water," Temric told her. "I've been paying attention, and not just to our language lessons, Billie. I was careful to respect your feelings. If I thought you'd be open to me gifting part of your share back to you, I would have asked first."

It made her happy that she could, and did, believe him. "Thank you." Those words were so inadequate. She wanted him to understand that she wasn't ungrateful. "I just … I don't want to be a burden." It was true, but it felt like a lie. What really mattered was if she'd have enough to get home. She wasn't sure she did.

"You're not a burden," Aliiren said softly. He stepped over Edrion's and Temric's oars, then settled across from her at the seat nearest the rudder and handed her a napkin full of food. He'd arranged the dried fruit, sliced ham, chopped herbs and soft cheese into tidy little rolls as if they were appetizers at a fancy Sothron party.

She tried to find words to thank him for the extra care without sounding like an idiot, or making too much of it. She ate in silence, mulling. Finally, she said, "these are very good. Thank you."

"You're very welcome."

She tied the rudder to keep it steady once Temric got them on his new course and then curled up awkwardly on her side in the little space on the rudder seat, her legs hanging off at a vaguely comfortable angle. She expected Aliiren to take Edrion's favorite sleeping place behind the forward rowing bench, pillowed by someone's wool blanket. Or maybe he could go to the slightly smaller space at the bow, nestled amid the dubious comfort of their supplies.

Instead, he tucked himself between Temric's feet and Billie's. He pillowed his head on the stack of her folded-up overclothes.

"I think this is a more comfortable place than where you're trying to rest," he said after a moment. "Please trade places with me."

But her eyes were already half-closed, and she didn't want to move. "If you want to sleep here, you'll have to fight me for it," she slurred.

Was there an unseen smile in that silence, or a frown?

Her eyes closed the rest of the way, and her aching body relaxed.

The next thing she knew someone had grabbed her shoulder. She surged up thrashing, sure that they planned to drag her somewhere and kill her where no one at the healer's college would hear her dying screams. Well it would take an army of them to—

"Easy, Billie! Billie."

It was Temric, his body faintly lit by the small light stones set at the bow and stern of the ship.

Otherwise, it was dark.

Actually, there were stars everywhere.

The moonlight glowing near the horizon was small and blueish instead of a silvery gold.

No, that wasn't the moon.

The ocean air held a new quality to it, filled with memories of a hot day in summer on a scree slope on Mt. Cross, but without that gritty edge of dust-covered glacial ice melting in a hidden crevasse.

Her senses caught a brief hint of smoke. It touched her face and then was gone in an instant, as if she'd only imagined it.

"Land," Temric told her. "We've found land, and there's a lighthouse to guide us."

## Chapter Eleven

◇◇◇◇◇◇◇◇◇◇◇◇◇◇◇◇◇◇◇◇◇◇◇◇◇◇◇◇◇◇◇◇◇◇◇◇◇◇◇◇◇◇◇◇

# A Silvery Green Light

◇◇◇◇◇◇◇◇◇◇◇◇◇◇◇◇◇◇◇◇◇◇◇◇◇◇◇◇◇◇◇◇◇◇◇◇◇◇◇◇◇◇◇◇

*Somewhere on the Coast of Arrak Thedra*
*2nd Gift Night of Sun Month*

"Now it becomes dangerous," Temric told them, once again sitting near the bow.

Edrion laughed. "*Now* it gets dangerous?"

Billie chuckled, but Aliiren didn't look amused. *He might just be in pain.* She certainly was uncomfortable, to say the least. As Edrion and Temric had worn themselves out rowing while she and Aliiren had slept, everyone decided to swap places. Now she and Aliiren rowed, slowly and steadily, across smooth, quiet water. An occasional breeze cooled their sweat. Her gift continued to fever her as it worked to keep her muscles from locking up. In particular, her elbows had begun to bother her even more than her shoulders.

This time she'd sat behind Aliiren so she could watch him while they rowed, to make sure he didn't push his body beyond its limits. So far he seemed all right, though his shoulders had swollen again.

After everything Aliiren had put himself through, she had no idea how he had been able to row without a strong native healing gift.

"Let's hold up while we figure this out," Temric told them.

Billie and Aliiren put up their oars. She was all too happy to rest for a while, even though they hadn't been rowing for long.

Edrion stretched out his legs, then covered his mouth with one hand while he yawned, steering with the other. "We can talk about it while we row toward the lighthouse."

"It's dark, and we still don't know where we are," Temric pointed out. "That lighthouse might be a small one, and we could be very close, or it could be tall and large, and it might be far away. The water is so quiet that we might not notice the sound of waves breaking over rocks. We could wreck on a big piece of driftwood or run aground on a shoal."

She hadn't thought about shipwrecking in the little rowboat. "Maybe, since the waves are lazy, that means it won't be that hard to get to shore."

"True, and we have Rill luck." Temric surprised her by his matter-of-fact statement, but it didn't surprise Edrion. He simply preened in response. "But it would be safer if we found a harbor, or a sheltered cove. We can't see those things at night. So it may be better if we anchor here and wait until dawn so that we can see what we're doing."

"If that's the right thing to do, why haven't we anchored already?" Aliiren asked.

*Because it wastes time that we don't have?* Billie answered silently.

"Because anchoring has its own problems. None of us are particularly skilled at running about in a rowboat on the ocean. The weather might change for the worse. The anchor might get caught in something, wasting precious time that we'll need to reach that lighthouse. And I'm sure there are plenty of other things that make anchoring dangerous that we don't even know about."

"I suggest that we row toward the light," Aliiren said. "It may be safer than anchoring, or it may not, but we'll get closer to the lighthouse. There should be a harbor near there."

"Billie, what do you think?" Temric asked.

He ought to have known her answer. "We go forward. You said yourself that none of us have the experience to do this properly. The less time we spend at sea, the less likely we are to make a fatal mistake."

"Edrion?"

"I want out of this rowboat," Edrion said. "If I wanted to be stuck in one place for a long time, I would have stayed on the island."

They all went quiet for a bit, while delicate, long waves gently lifted them and settled them down again.

Temric looked to Billie, and then to Aliiren. "Whenever you're ready."

Billie took up the oars, watching Aliiren carefully as he took his up. She didn't like how stiffly he moved, but they didn't have that far to go. At least, she hoped that they didn't. Every stroke of the oars made her shiver from the cramp-like ache in her shoulders and back. Judging by the way Aliiren moved, he wasn't having much fun either.

"I can see the docks," Temric said.

His next words punched her in the gut.

"It's not Ben Ariim."

She hadn't considered all the implications of not reaching Ben Ariim until Temric told them the bad news. She'd believed that it would be obvious whether they needed to travel east or west once they found land. But stars were the only lights she could see outside the civilization they rowed toward. They could only guess which way to go from here.

Half a chance wasn't good enough. They'd have to depend on the goodwill of strangers to find the fastest way to Ben Ariim.

"Are you sure?" Billie asked, hoping for a better answer.

"It's much too small," Temric said. "The great port of Ben Ariim is a city of nearly a million people. Judging by the number of lights, this is a village of perhaps a few hundred." He focused on the map with a scowl on his face. At last he sighed and rolled it up. He must have come to the same conclusion as Billie. The map would be useless until they figured out where they were.

At least they hadn't landed in a wilderness.

Temric tied the map to the bag holding his most personal and precious possessions, and then stood with a hand on the mast to keep his balance as they rowed in. Edrion steered them carefully around a curved mass of land that protected the harbor from large waves. A few well-placed sacred lights helped guide them past the rocks. Those lights glowed from within glass globes that hung from nets dangling from tall, stout posts with heavy iron hooks. The tops of the posts had sharp spikes on them. Was that to prevent hellions from interfering with the lights? She would have asked Aliiren, but something about the quiet and the dark made her reluctant to speak.

The small waves they rowed among once they rounded the rocky breakwater smoothed away, creating a watery mirror for the stars. Silence blanketed them, save for the soft plunge and dripping lift of their oars and the distant sound of sleepy waves rolling up against the breakwater. A gentle breeze carried a warm, dry scent of fragrant wood, warm stones, dust, and spices like she'd never smelled before. This was a new land, as different from Ruvall as Mount Cross.

The lights might not have been as numerous as Ruvall's or as Ben Ariim's were said to be, but there were plenty to illuminate the dark wood of the docks. Among them floated quite a few small but sturdy fishing boats. Most were rigged for sailing, but some were longboats and rowboats that were, with few exceptions, more substantial than their own little rowboat.

Edrion steered them toward a place with room for them to tie-in. Billie and Aliiren stopped rowing. Temric caught the dock with his long arms. After such a long time in the rowboat, moving as little as possible to save their strength, it felt awkward for all of them to move around at once. Billie picked up her bags. The weight of the straps on her shoulders was a new kind of agony.

"This is going to be too much for us to carry." Edrion kept his voice low, as if he didn't want to disturb the quiet either. "Let's leave most of it in the boat."

Billie heaved the weight of the bags off her shoulders, grateful for the suggestion.

"What if someone tries to steal it?" Temric asked. "It's too risky."

"I can stand guard," Aliiren suggested.

"You're the most respectable of us," Edrion reminded him. "The people in the village are more likely to be nice to you."

That made it obvious who should stay. "I'll stay," Billie told them. She didn't want to, but of all of them, she was the most likely to put someone off.

Aliiren shook his head. "They may speak a language here that I don't understand."

It pleased her that he had such faith in her, but … "I know only a few."

"More than any of the rest of us do," Temric pointed out. "I can stay."

Edrion laughed. "Would you let me make a single, clumsy mark on your precious map when we ask for directions? No. Which means that if anyone is staying, it'll be me. But do we really need anyone to watch over the boat? There's no one here."

"Just because we don't see anyone, that doesn't mean there isn't someone waiting to make off with our valuables as soon as we leave," Temric reminded them.

In the short silence that followed his words, a dog barked from within the town. It was a very lonely sound, and it seemed like a kind of warning, too.

Billie imagined Edrion trying to protect the rowboat by himself. She didn't like the idea at all. "We won't go far."

Edrion nodded. "Be careful."

Billie and Aliiren strapped on their blades. Temric reached for his spear. When his hand grasped the ash shaft, he seemed to think better of it, and took up his axe instead. He tucked the blade into a leather sheath that also had a cap for the sharp point opposite the curved blade, then slipped the axe into a loop on his belt.

They clambered out onto the docks and climbed the ramp from the docks to solid ground. The ground seemed to sway like water. She managed to shake off the feeling as they turned right to walk along the mortared pebble street that curved along the bay. High above the beach and dock below, they had a good view of Edrion as he tidied their little rowboat. The mortared wall that supported the street was built up from huge black boulders jammed with seaweed and driftwood. Farther down, steps led to a narrow beach where rowboats rested on a black sand slope.

Tidy stone buildings lined up with the street between them and the sea. A handful of larger, much-less-secure timber and brick buildings, now behind them as they walked, were built on pylons over the water.

She wondered what was inside those strange buildings. They didn't look like houses. Storage, or trades buildings, maybe.

Temric and Aliiren kept their focus on the line of stone buildings. Some had signs hanging above, beside, or on the doors. The pair of them read those signs so quickly that they didn't have to break stride.

"I don't recognize the lettering," Billie admitted. "What language is it?"

"Thedran," Aliiren told her. "Most of it is written in decorative script. That's why you can't read it."

It was kind of him to say, but they both knew that even if it was in block lettering, she still wouldn't have been able to read it.

Temric struggled to stay awake. He yawned often. Aliiren, she was sure, was just as exhausted, but he kept looking into shadowed places and behind them. She wondered why he was so nervous. His skittishness made her nervous, and she kept a wary lookout.

There were so many lights on all the buildings, especially the stone ones, that she wondered if everyone in the world was richer that the people of the Kilhells. Some of the doorways even had matching sacred lights. Many of the sacred light stones were held in colored glass globes similar to the larger ones they saw at the mouth of the bay, hanging from beautifully wrought bronze hooks. The lights within the globes weren't all that bright, though. Perhaps they were low quality and therefore more affordable. Some of them were dim enough that she could see the sacred light stone within them instead of just a glare. The stones were held in the center of the globe by glass spines, or perhaps thick, translucent strings? The beautiful, delicate construction fascinated her.

Aliiren stopped to touch the globe she'd been looking at. He scowled. "Something is wrong."

That made Billie even more uneasy. Did he recognize the culture? Maybe these were slave-keeping people.

Temric didn't seem to hear him. "That tea house might be the best door to knock on. At least they'll have a table and chairs where we can set up my map."

"Wait." Aliiren's voice was still soft, but the sharp tone halted Temric like a tug of reins on a pony's mouth. "Something malevolent damaged these lights."

"What?" Temric's hushed question was thick with alarm. Billie's gut tightened with a terrible, soul-searing dread. "Are you sure?"

"I can't be absolutely sure, but …" His chin lifted as if he wanted to see farther and taste the air at the same time. "I felt it as soon as we set foot on land. The god power here is in motion, but there's no one manipulating it. The Gods are eager for someone to channel them in opposition to an enemy."

"Are you serious?" Temric's eyes showed lots of white, reflecting the fear Billie felt in her heart. "Why didn't you say something?"

"I haven't felt this before." He sounded more afraid than defensive. A shudder traveled through him. "Ben Ariim and Ruvall are sheltered, and there are lots of people able to channel faerus. I thought this might be normal for this place." Aliiren sounded as if he desperately wanted that to be true. "But now I'm pretty sure that what I'm sensing is in opposition to settmin." Though his voice was calm and he wasn't trembling, something subtle told her that he was terrified. "The more I open myself to it, the worse it feels."

Every instinct in her body screamed at her to leave, now.

"But the lights," Temric protested in a harsh whisper under his breath. "If the town was defiled, wouldn't they all be destroyed?"

Billie did her best to stay calm as her gaze darted down the street. Nothing suggested that the things she'd heard of in stories—crucifixions, hellish fires, bonfires made of furniture and bones, corrals of frightened prisoners—had happened here.

Again, the lone dog barked in the distance.

Temric swept a hand through his mop of curly hair, exasperated. He shook his head. "We can't keep rowing through the night."

Did they have a choice? "If I have to, I can." And yet, there didn't seem to be any immediate danger. Was it possible that the hellions had taken what they wanted and left just before true dawn? "But first we have to find out which way to go." And, if someone had been hurt, maybe she could help. Sure, in principle it was wise to be leery of strangers. But as a fellow human living under the threat of hellion atrocities every true night, and as a healer, she felt obligated to do what she could.

"If we can figure out the name of the village, it might be on my map," Temric told them. She wished that he sounded more certain about that.

Aliiren's gaze slowly swept along the street. He'd gone pale. His hand trembled as he settled it on the hilt of his sword. He took an awkward step, then walked with more certainty down the street. Billie followed him as he turned at a corner to go farther inland a few paces.

A temple stood against the side of a steep hill, large compared to the buildings in Torath but tiny compared to the temples she'd seen in Ruvall.

The doors were scorched.

At least they were closed tight. Some of the blessings were dark, but the ones around the edges were lit with a rippling aquamarine glow as beautiful but also as faint as the sea's phosphorescence at night.

Billie halted alongside him, shocked by the signs of fire on the stone doors.

Aliiren's fears were justified. The village had been attacked.

But it wasn't true night. Hopefully that meant the hellions were gone.

Her hopes were flimsy things. She had a terrible feeling that a hellion was creeping up on them. She turned, putting her back to Aliiren's, her hand hard on the hilt of her sword. It was said that unless a blade was imbued with god power it would do nothing to a hellion, but she wasn't about to let herself or any of her friends be captured without a fight.

It wasn't a heroic feeling, nothing at all like she'd imagined when she heard the stories about fights against hellions. It was a terrible, lonely, desperate feeling. Her senses seemed to reach far beyond her body. She thought she could hear the dog panting off in the distance, could smell something rich—

Wait.

That smell.

She knew that smell.

Her heart pounded in her chest. "Meat," she managed to whisper. The sound of her own voice seemed like a shout.

"What?" Temric whispered.

"Cooking," she managed to choke out.

Temric took a whiff of the air. "I think I smell it too. Smells like … suckling pig."

"It's people."

Temric went rigid. "You're kidding. Don't joke."

"I'm not joking." The scent was gone with the breeze, then returned before vanishing into the night.

"We need to leave." But despite his words, Temric didn't move. It felt as if none of them could move.

"We need to help them," Aliiren said tightly.

"What?" Temric's voice hadn't raised much above a whisper, but it felt like a shout, making Billie jump inside her skin. "The three of us?"

"No. Just me. The two of you need to leave. Go to Edrion, find a way to the nearest inhabited place and get help."

"No." It wasn't just that she wouldn't even know which way to go. The idea of leaving Aliiren here to fight whatever might be here all by himself was too horrible. "I'm not leaving here without you."

"That's right," Temric whispered. "We're all leaving here together. Aliiren, there's nothing you can do. You're just one person."

Temric was probably right, but her heart shrank at the thought. *Aliiren is right.* She felt it deep in her gut. "We can't leave these people here like this."

"Aliiren's not even a mage yet," Temric countered. "Be sensible."

Aliiren's shoulders tightened up. He forced them back down. "It's my duty."

Thoughts of Brian fought hard against that word. Duty. She understood it very well.

Tilla would find her way if Billie didn't.

Could she, should she count on that?

But it was just as much her duty as a human being to stand by Aliiren and help these people if she could. Even if it was just one person that they saved. "Maybe what we can do is knock on the doors and let people know that it's safe to leave. We can all make a run for Ben Ariim." As soon as she said it, she realized that it might not be safe for whoever might be inside the temple to open the doors. Just because Bille and her friends were still alive and the village was quiet, that didn't mean that there weren't hellions stalking them at this very moment.

"They won't answer. They'll think it's a trick," Temric argued. "Listen to me. If we can figure out where we are, we can take one of the sailboats to

Ben Ariim and send help back. That's going to do a lot more good than one protector against who knows what is here."

"It's Gift Night," Aliiren said quietly. "True night falls tomorrow. These people are nearly out of time, and if we don't find a secure shelter before sunset, we'll be out of time too."

"Which means we have to convince them that it's safe to leave," Billie realized aloud. *And convince them to take us with them. But will they trust us, and can we trust them?*

"It might not be safe for them to leave, not unless I face whatever is here." Aliiren firmed his grip on the hilt of his sword. He didn't look more determined, though. He looked even more scared. "I'm not perfect." He muttered the words sharply, as if they were a rebuke both to himself and to them. "I can only give all of myself, completely, to the Light." His gaze, eyes too white and wild like an animal on the verge of panic, locked onto Billie's face. "As you must give all of yourself to your tribe. Go home, Billie."

The way he held his body, damaged from all the rowing they'd done, the terror ...

The fear within her was familiar. She'd felt this before. She knew that if she died, it would hurt, and how much. She'd been battered, cut, overwhelmed by the skill and determination of another being trying to destroy her.

But she also remembered what it was like to fight for people she cared about. And she remembered that she'd won.

Her mother could have screamed for Billie to run home. But she hadn't. She'd screamed one word.

*Fight.*

That word had exploded through Billie's body like a lightning bolt and fired her soul with power like she'd not felt since.

That memory gave her the strength to say, "I'm staying with you."

"Don't be foolish," Aliiren whispered sharply.

Running to Brian—running away from whatever horrors they might face here—tempted her.

*No.* "I may not be a protector, but I'm a follower of Life. I can't leave these people any more than you can. Not when there's a chance I can help."

Temric shook his head, but then he drew his axe free of his belt and pulled off the sheath, letting it drop to the ground. So often he seemed as awkward as a leggy colt, but the way he passed the axe from hand to hand, reminding himself of its weight, was well-practiced. He let out a shaky breath. "Then let's help if we can. All three of us."

Temric's words seemed to act as an antidote to the fear liquor coursing through Aliiren's veins. He strode with purpose deeper into the village.

Billie followed him, her body alive with flashes of hot and cold. She drew her blade. Her gaze switched from side to side. Sometimes she turned as she walked to look behind them. Aliiren might be able to sense the hellish god power in the village, but she couldn't, and she wasn't sure if the hellions might not have some way to conceal themselves from him.

Temric walked alongside her, less watchful but twitchy, his body reacting to sights and sounds she couldn't detect herself. She suspected that fear liquor was affecting him badly. She'd have to take care in case he mistook her for an enemy in the corner of his eye. She knew from stories of battles told on Mount Cross that such things happened sometimes.

The buildings connected to each other in long rows in this part of the village. Their stone roofs slanted from their high fronts toward the rising ground in the back. Little alleyways, sometimes steep and sloped, sometimes stepped, cut between sets of buildings to the next street up. The buildings gave her the impression of broad wedges that had been hammered into the rock. Those rocky slopes cupped the village and its harbor like a mother protecting her children within the curve of her arms. The building faces were flat and heavily carved with large blessings that were then lime washed, making them seem to glow almost as brightly as the sacred lights hanging by the blessed stone doors.

God power gleamed faintly along some of the blessings. She wasn't sure why they didn't all gleam. What would have been a matter of curiosity now fluttered fearfully in her mind. Was the village mostly defiled? Were most of the buildings occupied by hellions now?

The scent of cooking human, slightly sweet and unpleasantly appetizing, blew into her face on a breeze. The memory of boiling the thigh bone of the man she'd killed to make her flute came back in a rush. She gagged, spat. It took an extreme force of will to focus her mind past the lurching of her gut.

Survivors. They had to learn whether there were survivors.

She hoped that Aliiren had made a mistake, but in her heart she knew he hadn't. The hellions wouldn't have left behind cooking meat.

There absolutely were hellions here, then. They were actually here, right now.

Her heart thundered in her ears. Every instinct screamed for her to run away. Sharp tingles coursed through her body.

A door stood ajar. They all saw it at the same time, all stopped like deer that had heard a twig snap.

An eerie, strangely lovely, silvery-green light glowed from within. Steam wafted out from a hidden chimney, scenting the air with cooking human.

Aliiren drew his blade and took a slow step, and then another, and another, glassy-eyed.

She followed. Together they got closer, and closer. Her hilt felt loose in her hand. When Aliiren reached out and touched the door, she wanted to scream, *don't!* But he pulled it open.

Spiderwebs drew with it, snapping and crackling as he opened the door wide. The webbing was darker than spider webbing, a glittering silver-gray along which faint pulses of greenish light traveled. Aliiren's eyes widened even more, his pupils fully open. His irises gleamed like thin golden rings. Those rings sparkled with pale blue light.

Billie came up alongside him, stopped beside him.

Beyond the dark front room, within a small kitchen, glimmering webs surrounded something like a narrow, green and silver crab. A shield-like claw opened toward them in a gesture she couldn't translate. A pair of smaller, sharper claws shone with edges as long, hard and keen as her sword blade. Serrations reflected the being's green light like pale emerald points. Just above a pair of silvery, fuzzy fangs dripping with venom, a set of cat eyes—one pair set low, another pair on stalks—glowed with the same pale gray-green light as its body. The pattern of gray, silver and green around those eyes was hypnotically lovely, a series of waves and spots that reminded her of water flowing over rainbow pebbles. Beneath the fangs, a slitted mouth opened to reveal rows of serrated teeth set into ridges the color of rotted flesh. Those teeth curved toward its gullet; anything that went in would never get out.

The demon stood on two pairs of sword-like legs. Behind it, coiled with the promise of an agonizing death, an armored tail with twin stingers undulated back and forth above its eyes. Her nodes cramped in reaction to those living, poisonous weapons. Vinus rushed through her channels as if blood already spurted from her arteries, as if her bones had already shattered.

In all it was only slightly longer than Temric was tall, but she was absolutely sure that the demonic hellion was too much for them. It was on its guard, braced in the kitchen doorway, its largest claw covering the lower half of the opening. The pair of smaller claws lifted to protect its mouth.

It was ready for them.

Only Aliiren could protect them from the demon's powers, faerus that flowed from hellion gods of deception and devouring. Only Aliiren had a chance of killing it.

If she attacked, she would die here.

They might all die here, horribly.

But Billie could not run.

Because there was a child tangled in thick, silver webbing in the darkest corner of the front room.

Aliiren started to glow a faint blue, and the length of his blade sparkled with the same color. To her surprise, the hellion recoiled.

There would be no better time. With a scream of defiance, Billie charged.

Chapter Twelve

# The Child

*Somewhere on the Coast of Arrak Thedra*
*2nd Gift Night of Sun Month*

The demon moved so fast that she couldn't aim her attacks. She slashed, thrust and parried by pure instinct. Claws and sword-like legs came at her from all angles. Each time her sword made contact it felt like hitting stone. The shock sent jolts of pain through her hands, wrists and elbows. The pair of smaller claws with their gleaming, metallic edges flashed toward her face. She barely managed to bat them away. And still more attacks came in. Some she parried with her sword or dagger or both. Some opened hot wounds.

Any moment she would feel a flash of unbearable pain, and then nothing.

*It's too fast. I need a plan.*

She didn't have time to plan.

The demon gave her more and more fiery cuts on her arms, and bone-deep bruises on her legs and shoulders. Her body gradually buckled under the weight of its furious attack.

Her blades couldn't get through thing's armor. It was stronger than her. She could barely stop its weaponed limbs from spearing her.

The huge, shield-like claw opened.

If it closed around her arm, that arm would be amputated.

The claw twisted up toward her face.

She ducked and thrust toward the demon's eyes. A fang batted her point aside. Her sword skipped off the hard shell beside the eye. Billie twisted and ducked again to avoid the smaller pair of claws trying to scissor through skin and organs, even bone. She managed to sweep both blades against the hellion's living weapons over and over, desperately trying to survive. She realized she was losing—where was Aliiren?!— and thrust toward the mouth, the only vulnerable-looking thing she could reach with her blade.

Light burst from just behind her. Mercurial blue faerus flashed down the length of her blade.

Her sword sank deep into its mouth.

Light exploded from within the maw, blinding her.

The demon roared a rattling hiss. The stench of fish and a weird perfume blew into her face.

Billie yanked her blade free and thrust again even though she couldn't see. She aimed with a feeling clearer than sight, born of memory of where it had been and how it had fought. She dodged at the same time, hoping to make it harder for the demon to kill her.

Her blade sank in again, deeper this time. An icy, searing pain opened up along her arm as she pulled her blade free. She swept her blades in front of her body, instinctively defending against an attack she couldn't see. Her sword glanced off a claw. Her dagger missed. Furnace-hot air blasted out from the demon, sulphurous and spicy with something that reminded her of pepper. The scent of cooked person grew stronger, tainted with the sharp, dirty scent of singed hair. She bent over involuntarily and gagged.

Something hot and heavy struck her across the legs and raked up into her ribs. Billie spun away through the air. Her body twisted, her sword and dagger dangerously whirling along with her.

Her shoulder slammed into the ground, then her head cracked into something. Her head hummed as she rolled across the floor. It was all she could do to control her blades so that they wouldn't slash her open.

A horrible chanting in a language she didn't understand skittered through her mind. A flare of sharp green light pierced her blindness, unbearably bright, burning like fire. It took everything she had to resist the urge to claw her own eyes out. Someone was screaming. It might have been her. It might have been Temric, or Aliiren, or all of them together.

The chanting devolved into wet gasps and gurgles.

She'd become a prisoner in a world of endless blinding brilliance. She crouched, making herself as small as possible, and held her blades at the ready. Her remaining senses strained for anything that could tell her what was happening.

The screaming had stopped. *Are they dead?* Her heartbeat rushed in her ears. She choked on smoke, the horrid smells of cooked human and the hellion's perfumed stench.

Aliiren shouted something, and Temric answered. She couldn't make out the words, but their voices filled her with hope.

*They're not dead.*

The gurgling, snarling, and strange, chanted words the demon made were interspersed with wet gasps and wooden rattles. The tile floor was icy under her knee. Her body trembled uncontrollably and throbbed with heat from her vinus. She was bleeding. Her gift burned inside her like a wildfire, rushing everywhere at random. The smells and the taste of blood in her mouth made her gag again.

*Listen.*

It sounded like the demon was still in the doorway. From what she could tell, Aliiren and Temric were both fighting it.

She couldn't just charge in blindly and attack.

*I can distract it.*

Billie reached with the point of her dagger until it touched the wall and charged, using her dagger as a guide.

Something damp slapped against her arm and stuck, drying instantly in a patch as large as her palm. The thing pulled, hard. It made sticky, crackling sounds, sounds horribly familiar to her.

*Web. Spiders.*

She scrambled backwards against the pull, remembering the terrible twin stingers on the thing's armored tail. Her hip slammed into furniture.

The gurgling curses from the thing grew more desperate. The sound of a blade striking and ringing free sang out again and again, and again. Billie grabbed the web with her hands and pulled as hard as she could. A powerful crack and splintering joined the sound of the blade. The web tore and Billie stumbled back into finer webbing. When she tried to sweep it away it multiplied and became finer, as if she'd bumped a ripe dandelion head and the seeds, interconnected by magic, blew all around her.

Temric cried out something panicked and incoherent. That stopped her dead. She squeezed her eyes shut, and opened them wide again, desperate to see what was happening. She didn't dare scream his name for fear she'd distract him.

The demon screeched in agony. A faint, floral scent wafted through the room.

The brilliant blindness finally began to fade. Thank the perseverance of Life, she could make out Temric's silhouette swinging his axe toward the hellion's shield claw. Something like lightning arced into his axe blade from the ceiling and into the hellion right when the axe bit into the joint.

The claw sagged as the joint gave way, cut nearly through. Beside Temric, Aliiren glowed as bright as the sun, but cold and sharp, as crystalline as ice. Aliiren let out a soft, gasping cry as the point of his blade punctured the hellion's last remaining eye. The point went deep and the demon screeched in pain. Its arms and legs waved about and shook violently, the light of Aliiren's god glowing through its wounds and joints.

A terrible shudder passed through it.

It was dead. She'd seen enough things die that she knew. But, like her friends who kept stabbing and chopping at it, she was afraid to believe that. This was a powerful being of legends and countless stories of horror. When Temric staggered back, Billie rushed in to take his place. She barely managed to deflect a small claw that slashed toward Aliiren's side.

The hellion collapsed and shrank, like spiders did when they died. There was no vitality there, no reaction to pain and damage, no flinches.

Finally, it stopped twitching.

"It's dead," Billie croaked as Aliiren continued to stab it. "It's done. Aliiren."

The light faded from Aliiren's body enough that she could see his chest heaving as he gasped for air. His shoulders hunched as he sagged with exhaustion. Temric backed off another few paces, his body spattered with greenish and yellowish goo, his ax thick with it. The hellion dripped colorful fluids from its wounds, a grim rainbow of ichor. Around its eyes the fluid was the darkest, a deep brown. It smelled of fish and blood and the flowery scent had grown stronger. Her memory jolted her with recognition.

The floral scent reminded her of the wild, white daffodils that grew on a harsh, rocky hillside about a half-day's ride from Torath. That beautiful, lonely scent of home mixed with the fishiness and blood revolted her more than the scent of rotting flesh.

Every instinct urged her to get out, to get away from it, but she couldn't leave Aliiren and Temric.

Temric managed to stand tall somehow, but Aliiren was bent, braced on his knees. The light emanating from him flickered like ghostly flames.

Billie swayed as the room seemed to tilt around her. She walked to the nearest wall and tried to steady herself. Her hand made contact with more spiderweb, and she flinched away. The silvery webbing, no longer bright with lights, clung to her hand, and she found some more on her arm. She tried to sweep it away but instead it spread and clung to her.

That's when she remembered the child.

The light in the room was fading fast. She started to ask Temric to uncover the sacred lights in the room, but then realized that the hellion would have destroyed them. Hellions hated sacred lights. "The child," she tried to tell them. Her words slurred. "Aliiren. The child."

Temric must have understood her because he staggered her way. "Aliiren."

Billie pushed through the webbing that held the child off the ground. It was like drawing aside sticky curtains. Her hand touched the child's face. There was warmth there. The child was alive?!

Temric started tearing at the webbing. "Stop," Billie pleaded. "Wait. I need to feel ..." Both of the child's hands were buried too deep in the webbing to reach them quickly, but a foot was exposed. Billie knelt. Her hand curled around the sole of the foot, and she closed her eyes.

She forced vinus to flow through a large channel from her strongest node—the one connected to her womb—to her palm. With a hard push, she sent her gift into the child. There, the vinus acted like a part of her. Her inner sense sent back strange images of darkness, a feeling of something oily, of ...

Billie recoiled and fell back.

The child, a boy, wasn't warm because he was alive. "He's ..." She couldn't bear to say it. It gave the truth too much power, too much horror.

Aliiren's hand settled briefly on her shoulder before he reached in and touched the boy's face. Aliiren's light had steadied, illuminating him and the child as gently as the first light before the coming of dawn. It was a cool light, but full of the promise of warmth and renewal. "I have him," he whispered.

The room was so quiet now, she could hear his softly spoken words clearly, and the breath that came after.

Something simmered in the kitchen.

Aliiren bowed his head. "His soul ... I have to set it free before the defilement can do more harm."

"You can't save him?" Temric's voice sounded tight and small, almost as if he himself were a child.

"His heart isn't beating." Billie didn't want to say anything more about what she'd felt, but clearly Temric didn't understand. "He's not breathing. There's … there's no life to save."

"The soul is still trapped." Aliiren took another strained breath. "Look away."

Billie needed no convincing to do that. Besides, she had a horrible duty to attend to, one that her friends should never have to carry in their memories for the rest of their lives.

Her body felt weak and wobbly as she made her way to the kitchen. She didn't know what it would feel like to touch the demon, but she had no choice. She had to get past it.

The armored shell was cold, smooth, and despite the subtle gloss, not slimy like she'd half-expected. Billie stepped over its legs, and carefully pushed aside the large tail. Its stingers dripped an amber liquid that was thick as egg whites.

There were two adults dismembered there, with parts of their flesh and a hunk of bone missing, no doubt stewing in the large pot that sat on a coal-fueled stove. They'd been seasoned with something that smelled sweet and tart at the same time.

But that wasn't what shocked her.

There was a toddler tied into a basket made of thin strips of wood and ribbon woven together, bundled in a blanket smudged with blood.

Alive.

Large, brown eyes stared at her, uncomprehending. The baby was so terrified it didn't even try to scream.

Billie crouched immediately. It took a great deal of will to remember to keep her voice soft and low. "You're safe now." She drew her working knife from its familiar place in her boot, cut the ties, and gathered the little one up into her arms. The stench of urine and feces momentarily overpowered the rich scent coming from the stove.

Billie shoved past the awful carcass in the doorway once again. She covered the child's lovely brown eyes to shield them from the painful light of Aliiren's work, and escaped out the front door into fresh, cool air.

Her heart hammered hard in her throat. One child that she thought she could save was beyond her aid. One that might have been lost forever was safe in her arms. The feelings were just too much. She wanted to laugh, to cry, to scream in horror. Instead, she gently swayed back and forth, and hummed a wordless lullaby that her sister Stayce used to hum to Billie and Brian when she had charge of them.

An awful thought shocked her into stillness.

*There might be more hellions in the village.*

She strode back to the front room, keeping her body between the child and Aliiren's light as best she could. The baby began to sob, and then softly whine. "Shhhh." But there would be no soothing this babe, not in this place with the terrible smells and all that had been done. She expected that soon the screams would begin, screams for a mother that could not answer.

Aliiren sweated and trembled as he sat back on his heels beside the body, his face rigid with carefully contained grief. The light emanating from his body had faded, glowing like frost on his skin. His gaze shifted to her, and then his eyes widened.

"Aliiren, are there more settmin in the village?" Billie asked. "Can you tell?"

To her surprise the baby had quieted again. Maybe it was exhaustion. When had the baby last been fed? Changed?

Aliiren stood, his body rigid with fear once again. His trembling was more violent now, and he was still pale. "Take the baby to the rowboat. It's the safest place. I'll search the town for more settmin."

She didn't know if Aliiren would survive if he fought another hellion. The stories said that no two hellions were the same. What if the next one was larger, stronger, faster? What if the next one wasn't alone? What if Aliiren was ambushed?

She wanted to fight alongside him, but she couldn't. She had a charge now.

"Together," Temric added breathlessly. He looked to Aliiren with a pale courage that filled Billie with awe. "You and I."

"I'll need rags," Billie told them. She almost asked for milk, then thought better of it. Everything in the house might be tainted. Anyway, she had to get the baby to safety first. She'd start with a little water at the rowboat and then work from there.

A narrow doorway, the door shattered off its hinges, lay open on one side of the front room. A bedroom?

"Maybe in there." Billie gestured with her chin, rocking the baby that was quiet again. "And look for clean clothes."

Aliiren went to look.

"Are clean clothes really the most important thing right now?" Temric asked crossly.

He obviously didn't understand how fragile and helpless small children were. She did her best to keep her voice matter of fact. "If the baby has any open wounds, yes."

Temric looked away, scowling. Billie rocked the baby, deliberately focusing on comforting him and nothing else.

Aliiren found something in the room and quickly bundled it into a blanket, which he gave to her. "I'm so sorry," he whispered.

*For what?* But the baby's needs were urgent, and learning about what he meant could wait for later. "I have to go," she told him apologetically.

He nodded. "Then go."

As Billie hurried through the dark village toward the docks, flinching at shadows that she fancied had moved, something from long ago settled inside her.

After the attack on Billie's mother, her brother and her, the chieftain organized a pair of hunting parties. With his wife and his self as leaders, they would search for any other raiders that might be nearby. Billie had assumed that she would lead the way. She'd even boldly said, "I'll show you where it happened," to the chieftain's wife.

"You fancy yourself as brave as a Champion now?" Billie's father had snapped. "Stay home with your mother."

"But—" she'd begun to protest.

"Stay." He'd told her that like she was an ill-trained dog.

"You need to keep your own self safe," the chieftain's wife added gently. "For the sake of the tribe."

For a long time after she'd silently, in her own mind, argued with her father. She'd wanted to tell him that she wasn't proud—that all she'd wanted to do was help. Her gift was no good anyway because it only helped herself. She hadn't known at the time how to help anyone else with it.

But when everyone returned, her father had lavished so much praise on her that she'd just about forgotten the hurt she'd felt.

Later, alone together in the woods near the place where she'd killed her man, he'd guided her through the bone flute ceremony. While he poked at the fire, he'd spoken to her about Death's many kindnesses, so often overlooked because Life seemed so sweet and generous compared to Its dreaded lover. He also spoke about courage, and fear, and how they intertwined like Life and Death.

Without those lessons, she might not have been able to force herself to go into the kitchen. Without those lessons, would she have insisted on staying to fight at Aliiren's side, though the baby needed her gift?

*This is the worthiest thing I can do right now.* As she held the baby close, that feeling grew. *You're safe with me. I'll protect you with all my strength, with my gift, with my life.*

It wasn't until she got most of the way to the docks that she realized how broken her body was. Heat flared over countless bruises and cuts, and her shoulder and elbow felt hot on her left side. Sharp pains in her knee and hip made her limp. She managed somehow, because she had to for the baby.

"Hey," Edrion called from the rowboat. "I heard some weird noises and I was starting to get worried. Did you find—is that a baby?!"

"Yes. Can you clear a spot for us? And set this somewhere clean. There should be spare clothes and rags in there."

Edrion must have been organizing their things the entire time, because he had everything in order. He quickly made a safe space for the baby in the bottom of the rowboat. Billie peeled back the soiled clothes and rags. The child, apparently a boy, had red, raw skin and rashes in patches all over him. Edrion helped clean him up. Hopefully the fresh water eased some of the pain. The baby made harsh, protesting noises but to her surprise, didn't cry.

"What happened? You're bleeding." Edrion fussed with the baby's clothes while she used a clean, damp rag to do a final cleansing. "Are Aliiren and Temric okay?"

It looked like he'd organized the things inside her bag while she'd been away, which tweaked her a bit, but she had nothing to hide. Besides, his efforts would come in handy. "Can you find the case with my medicines in it?"

"Yes. It's close to the top." He quickly opened one of her bags.

Edrion's words—*what happened*—returned to her mind like an echo.

She didn't want to think about what had happened, but her mind swiftly conjured the child in the web, still warm to the touch, but gone.

"Aliiren and Temric are all right. We were in a fight," Billie explained as Edrion set the case on a bench within easy reach and then shifted his attention to the now-squirming baby. Thankfully Val had insisted that Billie take the healing medicines she'd made, and Tilla had packed them well. She used a cleansing balm that she'd made at the college to help prevent infection. She then thinly applied an ointment for burns to the raw rash on his skin, even in the places that seemed mostly all right, staying clear of his face and hands because she was afraid he might get it in his eyes. She washed her hands often in case she hadn't cleaned him as thoroughly as she wanted, so she wouldn't spread invisible films of filth on his skin. Though she tried to be as gentle as she could, it still hurt him. He screwed up his face and made painful squawks that cut into her heart. *I'm so sorry ...*

*He's an orphan now.*

"How badly are you hurt? Should I be worried?"

It was sweet of him to care, but the baby was more important. "No. I'll be all right."

"Who attacked you?"

"It was a settman. Aliiren and Temric killed it." She began folding the rags that would serve as a diaper around the baby's crotch.

His sharp intake of breath, and the forced exhale, was followed by a breathy laugh. "You're teasing me."

Edrion steadied the protesting baby by cupping his head and gently holding a foot while Billie tried to figure out how the baby's diaper cover worked. "I wish I was. If it weren't for them, I'd be dead. The thing knocked me around like—" *Like I was a child.*

The memory of the dead boy and how his defiled body felt cut through her mind as she tried to tie the diaper wrap on over the rags. The diaper wrap had been lovingly knitted in a sturdy, soft-edged pattern by someone that might be dead now. The knotting was a bit awkward—it was different than what she was used to—but she caught a mistake she'd made and retied it properly.

Edrion's smiling, hopeful expression closed up. "Where are Temric and Aliiren?" he demanded. "Are you sure they're all right?"

The baby seemed to be healthy, though he was thirsty and pale. Whenever he cried his voice was hoarse—no doubt from screaming in terror for endless hours. Billie lifted him up and held him against her chest, careful to avoid the spot where his original wrappings had soiled her clothes. "When I last saw them they were pretty banged up, but they're all right. Aliiren is looking for more settmin." She gently pushed the baby's palm against hers and used her gift to assess the boy, but that was about all she could do. His native healing was strong enough that her gift would fever him more than it would help.

It seemed that she needn't have bothered worrying about infection. She would have used the wash anyway, because every little bit would help him heal that much faster.

*He might have enough gift to become a healer someday.*

The healer's gift was a complicated blessing, one that would shape his entire future.

*I'm sorry. I'm sorry but this is your future now.*

Edrion, who had been gaping at her, speechless, found his voice again. "They're looking for *more* settmin?"

"Yes." Though she tried to be as tender with the baby as she could, he bawled even louder with his raspy, broken voice.

"I knew Aliiren was special," Edrion said weakly. "But this … he killed a settman?"

"Yes. Here. Hold him, please." She set the boy on Edrion's lap, and then dressed him in clean clothes, the softest and lightest she could find. The baby stiff-armed and tried to stop her, but he was only a baby, and she managed to get everything put on properly. Finally she wrapped him in his own blanket, and Edrion snuggled him close.

*Will he remember? Would he want to have memories of family, of love, even if that meant that he would also remember the horrible way that he lost them?*

He seemed settled now, so Billie did her best to clean herself up. The hellion had slashed through her sleeves in several places, and rents in her tunic and underclothes gave her access to a long wound across her ribs. She didn't find anything that needed stitches or surgery.

She cleaned the worst of the blood off, careful to leave the parts that needed to scab alone. The heat from her gift made her arms feel sunburned and her bruises like they were too close to a hot iron. She pulled some of her vinus back to her nodes. She'd heal more slowly, but she was less likely to complicate her injuries with a healer's burn.

She could have been killed. She got lucky.

Though dressed warmly, the baby started shivering. His breath hitched, and he wheezed out little cries of pain and fear, but he seemed stronger. "Don't worry," she soothed. "Edrion is going to take good care of you."

"You're going back." Edrion spoke the words flatly, like he'd expected as much, but didn't like it.

"I'm going to find them, make sure they're still all right."

"Maybe I should go look instead?" His voice squeaked and wavered. "I *am* lucky."

"But you're not a healer. What if they need me?"

"What if the baby needs you?" he asked in a small voice. Before she could answer, his gaze jerked toward the village like a hungry lion sighting on an old, crippled deer. He relaxed just as she turned to look in the same direction. "It's them."

They weren't running, which was a very good sign.

It seemed to take a lifetime for them to reach the rowboat. The lights on their little boat revealed a nasty cut along Aliiren's neck. Blood drenched his tunic. He had something like a burn along his sword arm, too. A destroyed sleeve hung from a loose cuff, the opening revealing shiny pinkness in a long, narrow stripe. He was sweating. He probably had a nasty fever from using faerus, and he shivered, with fever or fear or both, she couldn't tell. Small patches of fine cuts as delicate as scarlet thread dotted his face and arms and covered his hands. Those didn't look like they came from something sharp. They looked very strange, almost like a delicate, hot metal net had scalded his skin.

*It was the spider web. It burned him.*

Temric's left hand, his dominant, was badly swollen and he walked with a slight limp. But otherwise they both seemed like they weren't in danger.

"The settman had broken into other homes." Aliiren sat wearily at the edge of the dock and drew in his legs, hugging them hard against his chest. He rested his head on his knees and trembled.

Temric gave Aliiren's shoulder a tentative touch, then looked away from him toward Billie and Edrion with weary but wide eyes. "We think there are people still locked in their homes and at the temple, but no one answered when we knocked. How is the baby?"

"He seems fine, considering."

Temric climbed into the rowboat and put a hand on the baby's head. He started to say something else, but then his gaze snapped to the largest of his bags and his hands jerked to his hips. "Did you open my bag?"

Edrion's brows tightened together, and he rubbed the baby's back possessively. "Of course I went through your bags. I was bored, and curious."

"My things are private," Temric snapped. He leaned ominously toward Edrion, pointing toward Edrion's eyes.

Billie put her body between them, rocking the boat violently in her haste. "Stop it. You're going to upset the baby. We can talk about this later."

Temric huffed and crossed his arms, then turned his back on Edrion. Edrion didn't seem offended. He focused instead on murmuring something in his smooth, tumbling native language to the baby boy. The boy had stopped crying, but his face was pinched like he was thinking about crying again, and he punched Edrion repeatedly on the chest. It was like he wanted to push Edrion away, but at the same time he didn't want to be set down.

"We have to find the baby's next of kin." Aliiren's soft voice was tight with pain.

Yes, they did.

"Maybe in the morning," Edrion suggested. Somehow he'd gotten the baby calmed down. Or maybe the little boy was growing weaker?

They had to get him something to drink. Billie got into their water supply. He was probably too little to drink from a canteen, but what else could she do? "Here," she told Edrion as she approached with the canteen. "Hold your hand under his chin and try to catch the water so his clothes don't get wet." She pressed the canteen against the baby's mouth.

The baby violently turned away with a protesting squawk.

This was not going to work.

She kept trying anyway.

By then Temric had calmed down and turned back around to face them. "We need to find a way to talk to whoever might be in the temple. We didn't find that many ..."

*Bodies,* she guessed he didn't want to say.

"There could be several hundred people in that temple. Hopefully the rest escaped to safety." His voice wavered. "I suppose some have been taken away."

*They might have taken their own lives rather than risk having their souls devoured by hellion gods, or live out their lives as slaves.* She didn't want to say that out loud.

"I'm sure someone is alive inside the temple, but they're afraid," Aliiren said. "They probably thought that we were part of a settmin deception to lure them out."

Aliiren was a Light Protector. Maybe he was too overwhelmed by all that had happened to think that through. "Use Light," she told him.

"What?"

Maybe he was going into shock. She reached to touch him, but he tensed so she backed off. "Use Light's faerus to convince them," Billie suggested. "Reinforce the blessings around the door, or something." She realized that she didn't know what she was talking about and shut up. He'd probably channeled too much faerus as it stood. The fever was already making him sweat.

"We have to try." Aliiren braced himself back up to his feet.

"It can wait until morning," Temric said wearily, interrupting Billie's attempt to ask if Aliiren needed her to use her gift on him.

"The closer it gets to true night, the less time these people will have to get away," Aliiren reminded them. He turned and walked back toward the village.

"Aliiren!" Temric called, and then he shook his head.

"Here. Let me have a look at your arm," Edrion told Temric.

After a moment's hesitation, while she assured herself that the baby was safe in Edrion's care, Billie followed Aliiren back to the village.

## Chapter Thirteen

# Trust

Side by side they walked through the dark village toward the temple. With all that had happened she felt like it ought to be dawn by now, but it was as dark as it had been when they'd arrived. She was limping, and everything hurt, but she hadn't suffered any truly debilitating injuries. She'd been very lucky. Aliiren was walking well, but he cradled his right arm, and he was still shivering. More than once she thought about asking him if she could at least assess his injuries, but he was closed off and his face was tight with concentration.

Aliiren took in a deep breath, then spoke so softly that she could barely hear him. "I hope you will forgive me."

Had she heard that right? "For what?"

His fingers on both hands curled but didn't close into fists, probably because it hurt too much. "I—I panicked. And I didn't expect—is your eyesight damaged? From the faerus I channeled?"

*Oh.* "I'm all right." She wasn't actually sure, but he didn't need to know that right now. She would know more after sunrise.

He winced. "I couldn't move." His voice had grown in strength, but also in bitterness. "I just stood there while you fought it alone. It wasn't until—" He paused and shook his head. "There was a moment when your body and your sword aligned. It was … perfect." He crossed his arms, his tone suggesting that he'd had to struggle against his aversion to the word, after being unable to find a better one, even though they'd switched to speaking his native Thedran. "And I called on Light. I called, and Light answered. I didn't think. I just channeled into your blade with everything I had. I didn't know it would flash like that. I can protect my eyes. We're trained to do it without thinking. But you were unprotected." His head twitched in a forceful negation. "I thought I'd blinded you."

"Well—it was temporary," Billie assured him.

"But it could have been permanent." His words were thick with regret.

"But it wasn't. And if you hadn't done that, the nefarin would have killed me. So, thank you. For saving my life."

He saved my life.

Until she'd said it aloud, she hadn't realized that their friendship had grown to the point where the fact that he'd saved her felt as natural as if someone from her tribe had done it. While she'd fought the hellion, she'd trusted that he would protect her if he was able, just as she would do anything to save him if his life was in danger. It had been a long time since she'd felt that kind of trust, perhaps never outside of her tribe.

They walked the rest of the way to the temple in silence. She couldn't think of anything else to say that would ease his misplaced sense of guilt.

The faint, aquamarine light glowing from within the carved blessings on the temple was only a bit brighter than starlight, but seemed brilliant in its own way. She noticed now that the main blessing on the stone door had sacred light stones embedded in it, but those didn't glow at all, and one had been picked out. Her gaze fell with Aliiren's. He found the large, round agate first, and reached for it. His hand flinched back just before he touched it.

Had a hellion done something to it to make it dangerous, or was it just a lingering taint that made him flinch? Just in case, she made sure she didn't go anywhere near it.

The door had obviously been defiled, but the rest of the blessings on the temple's thick stone walls looked strong, at least to her uneducated eyes. A disc surrounded by several flames represented the sun in each corner around the door. Lines representing light rays radiated from the suns across the walls, where they interconnected in beautiful ways. Small light stones or small carved suns gleamed at the intersections.

Her gaze returned to the door. Claw marks through those lines, scorched and coated with reddish ash, marred the design on the stone. The marks didn't look like they belonged to the hellion they'd killed.

Something with clawed fingers or a paw did it, or talons. Whatever did it was strong enough to score the door's stone face.

Aliiren reached into a hole beside the door. His arm flexed. The faint sound of a bell rang within the temple. For a moment he did nothing, and then a gentle light began to glow within the hole around his hand. "I'm Aliiren, Light Protector," he said. "My friends and I have killed the nefarin. Please let us in."

No one answered.

They waited a long time. Aliiren, at least, had stopped shivering. He was still sweating. It was probably fever from using so much faerus. She hoped he wasn't in any danger.

Why wasn't anyone answering?

She just had to wait, she supposed, for them to decide if it was safe or not.

Aliiren had used faerus channeled from the God of Light. Wouldn't that be a sign that there weren't nefari nearby?

Her impatience got the better of her as they stood by the door, waiting for perhaps no one.

"Are you sure there are people in there?" Billie asked.

"The blessings have been renewed recently, and the strength of them comes from the other side of the door. Someone is inside. Or at least they were at some point." The light around his hand went out, and he backed away a step with a sigh. "I don't think they trust us."

"But you channeled Light," Billie protested. "Nefari can't do that."

Aliiren nodded. "Maybe they believe that a human slave to nefari could."

"Why would nefari keep a human that could channel faerus? Wouldn't someone like that be able to hurt or even kill them?" Billie asked.

"I don't think the nefari would risk it," Aliiren answered. "But the people inside the temple might be too afraid to think that through."

"What are they going to do?" she whispered to him. "Starve? They have to come out before the next true night, before the nefari return."

"If you tell them that, it will sound like a threat," he pointed out. He let out a sigh. "Maybe the best we can do is to take the child to safety. But which direction?"

Billie set her hand on her sword and scuffed the ground in front of the temple with her feet, her gut tight. If these people stayed in the temple until the next true night, it might mean that any hellions that came here would blame them for the death of their—did hellions have family and friends? Anyway, she feared that they would go to extreme lengths to punish the people of this village for fighting back.

The dog began barking again, this time closer.

That gave her an idea. "Wait here. Keep talking to them."

Aliiren made a funny noise in his throat and his brows furrowed, but he didn't protest as she went looking for the dog.

It didn't take her long to find it. The dog was bigger than she expected from the voice. Tall, leggy, and lean, he had a coarse, gray coat that was frosted white around the muzzle. He had a handsome beard and longer hair around his upper lip, and feathering around his hind legs, but otherwise his shaggy coat was short and coarse. A thick, long tail whipped back and forth as the dog tried to decide if he wanted to be friends or warn her off.

"It's okay," she promised in Thedran. "Good boy." His head ducked; he seemed to understand Thedran. That was something, at least. "Good dog. Come here."

He took a step toward her.

She slowly crouched down to make herself smaller. "Good boy. Come here. Come on." His ears perked at 'come on' and he let out a long series of warning barks. But then his tail tucked and his head slumped as he approached her with crouched, minced steps. He was good and scared, that was for sure. "Good boy. Come on." When he stretched out to try to sniff her, she lifted a hand and slowly offered it.

He took a step forward and sniffed her hand. "Good boy," she told him softly, warming and drawing out her words. "Good boy."

He sat and sniffed her hand again.

Billie rubbed his head gently, then stroked his neck and gently scratched his chest. A shiver went through him, and he started panting. "Good boy," she told him brightly. She started walking toward the temple. "Come on! Let's go."

He hurried after her and then took off running toward the temple, as if he knew where she was going.

Or where his family might be.

Billie trotted after him. He beat her to the temple, of course. Aliiren had crouched down and was murmuring something to the dog. He straightened back up, a hand on the dog's neck. As tall as the dog was, Aliiren didn't have to lean over to keep his hand on the dog's head. "You made a friend."

"Maybe. The point is, the dog wouldn't be anywhere near us if we were nefari, right?"

"But how will they know—" Aliiren's words were drowned out as the dog started barking and scratching at the door.

"Good boy," Billie told the dog. She gestured toward the door.

Aliiren took her hint and put his hand in the hole again. Once more, the light glowed within. "We're here to help," Aliiren told them. "We've rescued a baby, and there's a large, gray dog here too. I've searched the entire village. There was only the one nefarin. Your best chance is to escape to Ben Ariim, or some other well-fortified place, before the next true night."

"Stormy?" The woman's voice barely sounded through the door, but the dog perked up and barked enthusiastically.

Billie made out faint talk behind the door. She backed a step. Aliiren followed her lead and backed away as well.

The door opened a crack. The dog whined and pawed frantically to get in. The door opened a little farther, and young woman with dark, very curly hair peered out at them with large, brown eyes. From behind her a brilliant light shone. Billie couldn't see past it.

The woman drew back from the door. The door opened even wider. The dog wormed inside.

For a breathless moment Billie feared that the door would slam shut. Before she could move to stop it, the door swung wide.

A short, stout woman dressed in simple white clothing pointed a sword at Billie's eyes. The edge of the blade gleamed with a sharp brilliance, like it had been heated in a forge. Her face, especially her eyes, glowed so brightly that Billie couldn't make out much of her features. Graying hair curled around her head and down to her waist.

Aliiren held up a hand and a light glowed in his palm.

The light faded from the woman's eyes, revealing a face deeply lined and weathered by the sea. Her brown eyes were light and warm as amber. Behind her stood a substantial group of people, though shy of what Billie would expect from a village this size. *Is this all that's left?*

"I'm Protector Aliiren," Aliiren told them. "And this is my friend, Billie."

"How did you find us?" The woman sounded suspicious, and her gaze kept shifting past Billie and Aliiren to the village beyond.

"Our ship wrecked near the Embrer lighthouse," Aliiren explained. "We rowed from there to here, but we're lost. We're trying to reach Ben Ariim."

Billie cut in just as the woman started to ask more questions. "We found a baby, a boy, still alive."

The woman started to say something, but then seemed to think better of it. "Where is he?"

"At our rowboat with our friends. He's not badly hurt but he's thirsty, and he could use some comfort from someone he knows."

Aliiren's gaze stayed focused entirely on the woman. "None of you will be safe here over the next true night. How far is Ben Ariim?"

"If we leave in the morning, we should get there before true night," someone said from behind the woman.

If anything slowed them down, it would mean disaster.

"There are bodies that need to be consecrated," Aliiren said gently.

The point of the woman's blade dropped with a loud exhalation. His words shocked Billie too, though she felt impatience, not grief. *How long is that going to take?*

*Stop it. After what they've been through, they're not going to rush to the docks to take you to Ben Ariim.*

The woman turned from them and addressed the people behind her. "Daisy, pick some people to help you get the boats ready. The rest of you, come with me. I'll check your homes, and then you can go in and take what's most precious to you. We have to leave the village." She then looked to Aliiren. Her strong expression wavered. "Will you help me consecrate the dead?"

Aliiren nodded. "We should begin at the house where we found the baby."

"I'll go with you," Billie told him. "You'll need help." She hoped to protect him as much as she could from what was in the kitchen.

"Is it Rosie?" someone with a deep voice asked. "The baby. Is it Rosie?" A large, heavy man made his way to stand just behind the woman in charge.

"I can't say." Billie looked to Aliiren.

"The name beside the door on the house was Bucket."

A sharp intake of breath provided an answer to every villager in the temple. The man turned to the woman with the sword. "I'll fetch him back here. It's probably the safest place for him until we head out."

"I'll stay here and see to him," a boy offered. "He likes me." His breath hitched, and he sobbed.

The woman with the sword nodded. "Let's get to work."

As horrible as cleaning the kitchen turned out to be, the bodies had belonged to strangers. She understood that some of villagers might want to say goodbye. If it had been her family, she might have begged to see for herself. But it would have been a terrible mistake. Their nightmares wouldn't just have the sight of it, but the smell.

She gathered the remains from the floor and the stewpot into whatever sheets and blankets she could find. She bundled them tightly and, one load at a time, found Aliiren or the village's priestess to consecrate the remains before setting them by the stairs that led from the top of the sea wall to the beach. The dawn's light gleamed on the blue-green waves by the time she carried the last bundle to the black sand beach, adding stones to make certain it wouldn't float.

By then a group of people grieved and wailed near the sea wall's far end, too consumed by loss to notice her. A few more people pleaded with neighbors that stayed shut within their homes.

She could imagine trying to argue with her father if he'd barricaded himself inside their house. Would he have believed her if she'd told him that the hellions were gone, and that it was safe to come out? Or would he have believed that she'd allowed herself to be coerced by the hellions to beg him to come out?

Amid all that crying and pleading, survivors carried clothes, valuables and food to their boats.

Billie made her final journey to the black sand shore. There, with a silent prayer that the souls of the people who'd died had not been destroyed, she crouched and gently overturned the stewpot into a receding wave. She used the sand to scrub away any hint of residue.

The waves churned the milky fluid among the rocks and drew it away by the dawn's growing light. The scent was mainly gone, rinsed away by the bay's fishy water, but it lingered in her mind, mingling with the memories of making her flute.

She forced herself to turn away from her thoughts of death and walked briskly to the village, toward the living.

When she got back to the Bucket house, she found Aliiren sitting on the ground in the corner of the front room, silently weeping.

Her heart leapt with concern. She set the pot aside. "Aliiren?"

He lifted his tear-stained face to look up at her, searching for answers to questions she didn't know.

Billie sat beside him and crossed her legs. He turned his gaze to a spot on the roughly woven wool rug that filled much of the room's floor. There was a blood stain there, a big one, the kind of blood stain that pooled under a person that was dead or dying.

"I couldn't save them," he whispered.

"You saved Rosie," she pointed out gently. She didn't dare ask about the soul of the boy who'd been hanging in the web.

"It cooked them."

Billie nodded. She glanced toward the demon. It seemed fragile now, its armor translucent like an agate. The morning light angled through the open door, a sharp brightness that barely lifted the otherwise shadowed spaces where people had once lived and loved one another.

"You didn't recognize the scent from a funeral pyre, did you."

It took Billie a moment to realize what he was talking about. The sense of shame she'd felt in Ruvall was gone, leaving a cold weariness in its place. "It's a tribal ceremony. I didn't eat anything, not even a taste. We're not like that. Not on Mount Cross."

Aliiren covered his face with his hands and heaved in a breath like he'd been holding it for a long time. "You promise?" His hands slid down, and he looked at her askance, his brows pinched up with sorrow. The whites of his eyes were bright pink with grief.

It was such a strange question. If he didn't trust her explanation, why would he believe a promise? But she looked back into those golden eyes and told him the truth. "I swear. It was to clean a bone. To make a flute." She didn't want to go into more detail than that.

Now it was her turn to stare at the blood spot.

"I ... thank you. For cleaning up the kitchen. For wrapping the body parts, and ... cleaning the pot. So I didn't have to see."

She hadn't expected him to realize that she'd been trying to protect him. "There's no reason for both of us to have that in our heads."

He wrapped his arms around his legs, folding himself up tightly. "Why did you make the flute?"

She'd hoped he wouldn't ask, but at the same time, she wanted him to know. "I killed someone. The flute .... It's a reminder. I could have been the one who died. Or I could have become a slave. But I lived, because I killed him." Saying it made it clear in *her* mind, but he wasn't Kilhellion. "It's a reminder of what I did, of the price of my survival. And it's a warning for others. When an enemy hears us play our flutes, they'll know there may be a high price to pay if they attack us. It's not a trinket, or a war prize, or a souvenir. It's ...." She remembered the poem the chieftain spoke after the first time she'd played it for the tribe. One line in particular seemed to explain better than she ever could. "Life breathes into the flute, and Death shapes Her breath into music."

Aliiren shuddered, but then he said, "I think I understand."

It should have felt good to hear him say so. The only problem was how reluctantly he spoke those soft words.

"There's nothing left to do here." He stood up abruptly, wiping the tears from his face. "We have to go."

*Yes, we do.* She wanted nothing more than to put all this behind her, hopefully to never think of it again.

As they walked toward the docks, the village already felt empty. She didn't know if the villagers would ever come back. At its core the village would probably be as safe as Torath once repairs were made, but that wasn't saying much.

The priestess—the mage, Billie assumed—waited for them at the ramp leading down to the docks. "Your friends have convinced the Diir brothers to take you to Ben Ariim on their boat." She sounded upset, but then her gaze on them gentled. "Thank you, for what you've done for us. I know thanks are small, and what you've done is too great for any of us to be able to repay."

Aliiren blushed, and by the set, hard line of his mouth, it wasn't from modesty. "I wish we could have done more."

The mage smiled uneasily. "I would like to find you in Ben Ariim, if you don't mind. I have questions. I think you might have some answers."

"I'm returning to my temple in the Rushes Quarter in Ben Ariim. Ask for Aliiren. I'll be expecting you."

"And you?" the mage asked Billie.

The mage's regard surprised her. "Oh. Uh, I have to go to Port Sellon. I won't be staying in Ben Ariim." Saying so filled her with fresh strength. *I'm going home!*

The mage gave her an enigmatic look. "Well, then. Safe journey, both of you." And with that, she strode away.

Aliiren frowned at her back. Billie wasn't sure why he was frowning. It was probably for reasons that were complicated, related to Light maybe.

She'd miss him, but she wouldn't miss how uncomfortable she made him, or the way he tensed when he thought she might touch him. It would be good to be among her people again, people who loved her and would hug her and kiss her hair, people who would celebrate her return.

As if he'd sensed her desire to leave, Aliiren set off down the ramp. Billie followed him, toward her brother, toward a world that loved her like Rosie was loved.

THEY WERE ON THEIR WAY AGAIN TO BEN ARIIM, AND THIS TIME SHE didn't have to row or worry about whether they were going in the right direction or not. She was well fed, dry, and in clean clothes. The Diir brothers had her and her friends comfortably set up inside the sailboat's modest cabin built half above and half below the deck. There were a pair of bunks, a table, and some cabinets. It would have been tidy except for Billie's bags and the rest of their belongings cluttering things up. A single sacred light with several different covers was mounted in the center of the ceiling. At the moment they had drapes over the small, round port holes and a red-tinged glass cover over the light stone so that Edrion and Temric could sleep without being bothered. Billie and Aliiren sat at the edge of those bunks on opposite sides of the table in silence. Aliiren had his eyes closed, his hands placed palm-to-palm, meditating.

She wished she could meditate. It had to be nice, to relax and not think. Assuming that's what meditation was. She really didn't know. Maybe he was communing with his God.

She was exhausted, but Billie couldn't sleep. She couldn't rid herself of the sick feeling that her brother was dead.

She massaged her hands, working each finger and then running her palm against the table to work out the adhesions that had formed from the overwork she'd put them through rowing. She'd already cleaned up and dressed Aliiren's and Temric's injuries as best she could. Temric's wounds weren't too bad, but the burn-like marks on Aliiren's face and arms, caused by hellion faerus, had to heal on their own. Her gift would only make them worse. At least she was able to clean up and salve the nasty cut on his neck.

*Why is it that now, when I'm getting closer to Brian, I feel worse instead of better?*

She wished she had something useful to do. She'd washed her clothes. She'd tried to mend them too, but Edrion had made an exasperated noise and took that away from her after watching her struggle with a needle and thread.

There would be no more language lessons, no more writing practice. Just waiting while the sailboat rushed through the smooth waves of the Cerulean Sea near the rocky, arid shores of Arrak Thedra. Waiting to part ways with the people she'd grown to trust with her life.

*There's one more thing I can do.*

Billie sorted the lengths of cord left over from tying a knot for Tilla and began to tie another.

"I noticed you doing that before," Aliiren said even more softly than usual. She wasn't sure when he'd started watching her. "What is it for?"

"It's my signature knot." She kept her voice low so as not to wake Temric or Edrion. "We use them in the Kilhells to prove a message came from us, to bind promises," her cheeks warmed, "as love tokens …."

He silently watched her tie the knot.

She liked him. She liked his honesty. She liked the scent of incense on his skin, and his courage, his strength, and his patience.

Once they reached Ben Ariim he would go to his temple, and she would never see him again.

She had no idea where Temric would go. Wherever he went, he was eager to go back to his own home. He wouldn't be in Ben Ariim for long. None of them would have gotten far without Temric and his map and compass and wisdom. As much as she'd tried to teach him what she knew of languages, he'd taught her so much more of the world. He'd encouraged her to learn more than she ever thought she could.

Edrion might stay with her for a while at the docks while he waited for news of his sister, but then Billie would sail away, leaving him behind.

Edrion had left his sister to help her. Judging by the way Edri and Rani were around each other, they weren't much apart, like Billie and Brian had been almost always together. He probably missed his sister and worried for her as much as Billie worried for Brian.

She liked these people, and she would miss them. She wished that she could bring them home with her.

There was absolutely nothing in Torath for any of her friends. Mount Cross had no great cities, no elaborate festivals, no treasures, and there was no one there who loved them.

Except her.

She'd weathered a loss like this before. In time the pain would heal, like the pain in her hands as she worked.

She finished and gave the knot to Aliiren. "Here. Something to remember me by."

He took it and looked it over carefully. "Thank you."

"You're welcome. If you ever choose to go to the Kilhells, it will show people that you gained the trust of a Kilhellion at least once before. And if it's recognized by someone, they'll know to treat you as my friend."

"Thank you," he said again.

Thinking on it, she didn't like the idea of Aliiren wandering around the Kilhells alone. "It's not always a welcoming place for foreigners." She wished that wasn't true.

"It's not uncommon," he said gently. "In Ruvall, I wasn't able to shop for myself until I was properly introduced by another follower of Light. Not even to buy a cup of chocolate."

She didn't know Aliiren all that well, but the idea that he would want to buy a cup of chocolate surprised her. He lived so simply, she'd assumed that he didn't indulge in anything so luxurious.

Or maybe he just lived in an austere way while he traveled.

"I didn't leave the campus much," Billie admitted. She'd had such dreams of Ruvall. Now all she wanted was to get home. The more she thought about it, the more she realized that she didn't care if she never saw Ruvall again. *Axe and bury it,* she decided. "I'll be glad to be home. What about you? Have you missed your home?"

Aliiren shrugged, surprising her again. "Sometimes."

"I hope you're in time to see your teacher," she told him, meaning it with all of her heart.

"Thank you." He said it so sweetly.

Gods.

Soon, she'd wake up in the Kilhells, and all this would be as if it had been an elaborate dream.

Aliiren stretched out his legs and then put away her knot in his bag. When he settled again, he leaned over the table between them. His hands rubbed on the scratched and dented surface. "My teacher is dying. Any time I have with her will be short. There's hope that you'll have many years with your brother. If I had the power, I would give my time with her to you. She would understand."

She couldn't speak. All she could do was nod.

"If he's anything like you," Aliiren said, "he'll survive."

She gazed into his eyes, basking in the warm of his gentle, golden gaze. Yes, once she was home, this would very much seem like a strange, confusing, but exquisite dream.

She'd go home, and the dream would fade. But gazing at Aliiren, she hoped she'd remember this for a long time.

## Chapter Fourteen

<><><><><><><><><><><><><><><><><><><><><><><><><><><><><><><><><><><><>

# Ben Ariim

<><><><><><><><><><><><><><><><><><><><><><><><><><><><><><><><><><><><>

*Ben Ariim, Arrak Thedra*
*2ⁿᵈ Somber Day of Sun Month*

From the moment she first spotted the edges of Ben Ariim, Billie marveled at the vast array of ships tucked in a maze of boardwalks, long piers, and docks, a floating city of traders and fishermen larger than the whole of Ruvall. Overlooking those docks, rooted in the sea, Ben Ariim's famed lighthouse was taller and brighter than Ruvall's, almost like a second sun.

Temric had many questions about the soaring, massive architecture, and Aliiren had answers for most of those questions. Edrion, meanwhile, peppered Aliiren with questions about the people. Aliiren wasn't always sure when Edrion wanted to know the meaning behind a red-edged cloak or why someone would wear a hat as tall as Temric's arm was long, but he could usually name the culture or practiced tradition of a given person.

Billie only half-listened as they sailed past the docks in the main bay, then up the broad expanse of a vast river. There was too much to take in, from a flock of white birds diving in the river and coming up with green shells edged in black ruffles, to a woman in glittering silks galloping her gold-coin-armored horse past high stacks of barrels and crates to vanish into a large tent.

The sun seemed to sink at an alarming rate. She started to wonder why the Diir brothers didn't just pick the nearest empty berth so that they wouldn't have to rush to find somewhere to shelter over true night. They did seem tense, but not concerned enough to look afraid. She had no choice but to trust them.

Aliiren fetched his bag and sat with it by his feet. That seemed like a good idea, so Billie got her bags and set them near the place where there was no rail, just a rope to cover the gap where people could easily get on and off the boat.

Not far up the main course of the river rose high city walls. Blond in color, they were etched with huge blessings that interconnected across immense stone blocks. Grand palm trees grew nearly to the same height alongside them, dangling what looked like nets of green oysters from their crowns. At the base of the walls, a broad field of stone tile paved a road where people could walk, talk, trade, and move their carts. Immense crowds could have done so without crowding. At the moment only a few people populated the road, and those moved toward the gates with urgency.

The sun was really low. Billie did her best to stay calm, though her heart started to race.

Bells began to reverberate throughout the city, deeper and louder than any she'd ever heard, almost like horns being blown. She didn't know their meaning, but it sounded like an alarm.

"The bells are a warning." Aliiren gripped his knees, his fingers digging into the joints. "True night will fall within an hour."

She wasn't sure what an hour was. It was a counting thing. But she had managed to develop a rough feel for it, as several of her classes were an hour long. Those hours were also marked by a bell, rung at the center of Nuvar College.

An hour sometimes felt like a long time, but not before the coming of true night.

The part of the wall that faced the bay was interspersed with inset doors, dark rectangles shaded by deep arches. Aliiren explained that many of the doors led to roads upon which people traveled only in one direction, and toward a particular district—farmers would go in that door, while cloth merchants would go in another. Others opened for roads that only led out of the city, to go to the grain fields, for example, or to a particular river dock. He told her that the north wall had fewer doors, but they were equally well organized to manage traffic between Ben Ariim and Kal Ariim—the crown city of Arrak Thedra. The west wall along the river where they sailed had far fewer gates than the south wall that faced the bay, so it wasn't as dramatic. Instead, colorful inset stones created elaborate blessings and murals with a jeweled beauty that complemented the river's abundance and the city's many peoples.

Every gate in the wall was framed in deeply carved blessings and huge statues. "Are those celebrated kings and queens?" A particularly striking statue looked like a lion wearing a long cloak. Another looked like a hollow egg with the walls carved into elaborate patterns, revealing hints of a light that glowed from within.

"No. Those statues are of ascended."

"Senti?" Temric asked Billie.

She nodded, proud of Temric for following so much of her conversation with Aliiren in Thedran. Her own people called them godlings. The unusual figures made more sense, she supposed, if they represented godlings rather than human leaders. But how could there be so many in one place?

"People sometimes leave offerings or pray to them," Aliiren told her. "Dozens of them inhabit the city, but it's nothing like Kal Ariim. They have hundreds of them, some of which ascended before the first true night."

"Really?" Temric sounded surprised. "People talk with them? Like prayer?"

"There is one in Ben Ariim that occasionally manifests—appears—in order to communicate—talk." Billie liked how Aliiren did his best to expand Temric's vocabulary without overwhelming him. "Mainly with followers of Death, but in Kal Ariim, there are quite a few ascended that are able and willing to speak with humans."

Billie expected that Temric would leave Ben Ariim for Kal Ariim come true dawn for even the slightest chance to speak to a godling. The realization that she would have loved to go with him tugged at her heart.

*I'm a horrible sister. I shouldn't have felt that, even for a blink.*

The Diir brothers took down the sails, then used long paddles to help maneuver their ship into a slip on docks that intruded like a fish's ribs into the river. By then, everyone had staged their bags near the gap in the rail. Edrion jumped onto the dock and tied them in. Temric tossed Edrion everyone's bags and then the rest of them rushed off the sailboat.

The sun was alarmingly low in the sky. All of them grabbed their bags and hurried toward the nearest gate.

The members of their group and the gate guards were the only people still about.

The bells rang again, this time more urgently and for a longer period of time. They all changed their pace from a quick walk to a trot.

The guards just inside the gates wore full plate armor. Billie slowed, startled and overwhelmed by their intimidating, martial presence. They weren't champions, were they?

Aliiren slowed as well, but he strode directly to one of them and addressed them as if they were any other person. "Where is the nearest public shelter?"

"I thought we would stay at the Light Temple," Temric said.

"The nearest one is too far," Aliiren explained. "We won't reach it before they lock the doors." His voice was calm but his words raced, and his eyes showed more white than usual.

"There's one on Pomegranate," the guard told Aliiren, his voice somewhat muffled by his helmet. He pointed the way. "Two blocks straight ahead, make a right turn. The shelter will be on your left. You should be able to make it in time. If I'm wrong, come right back here. We'll let you into the gatehouse."

"Thank you."

They ran for it. The streets were completely abandoned, feeling all the more empty by how wide and open they were, and from the height of the buildings around them. The buildings and city walls completely blocked the faltering sun. Thankfully sacred lights shone everywhere: on posts, on building walls, and on both sides of every door, such that there were no truly dark places. Down one street Billie saw light stones on long chains that zigzagged between poles over an enormous square. A lit fountain depicted strange horse-like beasts in the center. The animals looked nightmarish, what she would imagine a demon would ride. Or maybe that thought entered her mind because she'd never been outside on land this close to true night's fall before. It felt more dangerous than being out at sea during true night. She wondered if hellions roamed these streets every true night, searching for doors with weak blessings, hoping that someone had waited too long to find shelter just like them.

She caught a glimpse of something dark in the sky to the east, and there was an ominous rumble, like distant thunder. She didn't dare stop to get a better look.

The bells rang throughout the city, clamoring with urgency. The sound of them spurred everyone into a hard sprint. Her bags bumped against her, throwing her off balance and quickly wearing her out. She regretted taking them.

They reached a staircase going down below street level just as she'd decided to drop her bags and run full-out. Aliiren led the way and pulled a bell ring recessed within a blessed cubby hole. The entire stairwell was carved with Life blessings grown through with delicate lichens and tiny wildflowers. She doubted that the blessings would save them if the door didn't open for them, but Aliiren ... maybe Aliiren could use them as a kind of fortification and hold off the hellions just long enough ....

No. If they let themselves get trapped here during the storm, begging the people inside to let them in, they were all damned. If the doors didn't open before the storm came, they could leave everything behind and run back to the gate. It was their best, and perhaps only, chance to save their bodies and souls.

Aliiren rang again. They were all sweating and panting hard, but Aliiren especially, and his skin was ashen like it had been right after he and Temric had killed the demon.

The door suddenly opened. "Welcome," someone said from a brilliantly lit hall past the door. "Come in." Aliiren motioned for the Diir brothers to go in ahead of him. "No need to rush. You're safe now," the unseen person said. Temric went in next. "No horses or camels? Good. We don't have room for horses or camels." Aliiren put his hand on Edrion's shoulder and gently pushed him into the hall. "Turn to the right. We have plenty of floor space, and a pair of rooms left if you have coin."

Aliiren motioned for Billie to go through, but she used her bags to gently force the issue. "Just go," she told him gently. His eyes were glassy and his hands trembled, and yet he still was willing to put himself between her and the hellions he imagined were coming for them. "It's all right," she assured him. "We're safe."

She wasn't sure he'd heard her, but a breath later Aliiren went in.

Finally it was Billie's turn to go through. The person who'd let them in was dressed in red robes, and she got a flash of a brief smile that brightened when he set eyes on her. She smiled back, her cheeks warm with a strange flush of shyness, before she followed the others deeper into the building.

She could barely see in the hall, the light was so intense. But then she got past it, turned right, and a much less bright light warmed a large common space. Behind her, she heard the door shut, and the scrape of bars.

The common space was packed with people. Edrion noticed some Rill and they cheered as if they knew him. Maybe they did, though they didn't call out his name. He grinned and joined them, speaking rapidly in his native language.

Most of the families were Thedran, dressed in clothes with worn hems and faded fabrics. A few gave Billie and Temric wary looks, but for the most part they ignored the newcomers, cheerfully coddling their children and gossiping.

A group of people with veiled faces, cloaked entirely in dark brocades of blood red, black, navy, and other deep colors, had taken over the far corner where they sat on the floor or at a small, short table on pillows. They were dusty, and wearily braced against the wall, leaned on each other, or lay sprawled on the floor. No one ventured near them, and they didn't speak amongst each other.

A large pack of families, nearly as numerous as the Thedrans, also kept to themselves but they were much livelier. They wore little more than light tunics and half-trousers in little better repair than the Thedran families, and most were barefoot. However, they wore elaborately beaded caps or small hats, and some had bracelets of semi-precious stones or silver, even gold. A few wore amulets set with stones and beads. That contrast between the appearance of poverty and signs of wealth intrigued her as she watched them chatter and bicker in a language without a single familiar word in it, always holding themselves with clear pride that verged on arrogance. Though they seemed quick to argue, they also smiled a lot, revealing bright white, even teeth. They were short like Thedrans, but delicately boned; even the men seemed thin and frail. Dark-haired and dark-eyed, they reminded her a bit of Edri and Rani, though their skin was closer in tone to hers and Temric's, and their eyes, though large, didn't open as wide and were sheltered by long, dark lashes.

"Gurras," Aliiren explained. "Those aren't their street clothes. They're in their underwear."

She hadn't heard of Gurras. "Are they related to Rill?"

"No. They don't wander. Most of them work about the city doing small jobs or running errands. Most of them prefer to live in tents, and seek blessed shelter only during true night." He paused. "Why would you say they might be related to Rill?"

"I don't know. Something about them." Of all the people crowded into the common room, they were the only ones other than the Rill who behaved as if this place was their home. "Their confidence. And their smiles," she decided.

Aliiren charmed her with a faint smile of his own. "They do have that."

"I'm getting us a room," Temric told them.

"You don't have to do that," Billie said. "This is fine." It wasn't just for the sake of economy; she felt comfortable among these people. Some of them obviously didn't trust her, but they didn't stare, or sneer, or avoid her gaze. It was almost like being in the long house at home during true night, though the room was far more crowded, and these were all strangers.

"I know I don't have to get a room," Temric snapped. "You're welcome to share with me. Or don't."

Why was he suddenly so angry?

Edrion had settled among the Rill, talking and gesturing like he was telling a story. One of the Diir brothers, Daisy she thought, began a conversation with a Gurra.

Billie looked to Aliiren for guidance.

He was watching the veiled people, sort of. His eyes weren't focused entirely on them, but somewhere beyond, maybe remembering something.

She supposed that she would get more rest in a private room. And if not, well, she could always change her mind. "Thank you," she told Temric.

"Aliiren?" Temric asked.

Aliiren also hesitated, but then he turned his gaze to Temric and nodded. "Thank you."

Temric called out to Edrion, but Edri was so deep in conversation that he didn't hear, or didn't care to answer. "I'll ask him later," Billie promised Temric.

Temric hired the room, and they bumped along with their bags down a dimly lit narrow hall to the door. Like the doors at the college, it had a lock, but Temric had been given a key.

It was more spacious than she expected. All three of them could have stretched out head to foot from the door and not touched the far wall. It wasn't nearly as wide, though. A large mattress covered with blankets and pillows filled the far end of the room. A short writing table squatted in the corner beside the door with a fine pair of kneeling cushions—a firm cushion to protect the knees and feet from the tile floor, the other a soft cylindrical one to rest on the heels. One of her instructors in Ruvall used such cushions during class. The room's only sacred light was set in a wall sconce above the desk. There was a fireplace near the door opposite the desk, loaded with what looked like dry dung. A hook with a kettle hanging on it could be swung over the fire if they lit one.

Billie dropped her bags, one atop the other, at the foot of the bed where they'd be out of the way. Just then the light above the desk dimmed, and Aliiren's breath caught.

"Do you mind if I meditate?" Aliiren asked.

"No." Temric dropped his things in the middle of the floor and staggered to the bed. Somehow he'd hidden it, but now she noticed that he was limping, and had a painful hunch in his back.

This wasn't from the fight with the demonic hellion, not all of it, anyway. He wasn't used to carrying heavy bags and running long distances.

Temric had snapped at her because he was in pain.

"Temric, can I help?" she asked.

"What?" Temric looked at her as if he had no idea what she was talking about.

"I think you could use some healing. I can give you a massage, or use my gift, or …"

He was already stripping off his clothes as quickly as his overworked body allowed him. "Yes, please!"

Aliiren lit his meditation candle, lending a little more light to the room.

Other than his face, neck, and arms, Temric was just as pale as Billie. Smooth-skinned, unscarred, long of limb, he was fit but thin. She'd never seen his sort of body except on young boys before they came into their shoulders and beards. There was strength there, though.

A cute rosy blush spread from his cheeks over his face and to his ears and chest, but he didn't stop undressing until he was down to his under-trousers.

"Lie down on the bed, face up," she told him. "Close your eyes if you like."

He stretched out and closed his eyes. The look of hopeful anticipation on his face made her smile. "Oh Gods," he breathed. "I hurt everywhere."

Billie knelt by his shoulders, his head between her knees. The moment she touched him, he relaxed, and she hadn't even done anything. She suppressed a chuckle. "Let's work on your shoulders and neck first." She smoothed her hands down his neck and underneath, searching for hot spots and knots, planning her approach. His brows tensed, but he kept his shoulders relaxed as she started to work.

He made a soft noise in his throat that might have been pain or pleasure.

"Don't forget to breathe," she reminded him when she noticed he was holding his breath. So, it was pain. She backed off the pressure. Working muscles, she'd learned at the college, required sensitivity, patience, and adaptability. Though she could force a seized muscle to release, too much pain in the process could cause other muscles to seize, or a flinch could bruise ...

"Sorry."

"I should be the one to apologize," she told him. "You're doing fine. I'm not the best at this."

"I disagree. It already feels better. But I could use some distraction. Tell me a story ... of the first true night," he said as she used her knuckles and worked more deeply into the muscle.

A story of true night? She had to think about it, which helped her to stop worrying about the technicalities of massage and gave her intuition more freedom. Doctor Val had told her many times that her healing usually worked better when she didn't think about it too much. "On the first true night," she began in Kilhellion, and then remembered herself and told the story in Thedran so he could practice listening to the language in its poetic form. She told him about a Wind mage who'd lost her ability to commune with Wind during the first true night. It was a sad story that ended with the mage committing herself to Death. She touched a hellion as her first and last act as a new acolyte of Death, a consecration that bound the hellion's soul to Death. It destroyed his body, and hers with it.

"You think is possible?" Temric asked in subtly slurred Thedran. "To knot a nefarin with a human God?"

Billie had no idea. "I think you meant bind, not knot," she began. Then she realized that Temric was asking Aliiren.

Aliiren didn't shift his gaze from his candle. "Light teaches that nefari can't be destroyed through consecration, at least not in the same way human souls can be destroyed by hellion gods through defilement. But Death is a mysterious god. Light rarely illuminates Death's mysteries enough for humans to see more than glimpses. Most of what we know, we're told by Death's sages." He sighed out through his nose, obviously dissatisfied by his own answer. "I believe the story has some truth to it. But I have doubts, and questions."

Billie thought it sounded perfectly plausible. "There might be more to the story that I haven't heard. Can you ask someone at a Death temple? There's a big one in Ruvall. Is there one in Ben Ariim?"

"Yes, but there is one in Kal Ariim with better records." Aliiren changed from kneeling to standing on his hands. While she watched, he slowly removed one hand and stretched it out to the side, perfectly balanced. Only a slight tremor in his arm betrayed the strain he endured to meditate like that. As much as his body had suffered recently, he shouldn't have had the strength. He had to be channeling faerus, she decided, because the longer he held the pose, the more serene and relaxed he looked. In fact his body seemed to align in a way that mitigated some of the damage he'd suffered from rowing and from the fight with the demon.

She found the source of the worst of Temric's pain. Her gaze turned inward. His spine alignment was a mess. He had no noticeable healing gift, so she felt comfortable using her vinus to explore more deeply. She linked the nodes closest to her primary node, cupped the base of his skull, and pushed her vinus through his skin. She avoided the channels that splayed up into his brain and instead followed the multitude that wove among countless nerves in a complex braid down his spine and from there throughout his body. It was tricky, but she managed to avoid all his nodes, then sent vinus to explore his overall health.

Temric's pain wasn't just from his spine, nor the bound-up muscles from the rowing and sleeping on hard surfaces. His body was inefficient at removing waste and accepting food and oxygen. It was like he hadn't ever worked hard enough to become truly fit, and now his body was trying to build up after the strain he'd put himself through since *Silver Parrot* ran aground.

He did have strength in him, especially his arms and legs.

His flexibility, though, was awful.

She withdrew her vinus and got back to work. She knew what needed attention. It couldn't be done all at once, though. She had to prioritize.

In time, she had him in a much better place using physical manipulation alone. She only had to use a bit of her gift toward the end to help speed recovery from the cuts and bruises the demon had inflicted on him, and to move waste built up in his back and both shoulders.

By then he was well on his way to falling asleep.

"Aliiren?" she asked softly as she covered Temric with one of the blankets. "Your turn, if you like."

Aliiren had returned to a kneeling position. "I would, but ..."

She waited. In that pause, her body suddenly grew heavy, and she realized how tired she was. Her eyes closed against her will. She forced them open again with effort.

He knelt before his makeshift altar a moment longer, eyes half-closed, not looking at her, but he wasn't looking at the candle he'd lit either. His profile was just as striking as the first time she'd seen him, with those sharp cheekbones, the strong nose, the powerful jaw, all seeming to be cut from stone. The fine lines on his face from the hellion's webs looked painful, but hardly marred his beauty. "I don't want to offend you," he said at last.

He didn't want her touching him. "You ought to know me well enough by now. I'm not easily offended. And I know it isn't easy for you." She wished she knew what exactly bothered him about being touched, and why.

"I can only say yes if I'm sure that you won't risk a serious fever," he said before she could explain that he could tell her exactly how much, or how little he wanted her to do.

That made her smile. "It'll be easy. You're a protector. Besides, I don't intend to use much vinus. You might not need any."

Aliiren bowed his head and lowered his gaze. "All right, then."

She patted the bed next to Temric. "Right here."

When he turned and got a good look at her, he frowned. "You're exhausted. It can wait until you've had some rest."

"I wouldn't have offered if I didn't think I could do it." Something else came to mind, though it was hard to say aloud. She took a breath and concentrated so that she spoke the words calmly. "I won't have too many more chances to practice before I need to help my brother." Thankfully, her words didn't waver.

He removed his clothes with a self-consciousness that somehow emphasized his grace. She looked away, but too late. She was too aware of his incense and the power in his body as he stretched out on the bed alongside Temric. He must have noticed the ways in which she worked on Temric because he gave her plenty of room for her knees in case she needed to straddle him.

For the first time, she hated how attractive she found him. Because she was tired, her thoughts strayed to forbidden places. Because she'd almost died, her body craved pleasure and release. And since she'd just used her gift on Temric, her nodes were already active.

That made everything about working on Aliiren so much more complicated.

Her primary node was linked to her womb, rooted deeply in her sexuality. It wasn't as rare an arrangement as having the swan node in the brain or the coiled snake in the tailbone as primaries, but it was unusual enough to draw even more unwelcome attention from her classmates at Nuvar College. Apparently healers with the lotus node as their primary often went into some form of specialized sex work. She'd been told that it was celebrated by Thedrans, but it was obvious that it lowered her value and status in Ruvall.

The rarity of her gift's structure did have a major advantage. It meant that there were only a handful of other students in the class she took that taught her about the advantages, and consequences, of her gift's physiology. She felt like she could ask questions, and learn, in relative privacy among people who understood.

Most of the time it made no difference. Tonight, it did.

Fortunately, she knew how to deal with it.

She linked her primary to her lantern node, bringing in the distracting influences of her liver and kidneys. The lantern was the most common primary node among healers, effective against infections, ideal for cleansing, and it was the largest node in the body, a powerful source of vinus that forced her to concentrate almost entirely on controlling its flow.

She used her vinus very, very slowly, and in small amounts, so that neither of them would fever too much. She found that the cut on his neck was healing cleanly, but the burns and lines on his arms and face had begun to fester under the surface. She spent most of her time carefully flushing the damage out from within. Pockets of deeper infection had begun to form too. It was a good thing he'd accepted her help. By the time the infection would have gotten bad enough for him to feel more than somewhat tired and sore, Aliiren might have become very ill.

When she was too tired to control her vinus, she withdrew it and used massage, and pressure, and manipulation of his joints.

By the end of it he was asleep. She covered him, and then stripped off her clothes. Among the blankets she found a thin sheet of cool linen and wrapped herself in it. Fever licked pleasantly across her skin as she went to the light stone and covered it. In the darkness, the stripe of light that shone under the door helped orient her as she groped her way to an unoccupied part of the bed near the back wall.

As soon as she closed her eyes, she thought she heard Brian calling to her.

It was probably just a dream, or her imagination.

Whatever it was, it scared her.

*Soon,* she promised. *I'll be there soon, I swear.*

## Chapter Fifteen

# Safe Harbor

*Ben Ariim, Arrak Thedra*
*2nd Fear Day of Sun Month*

Billie had healed someone's sprained ankle in exchange for some dried fruit and nuts to snack on during her voyage home. She'd also managed to wash and thoroughly dry her clothes. Rather than cram her clean clothes and new acquisitions into her partially disemboweled bags, she decided to unpack everything and organize it so that the things she'd need close at hand were on top. Besides, she hadn't aired her cloak out since she'd left Ruvall. It made no sense to even try on *Silver Parrot*. Snug in their room, she hoped that the small fire they'd lit for heating water would help drive out the damp from the thick wool.

Sorting through her things felt like discovering hidden treasure. It had been so long since she'd worn her best vest, patterned in soft green, gray and white, she'd almost forgotten she had it. It was wrapped around a thick book bound in red leather, embossed with elaborate black writing edged in white. "This isn't mine."

Temric, the only other person in the room with her, turned to look at her from where he read at the desk by the light stone lamp. "Let me see."

She handed it over, then nervously smoothed out her vest over the bed.

"Hmm." He opened it, then raised his brows and nodded. "It's inscribed to you. From Doctor Val, in exchange for unspent tuition."

"Oh." She'd been sure Tilla had packed it by mistake. Now she had to wonder what the doctor meant by giving it to her. "What kind of book is it?"

He turned a few pages, his blue-eyed gaze moving swiftly across and down each one. "*When Alone: Medicine for Travel to Remote Places.*"

*What?* She grinned and let out a breathless laugh.

"Several authors. There's a wide variety of subjects listed in the table of contents. I'm not sure if someone bound different books together, if it's a commissioned anthology, or a collaboration. Regardless, it looks very useful." He closed it and handed it back to her.

"This ... this is exactly the book we need in Torath." Her elation faded. "It must be worth a fortune." It would cost a fortune to return it. And her people needed it. She felt a slipping inside her, a wrongness that dragged her irresistibly toward accepting that this treasure was hers now. It would be so much simpler to do what everyone else around her would do in this situation.

"Let me see it again."

Billie handed it to Temric, still warring with her feelings.

He opened it to a central page. "It's printed rather than handwritten, and the lettering is the same throughout." He closed it and looked at the top edge before he opened it again. He used his thumb to fan the pages to a different place in the book. "I think this was always meant to be one work, and was printed as such, rather than several separate works that someone collected and bound together. That suggests that many identical copies of this book were made, most likely all at the same time. The paper is sturdy, but a bit coarse, the cover is calf hide and utilitarian, the pages aren't cut cleanly, they didn't bother with headbands ..." If he had more thoughts, he kept them to himself as he looked at the inside of the cover, on the sides again, and finally shut it decisively. "It's not a rare book, and it was cheaply made."

It didn't look cheap to her.

He seemed to sense her skepticism. "There's another way of looking at its worth. To an explorer, or sailor, or someone from a remote place like you, the book is priceless. But most people live in large cities, and most people never leave them. I don't think it would be very valuable in a place like Ruvall, because almost no one would want it." He gentled his voice. "It's a gift."

That made no sense. "I don't understand."

"Gift? You know, when someone gives something to you, as a kindness."

She'd had no idea that the word could be used in that way. Bitter feelings tightened her throat. "I thought he understood how I feel, how my people feel, about charity. We'll find a way to pay him back."

"No. It's not charity." Temric looked exasperated with her. "You know. A gift. People give gifts to be nice, because they like you. It's not just because they think you need the help."

"I thought a gift is something you have, an accident of birth, like my healing gift. I don't understand gift in this other context."

"What about giving someone something for a special occasion? Like the birth of a child? Or a wedding?"

"The tribe gets together and makes sure that they have what they need."

He looked excited. "Yes! Those are gifts!"

"But he's not tribe. Tribe helps each other. It all stays in the tribe. If someone from outside the wedded tribes made something or gave something for a marriage, it would be—" She didn't even know what it would mean. No one would do that.

"All that is expected in return is a thank you. It's expensive to send a letter to Ruvall, right?" Temric offered her the book. "Send a letter of thanks, and the gift will be repaid. That's how gifting works in the Sothron Empire. I promise."

She took it back and hugged it to her chest. She wanted that to be true, for it to be morally right to keep it. She thought over everything Temric had said, doing her best to not to talk herself into it in a selfish way.

What he'd told her made sense in a place where everyone had so many possessions, and where people made so much of knowing each other's names and status even if they knew they would probably never meet again.

*I can do this. I can explain to everyone back home that it's a fair trade. Otherwise, Nuvar college would owe us if we sent more than what they expected in return.*

Billie let out a breath that she hadn't realized she'd been holding and gave the book a kiss. Long after she was gone, Torath would have this treasure to help keep her tribe healthy. But how technical was it, and would it assume that whoever used it had a healing gift?

The tribal scribes would read it and let her know. She set it on the bed beside her and stroked the cover, reassuring herself that it was hers to keep and that it would be all right, before she went back to unpacking.

Her cloak was at the bottom of the bag. As she pulled, she realized it was wrapped around something too, something heavy.

*Now what?*

The cloak wasn't just wound around something. The ends were stuffed inside—

Her heart leapt. "My drum!" Tilla had packed her drum.

None of the things she'd brought to Ruvall were missing.

*Except my flute.*

*Shush. I have my drum. My drum!*

"Wow." At first Temric's admiration seemed to be directed at her drum, but it turned out that he was staring at her cloak.

Billie set her drum aside to give the cloak the attention it deserved. She folded up her vest and smoothed the cloak out carefully over the bed. It had gotten a little musty between the damp in Ruvall and on *Silver Parrot,* but mildew hadn't stained it, thank goodness. It wasn't thick enough wool for winter in the Kilhells, but the so-called winter in Ruvall never got cold enough for her to wear even this dress cloak.

It was the nicest thing she'd ever owned. Woven into the soft gray wool, the broken outline of Mt. Cross was repeated in white, like arrowheads sailing toward the ground, lining both front edges. Along the bottom, the outlines reversed to point upward, linked together at their bases like teeth. Alternating loosely on either side of the mountain pattern, lavender irises streaked in black and gold seemed to dance on a hidden breeze. Framing the design, a silken green cord had been sewn on either side of the mountain and floral pattern around the entire edge. The cloak had a generous silver beaver fur collar to ward rain from her shoulders. A separate hood attached to the inner edge of the collar with a series of wooden buttons carved into flowers. The hood was trimmed in deepest black wool. Woven into the black were the outlines of Mt. Cross again, this time linked base to base and point to point in a broken-edged diamond pattern.

She could see her mother's handiwork in the irises, and her sister's in the careful way that the silk cords had been sewn invisibly, perfectly straight, perfectly parallel. Her father, she was sure, made the buttons. Marta had woven the wool with the design laid out in such even perfection. Billie remembered her working on it, but she'd never guessed that it was meant for her. The rest had been done in secret.

This … this was a real gift, full of love, like the simpler but equally beautiful vest, and the matching trousers. When Brian was safe and everything was settled, she'd launder it, carefully dry it, and put it away.

The next time she'd wear any of it would likely be to Stayce's wedding.

In contrast to the fancy clothing, her drum was simple. It had no embellishments on the shell aside from the natural grain of the burl, which rippled and swirled in patterns that reminded her of lichen. The goatskin head was dyed a pale spring green, again, with no embellishments. But the ropes that tensioned the skin, reinforced by more cordage that served as a handle and protection from scratches and bumps, was decorated by countless repetitions of her personal knot. It had a wine stain on the skin, and countless fine scratches on the shell from her lugging it around, but that just made it more beautiful. This was the drum she played when she and her friends and siblings scurried off to spend part of a day by the lake to play around, during true night after a meal, or when she was watching ponies graze and wanted something to do. It was her first real drum. Her aunt had made the shell. The chieftain himself had tanned and dyed the skin. And Billie, with the help of Marta's eldest son Jamon, tensioned the hide and tied all the cords herself.

She loved playing the big cliff drums, but this drum was like a friend.

She hadn't played it much in Ruvall. She hadn't had time at first, and later, she hadn't had much heart for it.

"Mind if I sketch this in my journal?" Temric asked, gesturing to the cloak.

"Not at all." The skin produced a shivering sound as she ran her fingers over it. Not bad, considering that she hadn't attended to it for some time. It felt a little dry, but the only clean oil she had on hand was a healing ointment.

Someone might have something suitable in the common room.

"I'll be in the common room," she told Temric. The familiar feeling of gripping the cords and slinging the drum over her shoulder made her feel more like the self she remembered before she'd left for Ruvall. "Want anything from there?"

He shook his head, already engrossed in his drawing. Billie opened the door and went out, shutting it quietly behind her.

The hall smelled like fresh bread, the milky, sour alcohol everyone seemed to favor, and a thin, insanely spicy broth that had been simmering since the glass of sand had been turned the morning of Fear Day. Someone was singing, and she found herself walking jauntily in time to the music.

It was even warmer and more crowded in the common room than when they'd first arrived. The mood was infectiously festive.

A pack of children chased each other, weaving around tables and huddles of people engaged in loud discussion, occasionally bashing into someone because there was barely room to walk, never mind run. Toddlers waved their arms in excitement and tried to join in, held back by their distracted kin so they wouldn't get shoved over. Children on the cusp of adulthood pretended to look down on the chaos, though some cast longing looks toward a group of younglings who played a game that combined dancing, jumping, and slapping each other's hands. Meanwhile, the adults busied themselves with small chores, gossiped, or played board games, cards, dice, or some combination of these things.

The only calm space was in the far corner among the veiled people. No one ventured within an arm's span of them, except Aliiren. He sat on the floor at the edge of the group, his back aglow from the fire's light, his arms clasped around his knees. He was listening, while a group member nodded as they spoke to him, their veil puffing with certain words. Their gloved hands stayed low but gestured frequently toward Aliiren or to one side or the other.

"Billie!"

Edrion's voice helped her spot him. He wasn't with the other Rill for once, but with the Gurras. She waved and carefully picked her way over to him.

The Gurras cheered. "Play!" they called to her, and Edrion clapped in approval. A Gurra produced his own drum. "Play with me!"

Billie accepted an offered stool and sat, bracing the drum between her legs. "Do you have oil?" she asked, rubbing the drum's head.

"Yes yes," he said, and produced a tiny bottle. She accepted a single drop, rubbed it on her hands, and then smoothed the trace of oil carefully over the skin. Together they exchanged, through play only, the terms for the rhythm that would complement the lone singer in the room. It took only a few phrases for them to understand each other. Off they went, and the rest of the Gurras stood to dance.

The celebratory mood exploded into a riot of dancing and clapping. Her drum sounded a bit thin at first, but gradually its voice grew fuller, the way she liked it. The oil was doing its work.

As soon as the original singer finished his song, the Rill took over with a raucous song that matched the drumming. Everyone in the room seemed to know it except Billie, and even the older children joined in. She managed to learn the chorus before the last of a short trio of verses came to an end.

"What language was that?" she asked Edrion as she and the Gurra took the rhythm down a step to let everyone rest. Most of the people who had danced still stood, swaying to the rhythm, chatting excitedly.

"My grandfather told me that they're just nonsense words. I learned it as a child. We used to sing it as we packed up to go indoors on Somber Day."

"Mindah, a dialect of Arrak," the drumming Gurra told her. "Not many outside the Arrak people speak it, but they know the song. It's taught everywhere in Ben Ariim and Kal Ariim. The song talks about sharing things. Very important in the desert. No sharing, no life."

Edrion's brows rumpled up, and then he shrugged. "Strange. But maybe not. Generations ago we might have roamed Arrak Thedra. I noticed some of the words weren't the same as I'd learned them."

"Mistranslation, maybe," the Gurra offered. "Or misunderstanding."

Billie wasn't as interested in the history as the message. She wished she'd understood the lyrics, so that she could compare the song's philosophy to the beliefs held by her tribe.

Maybe it wasn't that important. She wouldn't be in Arrak Thedra long enough to have to navigate the currents of a new culture.

A Thedran boy, egged on by his giggling friends, approached Billie shyly. "May I?" He gestured to her drum. "If it's allowed," he added hastily just before he shot a warning look at his friends. They flinched back in mock fear, giggling even more.

She laughed and offered him the drum, as well as her seat. "Of course."

He sat with the drum. Honestly, the height was a better fit for him than it was for her—she had to tuck her feet under the base to have the head at the right height. After a little experimental play, he set in with an odd rhythm that the Gurra picked up. It took her a moment to figure out that there was a spare at the end of each pair of phrases. Once the beat entered her heart and mind, her feet and hands carried it into dance. Edrion took her hand. Together they formed a very short line that swayed forward and back, then side to side while their feet tapped and stomped the floor to support the drum's melody. A little girl ran up to them and tried to join in. Billie let her in between her and Edrion, and she squealed and created quite a lot of chaos, but it didn't matter. Her glee filled Billie with joy, even if her parents watched with a certain nervousness.

And so they played and danced and filled up on the bread and fermented milk offered to them. Her first taste of fermented milk nearly choked her, which everyone in the room found hilarious. Even Aliiren laughed, and his laugh was like the first light of true dawn.

The drink was stronger than she expected, and thicker in the mouth, and sour. At first, she wasn't sure she liked it, though she didn't exactly hate it either. But then she realized that it reminded her of the special sourdough bread her mother made, though with more salt. Instead of taking deep gulps of it like she would drink beer, she learned to sip and relish it.

Eventually Billie found herself nodding off. She took her drum and slogged down the hall to their room. Temric was already asleep. Billie yawned, set her drum at the foot of the bed, and claimed her place at the far wall. In moments she'd sunken into peaceful bliss.

AFTER A DEEP NIGHT'S SLEEP, SHE LET HERSELF BELIEVE THAT everything was as it should be. And why not? At true dawn she would be on her way to Port Sellon. Once she got there she would heal Brian, and all would be well.

Maybe he'd already be under Tilla's care. Her father might be angry with her for that. But she could weather that as long as Brian was all right in the end.

Her good mood might have something to do with the fact that Aliiren gave her a massage as thanks for the healing she'd done for him.

Gods, she'd needed it. She closed her eyes and remembered …

*"Place the heel of your hand where your palm is …"*

*Wordlessly, he'd obeyed.*

*"More pressure, and glide toward the shoulder blade."*

*"Too much?" he'd asked softly.*

*"You won't hurt me …"*

Toward the end, he had her so relaxed and supple she could barely speak. Then he covered her with a blanket and left the room. He'd somehow forced out not only the tension in her body, but the doubts and confusion she'd felt about what he meant to her, and what she might mean to him. There was a connection, and that was enough.

It would have to be enough.

Lost Day and Blind Night passed quickly, though she slept far less than she usually did during true nights. She and Temric went back to practicing—Thedran language for him, and for her, memorizing more ridiculous letters than there were stars in the sky, along with the sounds they made. Between lessons, she played games with Edrion and his new friends who acted as if they'd always known him and he them.

By the time the glass of sand for the morning of Dread Day was turned over, just about everyone was at least friendly with everyone else. Even Aliiren seemed a part of this large, temporary family. He pretended to be completely uninterested in the Rill games, but he smiled whenever Billie or Edrion won. When Billie played, the prizes were almost always songs, dances, or stories, which made losing not at all like a loss.

Sometimes, when Billie played, Aliiren danced.

Gods, Aliiren could dance. Her favorite was a sword dance, displaying his strength and grace but also a sense of music that paired beautifully with the drumbeats. It wasn't entirely martial. He would balance the blade on his head, or his arm, or with the point pinched between his fingers. He preferred to move slowly, with total control, and so when she drummed for him she stretched the rhythm out, playing his body as if she had become his lover.

When he was worn out and sat heavily beside her, sweating, the rare smile and look of friendship he gave her was more powerful than any kiss.

Edrion caught her blushing when Aliiren got up to fetch them both some water. He waggled his eyebrows at her suggestively. She shoved him and he laughed, shoving her back. Then some people came around with food and everyone set into eating and drinking.

It turned out that there was a guild of inns, and the guild required that a portion of any earnings had to be used to supply free bread and fermented milk to those who stayed in the common room. It was a generous, hospitable way of maintaining safe shelter for the extremely poor of Ben Ariim. The lack of money exchange helped make her feel as if she was at a songhouse rather than a common room far from home.

She didn't think she'd had much of the fermented milk with dinner, but she must have because she dozed off in the common room. She woke up with her head pillowed in Edrion's lap. His fingers gently twined through her hair as he spoke with their friends. Someone had covered her with a blanket.

Somehow, the final glass of sand that marked Watch Night had nearly run all the way into the bottom.

Part of her didn't want true night to end. It felt like a betrayal to her brother to even think it, much less feel that sadness. But it wasn't just because she selfishly wanted to play with her friends forever.

Once true dawn came, it would be entirely up to her to find her way to Port Sellon. She had no plan, and no idea how things worked in Ben Ariim. Hopefully, finding a ship to take her home wouldn't be as fraught as it had been in Ruvall.

She fetched her bags and went to wait near the entrance to the hallway leading outside while Temric and Aliiren finished packing. She felt too nervous to sit in their private room with nothing to do.

The sand raced away. She'd thought to be one of the first to leave, but to her surprise the friendships she'd seen forged over true night frayed as easily as they'd been knitted. Everyone acted like strangers again, strangers that swiftly formed a thick, unmoving line of bodies all waiting impatiently for the door to open. She ended up somewhere in the middle with no sign of Temric, Aliiren or Edrion anywhere.

She hadn't even thought to tell them goodbye when she'd claimed her place by the hall. She'd assumed that they'd stand together for the last moments before true dawn.

She'd made knots for Edrion and Temric. She hoped that they wouldn't vanish into Ben Ariim's streets before she could give them to them.

A few of the people in line sighed with relief. And then bells began to ring, and the Rill began to trill while a few other people cheered. Billie didn't feel like cheering, though she was glad true night was finally over.

The line of people shifted. She was able to take a half step, and then waited, and took another half step. Her shoulders ached from bearing the weight of her bags for so long. She crept along slowly until all at once the people ahead of her flowed forward. She did her best to keep her bags from bumping anyone, but it was impossible. Fortunately, no one seemed to mind. She bumbled through the brilliant light of the entry hall, squinting against the sharpness of it, and then emerged onto the shadowed stairs into a cool, soft dawn in Ben Ariim.

The line carried her along up the stairs onto the street. She quickly moved sideways to get out of the way. For no apparent reason the veiled people stopped only a few steps away from the top of the stairs and decided to have a conversation. If they'd been in the Kilhells someone would have shoved them out of the way, but apparently in Ben Ariim that sort of thing wasn't done. Instead, the people emerging from the shelter simply edged around them with only an occasional dirty look.

She spotted Temric and hurried to meet him as he slowly walked onto the rapidly filling street, gazing about at the buildings with undisguised wonder.

"Temric!" she called, worried he'd suddenly stride away before she could get to him.

He turned and smiled at her. She grinned, but only until she realized that this would be goodbye. "I almost forgot to give you this." She groped for the knot she'd tucked into her sleeve and gave it to him. "My signature. If you ever go to the Kilhells, the people there will know you have a friend on Mount Cross."

He looked it over carefully, head bowed, his expression a complicated mix of smooth calm and sadness. "Thank you."

Just then she spotted Edrion and Aliiren. They led the group of Rill. Edrion was chatting with them rapidly, while Aliiren seemed to be hunting for her and Temric. She waved both arms over her head. Aliiren noticed her and took Edrion by the arm at the top of the stairs. Together they stopped before her and Temric.

An awkward silence fenced them in for a long moment as the reality of their parting settled like a weight on her.

"I guess this is goodbye," she told them, her heart sore at the thought of it.

"Maybe I should come with you." Judging by Edrion's tight expression, she could tell he didn't want to.

She gave him the other knot. "No. You need to stay here and wait for your sister."

Edrion hugged her tight. "I was hoping you'd give me a knot."

Billie reveled in his embrace. "Of course."

"I'm going to miss you."

"Me too." She squeezed him so hard he gasped out a laugh, and then she let him go. "Be safe. And please let Larani know I'm going to miss her."

"I will."

"Take care," Aliiren told her. "And please, take this." He drew a purse from his belt. It jingled with coins.

"No, please—"

"Just a few coins, so that you can send a letter to my temple and let me know you reached your family safely."

"Oh." Her protests left her in a heavy sigh. "Thank you. But once I'm home, I'll be able to make my own way. I can have Melissa write—"

"Please take it." He held out the purse for her.

He so rarely interrupted anyone. This meant something to him, maybe as much as it meant to her. "All right."

Their hands met as he passed a few coins into her hand. She couldn't hold back anymore. She hugged him, hard, which made him gasp. She quickly pulled away. Gods, she shouldn't have done that. "Sorry," she mumbled.

"No, I … thank you," he whispered, his head bowed.

"One more from me." Edrion hugged her, making her gesture toward Aliiren much less awkward and hopefully less intrusive by comparison.

Edrion held her for a long time, then kissed her on the cheek. "Good luck."

She got a long hug from Temric, who whispered in her ear to be careful. "I'll check with Aliiren at his Light temple for a letter. I want to know you're safe too."

"There are two Light temples in Ben Ariim," Aliiren told her. "Make sure it goes to the South Light Temple of the Rushes." He crossed his arms and seemed to reconsider. "It should be enough to write Aliiren, Rushes Light, Ben Ariim."

He'd remembered she'd pay by the letter. "I'll remember," she promised.

"I'll write it down for you." Temric set down his travel bags and set to it.

The Diir brothers surprised her by approaching. "We have just a quick stop at a business not far from here, but then we're heading back to the bay to find the rest of our village," Daisy told her. "You're welcome to catch a ride with us. Even with the stop, it'll be faster than walking through Ben Ariim."

Their offer amazed her. "Thank you." They looked eager to leave, so she gave everyone a last look. "I hope you all find what you're looking for."

"Blessings," Aliiren told her as she backed away.

"Good luck," Edrion told her again.

"Don't forget to send word of your safe arrival," Temric reminded her, handing her a paper with writing on it.

"Goodbye," she said, though the word choked her.

*Goodbye,* she thought to herself, and set off after the Diir brothers.

## Chapter Sixteen

<><><><><><><><><><><><><><><><><><><><><><><><><><><><><><><><><><><>

# Searching for Passage

<><><><><><><><><><><><><><><><><><><><><><><><><><><><><><><><><><><>

*Ben Ariim, Arrak Thedra*
*3rd Meet Day of Sun Month*

The Diir brothers chatted as if she wasn't there. They spoke about the tide and winds and beating it to the bay, whatever that meant. They also squabbled a bit about how late they had come in before true night. Daisy thought it worked out fine, while his brother argued that it was a foolish chance to take.

They led her to some sort of shop tucked in among a wall of similar shops, all shaded by colorful awnings. A bronze sign hung beside the door. To pass the time, she tried to read it, but then her impatience got the better of her. She waited outside on the busy street, feeling lost as countless people walked by, all eager to get the first chores after true night settled before everyone else. Amid the other things they bought and carried, it seemed like everyone had a fresh loaf of bread—huge, flat wheels as broad as the length of her arm and dimpled with salt-crusted thumbprints. Most people balanced the bread on their heads, though a few carried them within large cheesecloth sacks slung over their backs. The bread smelled delicious, rich with yeast and exotic herbs that made her mouth water, though she'd had a good breakfast.

What was taking so long? Would it really save her time to sail with the brothers rather than walk across Ben Ariim?

The air wasn't heavy and wet like it was in Ruvall, so though it quickly grew warm, she didn't sweat much. But the air tasted gritty, and it dried out her skin. Crusts formed in the corners of her eyes. She sniffed her hand to make sure it was reasonably clean, and scraped the crusts out with a fingernail. No wonder so many people had dusty or bleached clothes. She couldn't see dust in the air, and the stone or brick streets were well swept, but the dust was there nonetheless, invisibly coating everything.

At last the brothers emerged from the shop, all smiles and chatting much more amiably. They nodded to her, and then continued their discussion, this time about a cousin as they led the way to the city's massive outer wall.

She wasn't sure if it was the same guards at the same gate. It might have been. They stopped no one as people found their way to their river boats. The Diir brothers sometimes had to move quickly or wait among the packs of people and carts and animals. Fortunately, people stayed out of Billie's way. She wasn't sure if it was her height, or the fact that she was Kilhellion, that kept them from crowding her.

It wouldn't be long now before such things no longer mattered.

Once they finally reached the boat, the Diir brothers made a quick inspection. When they found nothing out of place, they untied the boat and pushed off into the water. Billie took up one of the paddles so that Daisy could start hoisting sails.

The river was almost as crowded as the street. Once the pair of sails started carrying them forward, the brothers told Billie to sit down and stay out of the way while they maneuvered carefully among the others on the river. Their visit to the shop probably helped them avoid the worst of the crowding. She saw a lot more boats downriver from them.

Billie turned in her seat to watch the shore recede. The streets that had once seemed generous now barely accommodated the hordes of people that flowed in and out of the gates, along the wall, and among the docks. People carried crates and boxes and bags to vessels of all sizes. Some had exotic birds in cages. Beautiful baskets with ribbons woven among straps of exotic, dark woods and reddish reeds stored exotic fruits. An odd-looking bull with very short horns and a shaggy mane pulled a large cart along the road, led by a tiny girl with ribbons braided in her hair. Gurras in bright patchwork clothes fetched and carried and darted through the crowds with the skill of dancers. Their beaded caps flashed in the morning sun almost as brightly as their pervasive smiles. A few Sothroners, most in butterfly-bright silks, towered over the mainly

Thedran population, their height and dark skin setting them apart from their neighbors. There were a few Arrak too. An Arrak woman stood out in particular, her belt heavy with coins and gems, bracelets flashing at her wrists in contrast to her coarse, pale robes. Her heeled boots gleamed with jeweled buttons that secured embossed red leather straps over her feet and shins. She stood on the shore, braced against a lamp post at the top of a ramp leading down to the river docks, as still as a statue.

Billie had heard it said that like sailors, Arrak nomads stayed in the open desert during true night with only the vastness of the dry lands, like the vastness of the sea, to protect them. Like ships, sometimes whole tribes vanished during true night. Somehow, though, most of them survived.

Though she couldn't see beyond Ben Ariim's high walls, she heard the crowds on the streets calling, laughing, hawking their wares, shouting in anger or delight to each other over the growing cacophony.

Honestly, she was glad she wasn't there. She longed to be back on the mountain, in the woods, where the only noisy thing she might hear all day was a waterfall.

It didn't take long to reach the bay. The brothers pulled down the sails and she helped paddle them to a convenient berth. "This is where most of the outgoing ships dock," Daisy told her. "You should be able to find a way home from here."

"Thank you."

"It's we who should thank you," Daisy said, his gaze briefly intent on her face before he looked away. "If we could do more, we would. This is the best we can do."

"It's more than enough. I'm grateful that you've taken me this far."

He nodded, his mind seemingly as empty of the right words as her own was.

As soon as she leapt off with her bags, they pushed away again.

"Good luck, Kilhellion!" Daisy called.

"Thank you!" she called back.

In moments their little sailboat was just one of many in the large but crowded bay. A great number of them sailed out to sea. It was dizzying, with all the ships, and all the people in motion. She adjusted her bags and started walking. The boards made hollow sounds as people tramped on them. At least it wasn't as busy on the docks as it had been on the street.

The ships were bigger here than most other places in the bay, and the people even more diverse than she'd seen in the city. She recognized a Lordmarkan crew by the language they spoke. Their dour, pale faces, numerous weapons, dark, unadorned clothing and warning glares contrasted sharply with everyone else. They seemed fond of curses and remarking on everyone else's shortcomings. It made her dislike them intensely.

None of the largest ships appeared to be sailing out just yet. Everyone was still loading up and organizing. Billie took a deep breath and started asking no one in particular, like her father had at Port Sellon when she'd left for Ruvall, for passage. "Port Sellon," she called, changing between Thedran and Sothron, as she didn't see any Kilhellions or their ships around. "I'm looking for passage to Port Sellon."

She won an occasional glance, but other than that everyone ignored her, even when a glance suggested that they'd heard her. Surely some of these ships were traveling westward from Ben Ariim. It was the way she'd been told that the current naturally flowed.

The lines of floating boardwalks mostly fanned out in straight lines, but then wherever there was space, other walkways would jut out at sharp angles like veins on a leaf. Maybe she'd wandered into the wrong area?

She still hadn't seen any Kilhellion ships. Why was that? She knew that there weren't many Kilhellion traders, but wouldn't there be a few here to sell steel, gems, and wool in the most famous trading port on the Cerulean Sea?

For that matter she had yet to see another Kilhellion. Where were they?

The air grew hotter, and she felt more and more lost. Obviously she wasn't going to find any outgoing ships bound for Port Sellon this way. She decided to head toward the lighthouse that overlooked the bay. It stood within the waters of the bay's mouth, but on the shore nearest the lighthouse there were people lining up near tents and tables set up in front of a large stone building.

If Ben Ariim was anything like Ruvall, the people at the tables and within the tents served the harbormaster.

A warm, sensuous laugh rippled through the air, distracting several sailors from their work. Billie moved over just in time to make way for a group of sailors that walked by, arm in arm and hand in hand, with the most beautiful people she'd ever seen. Bejeweled and swathed in silk, clear-eyed and elegant, they moved more smoothly than water, carrying with them a perfume as intricate as a bouquet of exotic flowers. These, she realized, must be the famed pleasurers of Arrak Thedra, the denizens of pleasure gardens, as costly to hire as healers. Their patrons were diverse: the sated, blushing sailors they now attended, wealthy merchants, craftsmen and royalty. They arrived at a nearby ship and began kissing the sailors goodbye, flirting at the same time with everyone who stopped to stare. And many stopped to stare. The pleasurers lured in a few bystanders for a kiss on a hand or a cheek.

Suddenly the pleasurers began to clap and sing and then danced as if they were one being. Their bodies undulated together like grass blown by wind. The spontaneous performance drew a ring of admirers so thick that Billie could catch only an occasional glimpse.

Billie tripped over a loose nail on a board and bumped someone. They turned on her, snarling an oath in Thedran, but when they got a look at her, they muttered another curse and hurried away.

She suddenly realized how high the sun had risen. *Have I really wasted so much time?*

Billie picked up her pace, ignoring the goings-on after that. It still took a long time for her to reach the harbormaster's tents. After inquiring several times, someone finally told her that anyone seeking passage westward had to wait their turn in that line there.

And so she waited. By then her shoulders hurt so badly from carrying her bags that she set them down and dragged them with her as she moved along with everyone else. She was frustrated, overwarm, and anxious.

For no reason she could fathom she remembered Aliiren's calm. Her temper cooled. The last thing she wanted was to arrive flustered as she had at the harbormaster's tables in Ruvall.

The line shifted and she stepped forward, dragging her bags with her.

At last she reached the front of the line. Unlike the Sothron harbormaster's people, there was no sign of leisurely conversations. The Thedran man glared up at her, stacks of paper organized loosely across his part of the long table, and showed every sign of seeing her as an irritation. "Where are you going?"

"Port Sellon."

A muscle twitched on his handsome cheek. He was heavier than most Thedrans, but he still had that same clear skin, fine symmetry and perfect coils of dark hair trailing down to his shoulders to frame softly brown skin and deep brown eyes with long lashes. "Name?"

"Billie Maiyem."

"Billie. Mayhem."

"Maiyem," she corrected.

"Want to spell that?" A smile twitched briefly at the corner of his mouth. Someone behind her snickered.

"No." What did he gain by being rude? The approval of an ass somewhere behind her?

"Where can you be found?"

"Excuse me?" She wasn't sure what he meant.

"Where can the quartermaster locate you if a ship heading for Port Sellon is willing to take on a Kilhellion passenger?"

It felt like Ruvall's port all over again, and this time Tilla wouldn't arrive to help her. "I need to leave this morning."

He grunted. "Homesick, are you?"

She doubted he'd care, but she had to try. "My family needs me. It's urgent."

He shook his head. "Everyone here has urgent business. What fare are you willing to pay?"

She had the coins Aliiren had given her, but she'd promised to use them for a letter. She took out her purse and emptied the remains into her hand.

There weren't many coins left, but there were a few nice sapphires, and a good-sized piece of amber.

He looked over the collection and wrote something down on the slip of paper.

"I can offer my cloak," she decided rashly, desperate.

"That might work with a Kilhellion captain, but you'd be better off selling it for real money if you want someone to take your offer seriously."

She added half the coins Aliiren had given her. *I can work to pay the scribe.* "Is this a serious offer?"

"Depends on the quartermaster, I suppose."

This was for Brian. Reluctantly, she put the rest of Aliiren's coins onto the pile. *How am I going to pay to send the letter to Ben Ariim now?* She hoped that maybe she could earn actual coins in Port Sellon somehow.

He seemed to approve against his better judgement. "Now, where can you be found?"

"Here," she said. "By the lighthouse."

"You can't stay here. No loitering allowed. And don't even think of camping on the docks, either." He rubbed his forehead as if it hurt. "Maybe a public shelter?"

"There's a public shelter on Front Street. It's probably full, but you can give it a try," the man behind her offered kindly. "They'll let you camp outside the door until there's space inside."

"Front Street Shelter," the man behind the desk repeated as he wrote. He folded the paper in half, wrote on the outside, and handed it to the person behind him who put it in a box thick with other folded papers. "Next?"

He hadn't taken her money. "Wait. How does the money work?"

"You keep it set aside," he informed her impatiently. "And you better still have it when a berth comes up."

"Set aside?" She wasn't sure if he was using slang she hadn't heard before.

He grabbed a drawstring pouch made of coarse sack cloth from beneath the table. "Put it in here, and don't lose it," he warned her.

She realized, too slowly for the helpful person behind her as he let out an impatient sigh, that they intended to do nothing more for her. She gathered up the money into the drawstring pouch, retreated to the narrow shade cast by a lamp post, and dropped her bags.

She had no idea where Front Street was.

All her life she'd wanted to see the world's great cities. Now she wished she could sling her bags over a pony and walk away from Ben Ariim forever. She wished she could hike up stony paths into the trees, drink from clear streams when she was thirsty, hunt when she was hungry, sleep under the stars wrapped in her cloak when she was tired. If she could, she would walk home. For a mad moment, she considered it.

But ships sailed faster than she could walk. They never tired, never slept, never had to hunt for food before traveling onward, and didn't need to find blessed shelter to hide in during true nights.

*I have to wait.*

*But can Brian wait for me?*

The Gurra girl beside Billie suddenly vaulted up from the wall where they sheltered from the sacred sun's glare on Front Street. "I carry your packages!" she offered cheerfully as the two women bustled by, their arms full of groceries precariously balanced while they tried to herd a pack of children along through the crowded street. "Very cheap!"

"Yes," one of the women said, and soon they chatted away with the Gurra as if they'd known her all their lives.

A Gurra who'd been squatting in the sun on the opposite side of the street quickly took her place at Billie's side. Billie edged over slightly to make more room for him, but there wasn't much to give. She was almost ass-to-ass with the Gurra on her other side as it was.

"I've been watching you," he said with a rakish grin.

She answered his grin with a smile she didn't feel. Was he flirting with her, or did he mean it in a more sinister way? "Oh?"

"You're not looking for work," he said. "But it looks like you need some."

His words made her feel like an idiot. Maybe she should have been looking for work all along. "I'm not sure what to do. I suppose I can carry things."

"They won't trust a Kilhellion for such work," he said. "They'll think something is wrong with you. But I can find you work maybe as a guard, if you can prove yourself. Are you quick with that blade you carry?"

"A guard? Someone would trust me to protect them, but not carry their bags?"

He shifted so he could look into her eyes without twisting his neck. "You wouldn't be working alone at first, and you would stand maybe at a gate during the night, or make sure no one bothers the animals in a stable. Then, in time, they might trust you to walk with someone important who needs to go to, say, see someone who doesn't like them very much."

She didn't have time for that. "Thank you, but no."

"It's very good work," he assured her. "You would be surprised how nice the wages can be."

"It's not that. I'm leaving Ben Ariim, hopefully soon."

"Ah." He nodded, then watched the passersby for a while. "What else can you do?"

"I'm good with ponies. I play drums." She stopped short of admitting that she was a healer. She doubted anyone in Port Sellon would find out, but her instincts had silenced her, and she didn't want to fight them.

"You could play a drum," he said. "You have one in one of your bags?"

Despite the shade on this side of the street, the heat was starting to overwhelm her. Thirst thickened her throat. "Yes," she admitted reluctantly.

"How are you going to make money if you don't play, and don't want to guard?"

She felt stupid for asking, but … "How can I make money playing my drum? Would someone hire me?"

"No. You play here, and if people like it, they will give you money." He took off his beaded hat and set it on the ground, top down, so it made a decent bowl. He tapped inside it. "They put the money in here."

He was kind to explain things that probably everyone in the city had known since they could walk. But this matter of money twisted her guts up inside her and made her want to throw up. It wasn't just the way the harbormaster had looked at her tribe's wealth, like she was offering pebbles she'd picked up on a beach.

The true night before the last, she'd believed she'd soon be in Port Sellon. Now, she wasn't sure she'd get out of Ben Ariim before the next true night.

"Are you hurt? Grieving?" He spoke more softly and leaned closer, his brows peaked with concern.

He deserved more than silence. "I'm waiting for someone to offer me passage to Port Sellon," she told him. "But it's getting late, and no one has come. And I promised all my money for the journey." She had a mind to go ask what was taking so long, but she was afraid that as soon as she left, someone would come looking for her and she'd miss them.

"I can help, cheap," he offered.

"I just have my clothes and ..." *My drum, and the book.*

She knew in her heart that he would be of more use than the harbormaster.

"Will you accept my drum?" It meant so much to her, but it was probably of little worth here. It would be a bad trade, but it was a better choice than offering him the so-called cheap healing book, which would be a priceless treasure in Torath. "I have to get to Port Sellon. It's for my brother. He needs me."

"Hmm." He gazed at her solemnly for a time, long enough for her to notice pox scars on his cheeks and neck, and the freckles that dotted his nose and cheeks. He looked younger than she first guessed he was, younger than when she'd bled the first time. "What is your name?" he asked.

"Billie Maiyem."

"Here is what I, Hova the Bird, can do for you, Billie Maiyem," he decided aloud. "I will leave my hat here, and you will play. Whatever coin people throw into the hat, half will be mine and half yours. But even if they give nothing, I will work for you and try to find you passage to Port Sellon. It is a risk, but the risk will be equal, because I will take half the money even if I don't find you passage to Port Sellon. Yes?"

She couldn't have hoped for better. "Yes. We have a deal, Hova the Bird."

He grinned. "Very good." He moved his hat in front of her, then wove his way quickly into the stream of people going by. In moments another Gurra had taken his place in the shade.

She made nothing playing her drum. She went on playing mainly because she'd agreed to do it, but it was frustrating. Several times people came toward her with their purses in hand, but as soon as they got a clear look at her, they left without dropping anything.

A woman sneered at her. When Billie met her gaze, daring her to say something, she stepped closer. "Why don't you go back to where you came from? No one wants you here." She looked around with her chin lifted as if to look for anyone who agreed with her. Most of the people ignored her, but someone else met her gaze and nodded before moving on.

A man who saw the woman's disdainful reaction walked over and dropped coins in the hat while staring into the woman's eyes. She sneered at him too and walked off.

"Thank you." His pity made her feel worse than ever. She stared at the ground so that she wouldn't have to see his reaction. Would he be angry because she didn't show more gratitude? Indifferent? Offended? At last her curiosity forced her to look up, but by then he was gone.

Three pleasurers passing through began to shimmy and sway to her music. It was the first time anyone had really reacted to her playing, and it buoyed her spirits. She played with more spirit, more like she felt when she was at home.

The pleasurers laughed. Were they making fun of her?

As if they knew each other's minds, they began to dance as one. It was the most incredible, sinuous thing she'd ever seen. They were so deeply, movingly sexual that her body warmed to them, and yet they seemed beyond the needs of a body, like light, or air.

She wasn't the only one captivated. Most of the crowd moving along the street stopped to listen and watch and clap along.

Someone joined in song. There were no lyrics, but the open-throated, resonant call conveyed a joy beyond words. The voice lifted her up and carried her imagination to a place of deepest love, soft breezes and clear water. People put money in the hat the singer held out, and tucked coins into the belts and down the vests of the pleasurers in their bright costumes. Then a flute player joined them. A few coins even went into Billie's hat, but she barely noticed. She lost herself in the moment, swaying and rocking in time with the rhythm. And then it happened. The music began to play her. She stretched out the silences between beats so that the agony of its absence fired her to strike the drum with a force that felt like the pulses of an orgasm. The dancers cried out with those beats, and a Rill trilled when Billie ruffled the drumhead with tender, rapid caresses between the strikes.

The Kilhellion chant came to her, speaking to her from within the drum. They were soul words, sounds without strict meaning that came to Kilhellions during drumming, or battle. They mimicked the sounds of the drum, and of rivers, of avalanches, and wild beasts.

Some of the people in the crowd stopped in shock, and she faltered, but then the pleasurers whooped with enthusiasm and the chant returned to her. She screamed with joy and the crowd gasped, and Rill trilled, and the pleasurers cheered.

The power of their reaction inspired her to chant the names of her tribe and the short poems associated with each member, and she chanted the names of the people she'd lived as in previous lives. The crowd drank it in. It was like a festival night, but among strangers.

Her hands started to buzz and feel bruised, and the dancers were tired. She wrapped up the music with glances to the singer, the dancers and the flute player so that they all came to a halt together. A great cry went up among everyone—players, dancers and the people in the street—and she howled with delight.

The crowd melted away. In a few heartbeats she couldn't tell that it had happened at all.

Except, in the wake of the music, she felt hope.

One of the pleasurers approached her. "Thank you for that," he said from behind a delicate veil. He lifted it, and his face was flawless, powerfully masculine but with the refined elegance and delicacy of his Thedran ancestry. His brown eyes reminded her of banked coals, a warmth that could flare into flame in an instant.

He kissed her lightly on the cheek, and a shiver of pleasure went through her. And then he handed her a purse full of coins. "For the wild drummer," he said, and then with a light laugh as free as a songbird, he followed the others into the crowd.

She felt as if she'd been touched by a godling. And maybe she had. She couldn't be sure. She'd never seen anyone that perfect before, without a scar or blemish, with such symmetry, glowing with health and balance and lightness of spirit. It wasn't just that he seemed untouched by the harshness of the world. It was as if he could soothe that harshness with a touch or a smile or a dance, erase scars, maybe even charm Death into waiting a while longer.

She stroked the drum head. Thirst suddenly seized her like a pack of wolves, and hunger too. The coins she'd earned, though, were not hers to spend, and she couldn't leave anyway.

Except ...

She looked over at the Gurra woman beside her and considered. "I'm thirsty," she began. "Is there drinking water nearby?"

"There is a public fountain just down that way," the woman told her, pointing. She spoke the words kindly, and with a smile. Billie wondered if she expected money in exchange for that kindness. It didn't seem so, but she didn't understand this place. She hated the constant worry that she was being unintentionally rude.

"Thank you." Billie considered her words carefully before she spoke. "I'm waiting for word of passage from the harbor. I wonder if you would listen for my name if someone asks?"

The woman contemplated this. "Your name?" The smile had faded a bit.

Billie realized that it was asking too much to hold this woman here when she was hoping to find work at any moment. "I have little to offer. The coin I earned isn't mine to keep."

The woman's brows furrowed. She was about Billie's mother's age, now that the wrinkles showed more. "Who is it that you earn for?" she asked.

"Hova the Bird, and my brother. My brother who is ill."

The smile returned, this time laced with sympathy. "I will listen for you."

"I feel I should give you something." The goods she had with her were too valuable, except for the bit of rope she still had, but that was absurd. Unless ... she could give the woman her signature knot.

No, that would do the woman little practical good in Ben Ariim.

"We will make a deal with Hova," the woman told her. "Go ahead." When Billie reached for the strap of her bag, the Gurra woman put a hand on her arm. "I will also watch your things."

Billie hesitated. Could she trust her?

"On my honor," the woman assured her with a smile of encouragement.

The other Gurras were watching now. It felt like a test. She didn't know what she would win if she got it right, or what she would lose.

She stood to lose everything.

*Please, earn my trust.*

Billie picked up the bag with her spare set of clothes and the medicines in it, and left the other with her costly clothes, along with her drum and the hat with the money. "I won't be long," she promised.

The woman grinned with what Billie hoped was approval and not victory at winning the hat, coin, drum, and a bag of treasures.

Like everywhere else in Ben Ariim Billie had walked, the way the Gurra had pointed was crowded. If she hadn't seen it for herself, she would have not been able to imagine so many people filling the large square at the end of the street. And in the center, in tiers, was the fountain.

Her instinct was to hurry, but she knew that if the Gurra intended to steal her things, they were already gone. She needed to be careful and just watch for a moment.

She was glad that she had.

The fountain's lowest levels were large, terraced ponds divided by the central structure, which looked like a fanciful castle. She'd imagined Markan fortresses would look like that spiraling series of gardens, walkways, balconies and towers. People let their children splash and play on one side of the lowest pond, and on the other lowest side they did their laundry and washed their hands after doing filthy work. On the next terrace up, catching the water spilled from the castle, were square pools. There the people let their animals drink and washed their hands and faces before eating. To reach drinking water for humans, they could wade through the swimming part or the laundry part where a few steps led to the top level. There the clearest water pooled before flowing down to the troughs and ponds. Sedges and reeds were planted around the top tier, as well as massive irises far more voluptuous than the delicate blue ones that grew on Mount Cross in early spring. The lush iris blossoms had delicate, ivory petals brushed with bright yellow pollen.

Trickles of water flowed out of the top tiers, splashed down stepped waterfalls, to fill small basins in the shape of stone lilies. A thin stream flowed out of those lilies of the lowest pools, a pair for each side. Those trickles would take a long time to fill even a small bucket, but anyone who might struggle to take the steps to the top could catch clean drinking water in a hand, a cup, or even directly into their mouths if they had to.

Billie opted to go wading and climbed the steps to the top tier. Though the water was murky, it smelled clean, and she immediately understood why. Death symbols were carved into the base and interior sides of the fountain. She could have had a drink from the swimming side—it would have been safe—but she doubted she would have enjoyed the flavor.

The cool water filled her gurgling, hungry belly, satisfying at least one of her needs. She filled her canteen, then bathed and washed her clothes on the laundry side. She washed her shawl first so that her face wasn't exposed to the sun too long. Even in that short time her skin tingled from the sun's kisses. The wet shawl dripped down her face and body, quickly cooling the sting.

The modesty people exhibited was different than the Sothron Empire, which was to say that they exercised some at the fountain. She gladly imitated them, as that was closer to her own culture's sense of modesty, and kept her underthings on while she washed. She blushed to think of Aliiren and how she'd stripped down half or completely naked in front of him so many times. But then, he'd been in Ruvall for a time, where public nakedness around fountains and pools was not just tolerated, but expected, and where wearing clothes into the water or doing laundry was frowned upon. He hopefully didn't take too much offense at seeing her bare body.

By the time she finished she was tired and ready for a nap. Her clothes had dried quickly after laundering. It shouldn't have surprised her, with the heat from the sun and the heat on the stone walls of the laundry pool where she'd laid out her woolens. She slipped them on and made her way back to the public shelter.

The Gurra woman was still there, and so were Billie's things, and the hat, and the money.

Billie settled beside her. "Thank you."

"You have had a hard day," the woman said. "Sometimes, a little help is needed. And also sometimes, help given comes back multiplied when it is needed."

Maybe that meant that Billie owed her. She wasn't sure. Her experiences since she'd left the Kilhells often overwhelmed her ability to comprehend and contextualize. It seemed best not to say anything, especially to avoid making a promise she might not be able to keep, though that didn't feel right either.

"I will give advice, for nothing," the woman said. "The advice is what my people say. When things are bad, we look around beyond ourselves and our troubles. We look, like there, where that child is having their first drink of chocolate."

Billie saw him, and the light of wonder in his wide eyes, even as he scowled a bit at the chocolate's bitterness. He sipped at it again and laughed and looked for approval from his mother.

"We say, life is good. Life, is good."

The boy squawked in protest as his mother took the cup away. Apparently it was hers and she'd indulged him when he'd asked for some. She laughed and gave it back to him. He cradled it like it was a jeweled bauble more valuable than the whole rest of the city. And maybe it was.

"Life," Billie said. "Is good. How do you say that to another Gurra?"

"Sah mem."

"Sah mem." Billie clung to the sentiment, holding it close inside her. Life was good.

For now.

## Chapter Seventeen

◇◇◇◇◇◇◇◇◇◇◇◇◇◇◇◇◇◇◇◇◇◇◇◇◇◇◇◇◇◇◇◇◇◇◇◇◇◇◇◇◇◇◇◇◇◇◇◇◇◇

# Letters

◇◇◇◇◇◇◇◇◇◇◇◇◇◇◇◇◇◇◇◇◇◇◇◇◇◇◇◇◇◇◇◇◇◇◇◇◇◇◇◇◇◇◇◇◇◇◇◇◇◇

*Ben Ariim, Arrak Thedra*
*3rd Trade Day of Sun Month*

"The trouble is," Hova explained, "is that no one I've asked so far wants to take a Kilhellion on board. And I fear if I do not tell them, they will turn you away once they see you. But I will keep trying."

True night would fall tomorrow at dusk, and she was still stuck in Ben Ariim. Her frustration boiled over and she started walking to the harbor.

"Billie, where are you going?" Hova called after her.

Even in the evenings when most people would be sitting at their dinners, Ben Ariim's streets were crowded, and hot. The scents of savory, spicy foods filled the air, more potent than the sweat and incense and perfume. The abundant food all around her haunted her. She would have sucked blood from her own wrist to sate her hunger if she thought it would help. On and on she wove through the city until finally she reached the tents near the lighthouse, where she had to stand in line like she had the first time she'd come here.

She stood, and stood, raging, her eyes blurred with frustration and fear for her brother.

No one cared.

She doubted anyone would leave for Port Sellon now.

Well, maybe first thing in the morning. She could hope.

Her hope had worn thin.

*What am I doing here? They're not going to help me.*

And yet she couldn't bear to go back to the alley without trying for herself one more time.

A richly dressed Thedran woman jingling with jewels walked past her and started to chat with someone in the line. Before long she'd inserted herself as if she'd been waiting there all along. Billie worked her jaw, fuming. She looked around. No one else seemed perturbed. Weary, yes, bored, but not angry. How could they not be upset? Now everyone had to wait longer.

And when the woman got to the table they laughed and talked and had a wonderful time gossiping about the grand council members of Ben Ariim.

Billie thought of Aliiren, and his patience, and wondered if he was that way because he was deeply spiritual and kind, or if it was because he'd given up fighting against the injustices he saw all around him. Or maybe, because of who he was and how he was, he never suffered anyone's inconsiderate behavior.

Wealthy Thedran behavior, specifically.

Finally it was her turn. "Billie Maiyem," she told the man there. She remembered him. She doubted he remembered her.

"Ah yes. Billie Mayhem," he said. "Your Gurra comes twice, three, four times a day, raising your offer of fare."

"So why has no one taken my offer?" she demanded.

"There are other people who want to go to Port Sellon. See all the tickets?" he said, showing her the box. "They applied before you, so they get first chance at a place."

"I think mine is the oldest. It's worn and stained."

"From changing the fare on the ticket," he said with a smile. "Shall I change it again?" He pulled her ticket out.

"Why isn't anyone taking my offer?" she asked tightly. She wanted to take the paper and cram it in his mouth.

He placed it back with a sigh. "It's only been two days. Soon a Kilhellion captain will come along and take your ticket. My advice? Stop raising the fare. Either it's enough, or not. Eventually someone will take your offer. So stop sending the Gurra, all right? I have enough work to do without him pestering me. Next?"

"Eventually? Is it not enough? Why won't you tell me if it's not enough?"

He groaned. "It's not my job to tell you how much you want to pay. Only you know that."

"My brother may be dying. He needs me! Put that on the ticket."

He sighed. "It won't help, but if it'll satisfy you, fine." He took the ticket back out of the box. "Brother, dying." He wrote it, and a chill passed through her, as if writing it made it certain. "Next?"

"Did you put on the ticket that I'm Kilhellion?"

"Yes," he said with a tight, overly bright smile that showed off too many teeth.

"Take off the part about me being Kilhellion. I'm not any trouble," she told him.

He laughed. "You're being trouble now!"

She grabbed him, a snarl filling the void in her belly and suddenly everyone was shouting, clawing at her but she didn't let go. "A man is dying! Don't you care? *My brother!*" She shoved him away, back into his chair, which rocked precariously on the edge of balance but didn't tip him onto the ground. Her heart thundered in her ears. "Son of a gnat," she snapped in Kilhellion. "You tell them," she told him, reverting to Thedran, "you tell them to act like human beings and help me save my brother. You tell them that if they love the gods, and have any decency, they will suffer my presence long enough to dump me in my homeland so that I can be with my family again. It'll be better for you, better for all of Ben Ariim if I'm gone, don't you think?"

A pair of men, one tall and very dark, the other shorter but thick armed in the way of a swordsman, came over. They were armored. She wondered if they served this fuck waste, or if they simply defended anyone confronted by a Kilhellion. "Is there a problem?" the shorter one asked.

"No problem," Billie assured them, moving on because if she stayed, she was going to beat someone near to death.

"She assaulted my person!" the harbormaster's man shrieked.

She suspected that meant something here, something bad, something they might even use as an excuse to execute her. "I barely touched him," she protested, angry that they looked at her as if she was lying about it. "See? He has all his teeth. There's no blood, no bruises."

The tall Sothroner sighed and rolled his eyes before looking to the harbormaster's man. "Are you hurt?"

"There's probably a bruise on his chest," the person now at the table offered unhelpfully. Billie resisted the urge to snap at him. Barely.

The harbormaster's man fumed at her, and she realized she'd ruined all chances of leaving this place. Before the tears could swell and spill over she stalked off. *I will not cry. I will not cry!*

"Hey," the Sothroner called after her, and more faintly, she heard someone else say, "Just let her go."

The threat of sobs and tears warred against the wall of rage that held them back. She couldn't see where she was going for the longest time. Just away. And then she found herself in a strange part of Ben Ariim where there were fewer people, but they were all finely dressed and enjoying meals at tables set out in the street. There were Gurras within elaborate tents selling beautiful clothes. Somewhere hidden, a group of people played instruments and sang a song in poetic Thedran about a lost horse.

She was lost.

A Gurra gave her directions and she was able to find her way back to the public shelter.

"What happened?" Hova asked.

Billie started to say, but the tears threatened to win past the anger, and she had to swallow them down hard.

"Oh no. Here. Sit here." He pointed into the shade and the Gurras there made room for her.

Billie sat and did her best to calm herself. Crying like a lost baby wouldn't save her brother. But what could?

She hoped Tilla had reached him.

"You need to eat, Billie," Hova told her.

"I can't. The money is for my brother." Only now she had a little to spare, because …

No one would take her at any price. The harbormaster's man didn't say it. She just knew it.

"Tilla will save him," she told herself in her native tongue. "Tilla."

No one came the next day, and of course she spent true night in the public house. Hova made her spend some of the coin she'd earned on Somber Day on food better than the bread and fermented milk. She ate, and she drank plenty—probably too much. It wasn't just because it was free. She needed to fill the emptiness somehow.

Come true dawn she stayed inside with everyone else, as a dust storm was sweeping the city. She felt sick from thoughts of what her brother must be suffering. By the time it was safe to emerge from the shelter it was midday, and hot again, and busy. Dust still clouded the air, dimming the sun, making her and everyone else cough. Tying her shawl across her face only helped a little. The fine yellow powder worked its way into everything, even under her clothes. She waved a desultory hello to Hova before she went to the fountain where she soaked in the swimming area and drank water and soaked some more until her head felt halfway clear.

On the slog back to the street outside the public shelter, she felt nothing but defeat.

Hova must have been watching for her because he came running, a huge grin on his face. "There's a captain that wants to meet with you!"

For a moment she didn't think she'd heard right. "What?"

"A Kilhellion captain. She has accepted your ticket."

A thrill shocked through her so powerful it verged on pain. "Gods." She hugged him so hard that he gasped. Her breath sobbed with joy and relief. "Thank you!"

"I did nothing," he assured her, blushing.

"But you did. You did." She kissed him on the cheek, which made him blush harder, and then she paid the Gurra watching her bags and hugged her too before cross-slinging her bags over her shoulders. *I'm going home!*

"I'll take you there," Hova said, and led the way through Ben Ariim's dockside streets and onto the floating boardwalks, out to the ships. He moved as quickly and surely as someone who had done this all their life. She could barely keep up, but the last thing she wanted to do was ask him to slow down, even as her heart threatened to pound its way out of her chest.

She saw it before they actually got there, a Kilhellion trade ship rigged with pale green square sails. It was armored against pirates; maybe it carried Kilhellion steel, or sapphires, or both. The ship had a sturdy look to her, much like her crew. There was a tall man, and a short man who worked with a thicker man that looked like he might be the short man's brother. A tall woman, apparently a scribe, was writing something … and finally there was an even taller woman who looked to be in charge. She had the pale red hair that Kilhellions called flame red, with some wisdom frost that made it sparkle. Her fine tresses spilled out from under a brief, sky blue scarf that tidied all but a few wisps around her face. Her skin had tanned about as much as Kilhellion skin ever tanned, which was to say it was still paler than a Thedran pleasurer's. Splendidly dressed in white and green woolens almost as light as Sothron silk, her clothes flowed around her like the layered petals of a flower from the waist down—a skirted coat to mid-thigh, tunic to the knee, working skirt to mid-calf with large pockets and probably some hidden ones, and white hose so delicate they were translucent where they peeked between the skirt and her boots. Billie doubted that she sailed in such clothes. She probably worked in clothes similar to what Billie wore every day: a knee-length tunic over a light supportive undershirt that ribboned snug under the bust, worn with skirts and leggings over undershorts.

This woman was dressed to do business. Her unbraided hair suggested she was looking for a lover.

Billie wanted to drop her bags so she could run and hug this woman she didn't know. Then the woman saw her and reacted with a scowl that slowed Billie's approach. Billie felt a little faint as she took the last steps to meet the woman, who'd used some rigging to swing out and drop onto the deck in an intimidating show of strength and grace.

Something was wrong. She didn't know what, but something was definitely wrong.

"You, Gurra," the woman said roughly in Thedran. "This is private business. Leave."

It was within her right to speak this way, and in fact it was common for a chief, elder, or other person of importance to speak like that to inform outclansfolk that they were unwelcome, but growing up with a perpetually-polite chieftain and after all the time Billie had spent among other peoples, it jarred her almost as much as a slap.

"I have to pay you," Billie said to Hova, reaching into her sleeve.

"No. She paid," Hova said. "Rill's luck to you," he told Billie in Gurra, and left.

*What? The captain paid ... paid what?*

For a moment Billie wasn't sure what to do. She started to sling a bag off her shoulders, but the woman said, "No. Wait."

Was this an enemy of her tribe?

"You're Maiyem," the woman said.

Billie nodded warily.

"Billie Maiyem, daughter of Dayna and Ronheld Maiyem, from Mount Cross."

Maybe she was being exceptionally formal because this was business. Billie hadn't done any business on her own with Kilhellion outclansfolk, but she'd watched her parents trade and didn't recall them being treated so coldly.

She had noticed, though, that port tribes behaved differently than mountain folk. Maybe this wasn't as bad as it seemed. "Yes."

The woman scowled even more deeply. Gods. Maybe she had bad news. Was it about Brian?

*Stop panicking!*

Her hands trembled. She stilled them by gripping the straps on her bags.

"Look at me."

Billie was already searching for some sign of what was to come in the captain's face, but she obeyed by focusing on the woman's blue eyes.

There was only silence.

*What is happening?*

Billie braced herself.

The woman crossed her arms and looked away for a moment before she looked back into Billie's eyes. "You're no longer a Maiyem. Understand?"

No.

No, she didn't understand.

"What?"

The woman worked her jaw and then sniffed. "You don't have a home anymore. You're disowned."

That made no sense.

The captain uncrossed her arms and turned aside. Her gaze searched among the ships in the harbor before returning to Billie's face. "Nod if you understand."

That was not what she was expecting at all. It felt strange, like expecting a slap across the face and getting stabbed in the gut instead. It stole her breath, stole her thoughts. Had she heard right? "What?"

The woman lifted her chin. "You heard me. Disowned." She pulled a tube of paper from a pocket on her skirt and offered it. Billie recognized Melissa's handwriting on the leather tube, and Melissa's knot, and her father's knot, holding a precious piece of vellum within the leather in a tight roll.

Billie shied away from it. "No." That couldn't be.

The only way that could be was if ...

"No."

Brian was not dead. He couldn't be. No, that wasn't true. This was all a mistake. Maybe her father was so angry about Tilla that he'd pressed for his right to do this. She could beg for mercy from Gareth and explain what had happened.

Her tribe wouldn't let this happen.

She wouldn't let this happen.

She steeled herself. "Are you going to take me to Port Sellon?"

"You're not listening to me. You could go to Port Sellon, but then what? If anyone in your tribe sees you, they'll kill you. You're better off staying here in Ben Ariim."

"There's been a mistake." This was all a mistake.

"Go," the woman told her. "Don't try to go home. Don't go back to the Kilhells at all. It's not ..." Something in her relented just a bit and Billie felt a surge of hope. "The world is bigger than the Kilhells," the woman told her gently.

She'd secretly dreamed of having a life outside of Torath, but not like this.

"You're still a Kilhellion, maybe not in name anymore but you're stronger than anyone that's spent their whole life in a city." Each word hit her like a punch from her father, demanding strength while bruising her. "You have your eyes, your hands, your feet, a blade. What else could you want?"

*My family. My brother.*

"I need to …" Billie stopped herself as the captain's words finally broke through and shattered a place inside her that had felt as solid and safe as the songhouse. They wouldn't accept any explanations. Alive or dead, Brian wasn't her brother anymore. But hadn't Tilla …

*Did Tilla make it to Port Sellon?*

*What happened?*

Gods. If something had gone badly, if the ship sank, or Tilla made it to Port Sellon and there was a fight …

Tilla might be dead.

The world seemed to bleach out around her, then dimmed.

Brian. Tilla. Her parents. Her sister. Torath. Mount Cross.

Gone. She didn't know who was alive and if anyone died. The only sure thing she knew was that to her family, to her friends, to her tribe, Billie was dead.

Her mind spun, unable to grasp what she had to do.

*What about Tilla?*

*Tilla might know what happened.*

*If she's alive.*

Billie couldn't go back to the healer's college. Even if Billie earned enough fare to go back to Ruvall, she wouldn't earn enough to pay for the schooling. But she could make enough to send a letter to the college, maybe, and find out if Tilla returned.

*Does Tilla know what my tribe has done? Would she understand? Would she care?*

She realized she wasn't thinking straight. The things that didn't matter very much had tangled up with big things that she couldn't see around, big things like what in the hells was she supposed to do now? And Brian …

The captain had turned away and walked a few paces to give Billie some privacy.

The captain had come a long way to deliver this message. And how did she know Billie would be here? Was there another captain, with another letter, waiting in Ruvall?

For a moment all she could think about was the wealth they'd spent to tell her that she was dead to them now. She wanted this to be some trick, wanted this woman to be her enemy, but her father's knot, and the scribe's, made that impossible.

Billie gazed at the Kilhellion ship with its lovely pale green sails. If she could only get to Port Sellon, she could find her family and …

And they would kill her.

She was disowned.

This was happening.

*But I have to go home. I have to!*

The world had gone very still, and silent. The only color she could detect was the captain's copper hair, and the faded blue sky, tinged with the yellow dust that, in the storm's aftermath, lingered everywhere. Everything else had gone gray.

She was breathing, and her heart was beating, but she didn't feel alive anymore. Something vital emptied out of her and it wasn't coming back.

The woman offered Billie the letter once more. This time, Billie took it, as if she was taking back something that was hers, without thought. The sensation of the leather tube in her hands stung like nettles. A shiver passed through her, and then she trembled, like aftershocks from an earthquake.

If there were any answers, they would be coiled within the leather, carefully printed on vellum. Her fingers traced her father's signature knot, as familiar to her as her own. He loved her, didn't he? How could he do this? She'd disappointed him more often than she'd made him proud, but this …

As she'd left for the healer's college, he'd asked her to make him proud. She hadn't realized that those would be his last words to her.

"Hey." The woman slapped Billie's shoulder. A sudden return of sounds and color jarred her from thoughts of her father's smile, and the strength of his arms as he'd given her a hug before sending her away. He hadn't hugged her like that since she was a little girl.

"Hey! Didn't you hear me? You have everything you need to make your way in Ben Ariim. You don't need anything else." The hard experience in her voice felt more like an attack than encouragement. "Forget Mt. Cross. Burn that letter, or throw it in the sea. Don't spend your money to have someone read it to you. It's no good to you." Her voice softened. "It'll break your heart. Just … live. Throw the letter away and live a new life."

*Forget my life?*

Her breath gasped out of her as the memory came, clear as daylight. Before her eyes her bone flute flew through the air, end over end, slowly like a well-thrown dagger, growing smaller and smaller until finally it splashed into the sea and vanished from her forever.

Throwing away her flute had not helped her live a new life.

She would not throw away this last thing from her father. Ever.

Billie backed away. She bumped into someone. He spewed foreign words at her that sounded like curses. She shoved him aside and ran.

She ran hard, blindly, pushing through crowds to sprint down a cluttered alley, then across a park. Her bags threatened to knock her off balance as they banged against her. She ran along a shady canal, and then into the hazy sun of a busy square. No matter how fast she ran she couldn't escape the meaning of the letter she clutched in her fist. Her throat tasted like blood and mud. Exhaustion dragged at her legs and stabbed her side. Her bags staggered her steps and bashed into people but she couldn't stop, not even to apologize because her words, her life meant nothing to anyone anymore.

"Hey!" Someone grabbed her. "You're going the wrong way on a blessing road!" Billie tore free of him and tried to keep going, but someone else grabbed her. "What's wrong with you? You're on a white road!" He shoved her into an alley. She staggered, then pushed past some crates onto another road.

"There she is!" she heard someone yell. "The Kilhellion!"

She ran harder. She couldn't breathe, couldn't breathe …

She slammed into a tiny woman as she rounded a corner. Billie spun around with her, using all her strength and a fragile sense of balance to keep the woman from falling. They staggered in a mad, whirling dance until finally Billie could safely let her go. The woman took a few unsteady steps but didn't fall.

Billie slammed into a stone wall so hard it dazed her. Her lungs rebelled and she succumbed to a coughing fit that seemed to suck in more dust than it forced out.

The woman stared at her, wide-eyed, and then ran, abandoning the sticks of bread she'd been carrying. Someone stopped the woman and she babbled, pointing at Billie with a trembling hand. At last, the coughing fit subsided, leaving her breathless.

A trio of men gathered and stalked toward her. "Kilhellion shit," one of them snarled.

She laughed. She didn't mean to. But this was too much. They were shorter than her, and young like her, but so angry and certain of their power—it was like being stalked by kittens. And it was so absurd, because it was an accident, it was only an accident, and the woman was shaken but she looked all right, and yet they were acting like Billie had murdered her.

Her laugh stopped them short.

"Thank you," she told the one who'd insulted her. "But I'm fine. The bread, though, is ruined. Sorry about that." She grabbed the purse from under her belt and dug out the few coins she'd earned that day. She threw the money at them. They all flinched, though only the biggest of them got hit by a lone coin. The rest of the money scattered across the brick paving. "That's for her, so she can buy more."

She strode away. She shook as if she'd begun to freeze to death on Mt. Cross. It wasn't funny anymore. She was angry at herself, and them, and the city. She expected them to ambush her, but they didn't. She wished they had. Fighting for her life would have felt better than running from the desolation looming behind her like a growing storm.

Billie rounded the next corner. Buildings across the street rose to immense heights, shading the pavement to the foot of the buildings beside her. Indented panels of gold-streaked marble cupped around doors spaced along walls as white as good wool. The delicate blessings carved around the doors and at the edges of the buildings looked like lace spread over snow.

The street was busy, but not crowded, and people walked at an unhurried pace. The businesses arrayed to either side of her shared walls and roofs for the length of each block, with stairs at the corners leading to upper levels. They had their doors open. Some had outdoor tables with wares that shoppers perused, or containers filled with blooming plants, or benches where people sat and snacked and talked. Everyone behaved as if nothing was wrong.

For them, she supposed, nothing was wrong at all.

Only a few people noticed her. Some gave her a quick, wary glance in passing. A man slowed and leveled a challenging stare. He smirked with satisfaction and moved on when she did nothing, said nothing. The rest flowed around her as if she were a minor obstacle.

It didn't matter. The world had become a distant thing, a confusion of whispering sounds and muted colors like autumn leaves blowing around her. A dizzying number of languages blended into babble.

They didn't know her. No one knew her. She was surrounded by people, more than her mind could comprehend, and yet she was utterly alone. Suddenly, the customs of the Sothron Empire made terrible sense. To be known wasn't just a matter of who to trust in commerce.

It gave meaning to a life.

"You."

Billie turned to see an Arrak woman in leather armor stalking toward her. She wore a long blade on each side, one slightly shorter than the other. "Kilhellion," the woman added. Though she was short compared to Billie, only slightly taller than a typical Thedran woman, and had delicate hands and a thin, bony face, she carried herself with a fearlessness that demanded respect. The gray strands that streaked her smooth, black hair matched the experience lurking in her deep brown eyes. This would be a formidable opponent if she decided to attack. "You went the wrong way down a blessing road."

"I—I didn't mean to," Billie confessed. "I don't know what a blessing road is."

The woman's shoulders relaxed, and she let out a sigh. "The painted roads are blessing roads. The herringbone pattern in the paving points in the direction that you must travel."

"I wasn't looking," Billie admitted. "I'm sorry."

"As long as everyone travels the same direction on the blessing roads, it helps build the protections that keep hellions out of the city," the woman informed her coldly, and then she sighed again. "Look. It's not hard. If everyone is walking in the same direction, just follow along. Think you can manage that?"

"Yes." Her cheeks stung with shame.

"All right." The woman frowned at her, then walked away.

Billie didn't know what to do, or where to go. She thought of Hova, and Hawa, the woman that watched Billie's bags sometimes. They knew her. But she didn't know where she was anymore. Maybe finding them wouldn't help, but she had no one else. "Front Street?" she asked someone, but they kept going. "Excuse me," she tried again, but the person hurried on their way.

Did it matter?

What would she do?

She thought she'd be a healer in Torath.

*I can't be a healer anywhere. I'm nothing.*

A wave of dizziness overcame her. She eased herself to a narrow strip of shade beneath an awning against a wall and unburdened herself. The dizziness grew worse. She sat heavily between her bags and rested her head against her knees. *Slow, shallow breaths.* She closed her eyes. Her mind traveled into her body. Her lotus node gave her a quiet resting place before she linked it to her lantern node and sent vinus out from that dark lake of power throughout her body. Her insides felt flaccid, and her heart struggled to fill her vessels with blood.

She was hungry, and thirsty. Her stomach had forgotten its hunger, or had given up for the moment, but her mind and her muscles demanded food and water.

Billie relaxed her control over her vinus and opened her eyes. The city seemed to be made of gold and blinding whiteness until her eyes adjusted again, filling in the brilliantly colored clothes of Sothroners, Gurras, Arraks, but most of all Thedrans.

Across the street, a familiar, tall figure emerged from an austere building, books in his arms. He angled toward her just enough so that she could see his profile.

Temric.

He glanced past the wall of businesses on her side of the street, crossed, and vanished into the crowd. For a moment she wondered if she'd imagined it. Temric? Had it really been him?

Temric. But of course he was here in Ben Ariim. If she'd realized sooner that it really was him, she might have called out or run after him.

And say what?

The thought of looking into those innocent, inquisitive eyes as she told him what happened threatened to shatter the vestiges of calm that she clung too.

Aliiren was in Ben Ariim too, and Edrion.

She wondered if Edrion had found his sister.

Her eyes, ridiculously, teared up at the thought that the siblings might not have found each other. She moaned and shook her head. *It's stupid to imagine such things. It's bad enough that Brian …*

Her gut felt like it was full of mud. She wasn't hungry anymore.

*I don't want to know if something happened to Larani. I can't. Not now.*

Of all of them, she wanted to see Aliiren the most. Aliiren, calm and quiet and undemanding, would listen to what she had to say, and if she had no words, he wouldn't demand answers.

Aliiren would be with his dying teacher, struggling with his own grief. *I'm alone.*

Even in Ruvall, she didn't feel this alone, because in her heart, her tribe was with her.

The Kilhellion captain had told her that she had everything she needed to survive in this city, even thrive, but she had nothing that anyone wanted. The best she could do was drum for bits of coin and sleep in a public shelter over true nights.

She shook her head again and silently cursed herself for succumbing to self-pity. She took out her purse and poured the few remaining coins into her hand. The sack cloth pouch with her fare dropped out along with them.

*This wealth isn't mine.*

*I don't know how much I began with in Ruvall.*

*I don't know how to count what's left.*

This city and its people demanded counting, and measuring the worth of one sort of coin against another. She had to accept that though she couldn't eat money, it could buy her food, food that could not be gathered in the city like it could be in the forests near Torath. She would have to become numerate. She would have to learn, at minimum, to count, add and subtract.

She hated money more than ever. It couldn't send her home. It could never buy back her life.

It might help a friend.

Maybe she should try to find Edrion. Maybe she could help him find Larani. But how?

The docks seemed like the logical place to start.

She thought of Temric again, and how he'd tried to teach her to read. She still remembered some of the letters. She looked up at the sign nearest her, hanging from a bracket high up on the wall above a broad stone door carved with leafy Life blessings. She didn't recognize a single letter. She hoped she couldn't read it because it wasn't written in block script, not because she had no hope of combating her illiteracy.

*Will I have to learn to read to survive? How? Temric is leaving. He won't have time.*

Without Temric to help her, learning to read and count felt impossible.

She tucked the pouch, along with the letter, deep down into her bag. Her belt pouch had only a few small coins inside. She didn't know how long they would last. She didn't know if she'd earn enough drumming to keep herself fed, and she didn't know where she would stay between true nights. She suspected that hiring a room would be expensive, based on how many people slept on the streets between true nights, when the public shelters opened their doors to Ben Ariim's poorest residents.

She was tired, and hungry. She didn't want to think about anything anymore. At the same time, she wanted to accomplish something, or at least decide what to do next.

*I want to help Edrion find his sister. There. I've made a decision.*

But first she had to rest. When she woke, she'd find her way back to the docks.

Billie closed her eyes. Around her, the crowd's movement and sounds became as a mountain creek flooded by storm rains and melting snow. She drew in a deep breath, sighed it out, and used her gift to lull herself to sleep.

## Chapter Eighteen

# Foundlings

*Ben Ariim, Arrak Thedra*
*4ᵗʰ Meet Day of Sun Month*

"Theh."

She was riding her favorite pony, Waygirl, when she heard the sound. The mountainside, covered with impossibly beautiful wildflowers, began to fade into a grayness like death. Waygirl was gone, and Billie stood alone on an unfamiliar scree slope. The mountain looked strange, dark, barren. She was lost. She tried to call out, but she couldn't raise her voice above a whisper.

"Theh!" Wasn't that the Thedran word for *you?*

She opened her eyes. A pale sunset lit fragile wisps of cloud to a delicate pink edged in gold. Those lovely pastels silhouetted a dark figure. There were incredibly tall buildings around her. She felt the loss of Waygirl, who they'd sold to fund Billie's education.

Waygirl had been separated from her herd, and her human family, for nothing.

That loss felt like a fresh wound as she realized she wasn't home, and would never be again.

Worst of all, she wouldn't see Brian again. It was Brian she wanted to hug, to make sure he was all right. She needed to see him, to hear the warmth and mischief in his voice.

"You can't sleep here." The silhouette, apparently a man, bundled in a light evening coat to ward the trace of chill in the desert air, was speaking Thedran. Her understanding of the language came back to her. He glared at her in anger, his soft brown face darkened by a blush, but when she glared back at him he sobered and took a step back. "Go on, now. There are public shelters all over the city. Go bother them. We don't want you here."

Billie stood up and the both of them at once realized how very much taller she was than him, and the fact that the little wisp of a blade he carried wouldn't slow her sturdy Kilhellion one down at all. She didn't like his ungentle manners, but he was in the right. She did her best to cool her temper. "I'm sorry."

Like a foolish pup mistaking a mountain lion's retreat as a sign of weakness, his eyes flashed with victory. He gave her a prideful smile. He grew even braver when he realized he had everyone's attention and approval while he put this Kilhellion in her place. "We don't permit Gurras and other vagrants to sleep here. You're welcome to shop, but if you want a place to beg, don't come back here."

She stepped up to close the distance between them and that smile faded.

She'd meant to intimidate him. It didn't feel right, but she didn't want to back off either. "I don't intend to stay."

"Well … good, then." He stepped away again, and again, and wrinkled his nose. "There are public baths near the shelter on Front Street. But you have to buy the soap." He drew a coin from a pocket inside his coat and flicked it at her.

She let it drop, heat rushing to her face. "I don't want your money."

He sneered, tucked his hands into his coat, and puffed up his chest. "Heh. Typical. Mistaking compassion for insult."

"I think the mistake is assuming that because I haven't pounded you flat, you can talk to me any way you want."

He paled, but lifted his chin. "You can't touch me."

Was he an idiot? "Oh?" He flinched when she lunged but she had no trouble poking him in the chest before he could step back.

The remaining color bled from his face. "Leave me alone!" he cried as he fled.

Now everyone close by was staring at her like she was a monster.

"Billie?"

She whirled toward the vaguely familiar voice. Heat rushed to her face as embarrassment flushed through her, even as she prepared to argue that she hadn't done anything wrong.

It was Temric. For a moment she couldn't believe it, but he was unmistakable. He towered over the people who'd stopped to stare at the entertainment she'd unwillingly provided for them. He still had books tucked under his arm, or maybe they were different ones. Her embarrassment washed away with a feeling of pure joy at the sight of his pale blue eyes, long-nosed, narrow face and mess of curly hair, even if he looked perturbed.

"Temric." Speaking his name made everything feel more real. She wasn't alone.

"What are you doing here?"

Something scuffed behind her. A child snatched the dropped coin and make a run for it. She didn't care. Somehow, Temric was here.

She didn't want to answer, but she owed it to him, after all he'd done for her. "I'm lost, I guess." Her eyes suddenly burned as she thought of why she was still in Ben Ariim. Temric and everyone else around her faded into blurred spots of color, and her throat ached.

"Why aren't you in Port Sellon?"

The full force of what had happened to her rushed back and threatened to drown her. She stood still, certain that if she moved, something inside her would break.

"Are you all right?" he asked, obviously concerned. "Why were you arguing with that man?"

It took effort to speak, far more than she expected. She had to force every word. "He thought I was a beggar." Really, in most of the ways that counted, she was in fact a beggar. Her experiences near the docks had proved that being a beggar wasn't something to be ashamed of, but here, standing before Temric, in this place that didn't want her ... this matched what she'd been taught about a beggar's life. Whether she ought to be ashamed or not, people looked down on her and she felt it to her core.

Hova the Bird made life on Front Street bearable because he'd helped and protected her. Without him, she would have starved.

Temric gazed at her, obviously wanting to say something, but then he glanced over at the building behind him, and at the people loitering nearby, eavesdropping. "I have to return these," he said, gesturing at her with the elbow that held the books. "Will you wait?" And then he put a hand on her shoulder. The contact both surprised and steadied her. "On second thought, will you come with me?"

The gentle way he asked, almost as if she was a frightened child, made her uneasy. "Why?" Her voice sounded stronger than she felt, and sharp with suspicion.

*I sound like my father.*

This was Temric. He didn't deserve that. She crossed her arms, ashamed of herself.

He offered her a smile, the first she'd seen since her world had fallen into a bottomless crevasse. "Why are you making things difficult, Billie?" The soft, soothing way he asked her threatened to collapse her fragile composure. "Do you want to accompany me, or not?"

Regardless of how or why he asked, the answer was obvious. She forced herself to answer his smile, though it felt stiff on her face. "I'll come with you." She did her best to speak as if her life hadn't ended, but her voice faded along with her smile. "I'll just grab my bags." She fetched them from their place at the wall and slung them by the straps over her shoulders.

"I've been learning some things about the Isle of Winds," he told her as they walked. "But not as much as I'd like. Just about everything they have here at the library about the Isle of Winds is written in Markan." He looked at her sidelong and pursed his lips speculatively. "I seem to remember that you know Markan."

She wasn't sure if he was trying to be funny or not. "I can't read anything, never mind Markan."

He blushed. "I didn't mean … I meant to ask if you spoke it. If you do, I think I can learn how to pronounce the written words, and then I could read them to you."

Considering how long it took her to learn even a few of the sounds that Thedran letters made … "I don't see how that would work."

"It's a phonetic …" He seemed to remember something and shrugged instead of finishing his sentence. "We'll make it work." They reached the doors and Temric opened one inward, holding it so she could go inside without bumping through. "I'd offer to carry one of your bags, but I don't think I'm strong enough," he remarked.

Billie halted in the doorway, stunned by the sight.

Books.

Everywhere, books, and scrolls too, and ornate boxes, and she realized that they were full of words. Stories. Histories. Other things she couldn't even guess at.

She didn't know that there were this many words in the whole of the world.

There were shelves and shelves of them so high that they had tall ladders to reach them. The ladders angled between large, narrow wheels at the bottom and smaller wheels on tracks at the top that ran on brass rails. Small light stones that dangled on wires from the ceiling or glowed within delicate lamps that hinged from the shelves glimmered like lights in a night sky.

This was a sacred space. Maybe that wasn't strictly true in the sense that the Gods were present, or faerus imbued the library. But the incredible volume of books held their own kind of power. Her rudimentary understanding of books expanded so quickly that she felt dizzy. In a way, these things were a living connection to the passions, ideas and skills of countless people, though the people themselves, and everything they'd embraced, had long since perished. It challenged her belief that the written words of dead people didn't matter as much as the word of the living.

Though she suddenly felt very small, nothing more than a butterfly fluttering through a brief summer, this place seemed to welcome her, even embrace her. *Come look,* it seemed to say. *It's all here for you.*

But in actuality she was as shut out as if the doors had been barred against her, because she couldn't read.

It didn't matter, any more than it didn't matter that she didn't know the names of every star in the sky. It inspired her just the same.

In the center of the vast room there were long counters set in a square with doors on each side, and in the center of those counters were a few people. There was a short, thin Thedran, and a large woman with dark skin who didn't look Thedran except for her dark, coiled hair, and a very old person that sat on a tall stool and hunched over a large, stained, leather-bound book. The book was supported on a beautiful brass stand on the counter, and he wore gloves to protect the pages. But he didn't turn those pages. Whatever he gazed upon engrossed him.

The short Thedran saw them and bustled out through one of the swing doors toward them while Billie continued to turn in place, drinking in the sights. There were doors leading out of this room on either side and beyond the desk. She wondered where they led, and what other wonders this place held.

"You can't be in here," the man said.

"I was here," Temric protested awkwardly in Thedran. "A sip ago." He probably meant a moment, not a sip.

"Not you, *her.*"

Billie didn't care to argue, but she didn't want to leave just yet, so she ignored him.

Some of the books had gilded letters on the spine, and she recognized a few of the letters. Maybe the things Temric had taught her weren't entirely a waste.

"She with myself," Temric informed him coldly.

"Oh." The man made a soft, protesting noise in his throat, and then smiled a broad, unpleasant smile that narrowed his eyes and wrinkled his nose. "Technically, we don't permit the public in here. You were granted access, but that privilege doesn't extend to random people that you know. This place is here to help expand learning. If you want to entertain your friend, a pleasure house would be a more appropriate setting." He spoke more slowly than most Thedrans, maybe to help Temric understand, but if so, he should have used simpler, more common words.

"What if my friend wish to expand her learning?" Temric shot back. That impressed her. He'd understood enough of the man's educated Thedran to answer him correctly, and he'd even echoed the man's phrasing perfectly.

The small man fumed a moment, and then he cast a speculative look in Billie's direction. "She's here to read?"

That annoyed her, but she didn't want Temric to lose his privileges by saying or doing something rude. Besides, the Thedran wasn't wrong. This place wasn't meant for her. She walked back to Temric and leaned in close. "I can wait outside," she told him quietly in his dialect of Sothron.

"She is my teacher," Temric told him. "I want her with me."

"Teacher?"

"She speaks much languages."

That didn't matter to anyone, really, but like a tiny mountain flower opening from a bud, a little gratitude, a little color, opened inside her. Temric was a good man, and he was being a good friend.

"How many languages do you speak?" the man asked, and then he smiled that same unpleasant smile as before. "Just curious."

She'd met with this mocking disdain at Nuvar College nearly every day. She dared him with a long stare to tease her again.

She had to be careful, though. Temric needed to have access to this place. And what good was her pride anyway? She was no longer a Maiyem. She could shame herself utterly, and it wouldn't touch her family. It wouldn't matter to anyone at all, except herself.

Maybe not even herself, she realized with a growing unease.

"Billie, would you mind naming the languages you've learned?" Temric asked her in Sothron.

She didn't want to. She would do it, though, for Temric. "Kilhellion, conversational Thedran, poetic Thedran, classic Sothron, Sothron Ruvall dialect, Nuum dialect, Varas dialect, Kenta dialect, and Gahem dialect. I've begun Gurra and Arrak." There was something else. Temric had just asked. "And Markan." Her voice failed her toward the end. She didn't want to be here anymore.

"I think teacher isn't the right word," he told Billie quietly in Sothron. "How do you say interpreter in Thedran?"

She told him.

"Interpreter," Temric told him, a victorious tone in his voice. He stood straighter than he usually did, shoulders back, and offered the man the books in an imperious way. "I finished with these. I be back tomorrow." And with that, Temric turned and walked toward the doors.

Billie followed him back out into the sunlight. The gentle wind blowing from the sea had cleared the worst of the dust, and the sun glowed with a piercing brightness. Instinctively she set down her bags so she could check her shawl. It was still pinned in place. She adjusted it so that it no longer covered her mouth.

"Now I understand." Temric waited until she picked up her bags, then strode angrily down the street.

"Understand what?" With the bags weighing her down, it wasn't easy to keep up with his long paces. She hoped he wasn't doing that on purpose because he was angry at her. She didn't have the heart to fight back if he was.

"Why you were arguing with that man, and how you could be so enraged that you'd want to kill him when he suggested that you were a beggar," Temric ranted. "I'm ready to kill him myself."

She struggled to follow his logic. "Because they didn't want me in the library?"

"Because of the way that people treat you." He let out an exasperated huff. "The sailors, I assumed, were just being crude and rude because they were bored and wanted to pick a fight with you. Are people always this disrespectful to you?"

She stopped, overwhelmed by a rush of emotions that only had a little to do with how she was treated by strangers.

Temric realized belatedly that she wasn't alongside him and walked back to her.

She wanted to say yes, everyone treats me as if they've hated me their whole lives, but that wasn't true. "It just feels like it sometimes. Like today."

They'd reached a crossroads. The sky was darkening, and the numerous sacred lights on posts and buildings now seemed brighter in the growing shadows. The streets were just as crowded as ever, flowing around them as if she and Temric were a tiny island. She stood in a small place where she mattered, surrounded by a sea of indifference.

Temric gazed at her with worry carved deeply into his face. The fine particles of dust in the air caught the colors of sunset, lending a golden quality to his skin, and warming the buildings around them with a glow like firelight.

He'd said that he'd hoped to finish his business in Ben Ariim quickly so that he could return home. She understood. She'd wanted that for herself.

"I know something is wrong. Something happened." Temric touched her shoulder, then pulled his hand back when she looked at it. "Please," he said softly. "Will you do me the honor of confiding to me the cause of your distress?" The unusual formality of his words overflowed with respect. He might not have spoken to her that way if he knew …

*I'm disowned,* she tried to say, but she couldn't force herself to say it.

This hadn't been the result of her father's momentary rage.

Billie dropped her bags, unable to bear their weight along with the growing understanding of not just what was happening to her, but why.

In their place, she would have done the same thing.

*Brian has to be alive. He has to. Even if he wanted me to be disowned, I just want him to be alive.* Billie clung to that hope as tightly as she could.

If he was still alive …

If he still lived, she could endure anything. "I've been disowned." An unexpected chill passed through her, as if a gust of wind from Mount Cross had passed through her. She hugged herself for warmth. The thought of her family, friends, and the tribe turning their backs on her stabbed deep into her empty gut. She tried to tell Temric that she'd learned about it earlier today, but she choked.

Gods, this had to be so awkward for him to see her like this.

Somewhere nearby a seagull let out a long series of cries that sounded intensely lonely and filled with pain.

"Disowned?" He whispered the word, and she knew then that he understood her shame. "Why?"

"I don't know, not for certain." *I don't want to know. Not really.* She struggled to speak. Her throat swelled and her vision clouded. He kept looking at her. A Kilhellion might have turned their back, might have given her time to compose herself. She turned away instead and pressed the heels of her hands into her eyes, sparking flashes and spots behind her lids.

"How did you learn about it?"

When she crossed her arms, the heels of her hands were wet. "A ship's captain. A letter."

"What did the letter say?"

"I don't know. I can't read. You know I can't read!" She sobbed with frustration and sucked in a hard breath. She had to stop thinking about it or she'd start to wail and this wasn't the place, the time …

"Do you want me to read it for you?" he asked gently.

Billie turned on him, shocked by the idea. "Gods! No!"

He backed up a step and held up his hands, palms out, in surrender. "I'm sorry."

He didn't deserve to have her yelling at him. "No, I'm sorry." She had to not think about it. She was afraid if she thought about it too much, she'd lose her mind.

He lowered his hands and cautiously stepped closer again. She forced herself to look into his eyes. They were blue, one of the most common colors among Kilhellions, but his long face, the smallness of those eyes, the unruly curls of light brown hair, and his unusually long limbs, were foreign. It made it easier to shove as much as she could about home out of her mind. "It's a gracious offer. But …"

"But not here, not now," he said tenderly. "I understand."

"Thank you." She whispered the words and then breathed through her nose, which had begun to run. She sniffed and swallowed the salt and then rubbed her face across her sleeve. The wool was so fine, so soft. It was the best clothing she'd ever worn.

Now wasted on her.

"Billie."

She looked up into his eyes again, determined to keep her chin up this time.

He took her face in his hands. Once again his touch steadied her. "You're not alone. Do you understand? You're not alone. You have friends. You have me."

It shouldn't have hurt. It should have made her happy. But she knew what he apparently had forgotten.

He still had a home, and he was leaving for that home as soon as he could.

Nonetheless, she was grateful, more grateful than she could say at the moment.

He released her face and offered his hand. She slung her bags onto her shoulders and took it.

They walked hand in hand. For a long time he said nothing. It gave her time to stop thinking about all the things that hurt. Instead, she looked around at the buildings. She didn't really see anything, though. Her mind felt numb.

"Have you seen much of Ben Ariim?" he asked.

Thank the Gods that he didn't ask her anything more about what had happened today. "No, not really."

"Ruvall was big," he said.

"Yes," she agreed. Ruvall was vast. She made herself think about the buildings covered in vines, and the flowers and constant bird song, and the beautiful people, and their beautiful clothes, but avoided thinking about how much they hated her there. That part didn't matter. She would never go back.

"But Ben Ariim is something else," he said, his voice quickening with enthusiasm. "Ruvall is about the same size as my home city. I could imagine learning every street eventually. But this? And I hear that Kal Ariim is even bigger."

"Really?" She wasn't all that interested, but she liked listening to him talk.

"I learned that there are almost a quarter million people that live in Ben Ariim," he said. "Would you like to know how much is a quarter of a million?"

She sighed. "They tried to teach me counting at the college, too. Once I figured out the measures without counting, they finally left me alone."

"Sorry." He squeezed her hand gently. "I think it's remarkable that you learned how to measure out medicines without calculating weights and volumes."

"It's all about seeing the proportions," she explained, weary of talking about it just a few words in. It would make no difference to either of them if he understood or not.

"Proportions are mathematical constructs," he offered a bit too casually.

"Not like that. I *feel* them. It makes me wonder if no one outside of the Kilhells can bake bread without using scales and reading the numbers. My mother measures by eye." *Mother ...* "I weigh things in my hands. There's more than one way."

"Yes. The bread-making comparison helps me understand. My ..." He hesitated. "A baker I knew measured all her cooking by eye and hand as well," he said. "She told me it was all about achieving the right texture."

He was hiding something there, but she respected his privacy. It was none of her business anyway.

"I've started to read Thedran aloud," he offered with enthusiasm. "And I try to talk to myself in Thedran sometimes. I know I'm still making a lot of mistakes, but I don't care as much as I used to."

"The reading and the trying will help," she assured him. "But speaking to people will help the most. You should speak Thedran with me from now on."

He made a face. "I hear Thedran all day. I miss Sothron."

Her mind darted in a direction she didn't want to go. She quickly jerked it back to the conversation. "Sothron is a beautiful language, but Thedran is beautiful too, and very charming, full of easy rhymes and synonyms. It's the perfect language for long songs and even longer poems."

"Synonyms?" He tried the word out and didn't find it to his liking.

"Words that mean the same thing, or almost the same thing. A related word is nuance. It's a difference between similar meanings that creates a small but important change to context."

"Thank you for speaking slowly. I think I understood most of that," he answered equally slowly.

"Your pronunciation is very good." Her voice was coming back, and she didn't feel so cold inside.

"I listen to people talk while I'm eating my meals," he said. "I'm starting to hear the—differences—between the letters now. When I began, I couldn't hear the difference between iim in Ariim and eam in dream. I can't reliably say it, but at least I can hear it. I've been practicing. Ariim. Dream. Ariim. Dream."

"That's good," she said, and it really was. Ariim still wasn't as bright as it should be, but he was capturing the deeper sound of dream, just a little further back in his mouth and wider in the mouth as well, as opposed to the forward, short, almost aggressive Ariim. "But you should practice Aliiren's name too. If you practice Aliiren and Ariim back and forth, your mouth will learn not just to make the sound following the arr but also the ell."

Aliiren. She wondered if he'd reached his teacher in time.

If he hadn't, he would bear his pain silently, staring into a flame, or quietly sketching sacred symbols as he so often had on the ship.

"You say arr different than I do," he observed with a short laugh.

"You're trying to swallow it," she agreed. "Arr is more … airy. Around the tongue close to the teeth. Not back in the throat. And you push a little air out at the same time."

"But not trilled."

"No," she agreed with a smile. "There's no trilling in Thedran."

They discussed more things of language and pronunciations, switching to different dialects of Sothron when Temric grew frustrated by his limitations. That helped her improve her understanding of Sothron culture as well as nuances in the language. She welcomed the distraction, the camaraderie, and the less crowded streets. In fact, where he'd led her was very quiet, with only a few people about.

Most of them appeared to be lovers.

"Where are we?" she asked.

"The pleasure district."

She blushed as hotly as she'd ever had in her life, mostly because it was so unexpected. Temric was undeniably handsome in his own, boyish way, but she'd never felt anything more than friendship toward him. He'd only ever behaved like a friend toward her too. Well, he'd blushed a few times, but Temric seemed to blush easily.

Now the hand holding, which had been comfortable, felt awkward.

He hadn't flirted with her at all. Not once.

Maybe he was shy.

She needed to know if his feelings had grown beyond hers. She fervently hoped that she'd misunderstood the situation. She'd seen a friendship destroyed by misplaced ardor. Even more horribly, she'd watched a friend fade into a shadow of themselves as their longing led them to sacrifice everything about themselves in service to someone in a bonded pair. "Is there a reason you brought me here?" Billie looked up into his eyes, searching for a spark, a blush, anything that would let her know if they were walking toward disaster.

"To meet Aliiren." He pronounced the Thedran name much better that time. "We've been meeting just about every good evening for supper, and then I spend the good nights and true nights with him in the Light Temple."

"Oh." Along with the embarrassment, which at least felt better than shame, disappointment weighed her down as much as the bags she carried. Not that she had ever expected that pursuing Aliiren would lead to anything. He clearly didn't want to be pursued—not by her, anyway. At least now she knew it was because he preferred men, and not because she was Kilhellion, or because he thought she smelled bad.

Which reminded her of that man who'd called her a vagrant. "Do I smell bad?"

His head jerked in surprise. "No. Of course not." Maybe he read something in her expression that asked for more detail, because he looked her over in a way that reminded her of how her mother used to appraise a pony's condition and gait. "You're a little rumpled and I suppose you smell a little sweaty, but it's not unpleasant."

The trace of relief she felt gave her a brief respite from thoughts of Aliiren.

"Don't worry about it. We're not going to a pleasure garden. It's a chocolate shop."

Aliiren had mentioned chocolate before. She'd only had it a handful of times. She wasn't sure she liked it. Its bitterness and rich, strong flavor was uplifting, like most good medicines, but there were much better-tasting indulgences, like honey cakes, or mint tea with milk and honey.

Temric pursed his lips. "There *are* bath houses all through here, and they're not as expensive as the pleasure gardens. It's the custom, I've learned, to have a bath, a manicure, a shave, and all those sorts of things before you visit a pleasure garden." The formality had returned to his words, and the sense of respect. "Would you like to take a bath? My treat. For helping get me to Ben Ariim safely. And," he added with a smile, "also because I think you could use some pampering. I would consider it a privilege, and it would give me great pleasure if you accepted. Besides, I haven't repaid you for the excellent massage you gave me."

The way he put it, how could she refuse? "Thank you." She didn't want to wait to see Aliiren, though. "How is Aliiren? Did he reach his teacher in time?"

Temric sighed. "No."

Maybe if he'd stayed with the ship instead of going with her, he would have made it in time. Did he resent her for leading him astray?

A shout interrupted her worrying. And it wasn't an ordinary shout, either. It was the sort of strangled, desperate cry she remembered from girlhood—a sound of pain, and fear.

Her despair fell away, and clarity took its place. The colors returned to the world, so bright that the street looked as if it was lit by red-stained daylight. Battle liquor began to flow through her veins, and her strength swelled.

Billie strode toward the sound. She hunted for its source, heart quickening. And then she heard steel on steel.

"Sounds like a duel," Temric said, trotting to keep up with her. "We should probably stay out of it."

Or someone innocent might be fighting for their lives.

She followed a long, blank wall with greenery behind it. The wall went on and on. Finally, she found a way around it. She turned into a narrow alley between a walled garden full of trees and another walled-in place where water gurgled and splashed. The sounds of a hard-pressed fight were more intense now: grunting, another softer cry of pain, cursing. And then someone cried out, "Watch out!" in Thedran.

Billie dropped her bags, drew her sword, and sprinted. The alley ended in an awkward crossroads with another alley, a wide place with a little building that could be used as an emergency shelter for anyone caught out over true night. In that awkward space battled a man wielding a rapier alongside a huge black horse, a man in silk and steel armor with two short swords, another man with a hooked axe, an unarmed boy in torn silks, a half-dressed woman with a dagger in each hand ...

... and all but the boy were trying to kill Aliiren.

## Chapter Nineteen

<hr>

# Blood

<hr>

*Ben Ariim, Arrak Thedra*
*4th Meet Day of Sun Month*

**B**illie could only guess what was happening. She had to trust her heart, and her eyes. Aliiren was trying to protect the boy, a boy who was the only unarmed person in the fight.

She knew what she had to do.

She launched herself at the armored man and swung, hard.

Her blade chopped through silk, flesh, bone, and took off his arm at the elbow.

"Shit!" The woman bolted down an alley.

A blink later the man began to feel the pain. He screamed with disbelief and agony.

Aliiren's eyes widened, and his mouth gaped in horror.

The man with the hooked axe whirled into Billie. She struggled to fend him off. Even the glancing power of his axe shocked her grip. It took all her skill and no small amount of luck to avoid taking a full strike on her blade, or worse, into her body. He was good, sure of himself, with a cold look in his eyes that told her he thought he'd have no trouble killing her, as he'd killed many others.

But he wasn't her first either, and he was no hellion. She let him hook her sword to yank her closer. His own strength helped her throw her weight into him. His eyes went wide as they overbalanced together, and he grunted as they hit the ground, hard. She felt him pull a dagger. She grabbed his wrist, slammed her forehead into his face. His teeth cut her forehead. He looked strong, but surprisingly he wasn't.

He wasn't determined and cold anymore. Terror shone in his eyes as he bucked under her. They wrestled for the dagger for what seemed like an eternity. Their gasping breaths seemed unnaturally loud, easily heard over his friend's pained cries. She twisted the dagger out of his hand while he tried to free the axe from her sword. She drove the dagger into his throat. He tried to say something. She looked away from his fear and suffering for several heartbeats while he weakened and his movements slowed.

His friend's screaming abruptly cut off into choking sounds.

She surged up, expecting that someone else would be on her, but the man with the horse had mounted and was trying to escape. Billie gave chase, her blood hot to catch the coward.

As he rode he stared back at her, something deeper than fear widening his eyes. Rage seemed to turn his pupils crimson, his bloodless lips pulled back to reveal clenched teeth in a grimace that reminded her of naked skulls.

"Billie!" Temric cried.

"Let him go." Aliiren's soft voice pulled her to a halt where Temric's hadn't.

Battle liquor still surged through her. It numbed her hands, but the rest of her body felt unnaturally alive. She wondered if this was what it was like to channel faerus. The colors in the world looked too bright, too vivid.

Then the trembling started.

It wasn't mortal terror that shook her body. The battle had gone well. Aliiren, and the boy, were fine. Temric was fine. That's what mattered the most.

No, it was Life and Death that overwhelmed her. They'd danced with her and the men she'd killed, moved through her, and through them. Those Gods didn't care who lived or died here. But Their power had swollen like a river in flood, had overflowed, and left behind this aftermath where she still breathed, and her heart still pumped blood within her. Meanwhile, the blood of others seeped onto the ground, their souls led away by Death, as hers would be someday.

Burned into her mind, the rictus grin and wild eyes of the man that had fled haunted her.

Aliiren shifted in her peripheral vision. When she looked up, their gazes met. He seemed haunted as well, but not by the rider.

He looked away.

Had she just done something monstrous in Aliiren's eyes?

Maybe Temric would find what she'd just done unforgivable.

She'd killed people.

At least, she'd killed one.

The other one was still, and silent. The scent of blood and piss was strong in the air.

To make certain, she checked each of the men to see if they were beyond a healer's aid.

They were. Very much so.

The one whose arm was off had a small but deep puncture wound under a steel plate in his armor. There was a lot of blood around that wound, as much if not more than what had come from his arm. The weapon that made the wound might have penetrated a lung, his heart, or a major blood vessel. Hopefully it quickly ended his suffering.

The precision behind that single puncture made her think about Aliiren's control when he danced. She wondered if this was his first, whether he'd wanted to do it, and how he felt about it now. He might have done it to end the man's life, as part of the fight, but he might have felt forced to do it to end the man's agony, agony that Billie had caused.

The boy they'd all been protecting wasn't exactly a boy, now that she had a better look at him. He was younger than her, like her brother, but still a man. Barely. He wore the fine silks and jewels and bells of a pleasurer. His large hazel eyes looked all the larger from his fear and the kohl painted around them. Even with his clothes torn and in disarray, a bruise swelling on his cheek and another on his forehead, dusty and scraped with his coils of black hair spiraling every which way, he was the most beautiful man she'd ever seen in her life. His skin, dusky in tone, was silken and smooth. Other than his wounds, there wasn't a single blemish or freckle. His poor bruised hands looked soft and manicured, and he was barefoot, with perfectly trimmed toenails and golden bells strung at his ankles. His youth and natural grace reminded her of the pure, effortless flow of a crystalline mountain stream.

She looked back at Aliiren. Once again he avoided her gaze and went to crouch beside the young man. "Are you bleeding?" A red gash on Aliiren's arm crossed the healed, branching scars from the hellion fight. The blood stain, almost black on his blue clothes, was still spreading and starting to drip.

The young man shook his head, then seemed to rethink the question. "I don't think so." His voice was warm and pleasant, but shaky. He touched his own face delicately, as if he might add to the bruises if he pressed too hard.

Billie settled onto her heels beside Aliiren. "Let me have a look at your arm."

He shook his head once.

"What in the hells is this?" Temric demanded.

"Thank you for saving me," the pleasurer told Aliiren, gazing with utter adoration into his eyes. It was a tender moment, but confusing too.

"Aliiren," Temric pleaded.

"I heard a cry for help," Aliiren told them. "It was four against one, and he was unarmed."

"So you don't know this boy," Temric said.

"No." Aliiren had his hands on the pleasurer now, helping him up. The young man looked like he needed the support. He was shaking more than ever and had gone ashen. She stood up and cupped his other elbow in case he fainted.

"Please tell me that Billie didn't just murder two people over a business dispute," Temric said.

Cold poured through Billie's veins at the thought.

"They tried to rape me," the pleasurer said shakily.

Temric's attitude softened. "I'm sorry."

The young man flinched from the commiseration. "I thought it was just the woman, and everything was all right, but then the men showed up, and they were rough, and I told them no." He clung to Aliiren's arm, back hunched. His perfume of jasmine, honey, rose and musk mostly covered the scent of blood.

"I'm a healer," she told him gently. "Is it all right if I assess you?"

He offered his right hand, palm up, without hesitation. She gently took his hand, closed her eyes, and chained all the nodes she could to her lotus node. Her vinus took only a moment to reach her palm and pierce his.

He had small channels almost like a healer, but they were unusually smooth, like a mage's. It made it easy to explore his entire body quickly without much risk of fever.

He was a mess. It was mostly bruises but his attackers must have punched him in the stomach several times, as his liver and spleen were not in the best of shape. She focused vinus on the worst of his hurts, allowing her gift to naturally enhance his own tiny flow of native vinus.

His blood pressure was low, his hands and feet were cold … he was in shock, and his whole body was still infused with fear liquor.

After a moment Billie withdrew. "He's not badly hurt, but he should see a healer. A proper healer."

"I just want to go home." His eyes teared up.

Aliiren put an arm around him. "Lean on me and tell me which way to go."

"And just leave the bodies here?" Temric asked, bewildered.

"We can deal with that after we get him home," Aliiren said.

"Oh Gods." Temric swept a hand over his face. "Gods."

The pleasurer took a few delicate steps, but then touched his hip. "My sword."

Billie spotted it near the little building. It hadn't been blooded. The delicate, jeweled thing was mostly decorative. It was brave of him to try to defend himself with such a light weapon against so many enemies. She picked it up, then saw a jeweled belt nearby. A broken link spoke of the force with which they'd handled him. Her heart hardened against the men she'd killed. The world was a better place without them. Maybe in the next life they would be better people.

She hoped so.

*Maybe there's a chance that I'll be a better person too.*

The thought penetrated her mind with the precision of Aliiren's blade. It implied things that she didn't want to think about, things that went against Life and all that It stood for. She shook it off.

"Maybe I should stay and explain what happened to the authorities," Temric said.

"A stranger in Ben Ariim with two dead men?" Aliiren gave him a sharp glance, then encouraged the pleasurer to start walking. "I wouldn't, Temric. If a Champion finds you, you'll probably be treated fairly, but what if it's a private guard, or a land holder, or a wealthy merchant? I don't want you to end up confined somewhere, being interrogated in who knows what way for who knows how long. Please. Stay with me." His golden eyes shifted to look into Billie's, and she felt the power of his strength, his mind, and the power to channel faerus within him like she was in the presence of a godling. "You as well." He looked away and the world felt colder for it. "Especially you."

Was he concerned about her, or did he want to make sure she wouldn't run so he could surrender her to justice?

She wasn't sure what justice meant in this place. Even so, she thrilled at the thought of meeting a Champion.

Anyway, things could hardly be worse for her.

Maybe Temric would defend her. She hoped so, anyway.

Or maybe, like her roommate at the college had been appalled by her bone flute, Temric might now be repulsed by her.

She picked up her bags and trailed behind everyone else.

It was full dark by the time they reached the pleasure garden where the young man worked, not because it was far, but because he walked so slowly, mincing his steps. He took them to a well-lit street edged by a high wall on one side, and businesses with ornately carved stone walls and doors on the other. Living spaces above the businesses had balconies with elaborately wrought rails festooned with flowers. The pleasurer led them to an innocuous-looking gate in the high wall. They followed him through the gate into the strangest, loveliest garden Billie had ever seen.

It was so overgrown that she could hardly see down the path through which the pleasurer led them, but what she could see sparkled with glass and false fruit made of gems intermingled with real fruit and tiny, star-like sacred lights. The scent of flowers mingled with the ripe fruit, creating an intoxicating perfume. Water trickled and bubbled and splashed in hidden places. A slight breeze stirred glass and crystal wind chimes to harmonize with the fountains and rippling pools—was that a living fish of gold whose fins stirred the surface of a dark pond tucked beneath ferns and fig trees?

Someone like her, stinking of sweat and blood, who'd done the things she'd done, shouldn't be in this place.

At last they came to a low building. The roof was covered with more garden, which made it hard to guess the building's size. As the others descended a few steps to a thick stone door covered in Life blessings, she lingered back. She'd severed the lives of two strangers from their families and friends. It was instinct, an instinct that she hadn't known that she had in her. She wasn't sure she liked it. Maybe she was too quick to fight. Maybe she was worse than an animal, because she had a mind and she hadn't used it.

"Jasmine!" The stricken cry startled her. "God of Life, Jasmine, what happened?" It was a rich voice, deep for a woman's, mid-tone for a man, ambiguous but lovely. "What did you do to your face?" Those last words sounded unpleasantly sharp.

Aliiren murmured something.

"Come in. All of you, come in," the voice answered warmly.

"Billie." Temric was waiting by the door for her.

Where would this lead her?

She thought of the public shelter, and Hova, and Hawa. Realistically, they offered a path she could manage on her own.

Hova and Hawa didn't know anything about what had happened on the dock, or what she'd done on a street not far from here.

They thought she was on her way home.

They could be anywhere, thinking nothing more of her.

*I could run. Hide. I could give myself a new name.*

"Billie?"

*Even if no one who knows what I've done ever finds me, I can't rid myself of who I really am.*

She gripped her arm over the place where the tattoo of the badger was forever inked into her skin. But covering it felt like sacrilege. She let her hand slip, let the tattoo show.

*Even if I could, I wouldn't want to be anyone else.*

She went down the stairs, no longer shaking, but once again the world seemed darker.

As she stepped through the door into perfumed air, air that was much cooler than the evening outside, she shivered. But once they moved through the large entry room with its mirrors and crystal and chandeliers filled with jeweled lights, they entered a warmer room.

No, it wasn't a room. It was a balcony overlooking a different kind of garden.

Amid palms and ferns and orchids, pleasurers engaged their guests in intimate conversations. Some were fully clothed, but many pleasurers were partially clothed at best, and the rest wore only jewelry. No one was having sex, but the air was thick with lust and incense and wine. A waterfall moved large fans that turned along the ceiling. Couples and trios sat by a large fountain made of a deep green stone, while others chatted at the edge of a pool edged in jade and onyx.

On sight of Jasmine most of the pleasurers made exclamations of horrified concern. Several of them hurried up the spiral stairs to fuss over him. They took him from Aliiren's gentle hold and led him to a suspended platform in the center of the balcony. People below, working a wheel, lowered the platform and opened a little gate on the rails. Jasmine looked relieved to be there.

"What happened?" The man who addressed them could have as easily passed for a woman. He was ethereally beautiful, though he didn't match Jasmine even in Jasmine's state of disarray. He was a striking figure, poised and confident, and the slight signs of age on him leant him a sense of power. His filmy skirt draped from a jeweled belt at his waist down to diamond anklets, and he had diamond rings everywhere, including a piercing on his belly button and many along his ears. The brightness of his jewelry made his deep black skin look even more striking. The satiny sheen of his skin tempted Billie to touch him, but she wouldn't have dared. Once again she was keenly aware that she had blood on her hands, blood staining her sleeves, blood splattered across her chest and legs—everywhere.

"I believe he was lured into an ambush by a woman he thought was a client," Aliiren explained. "They planned to rape him."

The man's lips pressed into a thin line, and he narrowed his eyes. "Worse than that, I think. What was he thinking? There have been murders all over the city, murder rapes, disembowelments, bodies thrown in the canals ..." He seemed to realize that he was speaking angrily at Aliiren, as if it was his fault, and softened his tone. "The Champions have been hunting for the ..." He shuddered. "Gods. If he wasn't so valuable—" He closed his eyes, lifted his hands up, then lowered them as if he was pressing something down. When he opened his eyes again, he was smiling. "But you saved him and I'm grateful." He put a hand on Aliiren's arm. Aliiren flinched back and with a silent apology the man eased away a half step.

Aliiren backed closer to Billie. "I'm sorry—I'm not used to being touched."

"Please, I'm the one who should apologize. That boy ..." This time he stretched his arms in front of him like he was pushing something away. He shimmied his whole body as if a simple denial wasn't nearly enough to express his upset. "Never mind. My name is Spire. Please, accept my hospitality."

Aliiren, oddly, looked to Billie. She shook her head. She didn't belong here.

"We would be honored," Aliiren said inexplicably. "Thank you."

Had he just spoken for her against her will? She wanted to be angry at him, but at the same time, where else would she go tonight?

Spire looked relieved. "Excellent." He clasped his hands together and smiled. "Wonderful. You have no idea how precious our Jasmine is to us. Please. Come in." He gestured down the spiral stairs. "Are any of you hurt?"

Aliiren looked to Billie again. She shook her head, though for the first time in her life, she wasn't sure. She didn't trust the lack of pain and fever. She felt hardly anything at all.

But Aliiren was hurt. He'd stopped bleeding, but the gash on his arm looked angry through the gap in his sleeve.

"What a stupid question," Spire said. "Of course you've been injured. May I have your name?"

"Aliiren. Protector Aliiren."

Spire smiled enigmatically. "I've heard of you, Protector Aliiren." Aliiren looked surprised, though he quickly smothered the expression. "Welcome." Aliiren made his way down the golden spiral staircase. "And your name, my most welcome guest?"

"Temric." Temric smiled, but his glazed eyes darted everywhere, and his lips were parted. Was he scared?

"Welcome, Temric." Spire watched him take the first few steps down, then looked to Billie.

"I should go," she said. It wasn't just that she felt uncomfortable here. These people were here to enjoy themselves. She wanted no part of that.

"You're Kilhellion?" His gaze traveled over her bloody clothes and back up to her eyes.

She nodded.

To her surprise, he smiled. "Welcome, Kilhellion. What's your name?"

"Billie M ... Billie." *I'm not a Maiyem.*

"Looks like you did the lion's share of the work to save our boy, Billie." His smile tightened with grim approval. "Please, allow me take one of your bags."

Aliiren was watching her from the base of the stairs. His brows peaked and he clasped his hands to his chest, silently pleading with her.

*Damn it.*

"The stairs are too narrow for you to carry both. Or, if you'd prefer, we can use the platform," Spire continued.

"No, that's all right. I'll walk." She offered her lighter bag. He took its weight well, reminding her of Tilla's strength, and gestured. Billie went down the stairs. The spiral gave her a constantly changing view not just of the exotic room but underneath the balcony where gorgeous people assembled trays of food and made exotic alcoholic concoctions with fruit. Her stomach lurched unpleasantly. It was probably hunger combined with the effects of fear liquor. At least, she hoped it was something simple like that. She drew in breaths through her nose and out through her mouth.

"We're full," Spire informed them. "But I have some neophytes who would be honored to serve you tonight. They're not permitted to give you more than a kiss. But later we can fulfill every desire."

It didn't seem right that it wouldn't really be their choice whether or not to kiss her.

"That won't be necessary," Aliiren said.

"Food and drink, please," Temric said in fairly well-spoken Thedran.

They were looking to Billie now. "I, uh ..."

"She's hungry," Temric said with an apologetic glance to Billie. "I don't know if she's eaten anything in days."

Aliiren frowned and looked away from her. Did that make him angry? Why?

"Let's start with baths," Spire said. "And attention from our healers, and food ... and then we'll see what the evening will bring." Though his smile never faded, there was something calculating about his look. He crooked a finger, and they all followed him like ducklings after their mother.

## Chapter Twenty

<><><><><><><><><><><><><><><><><><><><><><><><><><><><><><><><><><><><><><><><>

# What is Owed

<><><><><><><><><><><><><><><><><><><><><><><><><><><><><><><><><><><><><><><><>

*The Iris and Golden Pear Pleasure House, Ben Ariim*
*4th Bless Night of Sun Month*

Dressed in a borrowed silk robe of red and gold, Billie stretched out on pillows in a private room where thick, elaborate rugs had the give of well-made seat cushions. Murals on the walls sparkled with jeweled flowers and fruit. A neophyte rubbed her feet, while another massaged her hands with almond oil lightly scented of roses and pear. Her parched skin soaked up the moisture. Her hair felt soft as silk from an exotic soap, and her skin too. It had been a long time since she'd felt this clean and relaxed.

They gave Billie, Aliiren and Temric wine with little bits of fruit that had been soaked in a liquor made from king fruit. They told her that the roots of a king fruit were as big around as a person, and tapped so deep that even desert horses—assuming she'd heard right because horses couldn't dig all that well—couldn't get to the bottom of them. But it was the top part that they made the liquor from. The way they described it, the fruit was covered entirely in needles as long as hair pins, and when the fruit was ripe, it was as big as a boar's head. The spines had to be clipped with special shears or whoever tried to handle it would bleed to death from all the stab wounds.

Billie was pretty sure they were having her on, but she chose to believe it anyway.

She surrendered to their attentions in silence, inviting sleep to claim her. But it didn't. So she half-listened to the neophytes tell Temric, at his request, stories they'd heard about the first true night.

She didn't know who said what to whom, or how anyone had found them, but Larani and Edrion burst in, followed by a trio of neophytes. Suddenly the last thing she wanted was sleep. After greeting Aliiren and hugging Temric, they hugged her. Edrion kissed her on the cheek, and they sat close on either side of her. They were together! Brother and sister had found each other. She smiled so hard with relief that her cheeks hurt. Billie put her arms around their shoulders. It wasn't a dream. They were real, and they were here.

As soon as a neophyte brought her a cup of wine, Larani began the story of how the ship was freed, mostly thanks to her luck of course. She made it sound funny, and everyone else laughed, but Billie's gut knotted. *I chose wrong.* She drank to cover her pain.

*Silver Parrot* reached Ben Ariim just before dawn on Trade Day, the day before Billie, Aliiren, Temric and Edri arrived in Ben Ariim. Billie tried to keep her expression from changing, but her eyes closed against a rush of complicated feelings when Larani wondered aloud if Tilla got passage to Port Sellon right away. Temric's mouth tightened into a line. Edri must have noticed, because he interrupted by describing how he, Billie, Temric and Aliiren had to run for shelter just before true night.

It wasn't as if Billie wouldn't wonder about Tilla just because Edri changed the subject. She was just glad that no one asked her what had happened to Brian, and what she was still doing in Ben Ariim.

Temric picked up the conversation after that. He rambled about buildings called hives shaped like a half-buried birdhouse gourd filled with thousands of people. Billie didn't know what a birdhouse gourd was, or thousands were, but she assumed thousands was a lot, and when she said so Temric shook his head and laughed. She grinned back at him, because he didn't think less of her because she was illiterate and innumerate, and that made her happy.

Aliiren listened with his eyes closed while a neophyte warmed fragrant oil between her palms and then drew her fingers through his tresses, deepening the sun-bleached reddish tones in his hair to a ruddy black, and the rest to a deep obsidian. Then she combed his rippled hair into long, heavy waves that flowed over her thighs. The few times Aliiren did speak, he murmured poetry about Light. Those undulating, subtly rhymed words held them all rapt and silent as they strained to hear his soft voice. Then the Rill told a story and he laughed, covering his mouth and sometimes his whole face as if he was embarrassed by his own happiness.

These people—her beloved friends—made the evening bearable. She drank, and her vision blurred, and things seemed easier.

She would survive. She would find a way.

Temric, now swaying a bit and slurring, told stories about rivers of lava and palaces made of ice. And he scared them all with a story about a man who once saw a hellion marketplace. Billie secretly wanted to see it for herself. All except for the part where they were selling people as slaves, and other people, even babies, for, Gods, stew and roasts … like they were cattle.

Cattle.

The neophyte tried to soothe Aliiren's growing tension by rubbing his shoulders, but Aliiren sat up and shifted away from her. Billie and Temric were tense now too, thinking of the demon, and of the smell in the house where they'd found Rosie the now-orphaned baby. The hellion marketplace would have smells like that in it, and human beings, still warm, hanging in webs, their souls defiled and promised to hellion gods, hopelessly lost forever in the Deceiver's maze, the Devourer's gullet, or stretched and torn to nothingness by the Destroyer.

Suddenly Temric looked to Billie and pointed at her, his finger wavering in the air like a child trying to point with a sword that was too heavy for him. "The Old Gods vanished on the first true night," he said. "What if we found a way to bring them back? Would that stop true nights from coming?"

"Why are you asking me?"

Aliiren made a scoffing noise. "The Old Gods were destroyed."

Temric leaned sideways, like a tree with breaking roots slowly falling over. The neophyte playing with his curls gently pushed him upright before he lost his balance. "Were they? Is that what really happened?"

"Yes," Aliiren answered tightly.

His answer killed that part of the conversation. Still, Billie kept thinking about what the world would be like without true nights.

*I might have made it home in time.*

Trade would become less risky. Maybe even remote places like the Kilhells would see more foreigners, and that …

That might lead to more Kilhellions learning how to count, and read, and write, not just the scribes. It might mean that many more Kilhellions would travel, not just out of necessity, but to explore, to learn, to celebrate important occasions …

Maybe if there was more travel, more people would meet more Kilhellions, and realize that Kilhellions weren't all brutes.

She'd killed two people today, and part of why they were celebrating now was because she'd helped Jasmine, but she was the one who'd started the killing. Before that, although people were getting hurt, no one had died.

She didn't want to be here anymore, where Larani and Edrion sang a Rill song to try to lighten the heaviness that now filled the room. But where would she go? And she couldn't leave with the robe.

They had her clothes, even her belt and her blade, because everything had to be cleaned.

Even now, when she felt like nothing would be right again, she wondered if she would have reached home in time if there was no true night.

*In time for what?*

*What happened?*

She realized she didn't want to know.

Her restlessness drove away the neophyte rubbing her feet to work on Larani's feet instead. "Can I fetch you something?" the neophyte now rubbing her shoulders asked.

She didn't know why she wanted to look at it now. "I don't know. Maybe." Even if they'd finished cleaning the blood out of her clothes, they wouldn't be dry.

Just then the door opened, and Jasmine came in. The neophytes abandoned them all to hug him and kiss him and coo over him. He was groomed now, dressed only from the waist down in embroidered sapphire and gold silk skirts. A diamond necklace circled his neck and dripped teardrop sparkles down to a massive stone in the shape of a cat's pupil. But his beauty didn't reside in his exceptional figure or his glamorous costume. It was his face, as perfect a face as might adorn a God if they were human. An almost feminine tenderness balanced with clear masculinity, confident, cocky and coy. His hazel eyes were rimmed in fresh kohl, so large that they seemed to see all the world as clearly as Light itself.

He went to Aliiren. "May I hug you?" he asked.

Aliiren stood up, his body moving with the suppleness of liquid. "You may."

He'd given permission, but Billie could tell that the strength in Jasmine's arms and the tender way that he held Aliiren close was far more intimacy than the Light Protector expected. But Jasmine let him go after a breath, then gave him a sweet kiss on the cheek in parting. "You saved my life and spared me immense pain. In all things, Protector Aliiren, I'm yours." With that, he removed the diamond necklace and moved to place it around Aliiren's neck.

"I can't accept," Aliiren protested, leaning away as if Jasmine held a necklace of spiders.

Jasmine held up a palm. With deliberate grace he lowered the diamond jewel and then the diamond strand until it formed a glittering puddle in his hand. "If not for you, then for Light?"

Was this a gifting thing? Her hand had tightened on her glass. She forced herself to relax and set it aside.

"I wasn't the only one who helped you," Aliiren told him.

Jasmine smiled. His bruises were no longer swollen, but they were deeply discolored. Somehow they looked cute on him. He was a bit flushed with fever. He must have received a lot of healing. "I have gifts for the others too. Please? It's not just from me. The whole garden wants you to have it."

*Oh no.* Billie looked to Temric for help, but he wasn't looking her way. He was watching Aliiren and Jasmine.

Aliiren bowed his head with a sigh and the neophytes applauded while Jasmine draped it over his shoulders. The diamonds looked exquisite against his dark skin, but he looked uncomfortable in them. Billie didn't blame him. No matter how much Jasmine's life was worth, that was a horrific amount of wealth. She wondered if the gift would make Aliiren beholden to Jasmine and the garden. No doubt the necklace was worth more than a letter of gratitude.

"I'm being so rude!" Jasmine exclaimed as he turned toward the Rill. "Jasmine of the Iris and Golden Pear, Favorite of Ben Ariim. You must be Larani and Edrion."

"Thank you for hosting us," Larani said brightly as a neophyte settled in behind her and drew her into his lap.

Jasmine quirked his brows artfully at Edrion, which made Edrion laugh for some reason. And then Jasmine looked to Billie. "You fought to protect me."

She wasn't sure what he intended to do, but she was afraid she wouldn't like it and that it would be rude to refuse. "I'm glad you made it home safely, and that you're going to be all right."

"You also healed me," Jasmine said, making his way among the pillows in a way that was like a dance, but without pretense. "The healers told me that without your help, I would have had to have been carried home, and that I would have been sick for weeks."

She didn't know what to say. She didn't want praise. More than ever, she wanted to leave, find some dark alley, and throw up in it.

"I wish Kilhellion skirts were more fashionable in Ben Ariim. I love that they have pockets," he said as he untied the sash on his skirt. "Spire managed to find one."

She gasped as the silk skirt parted to reveal a velvet wonder in sapphire, navy and black with embroidery everywhere. The embroidery had been sewn in the traditional diamond and triangle patterns of the mountain tribes to which she'd once belonged. He slowly unlaced the sides and then let it drop to pool at his feet. He was naked beneath except for a diamond belt and golden bell anklets.

She'd been wrong when she'd thought of his face as outshining his body. He was beautiful throughout, no part lacking in perfection despite the bruises. It was hard to breathe, looking at him. She hated the thought that he sold that body to whomever could pay. She wanted him to choose freely, as Kilhellions chose. But then, maybe he didn't care about that. Maybe he'd feel sorry for her family as they labored to keep colts alive when they were born in the middle of a fierce storm. Would he pity her if he knew how her tribe struggled when their winter supplies dwindled?

She didn't know, and nothing in his expression gave away his secrets.

He put his gold and sapphire silk skirts back on and smiled at her.

He couldn't be serious. As much as she loved the skirt, where exactly would she wear it, and with what? "I can't," she told him. "It's too much." She wanted to tell him that the necklace was even more insane, but she didn't want to tromp all over Aliiren's business. At least the diamonds would go to his temple and not stay with him personally.

Jasmine poured the supple fabric behind her, just out of her reach, then sat beside Edrion. A neophyte gave him a cut crystal glass of what they called punch, rightfully so because it would soon beat them all unconscious. "I insist. And so does everyone else. You've earned far better."

He was wealthier than Mount Cross' wealthiest chieftain, or so he seemed. How he thought nothing of forcing this thing that was so costly and fine on her, when she didn't want it, filled her with anxiety. She supposed it would have been worse if he'd tried to give her money. But still.

Edri nudged her. She glanced over at him, and he smiled and mouthed words that reminded her.

Billie sighed. She did her best to forget her worries and confusion, so she could bring Jasmine's thoughtfulness and the quality of his 'gift' foremost in her mind. It was, after all, an immense gesture, regardless of its meaning and implications. "Thank you, Jasmine."

Rani rubbed her back reassuringly.

"You're welcome." Jasmine drank some punch, and smiled at Temric. "I have something for you too, but it won't be here until morning."

Temric's eyebrows peaked in surprise. "I didn't do anything."

*See?* She made sure both Rani and Edri noticed her gesture in Temric's direction, to draw attention to and emphasize his own confusion. *Even Temric thinks this is weird.* Edri smothered a laugh. Rani's brows rumpled, apparently not understanding Billie's meaning.

"You called Billie back from chasing that fiend," Jasmine said, unfortunately noticing, but kindly ignoring Billie's gesture. "And besides, this is my party. I can give gifts to whomever I want."

She really wanted to figure out how gifts worked, but gifting still made no sense to her. This didn't seem anything like what Temric had explained before. And the context—she'd fought to protect Aliiren and Jasmine. She'd killed to save Jasmine. Was that why this felt so different from the situation where her teacher had given her the book?

A word came to her mind that she understood better. Reward. In the Kilhells, rewards were offered in advance, a kind of agreed-upon price for a dangerous or difficult service that was well outside the duty or responsibility of anyone within the tribe. Bounties, in contrast, were sometimes offered to people outside of the tribe when necessary.

Rewards and bounties didn't strengthen the bond between people. Respect did that. Love did that. Trust did that. Rewards and bounties were neutral. The deed itself, if important or admirable, carried more weight than any compensation that might come with it. It was both an enticement and, if the endeavor was successful, a kind of earning, a wage given in exchange for the risk.

Maybe Jasmine's gifts were more like bounties. Rather than be drawn into a bond of friendship, born in crisis and nurtured by gratitude and appreciation, he could distance himself. It would reduce the intensity of what had happened by giving them these things as if the payment had been offered in advance. It might even be expected in this society, a kind of unspoken contract understood by the people of Ben Ariim.

If true, that made sense. The city—no, the world—was too big for things to work like they did on Mt. Cross. Maybe the way such a vast and varied society encouraged the sort of thing they'd done for Jasmine was through bounties, rather than a belief that everyone in Ben Ariim was part of one vast tribe. Maybe it was too impractical for every stranger to become an honorary tribal member whenever they defended someone's life or property, especially if such crises were commonplace in Ben Ariim.

Jasmine raised his glass. "A toast to my new friends."

*What?*

*I give up. I'm too drunk to figure this out.*

The door opened again. Neophytes brought in more food and drink and took away the dregs, even though they were still perfectly good. She wondered who they would give it to.

It didn't matter. Jasmine had implied that Temric had done something important when he'd told Billie not to chase after the man on the horse. "Why was it a good thing when Temric told me to stop?" Maybe she shouldn't have asked, but what she'd done, and how they'd reacted to her, still bothered her.

Jasmine's perfect brows rumpled artfully with confusion. "You might have gotten hurt. He wasn't worth it."

That made no sense. Either he was a rapist and murderer that had to be put down, or he wasn't. Stopping evil like that was worth the risk.

"Wait. What happened?" Larani asked.

"I'll tell the tale," Jasmine began eagerly in poetic Thedran.

"Excuse me, forgive me," Temric said, "but is Billie in danger? Aliiren, would you smart us?"

Aliiren looked to Jasmine, who looked a bit hurt, and she was sorry for that but at the same time she needed Aliiren to tell her the truth. He wouldn't pretty it up with half-truths and weak reassurances.

"Whether she's in trouble remains to be seen," Aliiren said with a frown. "It depends on who they were, and whether or not they were acting on their own."

On Mt. Cross, such words would imply a blood feud, a rogue tribe, or something even worse. Jasmine, though, didn't seem bothered by what Aliiren had said. "I've got an idea. You tell us what you saw." He took another swig of his drink.

"Everything?" Aliiren asked.

Billie realized that she had no idea how far things had gone with the attack before she'd arrived. At the very least, Jasmine had been badly beaten.

She knew what that felt like. Intimately.

Aliiren had seen at least some of what had happened to him.

"Don't worry about me," Jasmine told Aliiren. "I've suffered worse." As he drank, he gazed at Aliiren. His eyes seemed especially jewel-like over the glass' rim. When he lowered the glass, he had a very cold smile on his face. "Go on. I want to hear you tell it."

"I'm not going to tell a story," Aliiren told them softly, his gaze moving from one person to the next, ignoring not one neophyte nor guest until his gaze rested on Billie. She stared back into his golden eyes, dreading how he saw her. "I'm going to tell you all what my imperfect eyes saw, and what my imperfect mind understood."

*Do you think I'm a murderer?*

"I was taking the quiet ways between the gardens on my way to meet a friend," Aliiren began. "I heard a cry for help, and so I ran toward it, and I saw four people assaulting Jasmine. They weren't just trying to control him, or rape him. They weren't just trying to strip him naked, and they weren't drunk on lust. They weren't drunk at all, or angry. They were toying with him, and laughing." Anger tensed his face, and he took a breath. "Laughing. They were torturing him, and enjoying themselves. It was a game, and it looked well practiced. The fact that he'd managed to cry out for help was a miracle. He was so breathless and hurt ..." Aliiren shook his head. His voice had softened and warmed with suppressed rage, his mouth twisted with revulsion, and his eyes seemed to glow with his own unanswered questions. Why, he seemed to wonder, would anyone do that?

Billie could answer that, though she'd never hurt anyone who couldn't, or refused, to fight back.

It never had before, but it made her uneasy to remember how often she'd felt pleasure unleashing the power in her body in a good fight.

"I commanded them to stop, but they didn't, so I called on Light and got their attention," Aliiren told everyone. "That's when two of them attacked me. I didn't expect them to do that. I thought they'd be intimidated, or run, or try to explain themselves. But no. They attacked me and it took all of my training to fend them off. They were practiced, it seemed, not just at torturing people, but killing. And I wasn't." His gaze deepened on Billie's eyes. "I couldn't think. I had no time. I just reacted as I'd been taught. I was about to draw on Light to save myself when Billie arrived."

Everyone was looking at her now.

"She already had her blade drawn. In her eyes I saw that she understood what was happening. She knew what those people were. She knew

Jasmine and I needed help. She didn't hesitate. She went for the one who was the greatest threat to me before he even knew she was there, and cut off his arm. Then she threw her weight on the other like a lion taking down a gazelle and pierced his throat with his own dagger. She would have killed them all if Temric hadn't called her off." His tone was even, carefully controlled.

She still had no idea how he felt about what she'd done.

"The two survivors went in opposite directions, but I think she would have killed one and then hunted down and killed the other. Because she knew a fellow predator when she saw one." He lowered his gaze.

A predator? It was true, but it didn't sound like a good thing in the Thedran language.

"But unlike them, she doesn't prey on her own kind," Aliiren added. Was that approval, or an excuse?

"She was amazing," Jasmine enthused. "Like a Champion." Billie's mind spun with embarrassment. Jasmine smiled at her with a flash of inspiration in his eyes as bright as sunlight glancing off of water. "You should train at the Tower in Kal Ariim! You would pass the test. I know you would."

It wasn't just her father deriding her about it that made her feel like Jasmine was having fun at her expense. She'd heard stories of Champions her whole life, more than enough to know that she wasn't anything like a Champion. "Thank you," she allowed, her words on the verge of faltering. It was ridiculous. People trained in a Champion's Keep from youth, squired to Champions, and did great things before they even attempted to test.

Maybe Jasmine wasn't mocking her. Maybe he meant it as a compliment. She tried to take it that way while her cheeks burned.

"But will she be in trouble," Temric said, not-quite-asking.

"Why would she be in trouble? I witnessed it. Aliiren is a Light Protector. He witnessed it," Jasmine said. "I mean, it was shocking. Don't get me wrong. I've seen people executed but it's quick. Humane. People pray for them to take a better path in the next life." Her gut twisted with his words. Did he think she was cruel? Maybe she was, compared to the people of Ben Ariim. Maybe she was, compared to anyone outside the Kilhells. "Aliiren was almost right," Jasmine continued. "She wasn't like a lion. She was like …" His expression changed as their gazes met. "I'm sorry. I can see that it bothered you to have to do it."

Billie hadn't realized she'd been holding her breath until she let it out. "Yes. It bothered me. I know what it feels like to be cut, what they went through. And I wonder if I really did have to do it. I thought maybe Aliiren could have stopped them without killing them."

Jasmine looked like he was on the verge of laughing. She wasn't sure if she felt offended, or relieved.

Jasmine sighed and finished off his drink, then accepted another that was quickly offered by a neophyte. "It seems I'm going to have to tell this story the right way. Your version, Aliiren, was accurate. But you missed the injustices, the heroism, the dread, and hope. The horror, and the sweet relief of deliverance from a terrible fate. In short, all the important parts."

Larani clapped her hands. "Yes please! I would like to hear the way you tell it."

"Me too," Edrion pitched in enthusiastically.

"That is," Larani said with a look toward Aliiren, then Temric, and finally Billie, "if it won't bother you."

"Let me hear more," Temric said. Billie suspected that he wanted to understand Jasmine's thinking and the culture of Ben Ariim more than the story itself.

To be fair, so did she.

Aliiren sighed and nodded, his neutral expression veiling how he really felt.

Jasmine told it lavishly. He made them all suffer along with his sense of betrayal when the woman whistled for her companions to surround him. She could almost feel his terror and pain while he was beaten, mocked, and toyed with. Those people had promised that they would let him go if he went along quietly. He'd almost believed them, but then he'd sensed that once they had him where they wanted him, he'd never be free until his soul left his body.

Then he made her and Aliiren sound like a legendary Champion and a powerful Sage, with Temric as their clear-headed commander, taking charge when they were too impassioned by their heroism to see clearly.

All the while their glasses were never empty.

Aliiren fell asleep. Healers came to make sure they weren't in any danger, sent for by the sober and attentive neophytes. The healers prescribed water, and tea for everyone except Aliiren, who apparently had been drinking far less than any of them thought.

By then her clothes arrived, cleaner than they'd been in a long time. The leather sheath on her blade looked brand new. She had to check the knot work at the end to assure herself that it was in fact her own. She had a way of twisting the leather cord on parts of the knot that would be difficult if not impossible for someone to imitate. Someone had spent a lot of time with tiny brushes to make that come clean.

After the neophytes left, leaving with the ones that had brought her clothes, Temric got up and settled behind Billie. He leaned close and spoke softly so he wouldn't wake Larani, who was napping beside her. "I want to help you."

"Help me?" She'd spoken more loudly than she'd meant to, which drew Jasmine's curiosity, and unfortunately woke Larani.

She wasn't aware that she needed help.

And then she realized that maybe he meant money. "I'll be all right," she assured him, though she wasn't sure of that herself. What she absolutely didn't want was more gifting and rewards and owing and dependence on anyone, even if she liked them. She didn't know what it all meant, or even who she was anymore, to these people, or to Ben Ariim.

"Why does Billie need help?" Jasmine asked in very good Sothron.

Temric looked to her, and she shook her head. He sighed.

"What?" Jasmine demanded. "Please tell me."

"I, uh …." She didn't know what she wanted to admit. Nothing, really. But everyone seemed to expect it. "I guess I'm looking for work." That sounded too much like she was asking to be hired. "But I'm not good at anything, and …." This was getting worse and worse. "Never mind. I have—"

"But you're a healer," Jasmine protested.

"I only just started my training." And as she spoke those words, she realized that she didn't want to be a healer. Not here, and not like this.

"You're too modest," Larani told her warmly.

"I could make arrangements for you to apprentice with a healer," Jasmine assured her. "And when your apprenticeship is done, you could work here!" His enthusiasm woke Aliiren. Aliiren shifted, then sat up with a groan.

That surprised her. "I don't know," she admitted. It didn't feel right, looking after drunk guests, healing the occasional sprain, touching up bruises, or caring for someone after a beating like the one Jasmine had taken. These were worthy things, but … "In my heart, I still want to be the one to care for—" Her tribe. "For people who have no one else. Not because I want to be special." That was her father's accusation in her mind, words he'd spoken in anger when she became too proud of her gift and had announced to everyone how she would help the village. It was what they wanted, what they expected of her, what they'd told her all her life that she would have to be. Her father had taught her that being excited about it was too close to acting superior to others in the tribe. Her parents, especially her father, always reminded her to be humble and remember her place. "There are people who have no healers. I want to help them."

"Like the people of your tribe," Temric said, as if he'd heard her thoughts. She felt exposed, but his tone was gentle, and Edri and Rani's closeness protected her.

Rani and Edri exchanged a look past Billie. "Wait. I just realized. How are you here?" Rani asked under her breath.

"This is what we'll do," Jasmine told them, pouring tea for Aliiren. Though he didn't look at what he was doing he didn't spill a drop. "I'll have to check with Spire, but I'm sure he'll agree. We'll send you to Nuvar College in Ruvall."

"Jasmine," Temric protested while a chill passed through Billie's heart.

"It's the least we can do, after what you did for me. And not just me," Jasmine persisted.

"Jasmine—" Billie held up her hand to Temric, asking him to stop protesting on her behalf. It was said. It wouldn't hurt to let Jasmine weave his vision of her future. Meanwhile Edrion, who'd been quietly sipping tea, stared at the side of her face. It was like he was trying to read her thoughts.

"But for all of Ben Ariim," Jasmine continued. "I know in my heart that the people who tried to hurt me are the ones that have been raping and murdering people all over the city. You deserve a reward. A real one. So we'll cover your tuition and then we'll arrange passage home for you. After we throw you a big graduation party." Finally, he paused. "I'm missing something."

She'd steeled herself, hands cupped carefully around her cup of tea, head bowed so that she didn't have to look at their expressions. She didn't want to hear what Temric would say to Jasmine's proposal. She felt dizzy again, and she doubted it was the punch.

"What happened?" Aliiren asked in Thedran.

The Rill sibs exchanged another glance. Moving as one, they put their arms around her. In their embraces, she felt steadier.

"It is private," Temric informed them in Thedran.

Larani gave her a squeeze. "Maybe we should talk about something else."

"Secrets can be like cancer," Aliiren said ominously.

"It's not a secret," Billie protested. But it did seem like a cancer, eating her insides, becoming heavier, sapping her strength. "Whatever is in that letter can't be worse than what I imagine. Read it."

Aliiren leaned forward, concern tightening in his face. "What letter?"

Temric went to her bags and found the tube. It brought back the memory of finding it tucked against her body as she'd undressed for the neophytes. It had been hard to relinquish it. Somehow, it had become her most precious possession.

"Are you sure?" Temric asked.

Why did he have to ask that? "Do you want me to beg?"

"No, that's not what I meant. I'll read it." Temric broke the wax seal and took out a knife.

"Don't cut the knots!" she cried with horror.

Temric hesitated. "Maybe you should open it?"

"I'll do it." Jasmine held out his hand. Something about his calm, and poise, and the way he didn't act like she was fragile made her feel like she could endure this.

Temric, after a glance to Billie for approval, gave the letter to Jasmine. Jasmine carefully pried at the wax still stuck to the paper until it came free, then slipped the wax and knots off the tube. He laid them at his feet. In the Kilhells that would have been disrespectful, but with his jeweled rings and pedicured perfection, the knots seemed to be in an almost blessed space. She appreciated that, even as she gritted her teeth against what would soon come.

Jasmine unrolled the paper. His eyes moved across the page. He glanced up at Billie, and then down at the page again.

"What does it say?" Aliiren asked impatiently.

"It's in Kilhellion," he said.

"Do you know anyone who can read it?" Temric asked.

"I can read it." He looked to Billie. "Do you want me to translate it, or speak it as it's originally written?"

*Do I want them to know? When we all part ways, do I want them to remember me this way?*

Aliiren was right. No one else outside of Torath cared about her. There was no one else who she'd trust to help her carry this burden.

*Do I want to hear the words of my tribe before I tell my friends the truth?*

No matter how much time passed, or how well she prepared, she knew she'd choke on the words before she could get them all out. Her throat was already thick, and she had to fight to force the words out. "Translate it, please."

Jasmine's eyes traveled over the letter once more. He took in a deep breath, as if steeling himself, and then spoke very softly and gently. After the first few words, she knew why.

"If we had sent for your brother, he would not have failed you, and you would not be dead."

He was dead.

Brian was dead.

Brian's smile, his blue eyes framed by his curly hair, flashed through her mind.

Impossible. He was right there, in her mind, still with her. It wasn't real.

But her gut, hard as stone and colder than ice, said otherwise.

She'd held out hope that it was something else. That they'd been so outraged that Tilla had reached them before her, and that they'd been obligated to pay her when it had been Billie's responsibility, and duty, after all they'd sacrificed to send her to college and the money they'd sent to bring her home …

*Brian is dead.*

*They sent for me, and they waited all that time while he was dying, hoping in vain that I would rush to his side and save him. No wonder they disowned me.*

The knowledge hacked through her, splitting her, and all the horror of it bled out. She could imagine his last gasps, his hands balled into fists as he tried to hold onto Life.

And yet she could remember, more clearly than she felt the space and people around her, sitting beside him, watching the ponies graze while their father worked with a yearling on a lunge line nearby. Her father called to Brian to fetch a blanket for him.

Brian stood up and was gone.

Everything, and everyone she'd ever loved, was gone.

*I'm alone.*

*I'm dead.*

"That's it?" Temric snapped in Sothron, startling her back to the room and the strangers now staring at her. "I must be missing something. She didn't arrive when they expected her to and now she's dead to them?" He raised his arms for emphasis, hands pointed sharply to the letter that Jasmine held in a limp hand.

"Temric," Aliiren said tightly. "Her brother is dead."

Temric looked horrified. His arms lowered and a hand covered his mouth. "Oh. Gods." His skin became even more pale, a kind of gray, and his cheeks turned a wan pink. "I … I didn't think it through. Billie, I'm so sorry."

Larani and Edrion hugged her hard, but not hard enough to squeeze the knowledge from her soul.

It took a long time, just forcing herself to take one breath after another and forcing herself not to think about it, before she could say anything. She could feel that expectation from everyone, that she should say something. "I'm dead along with him. Disowned." She didn't want to go home anymore, even if she'd had a choice. Not when she'd have to go to her brother's shrine, knowing he was dead because she'd failed him.

"Oh, dear heart," Larani soothed softly, while Edrion rubbed her back. "I'm so sorry."

Dear heart. They were sweet word of affection, but she had no heart.

As if to remind her that wasn't true, her heart started pounding, and her head felt tight and full of nothing, an unbearable pressure like she'd never felt before. Her chest contracted, forcing her to fold over her knees.

All the while Edrion kept rubbing her back.

"There's a tradition," Jasmine said in his clear, calm voice, "Of drumming to the souls of recently departed Kilhellions, to let them know that they will be remembered forever. I'll send for a troupe, and when they come, we'll all help you drum to your brother, so he knows."

She had no right. She shook her head.

"If you change your mind—"

"I won't." But maybe she should. "It's not for you …" For the first time in a long time she found it difficult to speak Thedran properly. "It's not your responsibility."

"We want to help you," Aliiren said.

"I've had more help than I deserve." The words came out roughly, harshly, and she was angry now, so angry at herself that she wished she'd died on the ship. "It was my brother that needed help, and I failed him." She had to get out of here. "I … have to leave." She got up and it took forever to untangle her tunic and put it on.

"Billie, stay," Larani told her sharply. "I mean it. You shouldn't be alone."

"I *am* alone." She ran then. She had no idea how she found her way outside. She was lost in the garden. There was no way out. She tripped over something sharp and slammed hard into the ground, breaking something thorny. Her soul seemed to shrink within her and her body trembled, coughing as if her lungs had forgotten how to breathe. She gripped her hair and didn't feel a damned thing except fire along her scalp. She lost her balance forward, caught herself on her hands. Her fingers gripped the earth and pain shot up from under her fingernails.

*He's dead he's dead he's dead he's dead*

Her mouth opened and she thought she might throw up. Instead, a pitiful, mewling scream rasped out and faltered, leaving her gasping. She hadn't cried since she was little. She wished she could because whatever this was, it felt so much worse.

"Billie." It was Larani. She knelt and Billie felt strong, thin arms wrap around her. The pressure made her heart flutter, and stabbing pains flashed in her ribcage.

*I'm okay.* She couldn't speak. Words couldn't come out of her mouth, neither placating lies nor searing truth.

Was this what dying felt like?

"It wasn't your fault," Temric said from somewhere in the darkness. "This isn't fair. Let me write to them on your behalf. I can explain what happened."

*No!* "You don't understand!" They would never understand, no matter what language she spoke. "He was everything to my tribe! He would have been a mage!"

"A healer is just as valuable," Temric told her. "Why would they give you up? This must be a mistake."

"It's simple calculus," she growled. That awful word finally felt fit to purpose. "I'm not as valuable. Not even close. They sent me to Ruvall first because if something happened to me, they'd still have Brian, and the tribe would survive without me as it always has without a healer. But Brian—" She had to take a breath. She hated this, trying to explain what had happened to an outsider who stubbornly refused to accept what she was telling him. "Whether Ruvall killed me, or I'd abandoned my people, it makes no difference to them. I didn't come back when they desperately needed me, when Brian needed me, and now Brian is dead. So now I'm dead too."

"But you're still alive," Temric protested. "You're a healer. Eventually someone else in your tribe will need a healer and you could be that for them."

"Even if they knew everything that an educated healer is capable of, which they don't, and which I'm *not*, that gift is worth less than straw compared to what Brian would have done for my people for generations. What if they didn't disown me, and I went home now? The question in their minds would always be, where were you when he needed you? Why didn't you find your way back home to him, or die trying?"

"You almost did die. You could tell them what happened," Temric argued.

She let out a hoarse laugh. "That I was in a shipwreck, but somehow survived? That I fought a hellion, and survived? That I begged, but no one would take me to Sellon Port? Why would they believe a word I said?"

"If you don't want to explain what happened, fine. But please, allow me to argue on your behalf. I've arbitrated many times before. I can do this for you. Please."

"Why should they listen to a stranger who doesn't understand them? What would you tell them? The truth? I barely believe it, and I lived through it."

"But—"

"They *needed* me. Brian *needed* me. I tried. But it wasn't enough. And that will always be true. I can't go back. It's in the letter they sent to me. They'll never forgive me, and I can't face—" She staggered to her feet and Larani backed away. Behind Larani and Temric, his face gently lit by a sacred Light, Aliiren watched Billie with no expression at all.

Silence followed. Finally, they understood.

"That makes no sense," Temric swept his arm out for emphasis and then brought it down like a hammer. "Whatsoever!" His cheeks flushed pink, and his voice thundered with anger. "If they knew what you went through, they would know that they could rely on you more than anyone. *No one* would have worked so hard, or sacrificed so much."

"My father would have reached him," Billie shot back.

"Bullshit," Temric snapped.

Billie went for him, but Larani grabbed her and Aliiren thrust himself between her and Temric. She didn't fight them. Her body shook with rage, but she didn't fight them. She wouldn't have hurt him. She would have grabbed him, dared him to slander her father again.

"You're drunk," Temric told her sharply.

Aliiren placed his hand on Billie's chest to stop her. The light touch, so unexpected, set her back a step. "Temric," Aliiren warned, holding up an open hand near Temric's chest. "Stop. Now is not the time."

She was drunk. And strangely, she felt better in Larani's and now Edrion's tight grip. Light-headed, but better.

"He's just trying to help," Larani said, pressing on her. Billie yielded and took another step back.

Would she have hurt Temric? She wasn't sure anymore. For a moment she'd been a member of the Maiyem clan, defending their honor, and she was drunk. "I'm sorry." Her voice didn't sound like her own, especially speaking Sothron. "I lied. I don't have a father. I don't have a family." She wondered if the shrine they'd make for her would be close to Brian's.

*They might not make a shrine for me.*

"I'm the one who should apologize," Temric said. "Larani's right. I just wanted to help. Please forgive me."

"I—" Her words got lost in complicated feelings of gratitude, and loss. "I know you meant well."

Neophytes emerged from behind her friends. "We're here to guide you back," a neophyte said. "If it pleases you. Jasmine is asking after you. He's worried."

Temric, Rani, Edri and the most fiercely of all, Aliiren, gazed at her, giving her the choice.

They wanted her to stay with them.

These were her friends. They'd rowed with her from the ship, and Edrion and Larani had parted ways so that Edri could help sail her closer to home. They'd risked their lives, and had been unfailingly kind to her. They'd fought a demon, and murderers and rapists. And she'd treated them terribly, with suspicion and yelling and she might have hurt Temric if they hadn't held her back.

Their loyalty and forgiveness humbled her. When she'd needed someone, they were there, not just beside her but holding her up.

She was still lightheaded, but she felt steadier. "All right." Her voice broke, but it had some strength to it again.

Larani put an arm around Billie's waist as they walked back. "There's something I've been meaning to talk to you about. I want to thank you, for taking good care of Edri," she told Billie quietly. "He's not as lucky as me. I beat him at cards all the time. I don't how he won that dice roll."

A laugh escaped Billie, weak, but it was a laugh just the same. "Thank you for letting him come with us." If she'd known what was to happen, she would have never left Brian. Ever. Did Rani know the risk she'd run by letting Edri go?

"We're staying a while in Ben Ariim, but when we're ready to leave, I want you to join us in our travels."

Billie wasn't sure of what she thought of the offer, or of anything anymore.

"You don't have to decide right now," Rani assured her. Her warm, rough voice soothed Billie's nerves. All she could do was nod.

Jasmine's poise had frayed in their absence. He put his hand on Rani's shoulder, using her to guide everyone in, his smile a touch too bright, his gaze darting from one person to another. "You're all welcome to sleep here. Or I can arrange for an additional room." With every word he calmed down, until, at the end, he'd recovered his grace.

"We're happy to stay together," Edrion said, his gaze steadily on Billie as if he thought that she'd run if he looked away.

*Where would I go?*

Jasmine looked to Aliiren with a sudden, formal importance, and held out his hand. "Do me the honor of protecting me while I sleep."

At first Billie thought it was some sort of pleasure garden custom that everyone knew but her, but Aliiren looked as surprised as any of them. "Of course," Aliiren said, though he looked reserved. He hesitated to take Jasmine's hand. Jasmine lowered it as if that was how it was done, and maybe it was. But then he extended his hand to Billie. "Billie, will you also do me the honor of protecting me while I sleep tonight?"

Her mind was still somewhere between Torath and the garden and everything seemed to be happening incredibly fast. She didn't know what this meant, or what she'd have to do. She was filthy again, her face was smeared with tears and dirt, her eyes felt swollen and hot … but something about the look on his face warned her that a refusal would hurt him. Besides, what did it matter? She'd already decided she would stay with them. "I would be honored," she said, though mostly she felt confused and tired. She offered her hand, and he took it with a smile. His hand was very strong, and soft, and supple in hers. Touching her transferred dirt and blood onto his warm, clean skin. Her grubby, pale hands had gone cold. Why did she suddenly feel so cold?

"We'll see the rest of you in the inner garden tomorrow," Jasmine said, leading the way out. "Good night, everyone." He paused after he opened the door. "Oh, and that rope hanging in the corner there? Pull on that if you need anything. Food. Drink. Extra blankets. Sex. More pillows. It's all yours." He smiled flirtatiously as he led Billie and Aliiren away.

## Chapter Twenty-One

◇◇◇◇◇◇◇◇◇◇◇◇◇◇◇◇◇◇◇◇◇◇◇◇◇◇◇◇◇◇◇◇◇◇◇◇◇◇◇◇◇◇◇◇◇◇◇◇◇

# Trust

◇◇◇◇◇◇◇◇◇◇◇◇◇◇◇◇◇◇◇◇◇◇◇◇◇◇◇◇◇◇◇◇◇◇◇◇◇◇◇◇◇◇◇◇◇◇◇◇◇

*The Iris and Golden Pear Pleasure Garden, Ben Ariim*
*4th Bless Night of Sun Month*

Billie wasn't sure what she'd expected, but it wasn't spending the night holding Jasmine in her arms while he shed lovely, silent tears. After a while he slept. He woke twice from nightmares, and she held him then, too, while he trembled.

Between those fraught moments, he lavished her with attention. She should have been the one taking care of him, but he insisted on washing her face and hands the first time he woke, and seemed happiest when she passively accepted his coddling. He told her a story about a little girl that grew up to become a famous explorer, and he sang to her, and brushed her hair. He pampered Aliiren too, but without touching him. Mostly he recited sacred poems about Light, and he wrote them down on fine paper, which he decorated with chains of flowers and leaves as delicate as frost.

They were all overwrought, and it was a rough night.

Every shudder that passed through Jasmine's body reminded her of how he'd been hurt in mind as well as body. Though she hadn't finished her training, she was a healer, and he needed healing. So she murmured things to him, mostly in Kilhellion, trickled traces of vinus to help ease his pain, and promised him it would get better.

It wasn't a lie. More than once in her life she'd felt like she'd been steeped in blood and wrung out, but she'd felt better in time and so would he.

Maybe that meant that she would be all right this time too.

It was too hard to contemplate her future. Easier to focus on Jasmine, and to let Jasmine do whatever he needed to do so he could begin to heal.

She could tell that Aliiren wanted to help, but he was uncomfortable with the whole situation. She assured him with silent nods that his soft words and sitting nearby was enough.

After Jasmine's bold words that he'd suffered worse before, and how he'd behaved during their meal, she'd begun to believe that he'd just shrug it off. But although he was struggling, he wasn't weak. He'd been a kind and generous host. He'd given them his friendship. And though someone who'd been attacked as he had might have fled to the protection of family and friends, he chose instead to honor her and Aliiren with a trust so complete that he slept in their presence, even if that sleep was uneasy most of the time.

Jasmine clearly led a pampered life, but his courage was made of steel.

He was, she decided, a knot of contradictions and mysteries she'd never untie.

It had to be close to dawn when Jasmine woke yet again. He didn't moan or struggle to move or make choking noises like before. She wasn't sure what woke her. He hadn't moved. He was just lying there, breathing softly, gazing at her face. He looked so miserable, and yet still beautiful. She reached for him. His hair was damp when she stroked it, and the dim, amber lights in the room revealed satiny tear tracks on his flawless face. "Thank you for staying with me," he whispered.

Those thanks, unlike the gifts and the party and the way he'd spoken before, felt personal. "You're welcome."

He rolled over and invited her to spoon with him. She tucked her body close against his, naked skin against naked skin.

It surprised her anew that he wouldn't rather be with close friends or family. Maybe it was another part of his knot of mysterious contradictions. Or maybe Jasmine didn't know what to do with those powerful feelings that bled from a soul touched by Death. Maybe no one at the garden did. The garden, it seemed to her, was a place of illusion where only pleasure, and plenty, existed. How often violence broke past the gates of this place, she couldn't say.

She wanted to hunt those people down who'd fled, and kill them. It wouldn't help Jasmine sleep, but he might heal a little faster in his heart, knowing they could never hurt him or anyone else again.

And it would give her purpose.

"Is he asleep?" Jasmine asked as he gazed at Aliiren.

Aliiren sat cross-legged near the door, head bowed, eyes closed, hands resting loosely one atop the other, palms up in his lap. "I'm awake," he whispered.

"Will you teach me sword work?" Jasmine whispered, his voice painfully uncertain.

"Of course."

"Not the pretty stuff that I learned to entertain," he said. "Real sword work. Like you do."

"Yes." Aliiren glanced to Billie. She guessed what he was thinking, but she wasn't offended that Jasmine didn't ask her to teach him sword work. She didn't think she could teach Jasmine to do what she did, even if he'd wanted to learn.

No one would want to learn that kind of butchery. What Aliiren had was skill. What she used was brute force and the unflinching determination her father had instilled in her. Hold back, he'd taught her, her sister and Brian, and you die. Flinch, and you die.

Act too late, and you die.

Jasmine propped himself up on his elbow. "You should haggle. I'll pay you anything." It sounded like he offered something more luxurious than money.

"It would be my pleasure. You may donate to my temple if you wish."

It seemed that Billie and Aliiren had more in common than she'd realized. He'd been reluctant to accept gifts, rewards, or whatever these things were, too. Maybe he wanted to tread lightly in the world, just like she did, giving all he had to give to it, and being satisfied with the simplest, most abundant things that kept him healthy and happy with as little excess and waste as possible. Neither of them wanted to be a burden on the world, most especially to other people.

"I have to give you something," Jasmine insisted. "That's a lot of your time I'd be wasting."

There he went again with trying to buy … what? Freedom from a real friendship?

"If you learn well, it won't be a waste," Aliiren countered. "I have private time that I seldom use. I'll spend that time with you." He opened his eyes. "And what about you? Will the garden spare you the time to learn defense with a sword?"

"You have no idea who I am," Jasmine said, wonder in his voice.

Aliiren looked puzzled. Billie wouldn't have been surprised if Jasmine told them that he was a prince. With all his wealth, he could be anything he wanted.

He laughed softly again. "But I know you. Three of you were offered a gift for achieving the status of Protector. You're the only one who didn't spend the next true night here. I believe the other gift they offered was a journey to Kal Ariim."

"Yes, to see the palace."

"Was it beautiful?"

Aliiren smiled. "Very."

Jasmine rolled onto his back and the blanket slipped down to his waist. He tucked his hands under his head, showing off his lean, muscular chest and strong arms. "Your friends talked more about you than they talked about themselves."

Aliiren frowned.

Jasmine made a moue. "Don't assume it's all bad."

"I know the things they say about me." Aliiren stared at the space in front of his feet.

She felt a spark of protectiveness. "What kind of things?"

"I'm cold. Arrogant. Self-righteous. That I love only myself. That I believe the only thing worthy to touch me is the Light."

She could tell by his expression that Aliiren was afraid some of it might be true. "I suppose they're all perfect," she snipped, irritated.

He winced. "They say I'm perfect."

She gathered that it wasn't a compliment. "I don't have to be a follower of Light to see that they're either blind or I—stupid. Or jealous." She'd almost called them liars, but that would have been a very serious accusation against followers of Light, not to mention that she didn't know those people. "You're a good person, Aliiren."

Oddly, her words seemed to affect him. He looked up at her, and his golden gaze seemed full of gratitude. "Thank you."

"You're welcome." She had to look away, feeling weirdly shy all of a sudden.

Jasmine chuckled. "You two are so cute. I wish I could keep you both here with me forever."

Cute? No one had called her that before. It made her chuckle to think of herself as an awkward filly, or an oversized, adolescent hound.

"You can find me at my temple any time you wish," Aliiren told Jasmine. "Either of you," he added. "I'll always be there for you."

He didn't say it lightly. She could tell that not only did he mean it, he hoped for it. She wanted to grab onto that offer with both hands, but she knew there was no place for someone like her to stay at a Light temple.

*He'll be here*, she realized, as if it was a new idea. *This is his home.*

*Will it be mine? Or should I go with Rani and Edri? They offered too.*

*I'm not alone. It only feels like it because …*

She closed her eyes tightly to block out the rest of that thought.

*I need to look to the future. And I'm not alone in that future.*

It was true, but feeling it … she couldn't force herself to believe it.

Jasmine let out a sigh and rolled back onto his side, propping himself on his elbow again. The blanket wrapped tightly over his legs, and his black hair coiled over his smooth, olive-toned skin. "Aliiren, would you like to lay down beside me? I swear I won't touch you. It's just … you look cold, and the way you hunch your back, I think you'd be more comfortable here with us."

Aliiren looked pained. "I don't mind being touched. I just don't like how some people *pull* …" His brows furrowed and his shoulders hunched just a tiny bit, but she noticed, and Jasmine reacted with widened eyes and slightly parted lips. "… at me." His voice grew softer, and he looked at a silk pillow with jasmine flowers embroidered on it. "They want more than I'm willing to give."

That shocked her. Not that people wanted to touch him. Anyone would. But that he didn't fight back. One hard slap and no one would dare touch him against his will.

Or did the people here allow crude oafs to get away with prodding and pinching and grabbing at them? She couldn't imagine someone like Aliiren tolerating that. So maybe something else was happening, something she didn't understand?

"I'm a pleasurer," Jasmine said. "And not just any pleasurer. I'm a favorite." He lifted his chin with pride. "My body, my skills, my mind and my heart are imbued with the gift of human harmony. So, although I would gladly take you by the hand and explore beyond any limits of pleasure you might imagine, unlike your friends at the temple, I have control over my body and how I touch. I have control of my mind, and how I think of you. And I have control of my heart, a heart that would never betray your trust in me. That is, if you decide to trust me." He hesitated, which made Aliiren look up, and their gazes met. At that moment, Jasmine's hazel eyes were as glorious as a field of wildflowers, delicate blue blossoms floating above frost green leaves and damp, mossy earth, the reflection of Aliiren's meditation candle like a miniature sun.

Aliiren's pupils opened even wider in the dim light, and his irises seemed to luminesce with a phantom gold glow. "Will you trust me, Aliiren?"

For a breathless moment the two men seemed locked in deep, silent communication. Jasmine had leaned ever so slightly toward Aliiren, a slack hand on the fluffy, silk feather bed, rotating his palm up with subtle invitation. Aliiren's shoulders pulled back, and his chin lowered.

Aliiren unfurled gracefully, but he was tense as a cat trying to slink past the notice of a sleeping dog. To her amazement he crept onto the bed. The scent of his incense caressed her face.

Jasmine lifted the soft blanket that covered Billie and him and lightly took Aliiren into his arms. It was like watching Life embrace Death, beautiful beyond words. And Billie was witness to it, a part of it, as her body braced against Jasmine's, and his body conformed to Aliiren's. For a moment Aliiren lay excessively still, but then he relaxed, and he let out a sigh. Jasmine sighed as well, and his body seemed to melt against him.

Billie draped her arm carefully over Jasmine's hip and leg so that she wouldn't inadvertently touch Aliiren. Strangely, it felt as if she'd just become far more intimate with Aliiren than when she'd been with Crellan. It felt as if Aliiren had given something of himself to Jasmine, and to Billie too, that he hadn't when he'd allowed Billie to massage him and the neophytes to brush his hair.

Now that she understood him a little better, she was astonished that Aliiren had allowed her to enter him with her vinus, and to massage him at all. At the time she hadn't fully appreciated what that meant.

She trusted he would let her touch him again. She trusted he was her friend. And she trusted that he would stand by her side, no matter what happened next.

And Jasmine?

She'd never heard of his gift, or of favorites. She still wasn't sure of what she meant to him, and now she wasn't sure if the subtle, confusing feelings she had for him were born of a growing friendship, or if she was being influenced by a power she didn't understand.

*He told us about it, and Aliiren still trusts him.*

A little bit at a time, her body eased like Aliiren's had. She hadn't realized how tired she was until she closed her eyes. The warmth of Jasmine's body and the cool softness of his silken bed comforted her. She took in a deep breath, let it out, and surrendered. Swiftly, like a caress, sleep took her.

## Chapter Twenty-Two

<<<<<<<<<<<<<<<<<<<<<<<<<<<<<<<<<<<<<<<<<<<<<<<<<<<<<<<<<<<<<<<<<<<<<<<<<<<<<<

# The Champion

<<<<<<<<<<<<<<<<<<<<<<<<<<<<<<<<<<<<<<<<<<<<<<<<<<<<<<<<<<<<<<<<<<<<<<<<<<<<<<

*The Iris and Golden Pear Pleasure House, Ben Ariim*
*4th Trade Day of Sun Month*

They sat at a teak table in the inner garden among other guests and pleasurers and neophytes among the greenery and fountains and streams. Edrion was tossing grapes in the air and Billie tried to catch them in her mouth. Apparently this was a game Rill played, and like other Rill games it was designed to make money. The idea was to teach Billie how to do it. Once she was well-practiced, sometime in the future they'd call her from where she'd be drinking chocolate as if they didn't know her, have her miss a grape and then catch another in her mouth. They'd then offer to take bets from anyone who thought they could do better than her either with one of the Rill tossing the grape or a friend, their choice. It had taken the siblings some time to convince her it wasn't cheating or thieving. It was a simple skill, they assured her. It wasn't their fault if people overestimated their abilities, or underestimated Billie's nimbleness and aim. And it wasn't as if someone in the crowd might not have practiced the game themselves, since it wasn't a new thing, and it was a fun way to make money. No one they'd ever played felt like they'd been cheated, and everyone always enjoyed themselves. All these things were true, she supposed ...

She couldn't think too deeply on it, or anything else. After spending two nights at the pleasure garden, she felt frayed and fragile, like fabric that had been wrung too hard. Other than Jasmine, the pleasurers left them alone, as Billie and each of her friends had their reasons why they didn't indulge in the pleasure garden's most famous form of entertainment. Billie's reason was packed carefully away in a bag, her fate sealed by words she couldn't read herself.

Edri and Rani were the only ones who were able to somehow keep her from dwelling … not on the disownment.

That felt like nothing compared to Brian's death.

A neophyte arrived and stopped by Billie. "A Champion and his dog are here to see you."

The grape Edrion had thrown bounced off her nose, which made everyone laugh except Temric, who looked worried. Aliiren's mouth tightened into a line, and he looked down, his brows furrowed just enough to notice.

"Ooo, a Champion," Larani said lusciously. "Can I come with you? I've never met a Champion."

"Me too!" Edrion pleaded.

"Alone," the neophyte told them apologetically.

"It's all right," Jasmine promised. "I sent for them. Maybe something you saw will help them catch those other two murderers before they hurt someone else." Then Jasmine exchanged a look with Aliiren, a subtle smile in his eyes promising that it would be all right.

Aliiren crossed his arms, deep in thought.

She knew she ought to care, ought to ask. Instead, she turned in her seat from the table.

Temric hadn't missed Aliiren's expression either. He took Billie's hand and squeezed it. She squeezed back, then pulled her hand away. Temric needn't get dragged along with her like a rider who'd fallen off a running horse with his foot caught in the stirrup. Her life was already destroyed. Whatever fate the Champion had planned for her, she could endure it by herself.

Billie got up, feeling more resignation than trepidation as she followed the neophyte to the spiral staircase, up onto the balcony, up the steep stone steps, and out into full daylight. They'd been having their breakfast at midday. It shouldn't have surprised her. They'd all drunk too much and hadn't slept quite enough. If it weren't for her gift, and the tea, and the healer that came to help the others, they all would have been in worse shape even now.

The outdoor garden looked even more beautiful by day, lifting her spirits almost against her will. The blossoming vines and fruit shone in colors as vivid as the jeweled garlands and wind chimes. Light stones within suspended golden cages sparkled subtly in the desert sunlight. She hadn't noticed the pomegranates before, or the oranges, or the date trees that soared above the limes and lemons, whose young fruits were still green. Melons, newly in blossom, hung from elaborate arbors among exotic trees. And spidery, perfumed flowers blazed crimson, white, and pink everywhere in-between. Birds, plump from the Life's Day treats they were fed yesterday, chirped everywhere, no doubt hoping for more handouts.

Her tribe would have been astonished to see that such a place existed. Brian would have—

She had to let the scars form around that wound or she'd bleed to death. It was a kind of dying like she'd never imagined, full of aches in her chest and a belly that turned to stone with the slightest thought of home. She had no idea if she would ever heal from it. Maybe it would be simpler if the Champion executed her. Then she could live a new life, without the memory of all that loss.

It was sacrilegious to even think such things. Life forbade it.

The thought clung like a leech inside her mind, painful when she brushed it, but otherwise numb. She hoped that in time, just like a leech, it would drop off on its own.

The garden was very large, but smaller than she remembered it from coming here at dusk, and from being lost in it in so many ways last night. She could see the walls that surrounded it here and there between the greenery.

The neophyte pushed aside huge leaves and delicate fern fronds for her as they negotiated a narrow path that ended at a delicate timber structure. It had a roof but only a pair of sides that formed a corner. An elaborate table was set with tea and cakes, and at the table sat two armored men, their heavy steel helms resting on the ground at their feet. It confused for her a moment.

Then she realized that one of the pair was the "dog." She guessed that it was an honorific, meaning someone who was loyal, brave, fiercely protective, and would sniff out any danger or duplicity in strangers. Because the neophyte said, 'his dog,' she took that to mean it was a subordinate position to the Champion, but maybe a dog was like a herd guardian, some kind of overseer?

The taller and stronger of the two was also the younger, and he frowned at her. He looked Thedran, but was by far the tallest Thedran she'd ever seen. His coils of black hair seemed thinner than most, and he had a receding hairline and thick brows that made him look angry. The other was Arrak, a lean man with incredibly broad shoulders, which reminded her a bit of Aliiren. He wore his black hair extremely short, mere stubble, his jaw was stronger, and his skin was darker than Aliiren's. Like Aliiren, he had gold eyes.

She'd never seen armor like theirs. It was almost like bulky clothing made of steel, though the plates flared in ways that cloth could not. The younger one's armor was dented in places, and plain. The older one had decorated armor chased in bronze designs that interlocked sun patterns and flowers.

One of them would bear a famed Champion's blade that would cheat Death Itself. Was it the Arrak? His weapon was a surprisingly plain-looking brass and steel hilt and a dark leather sheath protecting a two-edged long blade. The only adornment was on the brass pommel, a six-flamed sun similar to a blessing on a Light temple.

Either way, she had to admit that she was a little disappointed. They were both impressive, but neither was any more so than Torath's chieftain or his wife. Neither of them reflected her favorite stories of Axe Champion, whose 'mighty thews threatened to split his skin when he flexed.'

"Sun Champion." The neophyte looked to the Arrak first. "Mangy Dog. This is Billie the Kilhellion." The neophyte gestured to Billie with both hands, as if she were someone impressive.

Mangy Dog seemed like a cruel name. She didn't think she could bring herself to call him that.

"I thought Billie was a man's name," Mangy Dog remarked. He looked at nothing in particular while he spoke, so he might have been talking to himself. She couldn't tell if he was just curious, or if he intended to insult her in some way. She herself thought it odd that some Thedran men had flower names, but it said nothing about them, good or bad.

Sun Champion gestured to a chair across from him. "Sit."

Billie accepted his invitation and settled onto a strangely soft cushion that gave more than she expected. She shifted closer to the edge so she wasn't slumped back.

"Did you need more tea or cakes?" the neophyte asked Sun Champion.

"No thank you," Sun Champion told her politely. Unlike Aliiren, he had a strong voice, and quite deep.

A Champion.

He was staring at her. Actually, she realized it was more like he was staring back at her, because she was staring at him.

The neophyte vanished into the greenery, leaving her alone with these people who might or might not want to do something about her. Not that she'd want to be anywhere else.

An actual Champion.

Aside from his golden eyes and fancy armor, he seemed remarkably normal, a person like any other person. Which, of course he would be. At least they looked ferocious, especially the Sun Champion, despite his more gentle manners. He was relaxed in a way that suggested to her that he trusted his body to react faster than any attack she could muster.

While she thought about this and looked them over, the Sun Champion watched her, judging her. He didn't let on what he thought of her, but she couldn't imagine him seeing anything but a broken thing, disowned and outcast and disgraced.

He picked up a delicate teacup in a strong, large hand. Both hands were almost completely clothed in heavy leather and steel. He took a sip, never shifting his golden gaze away from her. He set down the cup, interwove his gauntleted fingers, and set his hands out of sight under the table. "Tales of your exploits have already reached me," he said.

*What exploits?*

*Oh.*

"You mean, the men I killed." She wondered if a wise person would run. The Champion and his dog would be slower than her in their impressive armor.

She didn't want to. Something inside her, and something about them, made her want to stay. She'd thought her life had lost its meaning, like a shattered cup, holding only a few drops of its former purpose. But was she broken? Her heartbeat quickened, and every breath felt like an answer to that question.

*I'm still alive, and I'm not helpless.*

"And the man you assaulted by the harbor," Sun Champion said, still watching her carefully.

That wasn't fair! "I barely touched him," she protested. He held up his hand, she assumed to signal for her to hold her peace, but she wasn't about to have it. "My brother was dying and those people refused to help me find passage. And now my brother is dead." Saying it aloud filled her with cold pain that threatened to fold her in on herself. She silently dared him to tell her she'd done wrong as her hands tightened into fists.

"I'm sorry." He didn't sound sorry. "But that's not why we're here. Tell me what happened when you arrived at the place where the favorite Jasmine was being attacked. Tell me what you saw, and what you did."

They acted as if they had a duty, or something, to hear her out. That, and Jasmine's assurances from the night before, helped her trust that they weren't interested in judging her. They just wanted the truth.

She had to think about it, but once she started explaining the words came naturally about Jasmine with his clothes torn, Aliiren defending him, the massive horse and the rider who abandoned his friends, the woman who ran the other way without even a glance back. She realized that part of her had expected that Aliiren or Temric would go after the woman, or something. But they hadn't. "I would have gone after the man on the horse, but my friend told me to stop. So I did." The Sun Champion's expression gave nothing away. "I don't know what's counted as justice in Ben Ariim," she admitted. "Or to Champions. But I was only trying to protect—" To say that she was trying to protect Jasmine or Aliiren wasn't quite right. The danger was over. Her blood had been up, was all. And yet … "Where I come from, we don't let people like that run away."

"You tried to chase down a man on a horse." The Sun Champion hadn't said a word to interrupt her until he made this observation.

She wasn't sure if there was a question behind his words. "I would have caught him, too," she muttered, still upset at the thought that he'd gotten away.

*It doesn't matter anymore.*

Mangy Dog glanced at the Sun Champion before he spoke. "Did the men you killed put up much of a fight?"

She wondered why that would matter while she chose her words. "The one I got in the throat managed to pull a dagger, but he wasn't strong or clever enough to hold onto it. The other one never saw me coming, so no, he didn't put up a fight."

"Would you say that they were experienced fighters?" The Sun Champion seemed more interested in her answer this time.

"Yes."

"What makes you say that?"

She had to think about it. "Aliiren said that they were having fun until I showed up, playing a game they knew very well. And even after I came in, they weren't afraid, not until I killed the second one." The man with his two sons that had tried to take her mother, brother and her on Mount Cross had acted with the same confidence until her mother killed one of his sons. After that, he tried to recover but never managed it. Billie didn't remember much about him. At one point his expression changed when he started to lose, a kind of gape-mouthed horror. Pain had opened his pupils so wide his blue eyes looked like thin rings surrounding arrow holes into his head.

She also remembered the man's leer and the encouraging words he'd given his sons as they'd rushed out of nowhere from the woods. They'd gotten close before they attacked. They didn't have to run far to attack— the sons with Billie's mother, the father no doubt planning to scoop up Billie and her brother with little trouble. *Don't be afraid,* he'd said. *Work together. She's just a woman.*

Billie, a child at the time, would have seemed even less of a threat to him than her mother had. And yet, Billie had killed him. She had to, for her mother's sake, for Brian, for herself.

It had felt awful—to savage his body with her blade, to see his soul leave, to recognize the pain and fear in his eyes, to watch the love for his sons blossom into crushing grief before his soul joined theirs in Death's embrace. He'd spoken a name—Searvil. Was it one of theirs? A wife? A parent?

If she'd been dying, would she have called out for Brian?

Had Brian called out for her at the end?

"Had you seen any of the attackers before?" Sun Champion asked, breaking her free from the memory.

Billie shook her head to clear it. "No. I haven't been in Ben Ariim long. That would have been strange, if I'd seen them before. They weren't interested in me. Or Aliiren. They were after Jasmine. Aliiren and I got in the way."

"Yes, they were." The Sun Champion leaned on the table and rested his chin on his fist. After a moment he glanced at Mangy Dog and then settled his gaze back on her. "Do you think you could take the man on the horse, or the woman, if you saw them again?"

That was a tricky question, the kind her chieftain would pose to test her. Was he asking if she could kill them, or if she would try to kill them if she saw them again? "I surprised them," she offered cautiously. "Maybe there's a lot more to them than I saw." The memory of the rider, hatred burning in his eyes, his dead man's grin, sent a chill through her. "I think I could handle them." But the real issue was, "*Should* I do something if I see them again?"

"It would be worth some money to you, if you see them, to tell us where you saw them, and what they were doing." The Champion's tone was warm, calm, and oddly protective. Or maybe it wasn't so odd. Champions were supposed to be, at their core, protectors. "If these are the people who have been murdering and raping their way about Ben Ariim, we want them in the worst way." His words were edged with subtle though clear frustration. A deepening scowl on Mangy Dog's face suggested that he would have preferred to be out in the city hunting for them instead of drinking tea and talking to Billie. "But we want them alive. We think they're part of a larger group, and we want to be sure we get them all."

She thought she might be able to catch one or the other alive, but if they were together …

"I don't want you fighting them again if that can be helped," Sun Champion added.

Was that a smirk on Mangy Dog's face?

Billie had to remind herself that it didn't matter what Mangy Dog thought of her, not when a bladed Champion was right there, including her in a hunt.

Judging by the Champion's soft attention on her and the way he now leaned forward on his elbows, she hadn't mistaken his meaning. "Would you be willing to do this? Would you be willing to watch out for them, and then come to the Keep and tell us what you find out about them?"

"Of course." It wasn't much to ask. He could have asked a lot more of her and she wouldn't have balked. But this was enough. It felt good to have a task, and a purpose. That it was a task sanctioned by a Champion made it feel different from any other duty she'd been given in her life. It felt … important.

"I have another request." The Sun Champion shared an annoyingly enigmatic look with Mangy Dog before he addressed her directly. "Try to stay out of trouble."

And with those words her heart sank.

"Personally, I think Kilhellions are no better or worse than anyone else in the ways that really matter." Sun Champion sat back with a sigh. "Nonetheless, the rules by which you were raised up are very different from the rules observed in Ben Ariim, which means that you're more likely to offend someone, or worse, end up in a cell. Don't put hands on someone unless you intend to defend yourself from serious harm. The people who fight for fun in Ben Ariim are criminals, and you'll be seen as a criminal if you brawl or even slap someone for a slight."

There it was. Rather than feel rebuked, she felt like she finally understood why people treated her the way that they had. Whether she agreed or not, whether it was fair or not, her willingness to grab someone like that damned harbormaster's lackey would make her look like villain.

"No speech is considered so foul that it justifies violence in Ben Ariim," Sun Champion went on. "Also, rape is condemned as severely as murder in this city. You must never force your attentions on anyone, not so much as a kiss or an intimate caress, if it's unwelcome."

The idea that an unwanted kiss or touch might be likened to rape seemed extreme, but she would never do it. She supposed that in Ben Ariim, how welcome such things were might not be as obvious. In the Kilhells, if someone got too friendly, a quick shove or a slap along with a choice bit of profanity was enough to warn the person not to try again unless they wanted a fight. Which, of course, the worst of them did.

The idea of not having to fend off unwanted advances by force sounded pleasantly comfortable. But was it even possible to walk the busy streets of Ben Ariim without inadvertently touching someone? It didn't seem like anyone was bothered as people jostled each other on the crowded streets. Maybe what he was telling her was simply not to grope people. Which was so obvious, it made her cheeks warm to think that he thought she'd do something like that.

She thought of Aliiren and how careful Jasmine had been when offering to touch him and hold him. So maybe there was something more that she was missing, something that explained why she offended people so easily. With growing horror, she wondered if she'd frightened anyone by flirting with them. Was it possible that she'd violated people without even knowing it?

The thought depressed her.

Larani and Edrion had invited her to travel with them. *Maybe I should.*

And yet, she couldn't deny that what she really wanted was to find those rapists and bring them to justice.

The Champion and his dog had been watching her all this time. She wondered what they saw in her, and what they thought of her. If Mangy Dog's expression was any indication, he was now willing to tolerate her. The Sun Champion was measuring her carefully again.

"I understand," she told them. "And I will watch for those people, and tell you if I see them again. I don't know where the Keep is, though."

"We're not far from the city council building. Anyone in the city can tell you how to find it. Some call it the Champion's Tower. Once you're at the gate, ask for me and someone there will take you to me." The Sun Champion's voice wasn't just instructional. There was another warning there. She was not to act on her own.

She chafed at the restriction. What if they were gone by the time she got to the Keep and reported where they were?

"How long do you intend to stay in Ben Ariim?" Mangy Dog asked. His tone was a bit too casual, with an underlying invitation.

"Do you want me to leave?" She'd meant to challenge Mangy Dog with her words, but they wavered at the end. "Fuck it," she muttered under her breath in Kilhellion. She stood up. "May I—"

Mangy Dog stood up fast, rocking the table. She froze, the words, *go now,* stuck in her throat. Her hand was on the hilt of her sword, but she hadn't drawn it.

Mangy Dog had his hand on the hilt of his sword too. Sun Champion set his hand on Mangy Dog's forearm. "It's all right," Sun Champion said. Unwillingly, Mangy Dog relaxed.

Billie rubbed her hands, her palms suddenly sweaty, on her tunic at her hips and forced herself to knit her hands together in front of her belly. "Sorry."

Mangy Dog looked away. "I am too," he said to her surprise. "It's not you," he added softly, mostly to himself.

"Kilhellion," Sun Champion said before she thought to apologize more thoroughly for startling Mangy Dog. "You're welcome in Ben Ariim so long as you abide by rule and law."

It was a generous thing to say, even if it contained a warning like his other words. "Thank you," she said.

"You're welcome." Sun Champion's tone suggested that he meant it, on the condition that she behaved of course. Mangy Dog was staring off to one side, mouth downturned.

*Something happened to him, and recently.* "I'm sorry I was rude." She looked at Sun Champion when she said it, but she then shifted her gaze to Mangy Dog, offering a silent apology.

Mangy Dog didn't seem to hear her, or even see her.

Sun Champion swept his hand through the air in a casual dismissal of her words, as if her apology wasn't necessary. "Would you please ask Protector Aliiren to meet with us?"

"I will." She waited a moment to make sure that they didn't want anything else from her, and then she walked back into the interior pleasure garden to find Aliiren.

## Chapter Twenty-Three

<><><><><><><><><><><><><><><><><><><><><><><><><><><><><><><><><><><>

# The Desert Horse

<><><><><><><><><><><><><><><><><><><><><><><><><><><><><><><><><><><>

*Ben Ariim, a city in Arrak Thedra*
*4th Somber Day of Sun Month*

The pleasurers, including Spire and especially Jasmine, made a good show of begging Billie to stay over true night. But Aliiren insisted on returning to the Light Temple, Temric wanted to stay at the library, and the Rill said something about a huge party at a palace somewhere. So Billie felt it wasn't overly rude to tell them that she'd planned to stay with a friend, and set off for the public shelter where she knew Hova the Bird would go. Much as she enjoyed being around Aliiren, Temric, the Rill, and Jasmine, she knew she'd feel more comfortable among the Gurras than in a palace or a Light temple, never mind the pleasure garden where she'd be alone with a man whose intentions and gift were beyond her understanding.

Jasmine's gift …

Thinking back on how the pleasurer had convinced Aliiren to rest within his arms made her realize that Jasmine controlled a gift with terrible power. To not respect it would be a huge mistake. If he'd had ill intentions …

She had countless questions about favorites, and temples, and Champions, and the criminals she'd been tasked to hunt. Hova was wise, and kind, and would give Billie information and advice without teasing her about her ignorance.

But when she reached the public shelter, Hova and the other Gurras Billie had come to know were gone, replaced by strangers. Billie asked after him, but the Gurras there either shrugged or asked her if they could do some work for her in Hova's stead. One offered to find Hova, but Billie decided it might be best to save what money she had and find him herself.

Billie hunted for him until she was so hot, and tired, and discouraged that she wanted to sulk for the rest of her life. Instead, she stopped by a fountain, now utterly lost in the vast city with no idea how to find her way back to the pleasure garden, or to the docks, or anywhere in the city. She'd always been able to navigate easily enough in the woods. But Ben Ariim wasn't like the woods, or Port Sellon, or even Ruvall. It was an endless maze where the buildings and walls and streets looked much the same.

True night was coming tonight. She needed somewhere to stay.

A wild idea struck her, like a fork from a lightning bolt had flashed out from a storm in the Kilhells all the way into Ben Ariim to set her alight. She remembered Brian as a child, standing atop an ancient stump with his arms raised to the sky, his red curls lit by a beam of sunlight. "I'm a mage of Life! And you're a Champion, and we're hunting a hellion that kidnapped the chieftain. We'll track it all the way to the green hell if we have to!"

She'd spoken to a real Champion now, and though he was impressive, it wasn't like he was head and shoulders taller than her, nor did he have eyes that glowed like hot irons. It didn't seem like such a crazy idea anymore.

*I'm a healer, and I can fight. Maybe they'd want me. Maybe they'd train me to be a Champion, or at least a dog, whatever that means.*

*And if they tell me no, I'm no worse off.*

*I might even ask them, why not? I haven't spent my life training to become a Champion, but I've faced a hellion, and I can hold my own against just about anyone. I'm not sure I can knock down Sun Champion, but I can knock down Mangy Dog.*

*I'm pretty sure I can knock down Mangy Dog…*

*Anyway, I can prove myself.*

*If Sun Champion is anything like Gareth, he didn't just invite me to come to the Keep with information. He's daring me to prove myself.*

She didn't know if that proof would come by doing what he asked her to do, or by pushing beyond it.

*I have to find out.*

*I can do this.*

She asked for directions to the Champion's Keep and set off, determined but feeling light-headed, as if this was a dream, or she was drunk, or both.

She hadn't gotten far when alarmed voices rose above the general tumult of the crowds. She doubted it had anything to do with the people she was looking for. People like that preferred to work in private, quiet places. But it was some sort of trouble.

As she got closer the cries rose again. They were nearly drowned out by a raw, animal sound that sounded like a mix of a horse's cough and dog's growl, but louder than a human could scream. She trotted past strangers who looked in the direction of that strange sound for only a moment before continuing on their way. They seemed worried, but not terrified by that powerful, eerie noise, so maybe it came from something familiar to them.

Familiar maybe, but not welcome, because it looked like just about everyone wanted nothing to do with it and seemed very keen to put good distance between them and it.

The sound came again, very close, from within a dark, wide doorway.

It was a building like most in Ben Ariim, sharing walls with its neighbors so that it appeared to fill an entire block. The sound came from an open double door cut into the ground beneath the building, a huge one. The doorway had no awning, and it wasn't recessed into an alcove like most doors. Instead of stairs, a walled passage larger than the entrance to most mines sloped down to the opening. Heavy iron rails kept people on the street from accidentally falling a dangerous distance down onto the earthen ramp.

A loose semi-circle of people, mostly Arrak, loitered near the ramp, hands tucked in the pockets of their dun leather trousers or standing with their arms crossed. Nearly all of them wore calf-length skirts with split sides over their trousers. Some were bare headed with their straight or wavy dark hair flowing free about their shoulders, while others wore hats or were wrapped up in plain shawls and even veils. A few wore riding chaps.

Something like a lion's roar slid into a loud, hollow sound like some immense horn. It failed, at the end, though, and she could hear something gasping and snorting down beyond the doors.

Then there was silence.

She was just about to leave, since whatever was going on was apparently over, when a pair of Arrak emerged, a man and a woman. The woman shook her head and said something in Arrak about it being no good and sad. She took up a quiet conversation with another Arrak who'd been waiting by. Then those people left. A moment later a few more left.

"What is that?" Billie asked in her best Arrak, gesturing to the doorway.

He said something like currocatta, and then said to her blank expression, "desert horse."

The sounds she'd heard didn't come from a horse.

He said something about it being no good, and sad, and he left.

In fact, most people were leaving the streets. It was close enough to true night that they were heading home or to whatever shelter they could find. The few people still about on the street were on their way to somewhere, some in a leisurely way, some in an obvious hurry with worry hunching their shoulders and quickening their steps.

The bells hadn't sounded yet, so she had a bit of time.

Billie ventured through the doorway. It smelled of horses here, and hay, which reminded her a bit of home, but something else tainted the air, something she couldn't ignore.

Decay.

There was a corpse somewhere.

She drew her shawl over her nose and mouth and went in deeper, her eyes adjusting to the gloomy light cast by cheap, brown-toned sacred lights bolted unevenly into the rough stone ceiling. The space looked like a natural cave had been enlarged, straight walls alternating with rough curves that arched up toward a ceiling obscured by numerous support beams. There were some plaster walls as well, sectioning off small rooms. And then she found a long hall of wooden doors. Each door was split in the middle so that the top could open separately from the bottom. Near the hall's entrance, a dark horse peered out at her through the open top half of a door. He stretched his neck to get a better look at her as she approached. She let him sniff her hand, then stroked his velvety-soft muzzle. His eyes were gentle, and he leaned a bit into her touch.

This was a large, underground stable.

Most of the stalls were empty. She wasn't sure if this was usual, or if the scent of decay meant that something very bad was happening here.

A man and a boy emerged from a stall. They saw her and hurried toward her. "You have a mount?" the man asked in rough Kilhellion, smiling too broadly. "Very good! Very good. We're very cheap, but we have much of hay, and water, and good groom. We'll give you a cheaper because of the smell."

"I don't have a mount," she told him in Kilhellion, guessing he'd want the practice. "I heard the noise. I wanted to see what was going on. Is there a dead animal in here?"

His expression melted into a frown. "This isn't a drum day. You want to … jump? your life for to get that damned animal out? If no, you need go."

"What animal?"

"Currocatta," he said. It sounded like an Arrak word, one she hadn't heard before. "A desert horse," he said in Kilhellion. "If you get it out of the room? … stall." He seemed surprised to remember the correct word, then continued with a little more confidence. "Or outside or in an other stall, I don't care not which now, you'll have a cheap place and all the food and bathing you want. Hells, I pay you to get it out."

When the mine petered out her family began to raise ponies. She wasn't exactly born to it, but she also didn't remember a time without ponies. Horses were bigger, but their character was much the same. She had to wonder, though, why the Arrak had failed. Even in the Kilhells, Arrak were famed for their horsemanship. A common boast in Kilhellion stories about heroes was that they were as skilled in horsemanship as an Arrak nomad. Despite her doubts, she was curious. "I'm willing to try."

"You have one hour, then I'm close the door," he said, briefly switching to Thedran for the time and number. He shouldn't have bothered. It meant nothing to her, though she guessed that he wanted this done before true night, with time to spare. "If you want to stay all true night, yes, but it's very foul. His owner died, and the horse won't let us close."

"I see." It didn't seem like that big of a problem. If nothing else, they could just lasso the poor beast's front legs and head and hopefully pull him out without hurting him or getting kicked. And really, a kick from a horse might be bad but seriously … why was this so hard? Was it something about the size of the stall?

"You might sick."

So that was it. Dead bodies carried the risk of becoming infected with something serious.

It was a problem for most people, but she was a healer. It was nearly impossible for her to get an infection of any kind. "I understand. I'll manage."

"One hour," he said needlessly, holding up a finger. He gestured for her to set down her bags in a stall set aside for tack, and then he and the boy led her deeper into the stables to a broad, short hall running between empty stalls. The stench grew worse until it threatened to gag her.

Halfway down the hall they stopped and gestured to an open doorway thick with flies.

It was a huge doorway, too. All these doorways were. Maybe it was a charger of some sort, maybe the kind that Lordmarkans used while wearing full armor and lances and big, heavy cavalry swords, all things she'd never seen but imagined.

Well, she'd seen full plate armor now. And it was impressive, and it looked heavy, and hot. The sort of horse that could carry a large man wearing that sort of armor, plus armor of its own, would be a sizable animal.

None of that explained the sounds she'd heard.

The man and the boy didn't approach the open stall door, a thing of heavy oak and iron, with the lower half almost as tall as her, and the upper higher than she could jump to touch the top. She wondered if the riders had a habit of riding their horses in, with room to spare to swing a long weapon around comfortably. With the latches set at about eye level on the lower door, and in arm's reach for the upper, a person wouldn't have to dismount to open the doors.

Billie set down her bags. She drew her shawl more tightly over her face and peered into the dimly lit stall. Even with the shawl she felt compelled to press her hand over her nose and mouth, not that it kept the smell out.

It wasn't a horse.

Smell forgotten, she stopped dead. A brown eye, gleaming with intelligence, reflected the amber light in the stall. Its gaze followed the motion of her hand as it dropped from her face to her blade. A massive mane lifted and flared like a porcupine bristling and brandishing its quills. Nostrils big enough to put her fist into opened to show the delicate red tissue within.

It kept its head lowered to keep its ears from brushing the ceiling. The head was in fact horse-like, but it had tusks. The bone that supported those tusks formed a ridge from a hollow place under its eyes down to emerge from its mouth, where they curved gracefully into ivory weapons as long as her arms. It had a mane like a horse too, but in a long curtain that nearly touched the ground. A lock draped between its ears to cover part of one tusk. The body was similar to a horse's, though at the withers it had a lump of fatty flesh bigger than a large sack of flour. She could see hints of a horse-like tail somewhere behind it as well. But its front legs had talons, almost like an eagle but much more muscular, and the skin below its knees was like dried toad skin, mostly hairless and thick and lumpy and ridged. Its huge, fuzzy hind legs terminated in broad, fleshy toes with thick, shovel-like toenails or talons. At her height, she wouldn't have to duck much to walk under the beast's belly. The size and weight of it loomed as an overwhelming presence, even in the very large stall.

She presumed that the pitifully small pile of rags in the corner was what was left of the human.

Her heart must have stopped, or she might have forgotten she had a heart for a moment. Now her heart pounded in her chest, staggering her breath.

She backed away, slowly. At least it hadn't reacted to her except to stare at her.

The animal—desert horse—shook his head and a cloud of flies lifted from him, only to settle elsewhere on his body or on the walls.

"His name is Roorah," the boy offered in a small voice.

At the sound of his name, the so-called desert horse huffed and shook out his mane more aggressively. Dust flared out of the stall door along with the flies, and the very air seemed to shiver in fear.

She hadn't noticed a halter or anything on him. "Is he halter trained?"

"Halter, bridle, saddle," the man told her. "Good luck getting a halter on him. The man who could do …" He pointed to the body.

"How did he die?" Billie asked, dreading the answer.

"Sick, I think. He looked no good when he come. He want to sleep there last true night. He never wake."

He'd been rotting in that stall since last true night? That was awful, like the flies, like the smell of decay, like the misery in the horse's eyes as he stared at her with a kind of weary hostility.

Normally she'd ask why they hadn't sent for a trainer, or a Mage, or someone with real experience with such beasts. But it was clear from what she'd seen coming in, and by the man's exhausted words, that they'd already tried everything.

She would be a fool to try. She didn't know anything about that … thing.

She started to turn away, but then she thought of how Roorah had held his head.

He wasn't just exhausted.

He was grieving.

He didn't want to leave his friend.

He had no tribe, no brother, no friend to comfort him. He was alone within a city of strangers that just wanted to get rid of him.

Billie put her back to the wall beside the stall door. Her heart steadied.

"There's food and water for Roorah," the man told her, pointing to the stall across the way. "He may grow hungry or thirsty? If you get him out, a Death Mage will carry away the dead."

*I might be Roorah's last chance. The Champion's Keep will still be there after true night.*

*It's not like they're waiting to take me in.*

A sense of impending defeat settled onto her shoulders. She doubted she'd save him, but … "I'll try."

"Luck of the Rill," he said in Thedran, and he and the boy left.

What a mess this was.

In a way, it was a simple problem. She had to get him to trust her. Once he trusted her, she had to convince him that his person was gone.

Simple, but she suspected it would be impossible. People who knew about creatures like him had tried.

The correct things hadn't worked. Maybe she'd stumble into something that shouldn't work, but would.

"Roorah." She had to remind herself to keep her tongue forward as she spoke, and emphasized the roundness in her mouth. His name felt awkward, but airy with a bit of a growl, like the boy had said it.

The desert horse blew out a warm breath that carried the scent of hay, and sugar, and a strange spice that momentarily rose over the scent of decay. A breath later it vanished into the overpowering stench. "Roorah," she said again, more gently, and Roorah sighed. He shifted, claws scraping, and something rubbed against the wall. She peered in. He'd settled beside the body, and had flared his horse-like tail over his legs and over the body to shelter it. On seeing her he arched his neck, and his mane flared away from his neck, splitting into locks, some of which stuck up higher off his neck than others. She'd never seen a clearer warning to back off.

Though it wasn't good training, she backed away out of sight. After a moment she heard him shift, and snort.

She feared she knew how this would end. The horse would die of thirst rather than leave his friend, and they'd cut up the body to take it out in pieces, because it was too big to move whole.

She wondered how long he'd last.

Billie sat down outside the stall, her back braced against the wall. Did she want to be a witness to this tragedy?

Unlike everyone else in this immense city, she had no pressing work she had to do, no one expecting her, nowhere to stay, no promising future to look forward to.

Roorah really needed her. He didn't want her, but she was all he had now.

The body had looked so pathetic in that stall. It had to be awful to watch the person he loved get eaten by maggots and rot. How horrible it had to be for him.

*How long will you grieve?*

*Forever,* Roorah seemed to say with his devoted, watchful silence.

She edged over so that she could watch him, and he could watch her. She sat with her back against the jamb where the gate would close, feeling pinned by the power of his baleful gaze. "I'm so sorry, Roorah." His ears didn't perk or shift, but somehow, she had the feeling he was listening to her. His ears had a thick, fuzzy front edge and then a more delicate, rounded edge, supported by the heavy side like a sail. She wondered if he understood the Thedran she spoke. She wished she knew more Arrak. She considered her words carefully, and tried to add in the few Arrak words she knew. "Your person was good to you. I can tell." This was more than goodness and friendship. This was loyalty, and love. Family. "You still love him, and that's never going to go away." In her heart a little defiance flickered to life, but the light quickly went out. She could love her family all she wanted, but she knew she'd never see Brian, or anyone else in Torath, ever again. Even if she tried to go home, what would that do but bring more death and more heartache? And yet … "You can't just forget and walk away."

*That's the problem, isn't it. For both of us.*

His eyes lost their focus on her, and half-closed. He was excessively still except for a tiny tremor that traveled under his skin. She wondered if he understood her. "When do we let go and get on with our lives? You tell me. You have to teach me. Because I don't know."

He probably didn't know either.

If she'd been with Brian and he'd died anyway, how long would she have stayed by him?

Until the rest of the tribe dragged her from him, she thought.

There was no dragging Roorah anywhere.

"What do you want, Roorah?" Maybe he wanted to be free. Maybe there were others of his kind living with nomads who were family to this man. Roorah might have a life beyond this stall. "If I led you out of the city, could you find your family?"

Or maybe Roorah and this dead person were alone.

"Would you rather be alone?" Kilhellions prided themselves on being independent and strong, on being able to survive on their own if they needed to. But in the end, tribe was everything. A Kilhellion alone was more miserable than a mountain lion cub without its mother. Roorah was obviously miserable without his human friend. Regardless of what he might have been like as a wild creature, he yearned for companionship now. "I'll stay with you," she promised. "So, at least you have me. All right?"

He made no sound beyond the deep rush of his breath. Was he resting? Was he in physical as well as emotional pain?

"You're good," she told him softly in Arrak. "Good Roorah." *Faithful Roorah.*

She'd been loyal to her tribe. What was she going to do with that loyalty? Keep it warm like Roorah tried to keep his friend's dead body warm?

"We're deep in the forest, you and I," she whispered to him in Kilhellion. "We've got to find a way out, or we're going to die alone."

## Chapter Twenty-Four

<<<<<<<<<<<<<<<<<<<<<<<<<<<<<<<<<<<<<<<<<<<<<<<<<<<<<<<<<<<<

# Within the Darkness

<<<<<<<<<<<<<<<<<<<<<<<<<<<<<<<<<<<<<<<<<<<<<<<<<<<<<<<<<<<<

*Deep within a stables under the city of Ben Ariim*
*4ᵗʰ Somber Day of Sun Month*

Roorah liked the sound of his name, and he liked the sound of the drum. Billie made up a chant and a drum rhythm just for him, playing it softly while she thought about how to approach him without getting killed.

She'd managed to settle just inside the doorway so that he could see her while she played. It had taken a lot of time to gain that small distance closer to him. If he had been a wild pony, she would have left him on his own for a while to think about her and what he might want, if anything, from her, and what they'd done together, which was mostly get used to each other's smell and the smell of the corpse.

Not that she could truly get used to it. It wasn't like shit or piss, where she could eventually ignore it. Every moment the air tasted as putrid as the last. No wonder the horse wouldn't eat or drink. The very idea of food made her want to be sick.

She had to leave the stall every time she got thirsty, too. Intellectually she knew she wouldn't become infected with a disease just because she was close to the corpse. Her healing gift protected her from that. But her body was sure that Death was near, ready to extend a hand and draw her soul into the realm of Gods. Her lungs didn't trust the air she breathed, and her stomach was sure all food and water was as corrupted as the body.

By comparison to the smell, the flies were a minor irritation. She learned to flick and swat them away without a thought when they got on her bare skin.

It didn't seem possible, but once the stable master closed the doors for true night, the stench intensified. Every breath made her want to gag. It took discipline to speak, but she made herself talk to him, just a few words at a time at first. She wasn't sure if he was listening, but every so often a large, fuzzy ear swiveled in her direction.

Roorah liked it when she drummed, spoke, and moved away from him. Everything else he warned off by huffing and flaring his mane. He even growled once, a sound that was more like thunder than a noise an animal would make.

But she couldn't allow herself to lose ground, so after each break away from the stall, she carefully moved closer, even if it was just a hand's length, and praised him when he finally accepted her and relaxed his threat display.

Talking to Roorah, and drumming, helped pass the time, time which she couldn't measure without other people about, or regular meals to eat. She slept only when exhaustion smothered her and woke groggily to the same dim lights and the same stench. She dreamt of death: Brian's death in a myriad of awful ways, the man she'd stabbed in the throat, the man whose arm she'd cut off. Horribly, she dreamt of fighting the hellion, and reaching into the dead child and feeling that evil warmth that had nothing to do with life.

She also dreamt, in a muddled, surreal way, of making her bone flute with her father. When she woke, she couldn't remember where she was until Roorah huffed. In that moment, home no longer felt like home, but like a bad dream, even as she yearned to return to it. She stroked the head on her drum and mulled on Ben Ariim.

She couldn't imagine this being home. It wasn't just a matter of being welcome or not welcome. She'd felt unwelcome in her father's house before. She knew such things passed, sometimes quickly, sometimes slowly. But eventually, Temric and the Rill siblings would leave.

They weren't her only friends, though. Aliiren would be here. She knew Hova too. And Jasmine, though she scoffed at the idea of going back to the pleasure garden to visit him. She didn't fit in that sort of place.

Whether she had friends or not, she would survive in Ben Ariim.

Surviving in a place didn't make that place a home.

She missed her family. She missed the mountains, and the ponies. She missed playing the cliff drums. At the festivals she'd play and play until she couldn't anymore. Then, drenched in sweat, she would rest until she had enough strength to play them again while others made thunder that struck the cliffs and rumbled inside her, inspiring her to dance and chant and scream. She missed running up, down and across the slopes, and climbing cliffs and stalking through woods with friends she'd known since childhood. She couldn't bear to think of their names, but they came to her anyway. She could hear them laughing and teasing her as if they were sitting beside her now.

How they'd gape to see Roorah. Billie smiled as she imagined their expressions, then sobered when she realized she'd never see them again.

She might not even see mountains again, or the stars in their full brilliance. The air on Mount Cross was so clear and clean. It always felt cool, even in summer, especially when a breeze lifted and carried the heat of the crystalline sun away. By comparison everything here seemed gritty and muddy. Even the color of the sky seemed tinged by a barely visible haze.

She stroked the drum again. She didn't want to, but she needed to say goodbye. Her gut lurched as she considered not just that, but a duty to Brian. She was sure that everything had been done at his funeral—

A sharp pain at the thought of his funeral sliced through her—

But he, assuming his soul hadn't already been born into a new body, would want to hear from her.

So Billie began to play to him. She played a rhythm they used to play together all the time, played softly at first, and then with love and pain powering every beat and stroke and rap on the wooden side of her drum.

It felt like Death had already taken her from her life and had poured her soul into a new one. But Death's touch hadn't mercifully cleansed her soul of most if not all memory of her life on Mt. Cross. She remembered.

If only she had died, it wouldn't hurt like this.

How sweet that would be, to not remember. What was the difference anyway, between this and if she'd really died? Wouldn't it be easier to just end it and start over clean? Who would care if she was gone? People who barely knew her?

For a breathless moment she imagined being gone. This city would sigh with relief. Her family could truly move on as, no doubt, Temric would find a way to send a long letter about her passing to her tribe. He would probably lace the facts with his opinions on the matter, hard opinions like the ones he'd expressed at the pleasure garden. Would her parents mourn her a second time? Or would her father feel as if Brian had been granted justice?

If an outsider did take her tribe to task for what they'd done, no doubt they'd be even more sure they'd done the right thing. They would only care if criticism came from within the tribe.

She wondered if any of her friends had protested, or if they'd even been told. Her immediate family, the chieftain, and scribes had the right to tell the rest of the tribe that she was actually dead. Either way, everyone would have gotten together, to mourn, to distribute her things to people who needed them, to drum to her soul. At this moment, someone was probably wrapped up in her blanket. Someone else might be playing her drum, carved from a burl big enough to bathe in. It had carvings of a badger playing, a badger fighting, and a little badger curled up, sleeping within a circle of apple blossoms.

Who got her walking stick? Her mushroom basket? Her canoe?

Strangely, it comforted her that those things would get good use.

*Maybe everyone is better off now that I'm dead to them.*

*Is that true? Am I better off dead?*

Perhaps logically, but something in her heart couldn't accept that.

*Enough daydreaming.*

Drumming to Brian had transitioned into drumming to her own death. It felt right, and her grief felt quiet, almost serene now. Her hands stopped abruptly on the skin, deadening the last beat. She forced herself up. Roorah shifted his weight restlessly. She took a careful half step toward him and turned sideways, keeping her face averted, listening. He settled again. "Good Roorah," she told him in Arrak.

The stable master had been teaching her more Arrak words to help her work with him. The words she'd been taught had become second nature to her now. More importantly, Roorah had learned to trust her voice and movements, even if he did fuss sometimes.

His fussing had the power of a whole herd of horses, not one, but she recognized that he didn't mean to kill her. Yet.

She left to take a piss in a nearby empty stall and then traveled farther to drink some warm water from a pail set up for her use at the far end of the complex of stalls. Though it wasn't as strong, the smell clung to her.

Death.

Goodbyes.

Maybe there was a way for Roorah …

She wondered if anyone else had tried it.

Billie went to the stable master's room and knocked on the door.

Fortunately, he answered fully clothed and in what appeared to be good humor, a book in hand. "Ah, Billie. How are things?" His tone surprised her with its welcome and kindness. But then his nose wrinkled and he edged back. She was sure she stank. Best to get this done quickly.

"I need to learn more Arrak." She explained, and he nodded and stepped out into the hall with her. It took him more time than either of them wanted, but she managed to learn what she needed. She also ate some bread and an orange that he offered. He wished her luck, she thanked him, and then she returned to Roorah.

She hoped that what the stable master had told her about desert horses was true. They were thinking creatures, he'd said, as smart as humans in their own way, and could understand a great deal more than even a very smart horse.

"Roorah," she said, slowly claiming a place another hand's length closer than before. Roorah lifted his head.

His wasn't a human face, but nonetheless his expression struck her like a slap. She knew it, not because she'd seen it, but because she'd felt it.

A person he cared for deeply, maybe the one person he cared about most in the world, was dead. He could be wondering, why am I alive? Wouldn't it be better if I died, and lived my next life ignorant of all that I've lost? Who would care if I was gone? These strangers are kind and express concern, but don't really know me. How long would they grieve if I died?

She had no easy answers. But Gods, it mattered even more to her that Roorah found a way, because she knew this loyal being deserved all the things that Life offered before he died. Every living thing was sacred, but his devotion made him even more special. She wanted him to have a future full of joy and love, adventure and honor, tranquility and pleasure.

She had to win through to him and show him not only that Life still had gifts to give him, but that he had gifts to give, gifts the world needed.

Her plan, though good, would not be enough. She had to find a way to express how much he mattered to her, and to the world. She had to convince him that the world would be a smaller, colder place without him. She had to convince him to live.

"Are you a healer?" she asked him in Arrak. "May I heal him? May I heal your friend? Roorah?" She edged closer to the body. His mane flared and he let out an intimidating huff that made her pause. The odor from the corpse was eye-watering. "Please, may I heal your friend, Roorah?"

The mane lowered and he sniffed toward her. Drool dripped down one of his tusks, and the talons on his front feet gripped the straw-strewn stone floor. She kept her gaze lowered and breathed as lightly as she could. His muzzle, wrinkled and drooping with a prehensile upper lip, neared her face. He sniffed, so close that the whisker-like hairs on his lip brushed her face. His mouth gaped open and the prehensile lip lifted, baring square front teeth between the tusks. His breath smelled like decayed hay. She exhaled, and he drew her breath into his body.

He arched his neck, which moved his head away from her, and then watched her askance out of one eye.

"Good Roorah," she whispered. For some reason he tensed. She hadn't moved. Maybe it was her tone of voice? "I'm here to help," she tried in a low, but not whispery tone. He chewed on nothing and nodded. She hoped that was a good sign, like it was in a pony. "I'm here to heal. Good Roorah." She eased farther into the stall.

His gaze focused on her keenly, but the mane didn't lift, and he didn't huff or growl. His stillness, though, felt like he was perched on the edge of an attack.

She'd come too far to back away safely. Billie sidestepped, facing him as she slid along the wall.

If he took exception to her now, she would not make it out alive.

Her body tingled with fear. Her heart swelled with awe in the presence of that much physical power. Death seemed a breath away. "Good Roorah. I will heal. Healing. Do you know the word healing?" Gods, she hoped she pronounced the words correctly.

He just stared at her, clearly wary.

She was only a few steps away now.

The mane flared again.

She stopped, heart beating so hard against her ribs she wondered if he could hear it. Those massive talons, those tusks … she'd been an idiot to put a hand on her sword when she'd first seen him. Yes, she might have cut him. But she would have never reached anything vital on him before he disemboweled her with a single swipe.

*This is the most idiotic thing I've ever done in my life.*

Was it just her imagination, or had he relaxed? "Good Roorah. I'm here to help your friend. Good Roorah." She started moving again, but this time much, much more slowly.

It took an eternity, but she eventually reached the corpse. She was close to Roorah's hind leg as well. If he kicked out, she'd be squashed against the wall. His tail was flared over the body to protect it, not that it guarded against the host of flies that buzzed and crept in between the coarse tail hairs.

What horror he'd had to endure out of loyalty, or love, or both.

She showed him her hand, then slowly lowered it onto his tail as she reached forward toward the corpse.

He probably didn't feel the contact, but he tensed anyway. She waited until he relaxed, and then told him, "Good Roorah." She took her hand away to hopefully teach him that she wouldn't force him to do anything, not that she could. He watched closely, but he was still relaxed. "Good Roorah." She reached again and parted the hairs. Underneath, the corpse felt warm to the touch, even through the stained, reeking fabric. Maggots made soft, slippery sounds amid the decaying flesh beneath the soaked clothing. "Healing," she said, though of course there was nothing she could do. "Healing." And then, in an exaggerated way, Billie bowed her head. She waited a moment before looking up into his eyes, knowing that was dangerous, but feeling in her gut that their gazes had to meet for him to understand. "He's dead. You know his soul is gone. We should sing to his soul." The emotions in his eyes were too intense to bear for long, full of pain and fear. She lowered her gaze and bowed her head again. "He's dead. We have to sing to his soul."

She hoped she remembered the Arrak funeral chant correctly. Fortunately, it was short, and the syllables fell into a simple rhythm that flowed well. While she chanted, she carefully lowered herself until she could brace one hand against the ground. She reached with the other toward his nose as she sat her ass down on the stone floor. The stones were filthy with his piss, excrement and old straw. As foul as it was, it smelled sweet and felt clean compared to the corpse.

Roorah just stared at the remains of his friend.

She shifted her position to sit at the corpse's head, or what she guessed was the head. The body had partly flattened into odd lumps and bumps under Roorah's tail. It made it hard to tell what was what.

Roorah did what he'd done before while she'd been drumming. He lowered his head and curved his neck so that his nose was near the corpse. Billie kept chanting.

Billie extended her hand toward his muzzle. She didn't quite touch Roorah's wrinkled, prehensile lip, just let him smell her hand while she chanted, and chanted, while her arm ached and burned from the strain of holding it out so still and for so long. Then, when she decided she dared, she set her palm on his nose.

It took a force of will to keep her breathing and heart rate steady, and her body relaxed. Like a horse, he lipped her hand, exploring. The skin was thick, tough enough to endure touching the things he ate in the desert, but it was tender and supple too, and softly fuzzy, and very warm. His hot breath blew over her.

She slowly lowered her body until at last she lay flat on her back and could rest. The straw had been flattened and soaked with foul things, but it still cushioned her a bit from the bare, cool stone.

Billie didn't know how long she lay there. Forever, it seemed. She dozed for a while. And when she woke, flies and a few stray maggots crawling on her, Roorah was sleeping. As far as she knew, he hadn't slept since she'd first met him. He probably hadn't slept while all those other people had tried to coax him out of the stall either. He must have been exhausted.

Watching him sleep felt like a rare privilege. She doubted there was much that could seriously hurt him, and yet he seemed vulnerable in sleep.

She could probably escape.

She didn't want to leave him, not when he'd finally accepted her presence. She wanted to be here when he woke up.

She edged closer to his head, careful not to touch him, closed her eyes, and rested as best she could.

She woke when he shifted. She opened her eyes and he snorted. She closed them again, trying not to tense.

Not so long ago she'd wondered if Death might not have been welcome. This horse could send her into Death's arms in a flash of movement. She didn't know how she felt about that anymore. She didn't want the pain and fear, but would it be so bad to have it over quickly?

The problem was, it might not be quick. She might end up broken, her gift extending her life for agonizing hours of fever, in a place where no one could get her out safely. She'd die in the filth, helpless, while Roorah gradually slipped closer to Death alongside her.

He snuffled her head, lipped her shawl, and tugged it off her head. The power behind that tug wrenched her neck, despite the relative gentleness of his demeanor. He was still lying down, the farther foreleg tucked under him, the nearer foreleg curled more loosely, and still within her reach. She extended her hand while he explored her face with his lip.

He could take off her head with the ease of a child plucking a dandelion. His tusks scraped the ground, two massive dull swords that could gore her horribly without effort.

"Roorah," she murmured. "Healing, Roorah." She slid her hand between his talons, heart hammering hard at the moment of contact. The deeply furrowed, thick skin felt silkier than she expected, and it had very fine hairs. He was hot, like a human with a potentially deadly fever. Was that normal? "Roorah. Healing." She linked her nodes. He didn't seem to sense that. She wouldn't expect him to, but she felt as if everything she did was against the pressure of a sword's point. "Roorah." She closed her eyes, then moved a stream of vinus from her linked nodes to her palm.

With great caution, she entered his body through the channel opening in the central point amid his talons, the place equivalent to a human's palm or arch of their foot. Her hand, nestled in the center of his forefoot, was no larger than the tip of her finger touching the palm of her chieftain's gnarled hand.

Something within him pushed back gently, like a breeze entering her veins. He had a trace of native healing, but there wasn't enough friction to ignite a dangerous fever if she persisted. She let her consciousness travel into him.

Her mind opened to a realm of water and lush livingness far more vast than any human's body, and more complex.

He huffed, perhaps in warning, but she was so dizzied by his physiology that she didn't think about what that might mean until the threat had passed.

He was definitely a mammal, and no, he wasn't sick with fever. He was dehydrated, hungry, but not dangerously so. She didn't know how long he might last, but he seemed strong enough to live for the foreseeable future.

The quiet, pervasive thing hurting him was his grief. She could feel it. It made each beat of his heart heavy. It tightened his two stomachs, which barely moved. She wasn't sure if that was normal, but she doubted it. His mind felt bright in only a few places. The rest of his mind felt dark, as if he was asleep and drowning in a grim, half-realized dream.

She didn't have the skill to do anything to his mind. Few healers did. Nor could she change the rhythm of his heart directly—she could tell without attempting it that he was much too strong for her. She could affect his blood vessels, but she wasn't sure that would help him. The only thing she could think to do was something intimate, a thing she wasn't sure he would welcome.

When she'd practiced it at the school, none of them had volunteered to let her touch their nodes with her gift. She had to practice with Dr. Val. At least he made it quick, his expression didn't change, and he made no comment while she felt as if his vinus occupied every part of her body at once. When her turn came, as soon as his vinus touched her nodes she'd sensed within him kindness, wisdom, openness, generosity, and a kind of far-seeing practicality. There was also a remove, a hidden place where he buried his pain and fear. She'd pushed his vinus out of her nodes after only a moment, unwilling to sense more than she already had. Afterward, Dr. Val had looked away and quickly returned to his place at the front of the class, but he didn't treat her any differently.

Roorah barely tolerated her now. If she offended him, or scared him, he might kill her.

She hoped that if she showed him who she was at her core, he might trust her enough to let her lead him from this tomb. Maybe he wouldn't sense how much she cared, and how committed she was to helping him. It would be unusual if he could see into her past, or feel her actual emotions. It required a rare gift to sense such things. But he would certainly get a sense of her soul.

He'd sense things in her that she couldn't sense in herself. Dr. Val explained that it would be like her own eyes trying to see themselves without a mirror. The comparison made sense, but she didn't understand why she couldn't know the nature of her own soul.

She had no idea how great of a risk she was taking by doing this.

*What if he doesn't like what he senses?*

If Roorah tried to kill her, there wasn't a lot she could do to stop him. "Roorah," she murmured, and sent her vinus toward his nodes.

As she drew closer, she could feel the outline of each node. Most reminded her of weird animals. His nodes were different from a human's—larger, with more limb-like structures—but their placement and how they connected to his organs were similar. That helped orient her. She was almost there …

He tensed. She backed from them, pooling her vinus near what appeared to be his dominant node, the one she knew as rabbit or the fists, also known as the fifth node at the healing college. The numeric designation didn't speak to her, though, and not just because she had difficulty understanding numbers and their use. Fists felt real. They were like a child's fists pushing against an adult's fists. She sensed that pressure within them. Rabbit made some sense too, especially since unlike in a human, his seemed to have long ears. At the college she'd been taught that this node anchored the soul. It was the node that went dark before the others when the soul started to slip free of the body. The lungs connected to this node, and the node stretched and contracted very slightly with each of his breaths.

He relaxed. She advanced her vinus toward the node more slowly this time. He tensed …

The contact with his rabbit node felt like dunking her hands into a hot river. She took a breath and allowed the feeling of his presence to fill the whole of her with that heat. It was impossible to defend herself. She had no awareness of the stall, or even of her own body. She wondered if she'd feel pain if he bit her head off or crushed her body against the wall with his hind foot, a foot that could cover her entire upper body.

But that didn't matter. All that mattered was floating with him, and the wonder of gazing about the palace that his living form made.

She slid toward his tail into the crab node, or so-called fourth node. It connected to his skeleton. She filled it with her vinus, lending fresh strength to an incredibly potent source of healing—his marrow.

All at once she lost contact. She blinked, disoriented as she became a being within a human body once more. He towered above her, his mane a pale curtain that draped within a handspan of the filthy stone floor. She'd forgotten how massive he was while they were both on the ground. Now, at his full height, she was no more than baby bird fallen from a nest at his taloned feet.

He lowered his head. His lip played through her hair. Billie held very still. She didn't know what had caused him to rise, and so she had no idea if she'd offended him, or frightened him, or angered him …

His head swung back to look at the corpse. He stared at it, something working deep within his brown eyes. Billie carefully backed toward the door, scooting on her ass and hands. She didn't feel safe, not even when she reached the doorway, not even when she got her feet under her and backed a step. Something about the way he stared at the body connected in some way to her. She knew that he wasn't ignoring her. If anything, he seemed keenly aware of her in a way that he hadn't been before.

Which made sense. He'd seen her through his nodes. He knew her in ways that she didn't know him, would never know him even if they spent the rest of their lives together. Perhaps, in some ways, he knew her better than she knew herself. Did he find her wanting in many ways, as her father usually did, as her mother sometimes did, and as, obviously, the chieftain and scribe also had, or they would have never disowned her?

His weight shifted and his head swung back toward her, those ivory tusks sharp enough to kill her. He took a step toward her. Cautiously, not sure if she was fleeing or leading him, she took a step back.

And another. He stepped toward her and stretched out his neck. In that moment he seemed very horse-like. It was the fearless sort of I-want-to-smell-you gesture that ponies often did. And then, keeping his head low and in reach, he arched his neck in a pet-me gesture.

She caressed the side of his neck from behind his massive jaw back toward his chest, then rubbed as he leaned into it. Gods. Was this really happening? "Good Roorah," she remembered to say. It came out breathless, because she was breathless.

He made a grunting noise she hadn't heard before. It sounded … happy.

She smiled. "Come, Roorah," she told him, remembering the word in Arrak more or less. He understood, anyway, and stepped toward her. "Good Roorah. Come." She led him out, but not to the stall across the way. The scent was too foul in this whole section of the stables. She led him down the broad hall, a bit nervous as he loomed with his head just above her shoulder and his withers, covered by the sack-like hump of fatty flesh with arm-length locks of pale mane sticking up every-which-way from its crest, high above her head. Those withers were close to grazing the high ceiling. He followed her to the hall's end, and around the corner, to the next line of large stalls.

She opened the door to the first one. She had to reach up to unlock the bars attached to the upper halves. He wouldn't be able to get through the doorway otherwise.

And he went in, sweet as child wanting a sleepy cuddle by the fire before bedtime. Billie followed him in. "Good Roorah. Hold." She stroked his neck. "Hold, Roorah. Hold." She picked up the bucket in the stall, left the door open and went out. When she looked back, he'd stretched his neck to watch her go. "I'll be right back," she promised in Thedran, and hurried to the nearest water spigot, filled the bucket, and brought it to him.

He drank even before she finished putting the bucket down. She stroked him and then ran for fresh grain and hay in the nearest hay stall. Once he started eating, she went back to find the other fodder that had been set out for him, and found some jerky. He loved that! Then she searched for and found grooming supplies. She got a chunk of soap, a brush and comb, and a bucket of fresh water so she could begin the work of cleaning him. She started to dry brush at his neck and chest where he seemed to like being rubbed the best, and then she went in with slightly soapy water. Working in sections was the only possible way to do it. She left his tail for last, letting the filthy, caked ends soak in the bucket while she worked. She didn't wash his face, though she went over it with her hands while he munched placidly. She was just being cautious, not sure how he'd tolerate bristles around his muzzle and eyes. Finally, she went over him again with clean water, wetting the brush, stroking him, wetting the brush again … And then she had to splash bucket after bucket of water onto him to make sure every last bit of soap was out of his coat.

By the end of it she was exhausted. It felt as if she'd scrubbed down her tribe's entire songhouse, floors, columns, walls and every bit of furniture, all by herself.

The stall was soaked with filthy water. She moved him across the way. She found fresh straw and created a thick bed of it.

Billie left him long enough to strip down to her underthings and scrubbed herself raw. She desperately wanted hot water and rags and to soak in soap for the rest of her life. Cold, soapy water would have to do. Despite her best efforts, the scent seemed to linger, if only in her own mind.

Shuffling footsteps alerted her before the lights revealed the stable master. "How is it going?"

Only then did she realize what had happened. "Roorah is free," she told the stable master, because it was true.

## Chapter Twenty-Five

◇◇◇◇◇◇◇◇◇◇◇◇◇◇◇◇◇◇◇◇◇◇◇◇◇◇◇◇◇◇◇◇◇◇◇◇◇◇◇◇◇◇◇◇◇◇◇◇◇◇

# Roorah in the Sun

◇◇◇◇◇◇◇◇◇◇◇◇◇◇◇◇◇◇◇◇◇◇◇◇◇◇◇◇◇◇◇◇◇◇◇◇◇◇◇◇◇◇◇◇◇◇◇◇◇◇

*Ben Ariim, a city in Arrak Thedra*
*1st Meet Day of Flame Month*

True dawn had long passed by the time Billie thoroughly groomed Roorah once more, took a long, hot bath in the stable master's rooms, and properly laundered her clothes. She thought that because Roorah had finally said goodbye to his former human friend that anyone would be able to manage him, but he bristled and growled at the stable master and his boy when they approached, so she took care of him on her own. It was nice to be wanted, and yet, she could have used the help. From a safe distance, the stable boy would suggest new things to do, like cleaning under the talons on Roorah's front feet and scraping under his strange, padded back feet with a fine rasp.

The stable master told her that if she set him loose outside the city, that would be the best way to find out if Roorah and she belonged together. He assured her that desert horses could full well take care of themselves, and that he'd be fine if he decided to run off.

Billie wasn't so sure. It didn't seem right. She'd seen the state that wild mountain ponies got themselves in, especially over winter. She just nodded and decided she'd ask someone she trusted about what to do. But first, she wanted a good meal.

The stable master had given her a handful of coins. She was fairly sure they'd buy her a few meals. With the reassuring weight of them tucked away within her belt pouch, she hefted up her bags, then headed for the ramp leading up to the street.

Roorah left his stall and followed her.

She stopped and looked back at him. He went right up to her, towering over her a moment. His front leg matched her height, and his barrel-like belly was equal to a good-sized boat. He sniffed her head, then passed her to go up the ramp.

Well, then.

She followed him out and blinked against the bright sunshine. He'd stopped on the busy street. People quickly got out of his way when he huffed and shook out his mane. Seeing him among Thedrans emphasized his immensity. He was closer in size to the buildings around him than a horse or a camel.

He really was a magnificent beast, and it seemed that he knew it. His true colors glowed in the sunlight. He was a deep gold. His forelegs and talons were covered with dull, gray, scaly skin with dark freckles and a thin scattering of dark gold hairs. His mane and tail looked nearly white alongside the gold coat. His eyes were not nearly so deep a brown as she'd thought, but more like burnished copper. His talons were like ivory at the tips and deepened into a color that verged on black. His ivory tusks seemed brighter in contrast to the grayish hairs around his muzzle and the dull, freckled gray of his prehensile upper lip. The water hump over his withers was covered with cockeyed, relatively short tufts of mane in a dull, brownish gray, making it appear like it had come from a slightly different animal. In all he was splendid and regal, but when she looked at his individual features, he was a very strange-looking animal.

"You saved him," an Arrak woman remarked in Thedran as she approached them. Roorah snorted at her, and she stopped abruptly. "Good Roorah," she told him in Arrak as she eased back a step. Her look of surprise scrunched up into a narrow-eyed frown.

"Do you know him?" Billie asked. Part of her wanted very much to put him into good hands, but she'd grown attached to him and she didn't know this person.

"Only by reputation," the woman told Billie, reverting back to Thedran. "I tried to help him, but he was having none of me." Her expression grew shrewder and Billie put a hand up on Roorah's shoulder. He snuffled Billie's hair, which pushed back her shawl. Billie pulled her shawl back on more or less into place. He lipped at it, and she pulled it away, hoping he wouldn't grab it. Thankfully he left it alone.

"What do you intend to do now?" the woman asked.

She had a feeling that admitting that she had no idea would be a mistake. "I guess that's mostly up to him."

The woman shook her head and walked away, mingling in the crowd. Billie quickly lost sight of her.

What in the hells was she supposed to do?

"Kilhellion."

It was the stable master. Billie turned to face him warily, wondering if he might take back what he'd given her for helping with Roorah.

He'd given up on practicing Kilhellion with her over true night, once he'd realized that she spoke Thedran. She suspected his language skills were poor in part because he didn't care to practice as much as he ought to. "The Death Mage is nearly finished with her work."

Death Mage? Billie knew one had been sent for, but she hadn't seen one go by. She supposed it was for the best. All she would have done was gawked, like people so often gawked at her.

"I thought I'd let you know, and also, I wanted to tell you I'm grateful." He placed both hands over his heart, and grinned.

His kind words and gestures made her smile, and her body warmed with a quiet happiness. "I'm glad I could help." Roorah lowered his head to her shoulder and steamed it with his breath, as if to remind her that she should be paying attention to him.

"I have a friend." The stable master offered her an envelope. "Murina is, among other things, a camel breeder and broker, though she also deals in horses."

Billie gazed at the envelope. "All right." She had no idea what that had to do with her, and she wasn't sure what accepting the envelope would mean.

"She can help you with him."

She wasn't sure she understood. "Are you saying that she might buy him? He's not mine to sell."

His smile faded into a concerned, apologetic look. "Sorry. I didn't mean that so much as ... You see, whether he's yours or not, you're his now." Roorah snuffled her scarf, and she placed a hand on his muzzle to distract him so he wouldn't pull it off of her head. "If that's not your wish, you'll need her help. And if it is your wish, you'll still need her help. Desert horses can be a lot of trouble, as you've already seen." He held out the envelope again.

Billie accepted it. She wondered what words it held, and if those words were meant for her, or someone else. Like the letter from her family, the envelope seemed to hold great power over her life, and she wasn't sure she wanted it.

"If nothing else Murina can give you some advice about keeping him happy and out of trouble." The stable master gave Roorah an admiring look. "He's loyal, and brave. I wish him long life and happiness. And you too, Kilhellion." With that he touched his forehead, held his hand palm out toward her, and then turned and walked back into the stables.

"Thank you," she said belatedly.

If he heard her, he made no sign of it.

He'd have a lot of nasty cleaning to do, she realized. His thoughts were probably cast ahead, trying to sort out how to make his stables welcoming again.

She stared at the envelope. It had letters on it. She was pretty sure she recognized one of them.

A Gurra boy caught Billie's attention. "Gurra," she called out, and he trotted over to her, smelling of sweat and sweets. Roorah didn't seem to mind him. If anything, he seemed curious about the boy, who held out his hand to be sniffed. "Do you know Murina the camel breeder and broker?"

His brow furrowed, but then he looked at the envelope and relaxed. "At this address?" he asked, gesturing to the envelope with his chin. Roorah lipped his hand.

"Yes," Billie said uncertainly.

"Very good. I'll show you!"

Billie followed him, and Roorah took up a slow-for-him, ground-eating pace alongside her. The massive desert horse seemed to be as tame as summer, though the power of storms flowed through his body, which flexed to the work of moving him as if his bulk was nothing to mind. She doubted he would feel her weight even if she hung from a fistful of mane with her feet completely off the ground. Could he be steered? Was he a companion, a protector, a mount, or a pack beast? All the time she'd spent in Ben Ariim, she hadn't seen anything at all like him.

They had to stop at a fountain where Roorah drank for a long time, and then continued over a broad, long bridge that passed over a swampy ravine. The bottom of the ravine was thick with reeds and irises with crinkled periwinkle blooms that smelled like warm sugar. Not far beyond they entered a neighborhood with houses that weren't connected to each other. Every house was surrounded by walled gardens. She cringed when

Roorah stretched his neck over a wall and nipped a large branch off an orange tree in passing. He munched on it as he walked, leaves, stems, and any fruit that didn't drop off before it got to his lips. She hoped the owner wouldn't come running after them, calling them thieves, or vandals, or both.

The stable master was right. Roorah could get her into a lot of trouble.

Many of the walls had patterned openings in them that revealed intriguing hints of lush plantings, elaborate benches and tables carved from exotic woods, tidy paths of rounded stones, and of course fountains. She'd been told that Arrak Thedra was part of a vast desert, but so far it seemed it had as much water as the lakes and streams all around Torath.

Torath: home that wasn't home anymore.

And this place … it was a forest, but instead of dells filled with ferns and meadows lush with grass and wildflowers, there were streets filled with people, and instead of cliffs and fir and oak and maple trees, there were buildings and palms and statues and fountains. She wondered if she'd ever learn to navigate the city, or if she'd always need a guide.

In this part of the city, the streets had fewer people, most of whom walked as if time had stopped flowing and pooled like a peaceful lake. They looked at her like she had strayed into their house and wondered if she'd leave on her own or if they'd need to help her find her way home.

The Gurra stopped by a fine iron gate set between stone pillars. The stone wall that extended to either side had so many small openings carved into it that it would have been lacy if the blocks weren't so thick. The Gurra looked at her expectantly. She pulled her money pouch from under her belt and fished around and from under the sackcloth pouch until she had several coins. "Is this enough?" she asked, holding them out to him.

A look of pity flashed through his expression. The warmth of shame in her cheeks felt familiar, and exhausting. "More than enough," he said, picking out two of the smaller coins.

*I'm not going home, which means I'm going to have to learn how to work with money.*

It felt like an impossible task.

She felt a sharp pang as she remembered something. "How difficult is it to send money to another place?" Most of the wealth in the drawstring pouch wasn't hers. It was tribal. "Like …" He wouldn't know about Torath. "Like Port Sellon." How would her tribe react if she managed to do it?

The chieftain was shrewd. He would accept that she owed at least that much to them, if not more. But what would it mean to her tribe? Would they think she didn't care, that the gesture was born of arrogant pride? Or would they trust she was the person they'd always known, not the best in the tribe, but someone they once cared about.

"Not hard, but risky," the Gurra said. "I might make a special arrangement. The more you spend on passage for the money, the safer it will be. Sending it cheaply …?" He shrugged. "Who knows?"

The thought of sending the coin home, regardless of its potential repercussions, gave her a strange if uneasy feeling of satisfaction. *Yes. If I can do this, I will, and more.*

"I will return with a price, and if you wish to pay, I will help you send your money to Port Sellon," he promised. "What is your name?"

"Billie." Speaking her name, even without including her family name, didn't fit right anymore, like a tunic with a big tear in it.

"Where will I find you? Here?"

"I don't know. I don't think so." She considered her options.

"If you trust me, I think I will be able to find you," he said with a grin. "You will be the only Kilhellion with a currocatta, I think."

Roorah tipped his head at the word, as if to get a better look at the Gurra. The boy put his hand up but withdrew it again with practiced calm when Roorah tossed his head and snorted.

"Steady," Billie told Roorah instinctively. She wasn't sure she ought to admit in front of Roorah that she wasn't sure if they would stay together. "I hope we'll be together," she decided to say.

"Either way, tell Murina where you will go next, and I will begin there."

She thought of Temric. "If that doesn't work, I might spend some time near the library."

"Which library?"

Hells, there was more than one? "Uh …" She tried to think of a distinctive marker nearby. The fountain, she suspected, wouldn't be distinctive enough. "There are shops across from it, and it's a nice street, but there are no Gurras there and when I stopped to rest one of the shopkeepers told me to leave. It seems that they don't allow vagrants there."

He kept smiling but his eyes narrowed. "I think I know which one. I'll find you." And with that he left her there at the gate with Roorah steaming her shoulder with his breath.

She was about to open the gate when she heard a door scrape open beyond it. She heard voices, and then a somewhat scruffy Thedran man walked to the gate. He was adorably sweet-faced with a wispy beard more fitting for a young boy. His hair was long and flowed over his shoulders in thick, dark waves, and his eyes were hazel, appearing bright beneath thick, dark brows that stormed not with anger or disgust but with puzzlement. "May I help you?" he asked in heavily accented Kilhellion. He was no longer looking at her, but at Roorah with even more puzzlement and no small amount of wariness.

She handed him the envelope. His gaze finally returned to her. "I will take this to Murina," he said. "Please wait here."

She nodded that she understood, and stroked Roorah's neck. She'd just reached up for another stroke when a woman barely older than Billie with a figure overflowing with lushness stormed toward her. Her ethnicity seemed Thedran, but her skin was darker, and her dark eyes gleamed with mischief. "You leave someone standing at the—" she began angrily in Thedran, and then saw Roorah. "Oh. Oh." And then she laughed boisterously. "Good Gods of humanity!" She glanced at the letter. "I'm Murina. My apologies, but he'd eat my whole garden in two bites if we let him in. Falidee, I'm sorry. I see now. Would you please bring a table and chairs and some refreshments," she called over her shoulder, and let herself out through the iron gate onto the street. "And you are …?"

"Billie Mai … Billie." She quickly focused on her new friend. His life was what mattered. "And this is Roorah."

"Roorah," Murina purred. "May I introduce myself to him?"

"Of course. But be careful. His friend died, and he doesn't know me very well."

She nodded. "If I lose a hand, it'll be my own fault." Murina focused on Roorah without meeting his wary gaze. "Roorah. Good Roorah." She purred the words in Arrak and stayed very close to Billie, their bodies almost touching. "Good Roorah. How magnificent you are. I'm honored."

He arched his neck as if preening in response to her words. It convinced Billie that he understood full sentences in Arrak.

"Have you come to visit me? I'm honored. Very honored." Murina went on in Arrak while Falidee set up a small square table with a hole in the center through which he placed the stem of a large, square umbrella. He continued setting a comfortable place for them as Murina spoke soothingly to Roorah in increasingly complex Arrak that Billie couldn't follow. Falidee put embroidered velvet cushions on the chairs, then brought out a crystal pitcher and glasses which he filled with thin slices of lemon and the clearest water Billie had seen since she'd left the Kilhells. Murina, between praises to Roorah, slipped in another quiet apology to Falidee for snapping at him. Falidee simply smiled and then brought out generous slices of dark bread, slivered candied fruits, and colorful pastes that Billie couldn't recognize and wasn't entirely sure were edible. He set out napkins and gold spreading knives with short blades, and thick gold pins with flattened handles on one end. At last he positioned himself against the wall, holding a pitcher made of unglazed ceramic decorated with camels and flowers.

Murina stepped back from Roorah, who'd deigned to sniff her hand and then her hair. "If you'll kindly sit, we can get to business," Murina told Billie. Her round cheeks and crinkled eyes looked like she'd been born smiling, and had smiled ever since.

Did she think Billie meant to sell him? It shouldn't have been a shock, especially after her conversation with the stable master, but it still jarred her.

She'd helped her father sell ponies before. It was hard, but it was business. This, though, didn't feel right. Roorah understood at least as much language as a child. That alone made selling him feel dangerously close to slavery.

Even within the part of Kilhellion culture that kept slaves, the correct path was to free him and return him to his home, as might happen to a slave if his owner died in the Valley of the Kings. Even they wouldn't just lay claim to someone else's slave and sell them again.

So, with great unease, Billie settled, and sipped water made all the more refreshing by the bitter-sour-sweetness of the lemon slice in the crystal glass while Murina read what proved to be a very long letter. The words filled both sides of a large piece of paper, as big as Billie's hands set flat thumb to thumb.

"So, you've only known Roorah for a single true night," Murina said.

"Yes."

"Were you raised with desert horses?"

"No."

That natural smile faded. "What do you know about them?"

"Very little," Billie admitted. "I've never seen one before I saw him."

Murina shared a glance with Falidee. "From what I've gathered from this letter, he had a single human friend. That could mean a few things. If he was born wild, he'll want to return to the wild. I would suggest that you try to do that as soon as you can," Murina told her, much to Billie's relief. "But if he was raised by that man, the man who died, who Roorah was trying to protect even after death ... he's probably very confused right now. He will have never known a life without his friend. He may not know how to care for himself very well. He may not know how to get along with others of his kind. Most colts raised by one person, bonded to that person, die unless they can learn to trust someone else."

"I don't know that he trusts me," Billie admitted.

"But he followed you here," she pointed out.

"I helped him grieve with a funeral chant. After that, I think he was just ready to see the sun again." She wanted so much more for him than a few moments in the sun. "He probably doesn't know where to go any better than I do. I'm afraid for him. I don't want him to die."

She set the letter on the table on top of the envelope in which it came. The inside of the envelope had a little writing in it also, but it seemed that Murina didn't consider that writing important because she'd paid it only a brief glance. "How long have you been in Arrak Thedra?" And then she shook her head before Billie could answer. "Forgive me. You speak Thedran well. Do you know Ben Ariim well?"

"I don't know the city at all. I came from Ruvall, but I wasn't long there either." She didn't mean to be so brief, but this was about Roorah, not her. "I'll do whatever he needs."

"Then you and I, after water, will go to the east side of Ben Ariim and learn what will be best for Roorah." Murina's smile returned, and Billie finally relaxed. This didn't sound like a sale or exchange. It sounded like Murina wanted what was best for Roorah too.

The stable master had done the right thing, sending Billie here. She felt a keen gratitude toward him for that, and all the other gestures of kindness he'd shown. He may have done it for his own sake, and maybe Roorah's, but he'd been fair and generous with Billie. And now Murina, with her cheerful sweetness, built a new sense of shelter and hope within Billie.

Maybe life in Ben Ariim wouldn't be so bad.

Together they would find a new home for Roorah, and then, maybe Billie would find a new home herself.

BILLIE DIDN'T KNOW MUCH ABOUT CITIES. COMPARED TO LIFE IN Torath, everyone in Ben Ariim was rich.

This was wealth of a different kind. It wasn't lavish and ostentatious like the pleasure garden. It felt more real, and in many ways more impressive.

It turned out that Murina had a large family, and she was that family's primary source of comfort. Some of that family, in the form of cousins, their spouses, their children, and Murina's two husbands—one of which proved to be Falidee—helped escort Billie and Roorah to the city's east side, picking up herds of camels and horses and lines of carts along the way. None of the people appeared to expect Murina's arrival, but they were all happy to see her and they all wanted to take their animals out of Ben Ariim with her. To a person they were kind, well-dressed, well-mannered. Mulina introduced everyone, assuring Billie that no one would be offended if she didn't remember their names. She included Billie in their conversations, and she made sure Billie ate and had fresh water over the long course of the day. That was a blessing, as this gathering took much of the day. Billie explained about the Gurra that would come looking for her. Murina, after a quick word to Falidee, assured Billie that someone would wait for the Gurra back at the house.

Maybe she was being a fool, but Billie set her hand on Roorah's shoulder, nodded, and gave her trust to Murina. It seemed that, in Ben Ariim anyway, that's what good people did. They helped each other.

Billie hadn't known what they planned to do at the end of that day, until they left through the city's eastern gates. Then much became clear.

They were leaving Ben Ariim along a broad trade road along the outside of the city's main wall. That vast wall, taller than Roorah could see over even if he stood on his hind legs and craned his neck, ran a mostly straight course due north. To the east, grain fields covered in knee-high grasses were fenced off by a shoulder-high wall that thankfully Roorah didn't step over.

The wall at her left shoulder dropped to shoulder height, revealing more tender grain fields. Ahead, she could make out a new wall. Some of it was stone, but most of it was logs as tall as ship masts, between which were strung nets. The gates through that wall were tremendous things, more like moving walls of stone and steel than doors, left open to a road that continued northward into the desert.

The river was visible to the left from the road at times, but often snaked away, edged in trees and surrounded by low scrub and stretches of tall grass. At a decorated stone marker, they left the main, paved road to travel east on a dirt cart road.

The ground was hard and dry, but tough plants flourished, many of them grasses, or shrubs with furrowed bark and small leaves. Every so often a huge tree cast some shade over them as the sun began to settle in the afternoon. Despite the dominance of stone in this dry, hot place, it was shockingly green compared to what she'd imagined the desert would be. The most common grass, rather than growing in a thick, lush blanket of deep green, was pale green or almost blue in color, and grew in thick tufts that created mazes of paths around it. Wildflowers, mostly white and yellow, grew between on tall, leafless stalks, punctuated by scarlet poppies or a mat of sky-blue flowers that liked to grow over stones. The trees varied from the size of an apple tree, up to those broadly spreading mammoth trees that cast shade over vast stretches of ground. Flocks of birds soared from tree to tree in the distance, flashes of white, black, red, and blue. Other birds behind their caravan would burst into the sky all at once like flies chased off a corpse, then descend again to what she expected were the shores of the Jeweled River. More drab birds flitted about individual trees and shrubs, mindful of the hawks that perched on high, bare branches or circled in the pure blue sky.

Camels and horses roamed free on these lands, intermingling much like the ponies and goats her tribe managed. Every so often the cart road would split, leading to a walled manor house with pastures, olive groves, and huge gardens. Some of the pastures surrounding those manor houses were walled in a combination of stone and hedges thick with ferocious thorns. Eventually she spotted a few desert horses in the far distance, and one much closer. That one had patterns clipped into her coat. Murina explained that the patterns identified who was responsible for them. Later they saw a black desert horse with a back bronzed brown and a gray mane. He was slightly bigger than Roorah, but the others had been smaller. Roorah, she gathered, was exceptional. The admiring looks Roorah received from the people who worked in the open, most of them tending gardens, herding animals, and mending walls, confirmed her suspicions.

For his part, Roorah seemed uninterested in the other desert horses. He kept close to Billie, steaming her shawl with his hot breath.

She'd seen drawings of antelopes and gazelles, so she guessed what they were, but she hadn't realized there were so many kinds of them of different sizes and coat patterns. There were other creatures, at a distance, that looked like gray blocks with tremendous, fan-like ears and strange, elongated prehensile muzzles. She tried to think of how they would compare if one stood beside Roorah. They looked far heavier, but possibly the same height or a little shorter than him. She thought, perhaps, they might be elephants, though she'd never even seen a drawing. From the one story the tribal scribe told of elephants, she'd imagined something quite different, with long, shaggy red hair, so she wasn't sure these were the same.

Most of the stone that interrupted the thin, yellow soil was either the same yellow, or gray with stripes of other colors through it. She took note of a ridge of slate-colored columns of rock so regular they looked as if they'd been taken from far away, carved, and stood up by the Gods. "Kiinah's Towers," Murina told her. "We're almost there."

Their large party walked and rode on until they reached a shallow river. Murina sent Falidee and Billie across while everyone else waited to see what Roorah would do.

He didn't hesitate. Roorah followed Billie across, then stopped with her on the far bank, where she let her feet cool off in the warm, muddy shallows.

*I don't want to do this.*

Murina had told Billie what to do, but Billie gave herself a moment to run her hands over Roorah first while he stood in the water and drank deeply. His appearance had put her off at first, but now she saw him as a being of gentle greatness, with a deep intelligence behind his eyes. He was graceful despite his size, and considerate of her, never treading too close and always mindful of his tusks. She stepped back to face him, and had to chuckle because face-on his tusks looked a little absurd, similar to how a buck-toothed child had an unexpected cuteness to them. It was a different way to see him. "Roorah," she said, and then sighed. She didn't expect it to be this hard. "Go on," she told him in Arrak. "Go play, Roorah. Go on. Get ha. Get ha."

He snorted, shook his head, and took off at a gallop. Her heart soared to see him gallop, his weight pounding the earth into submission, the sound of his talons and his heavier hind feet drumming a rhythm as powerful as cliff drums.

He was free. He would be wild, and he would be fine, and she wouldn't have to worry about him anymore.

So why did it hurt so much?

"It's good," Falidee told her gently. "Desert horses are very difficult to keep. They're better off as wild creatures. Better for them, and better for us. They can be a nuisance, getting into crops, eating pet cats and rabbits ... more than one human has died because a desert horse going through town took exception to them and they didn't get out of the way fast enough."

She nodded, not so much to agree, although she did, but because she didn't trust herself to speak.

She'd grown attached to a wild thing like this once before. She'd rescued a young raven so weak it couldn't hop even to the lowest branch in the brush where it had tried to hide. Her father told her to keep it in a box overnight, and if it was still alive the next day, she could try to nurse it back to health. And it did live, and it drank water from a bowl, and ate the grubs and worms and snails and eggs she and her brother fed it, and it grew strong extremely quickly. After a true night with them, she and Brian took it outside. It managed to fly, not very well, but got up into the lowest branches of a fir tree. They called to it, but it kept flying in short stretches to the next tree, and the next, getting higher each time, until they realized it was useless to keep following it.

She'd cried like a fool, even though she was glad it was all right. She'd thought …

She'd thought it had loved her as fiercely as she'd grown to love it.

Like she loved Aliiren, and Temric, and Larani and Edrion, though she barely knew them. She loved them, and her heart leapt every time she thought she might see them again.

Maybe, she realized, like she'd hoped Roorah would stay, they'd hoped she'd stay with them. But what would they do with her? Like the raven, like Roorah, she was a lot of trouble, and really didn't give anything in return but companionship.

And then she chuckled through her pain, and felt a bit better.

*I'm an impractical pet.*

She and Falidee crossed back over the river, and then they all went to Murina's mansion, because of course she had a mansion that was very large and grand but without a speck of gold or jewels on display anywhere. They had a celebratory feast of roasted lamb dripping with juices, luscious, tart pomegranate and vinegar dressed over crisp greens and slices of some root that reminded her of strawberries mixed with apples, and many other good things. All the adults sat at one very long table with the children at smaller tables all around, and everyone drank wine, though the children's wine was mostly water.

They toasted, and sang, and made speeches and cheered, because desert horses were special and rare and an important symbol to the people of Arrak Thedra. Because, Billie was told as she sat beside Falidee and ate toasted flat bread that she stuffed with feast food and washed down good red wine, desert horses represented freedom from true night.

They were the Champions of the desert.

There were even desert horses that could channel faerus, like elephants.

She'd had no idea that elephants could channel faerus, never mind desert horses.

Desert horses didn't just defend their own kind, she was told. They defended many of the beings that roamed the desert. The herds with desert horses among them were safer from hellions and lions and other predators than herds without them. And desert horses, though they traveled in small groups, loved mingling with other herding animals. It was a sight to behold, she was told, to see elephants, desert horses, gazelles, antelopes, rezan, and all other kinds of creatures roaming from south to north, and then back again every year, like a nomadic city. And among them traveled the wild Arrak. The Arrak near Ben Ariim and Kal Ariim were almost a different people, many of them born from seed children or who were seed children themselves. But the wild Arrak, the nomads … they were as special as the desert horses. They too represented freedom.

By then it was too late in the night to ask about what seed children were, and everyone went to bed. Billie, her heart empty but her head and her belly full of the feast of ideas and stories and endless food, lay in the bed of Eniid, a Thedran woman who'd invited her for pleasure. While Eniid slept, Billie stared at a ceiling dotted with tiny, faint light stones set in patterns of constellations. She decided that she was lucky, luckier than anyone. That luck had come too late for Brian, but if it was true that Rill were lucky, then Larani and Edrion had truly blessed her.

This loss of Roorah, so little compared to her brother, had nonetheless taught her more than all the comfort Temric and Aliiren and the others had given her. Every day she'd been met with wonders, generosity, and kindness. And to end up in a place like Ben Ariim? It wasn't home, but if she could make it home, she would be even more fortunate.

There was only one way to make Ben Ariim home.

She would have to earn her place, and the trust of the people who lived here.

She would begin tomorrow. She'd go back to Ben Ariim, and go to the Champion's Keep.

She closed her eyes, wrapped her arms around her lover for the night, and thought about Roorah running free until sleep took her.

## 1st Labor Day of Flame Month

SOMEONE WAS PUSHING HER. BILLIE WOKE WITH A GROAN, DISORIENTED. She wasn't sure why she was in a soft bed, or with whom. The small but richly appointed room brought her back to her senses as she sat up to face a strange man. It was only then that she realized that she was naked, but he didn't seem to mind, nor did he leer, so she relaxed.

"Roorah is here," he said.

"Really?" She grinned and groped around for her clothes, throwing them on as quickly as she could. She couldn't find one of her socks, but she decided to put on her boots without it. Her socks were full of holes now anyway.

If she'd been home, her mother would have fixed them for her. Billie had tried to learn how to darn socks herself, but she just couldn't figure out how to do the needlework her mother did so effortlessly and evenly.

But never mind that. Roorah was back.

Maybe she shouldn't be happy. He belonged better in the wild. But he'd come back, and that meant …

Joy gave way to uncertainty. Did this mean she was responsible for him now? What about going back to Ben Ariim, to presenting herself at the Champion's Keep?

Eniid rolled over, exposing exquisite breasts. She didn't even smile at Billie. She just turned back over and drew the light, silky blanket over her head. It didn't hurt Billie's feelings. Maybe later, they might find out if they actually liked each other.

For now, all she wanted was to see Roorah.

The man led her through the maze-like house out into the garden, which was full of blooms and fruits and rows of vegetables so swollen with goodness they seemed bawdy. He took her to a gate where someone big and fuzzy lipped through good green hay made from something that looked like snap pea greens. She strode to him, her heart full. "Roorah," she gushed, and then caught herself before she hugged him around the neck. They were, after all, still getting to know each other.

But he closed the distance between them in a pair of long strides. The gate closed behind her. It startled her, but then she realized that they probably just wanted to keep him out of the garden.

Maybe he'd wanted to get into the garden, and didn't give a damn about her.

But no, he put his huge head into her arms, and she hugged him and scrubbed his face and drank in his musky scent that was something like a horse but also a little bear-like. "Good Roorah," she told him. "Good Roorah."

"They have a remarkable sense of smell," the man behind the gate told her. "Near as we can tell, he tracked you here."

"You know me, don't you." She kissed his muzzle. "Good boy, Roorah. Good Roorah."

"We'll bring you some breakfast," he said. "Murina may join you. She's very pleased that he came back to you."

"So am I. But how can I keep him?"

"It can be troublesome," the man agreed. "But you're friends now. And once you've befriended a desert horse … that's for a life." He nodded, seemingly to himself, and then grinned at her. "You'll have to learn to use a curroket, I guess, and learn how to tack him up, and ride him."

Her plans to become a Champion faded in Roorah's massive presence. But that was fine. That—that had been a crazy dream. Roorah was real, and he needed her. "We'll work hard and find a way to keep you well, hmm?" she told Roorah in Thedran. "Starting with me learning more of your language, and maybe you'll learn a little Kilhellion too. If you like. And we'll figure out this curroket thing too, whatever that is."

By the relaxed way his lashes shaded his eyes and the gentle way he lipped at her clothes, he would like it.

## Chapter Twenty-Six

## Visitors

*The Estate of Murina, East of Ben Ariim*
*4th Trade Day of Flame Month*

Sometimes in her dreams, she hiked through the cliff-cut forests near home, often on the edge of falling to her death. Sometimes she rowed across the ocean surrounded by violent waves, each larger and taller than the last. Worst of all she'd be fighting hellions of all different shapes and sizes, each more terrifying than the next. But in each of the dreams Larani and Edrion called out encouragement from far away. She could barely hear them. Then Brian would suddenly be there, his soft, rusty hair and grey eyes as clear to her as if he was actually beside her. His face was all she could see.

He tried to speak, but she couldn't understand him. And then, she would start to fall, or start to drown, or start to be torn apart by a crowd that screamed murderer, murderer, murderer. And while she thrashed and tried to save herself all the sounds around her—of the trees or the waves or the crowd—would change and blur until she heard just one clear voice. It was her father's.

*Murderer.*

Sometimes she woke up screaming. Eniid tried, but Billie didn't blame her for deciding that spending the night with the crazy Kilhellion was too much trouble. And really, though Billie tried, and Eniid tried, they didn't care about each other the way that either of them wanted.

For hours after those dreams, that word in her father's voice would haunt her.

She'd wash, she'd dress, she'd work with Falidee and Roorah, and that word would linger in her mind, along with her dead brother's face so close to hers that she couldn't see anything else.

Billie tried not to think about it. She had every reason to be happy.

She smiled. She thanked Falidee every day, thanked Murina every day that Murina was there. She thanked the other family members who worked at the mansion for the food, for the companionship, for helping her with her laundry and helping her mend her clothes, which had begun to pull at the seams because they were very fine and so they wore out more quickly than the more durable wool she'd worn all her life in the Kilhells.

Murina and most of the family went to Ben Ariim for the whole week of the Sun Festival and the true night that followed. She stayed with Roorah, the members of the family with very young children, and the workers. She helped prepare the feast, and silently thanked Jasmine for the beautiful skirt when she wore it during the meal. Everyone seemed impressed, but she felt like she shouldn't wear it.

It almost felt like living within a tribe again. They gave her work to do. They asked her to heal minor hurts. They appreciated the massages she gave them after an especially hard day, and the extra work she pitched in to help them with like the grooming work that never seemed to end as they managed their camels and horses, which they sometimes called grass horses to distinguish them from Roorah.

But she wasn't part of Murina's family. She wasn't really a worker either, though most of them were kind to her, and all of them were respectful. Billie was a friend with useful skills and a desert horse that she was still learning how to manage. She was welcome to stay, but there remained an unspoken question.

How long?

Billie didn't know the answer. She felt safe here. Roorah needed her. She was useful.

Maybe, in time, they would feel like family to her, and she to them.

Over a week after the Sun Festival, she found herself trying to figure out why a particularly obnoxious blonde camel named Tricks had suddenly begun to limp. From what her gift could tell her, Tricks had strained a shoulder. She was so engrossed that it startled her when Falidee the

Kind, as she'd begun to think of him, knocked at the threshold of the stall. "There are some people here to see you. They say you're family?"

Her heart began to thunder in her ears. "Kilhellions?" Had they come all this way to kill her?

That couldn't be. It wasn't their way.

But she had sent the money back home.

*Gods, have they changed their minds?*

"No," he said, cocking his head and setting his hands on his hips. And then he smiled a puzzled but pleased smile. "I think they're your friends. As soon as the pleasurer said it, the tall one—I suppose he could be Kilhellion—started to argue with him and the Arrak with them—well, by your expression it looks like you know who they are."

She wasn't sure how she felt. Excited, yes, but anxious too, and too aware of how fine they would all look and how unkempt she'd become. After all, Roorah didn't care if her hair was combed, or if she had a hole worn through the fabric of her trousers over one knee.

Her father had told her to keep her clothes clean. When had that stopped mattering? It was as if who she'd always been had begun to crumble, with random bits falling off around the edges.

Everything else had begun to crumble too, everything except the bond with Roorah. That, at least, had grown stronger, strong enough that she slept with him in a stall or in the pasture during the good days of the week, blanketed by his mane and tail.

Billie followed Falidee out of the corrals, through the garden, around the mansion to the other side. Under a magnificent awning around a paintwood table in large, rounded-armed paintwood chairs, sat Temric, Aliiren, Larani, Edrion and Jasmine. They were sipping lemon waters. Her heart swelled in her chest to see them, and she grinned. They all looked so fine. But then all of them looked at her like she was a hurt colt except for Jasmine. It was all she could do to keep from bowing her head in shame.

"I told you she was here," Larani told Temric as she stood and hurried to Billie. She hugged her hard. "It's so good to see you," Rani breathed into Billie's ear.

"You too." Billie let her go reluctantly, but it was probably too late to keep the stable dirt from transferring to Rani's voluminous patchwork skirts.

Edrion was slumped in his chair, eyes closed, apparently napping beneath the broad brim of an Arrak nomad's hat that looked very out of place with his own flashy patchwork clothes. Jasmine was exquisite in his silks and frills. He had a matching parasol leaning up against his chair in case the sun suddenly changed course to attack his perfect complexion. Beside him Temric looked very pale, overheated, plain and thin in clothes cut from cloth too fine for the simple tunic and trousers he wore. His brows furrowed as he looked her over.

Aliiren, though, of all of them, looked exactly the way he did when she'd first seen him. Calm emanated from him like a shady pool of clear water. But underneath that steadiness, his strong features had a fragility to them, as if grief for his teacher had made his skin more translucent, revealing his soul's pain beneath. Her shame faded, replaced by tender feelings of concern for him, and soon after, for the rest of them. She knew each of their situations weren't easy. Of all of them, Jasmine looked the happiest, though he'd been attacked not terribly long ago. She supposed he was just expert at hiding his feelings.

Aliiren stood and pulled out a chair for her. She hated the idea of sitting next to him as she was. "I'm filthy and I smell like shit," she told him apologetically.

"We don't care," Temric assured her. "Please. We came a long way to see you."

"You'll care when the flies start to gather around the table with us," Billie joked, but she took the seat, self-conscious of her stench as Aliiren's incense-laden perfume caressed her. He sat back down close by with no change of expression on his face. Jasmine poured her a glass of water and Larani passed it to her as she sat down. Edrion finally sat up with a yawn and then smiled at her.

"So, what have you been doing out here?" Jasmine asked politely.

"Cleaning up after Murina's animals. Grooming. Healing injured animals. Training with Roorah."

"The desert horse that you rescued," Edrion said eagerly. "That's how we heard about you. All the Gurras have been talking about it."

"So it's true? You saved a desert horse," Jasmine marveled.

"Why is this such a topic for gossip?" Temric asked.

"You'd only ask that if you've never seen a desert horse," Jasmine said.

"You mean an elephant?" he asked, using the Sothron word and sounding impressed.

"No," Billie told him. "Roorah is not an elephant."

"Can we see him?" Jasmine asked eagerly.

"That may not be wise," Aliiren pointed out. "Besides, she only just sat down."

"Please?" Jasmine pleaded. "We hardly ever see them in the city, and the few times I've been in the wilderness, there weren't any in sight."

Wilderness. She chuckled. Was this mansion and the gardens all 'wilderness' to him? "I'd be happy to introduce you." At least she could contrive to stand downwind of them.

They got up, and she led them back through the gardens while they chatted and asked her questions that had simple answers because really, she hadn't done much since she'd left them. Meanwhile, Jasmine had apparently broken ties with a long-time client which resulted in tears and broken hearts, and Rani and Edri had been exploring the city, going to party after party and making friends everywhere. Jasmine asked for details, and so the three of them kept everyone entertained while they made their way past the corrals to the enclosed pasture where Roorah deigned to stay.

If he wanted to leave at any time, he could. The wood fence posts and rails between the stone corner posts, all of which were substantial enough and tall enough to daunt a grass horse, were little more than twigs that he'd barely have to hop to get over.

He stayed because he liked her. That never failed to soothe her heart.

"Good. Gods," Temric gasped. He stopped dead while the rest of them lined up along the rails and leaned on one of the lower ones to gawk at him. Roorah, who'd been grazing a good distance off, noticed Billie and trotted toward them, his long strides quickly covering the distance. "That is *not* a horse," Temric added.

"That was my first reaction too," Billie assured him.

The ground trembled as Roorah picked up his pace to gallop toward them, his taloned feet treading with the comparative lightness of a draft horse, while his massive hind feet struck the earth with the force of a lightning bolt. He slowed just before he reached them and viewed the others with suspicion, facing them at first with his favored right eye, and then with both eyes for a good, long look. As usual, from the front his face looked a bit unlikely, verging on ridiculous, with his tusks looking like he had two sticks in his mouth. But then he cocked his head to look at them with his right eye again and the saber-like curves revealed themselves in a different, more intimidating way. The bone that rooted the tusks formed a ridge that arced up all the way under his eye, hinting that he could use them as easily to dig through hard earth as he could eviscerate with them.

"Good boy, Roorah," Billie told him. "These are my friends. They're good people."

"Your Arrak is very good," Aliiren told her in Thedran.

Heat rose to her cheeks. "Thank you. I've had a lot of practice." She'd spoken in Arrak, and to her surprise Aliiren didn't seem to follow her words very well. And now he was blushing too. "I've been working hard at it," she added in Thedran.

Aliiren moved to stand closer to her while Jasmine speculated with the others about how many 'tons'—the measure they used with desert horses, elephants and other large beings—Roorah weighed. Judging by the scoffing noises they made, no one was really sure of their number. She doubted that it mattered whether he was three or seven or ten. He was massive, regardless. "What do you think?" Billie asked Aliiren. "Does it matter how much he weighs?"

Aliiren shifted his gaze to look out toward Roorah. "How have you been?"

He spoke so softly, it felt intimate and private. She had to remind herself that he always talked that way, and that he hadn't meant to sound like he was asking in any way other than as polite conversation. "Fine," she said. "And you?"

Muscles along his cheek tensed and she realized she'd made a mistake. "Well enough," he told her. "I have no cause to complain."

"The truth is," she began, then hesitated. She had his full attention now, with those gold eyes focused intently on her face. "I feel like I should be in the city, looking for those people that attacked Jasmine. But I have a responsibility to Roorah as well. And, realistically, how would I ever find them? Besides. These people want me here." *I'm a more practical pet here,* she thought, satisfied by the sharpness of her private joke.

"Do you like it here?"

Falidee wasn't around, so she wouldn't hurt anyone's feelings, and yet … the thoughts that came to mind would sound ungrateful if spoken aloud. "What's not to like?"

"That isn't what I asked." He sighed. "I just wonder if this is what you want."

All thought vanished as she gazed into his eyes. The first one that returned, said, *I want you. A family. Home.* But then more ideas came, of making a difference in the world, of fighting for something better than just survival, and helping people that really needed it. *I want to become a Champion.* "It's just so … easy." She had to chuckle. "What a complaint. But … *look* at all this. They did fine—better than fine! —before I ever arrived and if I died tomorrow, they'd go on being fine."

"Wouldn't that be true anywhere?" Aliiren asked gently. "Small contributions, large contributions...perhaps it's not the size or quantity, but the quality. Like Roorah. It doesn't really matter how many tons he weighs. His presence, his willingness to be here with you and work with you and learn how to be of help to you and this estate, is more important than the size and even the strength of him. The practice of contributing even a little every day is important. Over time a person who commits to daily, necessary tasks can accomplish much more than someone who only occasionally manages a grand act of heroism."

She grimaced, wondering what he'd think of her yearning to do just that. "Trust me. It's not about being a hero. It's just that back home ..." She'd expected a flash of pain, but it didn't hurt as much to talk about it as she thought it would. "My family, my tribe, really needed me. They're going to struggle without me and my brother."

"The fact that you're not with them now is not your fault."

She could have argued, but everything she could use in her arguments, he already knew. He didn't blame her for her brother's death. She did.

The more she thought about it, the more missteps she saw in every choice she'd made. Every one of those poor choices had been her fault. Which made all of it her fault.

She'd failed Aliiren and his teacher too. And yet, Aliiren was here. Hopefully that meant he forgave her. "And you? What plans do you have?" Learning about his life would be so much better than talking about hers.

He set a hand on the rail and tightened down. Roorah was now lipping Jasmine's hand while Edrion looked on in awe. "We're lucky, but that might not save your hand if he bites it off," Rani told Jasmine.

"He's sweet," Jasmine said, smiling prettily. "You would never do anything to hurt me, would you Roorah," he cooed in perfect Arrak.

Roorah suddenly thrust his head forward and grabbed Jasmine's parasol. While he took off with it, everyone stood in heart-pounding shock, grateful that Jasmine still had his head.

And then Jasmine climbed onto the rails so that he could wave at Roorah over the top rail. "Hey! Bring that back!" he called in Arrak. "Roorah! Please bring—" Roorah had tossed it in the air and it landed in the dirt. Roorah grabbed it by the handle and pranced around with it.

It was funny, but mortifying too. That parasol was probably worth everything Billie owned and more.

"I've hardly had time to think, much less plan," Aliiren told her wearily. "Although, technically, the Sun Festival is over, Games Day has, as usual, been treated as a continuation, and House of Light is involved in the competitions as well. When Jasmine invited me to come out here today, Mage Pomi kindly allowed it."

Billie nodded her approval. "I'm glad." According to Murina, the Sun Festival was especially spectacular this year. Maybe so, but to Billie it sounded noisy, chaotic and overwhelming. She was, more or less, glad to stay with Roorah instead.

"The plan," Aliiren said, his voice even more soft than usual, "is for me to study to take over management of the temple. My teacher believed that I'm the best choice to guide the temple to greatness. Mage Pomi concurs and has been tasked to guide me on that path."

Thankfully she noticed that he didn't look or sound happy about it before she gushed congratulations. "What do you want?" she asked carefully.

He seemed more fragile than ever now. "To follow Light wherever Light takes me." But then pain tightened around his eyes and mouth. "I always believed that would mean studying and serving in Ben Ariim. But … I'm restless."

"You're leaving?" It wasn't like she'd seen anything of him since they'd parted at the pleasure garden, but still, her heart sank. Temric would leave. Rani and Edrion would leave. And now, Aliiren.

"Part of becoming a mage is learning about the world. I've lived in Ben Ariim all my life. I have to go. I have to see it for myself." He looked sad, rather than excited about the idea.

She was sad too. They hadn't seen each other in a long time, but now she realized that the fact that he was in Ben Ariim had brought her comfort. "When? Where?"

"Not any time soon. I must find a course," he said. "Temric … Temric and I have been meeting."

She remembered Temric mentioning that the day that Jasmine had been attacked.

"I have questions." Aliiren glanced toward Temric, as if he was about to tell her a secret that he wanted to keep from the tall scholar. "Temric led me to them. I think I might find what I need to find if I go with him, whether it's farther north, or south back to his homeland."

"When is he going home? He was so eager to make his way back."

Aliiren nodded. "He's torn. He's homesick, but he's learning so much that it's hard to leave the promise of even more knowledge behind. Perhaps he's learning the wrong things, but Light teaches that sometimes you must look into a murky reflection before you learn to see clearly."

His words about murky reflections gave her a surprising amount of comfort. It felt like she'd been seeing her future in a filthy, broken mirror ever since she'd been disowned. Aliiren gave her hope that one day she'd no longer be staring back at her own inadequacies and instead would see a clear way forward. "I'd like to —" *Go with you, wherever you go,* she wanted to say. "—visit you, wherever you go, if that would be all right."

"Of course." He sounded surprised.

Billie smiled, buoyed by the invitation. "It's settled, then." She climbed between the fence rails into Roorah's pasture.

"Where are you going?" Aliiren's surprise tightened into alarm.

"To get Jasmine's parasol."

It was a game, of course, and Roorah stretched it out. First he wanted to be chased, which Billie obliged, albeit at a leisurely pace so she wouldn't wind herself. Then he wanted to play keep-away, jerking the parasol well out of her reach every time she stretched to grab it from him. The parasol looked a little battered when she finally calmed Roorah down with a healing touch. He lowered his head, his gaze drooping along with his head. "May I have it?" she asked in Arrak, and he gave it to her. "Thank you. Good boy." She gave him a good neck scratch, then carried the parasol back to Jasmine. "Sorry. It's really dirty." At least the silk hadn't torn. But it was filthy, especially the lace that fluttered from the brim.

"My hero," Jasmine gushed, and then smiled beautifully at her as he shaded himself. "I thought I was going to scorch in this sun without it. And don't worry about the dirt. I'll just have it cleaned by a Gurra. It won't cost a thing."

She sighed. Nothing to Jasmine was a lot of money to just about everyone else.

"I will owe you forever for rescuing me," Jasmine said more seriously. "And it wasn't your fault."

No one ever thought anything was her fault, except the people whose judgement she trusted above all. They were the people who knew her the best.

"I know you're grieving," Jasmine said gently. "If there's anything I can do to help."

It was a kind offer, but not needed. "Thank you, but I'm all right."

"I know," he said.

A shift in his body warned her. She could have stepped away, if she wanted.

Instead, she welcomed Jasmine's perfumed embrace. It felt good, and he smelled wonderful. It made her even more aware of how expensive everything about him was, and how bedraggled she'd let herself become. Why was he even here? He could have stayed at his pleasure garden. Was he really here to see her, or had he come here because Aliiren had come here?

"You're a good person," he whispered in her ear. "Don't let anyone convince you otherwise. Most of all, yourself."

She probably shouldn't have, but she let the words comfort her. "Thank you."

Her doubts about his real reasons for coming here suddenly felt unworthy. Somehow, he'd become her friend. They were all her friends, and she would miss them. She'd been missing them all along. She just hadn't realized it.

Jasmine was still holding her, comforting her, when he was probably still feeling fragile from the vicious attack made by people still free to do the same again. "Maybe sometimes I can come visit you," she offered. "If that's all right."

He released her slowly and looked into her eyes. "Of course it's all right. When no one could find you during the Sun Festival I started to worry. It's why I arranged all of this."

Jasmine had arranged for everyone to come see her? Her lips parted, and she looked over his shoulder to Aliiren. Larani and Edrion were now taking up Aliiren's attention, chatting about their work fixing little things for people all over Ben Ariim. Rani asked if anyone at Aliiren's temple needed any leatherwork or clothing repairs.

"Why haven't you come to see me?" Jasmine asked Billie.

She started to make excuses, but realized they were worthless. Her reasons—that she wouldn't have felt comfortable with the wealth, and the potential for more gifts which she absolutely didn't want, and that she wasn't really needed—now felt awkward and more like excuses than reasons. She mattered to him. He'd proved that. He mattered to her too. She cared whether or not he was doing well, and she wanted the memories of his fear and pain to heal just like his bruises had healed. "Because I'm an idiot."

"Well, please do the smart thing and come see me," he said. "And if you give me warning, I might even arrange for something special. Nothing too expensive," he added quickly before she could protest. "Something simple. But special just the same."

She looked past him at Aliiren, who looked thoughtful and as if he was only half-listening to Rani and Edri. She didn't have to force a smile when she looked back into Jasmine's eyes. Jasmine had no idea how precious this gift—the gift of coming here and bringing the rest of them here to see her—really was. Or maybe he did. "I promise I'll come visit soon. Before anyone goes anywhere, all right?"

She and Roorah had to come to an understanding. Either he had to behave well enough that she could trust him in town, or he'd have to learn to do without her for a day or more. That had to happen before her friends scattered like autumn leaves in the first storm winds of winter.

And after that, the Champion's Keep?

She remembered that first night at the pleasure garden. He'd told her that she could train to become a Champion. It hadn't sounded like a joke, or flattery.

It almost didn't matter if he was being ridiculous at the time, inspired by his rescue. He made that future feel possible.

A tiny spark of fierce purpose lit within her. She fanned it, and made that spark glow.

# Chapter Twenty-Seven

<<<<<<<<<<<<<<<<<<<<<<<<<<<<<<<<<<<<<<<<<<<<<<<<<<<<<<

# Messengers

<<<<<<<<<<<<<<<<<<<<<<<<<<<<<<<<<<<<<<<<<<<<<<<<<<<<<<

*The Estate of Murina, East of Ben Ariim*
*1ˢᵗ Labor Day of Wandering Month*

"You seem nervous," Murina said at breakfast.

They'd had many, many breakfasts together. Murina had left for Ben Ariim and returned to the estate many times, sometimes bringing Jasmine with her. Larani and Edrion had come to visit too. Recently they'd stayed for a whole true night so that they could try to convince her to come to the Feast Equinox celebration in Ben Ariim.

She'd stopped short of promising, but she wanted to. She didn't know how much longer her friends would stay in Ben Ariim. So she'd been working even harder to learn about the keeping of desert horses. Mostly it was about learning his language, a language that was as rich as human speech but with fewer sounds. The Arrak words, the gestures she'd learned, postures she'd learned to hold when teaching him, and the movements she made, all communicated to Roorah what she wanted of him. At the same time, he taught her what the sounds he made, the postures he took on, and his gestures and movements meant.

At first he stayed with her and trained with her every good day, then took shelter in the blessed stables at night where he could be reassured by her scent and hear her heartbeat. Then Falidee encouraged her to tell him to go run free during true night. Roorah was always waiting for her in his pasture at first light on Meet Day, safe and sound, much to her relief. Recently, she'd tried to turn him loose for an overnight during the good part of the week, so she could practice with the curroket to call him back in the morning. He played for a short time and came back in the middle of the night. Fortunately, he politely scratched on the stable door until she opened it for him.

Today Billie would go out a much longer distance with Roorah than usual, find a herd of camels or gazelles or something, turn him loose, and see if he would stay with other herd animals in the wild long enough for her to try using the curroket to call him. He already knew the buzzing roar of the strange instrument, as he'd watched her practice with it. "It would be good if you learned to trust each other more," Falidee had said. "You and Roorah are good friends, and work together well. This is excellent. But you should do things without each other. This way you will both know that just because you are not together, it does not mean that you will never see each other again. Then, at last, you can both relax and have real trust."

Falidee was interested in helping Billie and Roorah form a partnership, and Billie wanted that too, but his dependence on her filled her with dread. If something happened to her …

In this civilized, gentle place most people seemed to pretend that Death would always wait until old age to take a person's soul away. Billie knew better. Roorah needed to be independent enough to survive if she died. She was pretty sure that Roorah wasn't as attached to her as the person he'd loved before. Falidee seemed to want that for them both, but she did not.

She didn't know how, but somehow she had to train both him and herself to trust in their bond, while teaching him to survive on his own when they were apart. Maybe he did that just fine. But she couldn't help but imagine him out in the darkness of true night, curled up and shivering with fear instead of grazing, taking in water whenever he needed it, and being prepared to fight if anything threatened him.

She wished she could heal away his fear. She wished that she could teach him how strong and powerful he really was, and that he could live on his own for the rest of his life if he needed to. She didn't want him to have to, but neither of them had a Rill's luck. If anything, they had the opposite. They both had to be ready for whatever might come.

"Billie?" Murina prompted, concern creating delicate furrows on her brow.

"I'm going to take Roorah on a long ride," Billie told Murina. "And then walk back."

"No," Murina protested. "Take a horse with you, and ride back. It's not a good idea to roam the desert alone on foot, especially so close to the equinox. The rains could come early."

"I'm thinking ..." She swallowed hard on her nervousness. "I'm thinking of going to Ben Ariim for the feast days if Roorah decides to stay out in the wilds for a while."

Murina's face glowed with surprised glee. "Oh, that's wonderful! I've been hoping you would go. I think Roorah feels safe enough now."

Billie wasn't so sure. He was still grieving. Sometimes he gazed in the direction of Ben Ariim, and she could see it in his face.

"Soon you'll be better at working with him, and you can take him with you," Murina assured her with a smile. "But I understand. He's a lot of responsibility, and you need some time on your own. You need the freedom to go to a place without knowing where you'll stay or for how long, whether you'll meet old friends, or make new ones. In the same way he needs to become comfortable in the desert, to roam for a while and become more sure of himself." She nodded decisively. "Take one of the horses, lead Roorah out for some exercise, turn him loose, and then ride straight from there to Ben Ariim. The more often you tell him what you want, the more likely it is that he'll understand. And if he follows you to Ben Ariim, don't worry. The walls will hold even against a big boy like him."

Murina made it sound so easy. "I'll try." She could always ask a Gurra to watch for him, spend a little time with her friends, and then go back to the estate. She didn't want him clawing at Ben Ariim's walls in a panic for hours while she pretended that all was well.

If that worked, maybe at the end of next week, she could feast with her friends on Somber, and spend true night in Ben Ariim.

Maybe.

"I'll have someone pack a lunch for you."

A burst of nervousness escaped her, a chuckle that left her feeling chilled. "Not today, thank you. I'll leave first thing tomorrow. Today we're going to do more saddle work. Roorah is used to having a saddle and rider, but I'm still learning how to ride him. Besides, I promised him we'd go to the swimming hole today."

Murina tapped her finger beside Billie's plate, reminding her to eat. On the opposite side, lines of coins were laid out, representing the worth of Billie's breakfast, the silk place mat, the water glass ... Even the vase of miniature sunflowers had coins beside it—a line for the vase itself, and a pair of small coins for the flowers. This manner of teaching helped so much more than reciting numbers, and it helped Billie with her counting as well. "If you like," Murina said. "But I insist you take a certain horse with you when you take Roorah out, and ride him back. He needs the exercise. Everything close by is too easy for him. He needs to really stretch his legs, and his mind."

Murina meant Elino. Billie groaned, though secretly she was pleased. He was a horse from a dream, a huge black with feathering on his legs like a draft horse. Unlike a draft horse, Elino was quick on his feet, and he was a little wild. Murina had gotten him from a Markan horse trader that had driven him and a large number of other fine animals all the way from Midmark to Kal Ariim.

Kal Ariim, where apparently Temric and Aliiren would soon go. The only reason she knew that they hadn't left already was that they'd promised to stop by and see her on their way out.

They'd written her since their last visit, all of them. Murina had kindly read the letters to Billie, and had helped Billie write back by sitting beside her and helping her to spell out the words with Thedran block lettering. Each letter of every word took Billie a long time to draw. The marks she made on the paper seemed to shift and vanish and return unpredictably as she tried her best to sketch each figure. Murina had offered to write the letters for her, but Billie knew it would mean more if she wrote the letters with her own hand, and so she'd struggled on. "Will you help me write a letter to Aliiren first, before I go? So I can warn him that I might be visiting tomorrow."

Murina made a face, and not a pleasant one.

"What?" Billie asked.

"I went to see him when I last went to Ben Ariim," Murina said haughtily. "He's so … uninspiring."

Billie's heart skipped with shock, and then her face flushed. "He's my friend."

"He's lazy," Murina told Billie firmly. "He's lazy and he hasn't come to visit you, not once, while Larani and Edrion have come twice. And he only wrote the one letter, while Temric has written at least once a week."

She knew full well that Aliiren was very busy at the temple. And it wasn't as if Billie had managed to go see Aliiren herself, even for a half day.

Murina shook her head. "I see the way you look at him."

Billie's face burned hotter.

"He's not good enough for you." Murina tapped the table in front of Billie's breakfast plate for emphasis. "My sister refused to listen when my mother warned her about the good-for-nothing she saddled herself with and now she keeps two more husbands that do all the work and that lazy cat of a man doesn't help a bit around the house, or in the garden. He doesn't cook, he doesn't sew, he doesn't dye, or paint or anything! Now, Aliiren is a Protector," she allowed, "and well-placed in his temple. But he never goes anywhere or does anything except flex his muscles, practice his religion and meditate. And what if he is close to Light? What if he Ascends? Then what will you have? Some ethereal presence that watches you while you stir your pot and stare at the ceiling wishing for a flesh and blood man. Be wiser than my sister, Billie, and listen to me. Temric would be a much finer choice! And Jasmine. He'd lavish you with wealth! And there are countless other men if either of those don't suit you." Murina kept talking though Billie had drawn a breath to cut in with choice words of her own. "*Believe* me, I understand. Temric isn't warm to you in that way, and Jasmine … you'd have to share him, and that isn't always nice when it's half the city you're sharing him with."

"Thank you," Billie said sharply, standing up from the table. She'd heard more than she'd wanted to hear. "For your advice," she added more softly, though she still felt tight inside. She wasn't angry so much as frustrated. She did want a partner in life, and a family, but now wasn't the time.

*Even if it was time, Aliiren wouldn't have me.*

"I tell you these things because I care for you," Murina told her firmly. "I want you to do well in life. I see how you look at my children and grandchildren. You want a family. You want a good life."

Billie shook her head. It was true, but unbearable to hear.

"You do! And that man has nothing to offer you."

"I have even less to offer him," Billie pointed out. True as that was, it was clear that it was time to stop hiding. She had to try to see Aliiren. "Maybe today is a good day to send Roorah into the desert after all. I need to stop putting it off." Billie left before she said something awful.

It was a relief to saddle Elino and then Roorah, who was fond of Elino and treated the massive stallion like he was a colt.

Elino never knew what to make of Roorah. He was twitchy around him, and kept turning aside to him, as if he was thinking about wheeling and giving Roorah a warning kick, but didn't quite have the nerve to do it. Billie had brought sugared coconut candies for Elino to help reward him for being so brave around Roorah, and of course jerky for Roorah to keep him distracted from wanting to lip Elino's mane. So Roorah lipped Billie's scarf instead, and stole it a couple of times before she finally mounted up and rode Roorah out toward the swimming hole.

It was a relief that Murina didn't come out to lecture her more, and that Falidee hadn't come out to join her. She needed the time alone to think.

She *did* want a family in the worst way. That wish, that life, had been her destiny in the Kilhells.

She felt insane. All her life, all she'd wanted was to help her tribe, to do her part, and have a family of her own. All her life, that had meant becoming a healer.

Murina had offered to help her find an apprenticeship with someone in Ben Ariim or even Kal Ariim, and every time Billie had used Roorah as an excuse. The more she thought about it, the less she wanted to become a fully trained healer. Always having to mind how much she fevered, the massive responsibility as strangers entrusted their lives to her, the reading she'd never be able to do, the extra work of memorization she'd have to commit to in order to learn the proportions of critical medicines, some of which were deadly poison if given incorrectly ... and if she made a mistake, she might die, or the patient might die, or both.

On top of all that, they had high expectations in the city. In the Kilhells, her ability to handle critical injuries and infectious diseases, things a healer of modest capabilities could manage, would have meant a great deal to her tribe. In the city, they had access to the best healers, and the people expected to feel perfect all the time. Every little twinge, every little sniffle and they went running to a healer.

What would Murina think of Billie's hope to become a Champion? Billie didn't think she'd laugh, but she'd certainly let Billie know how much better it would be to pursue healing rather than chase after a life of danger and poverty, assuming they would accept her.

Gods.

For a while she'd considered that maybe she could become a healer in a remote village somewhere in the desert, but would they accept her? They might not even let her into their village. What if she simply traveled the distance to ask, but was shut out, left in the wild desert to die over true night?

All of those obstacles wouldn't have mattered if she'd wanted it badly enough. But clearly, something had changed.

Ruvall had changed her.

Brian's death had changed her.

Her friends had changed her.

Roorah had changed her.

She felt so different from the person who'd left for the healer's college, she didn't know herself anymore.

If she'd said something like that to her father, he would have laughed. If she'd said something like that to her mother, she would have scoffed and told her she was being an idiot. She was a Kilhellion. What else could she be?

She wished she knew what Brian would have said. When she imagined him, he sat beside her, his gray eyes and the tumble of rusty hair more like her mother's than Billie's. He smiled within his boyish, scraggly beard, but he remained silent.

Maybe he would have said that she was his sister, and she would have hugged him, and they would have gone back to minding the ponies grazing in the meadow, working at some chore while they sat in the shade because in Torath, no one could afford to be idle.

*I'm not his sister anymore.*

After she'd dismounted and unsaddled Roorah, while Roorah waded and splashed around in the swimming hole, she had to fight to hold back tears.

*What's the matter with me? It's done. I have a new life now. It's different from what I wanted, but at least I have a future.*

Her heart still ached while she rode out on Elino, coaxing Roorah to follow from the swimming hole to the wilder lands beyond. It didn't take long to find a mixed herd of camels and gazelles. They looked up at her from their grazing, ears switching, tails flicking in irritation. Her heart still felt bruised when she told Roorah to *get ha*. She watched him trot a few paces toward the camels. He stopped to look back at her as if he was worried, his tusks looking absurdly cute as he gazed at her face-on.

"I need some time alone in Ben Ariim. I'll be back at this time the day after tomorrow, all right? I need some time to run free, by myself. So, get ha."

Roorah tipped one ear back, showing interest in the wild herd, but his eyes still focused on her with concern.

*Firm, but respectful,* Falidee would tell her, *like asking an equal to quickly deal with something extremely urgent.* "Get ha!"

He ducked his head, then shook out his mane and trotted onward toward the herd of animals that now turned to warily face him. Did he understand?

She hoped so. And she hoped he'd be all right, and happy. She hoped he relaxed while she was away, protecting his new herd until she called him. Then she could practice using the curroket while he was at a long distance. It would be good for both of them, to learn to trust that they'd be able to find each other.

Maybe it wouldn't happen this time, but as she watched him settle in to graze a few long strides away from the outermost camels, he seemed happy, which made her smile. The potential was there, for both of them.

She was grateful for Elino as she rode back. If she'd walked the entire distance to Ben Ariim, she might not have reached the city until morning. Elino wanted to get back to his comfortable stable with his good-smelling mares and hay and brushes, so he needed no urging to take up a quick pace. She let him have his head and he spent most of his time in a canter, slowing into a fast walk when he got too winded. He only stopped a few times to make certain that a bright bird wasn't about to ambush him or that a stick wouldn't bite him like a snake.

She was just within sight of Murina's estate when Falidee rode toward her on a fast bay gelding. "Billie!" he cried. "Billie!"

It didn't take much to encourage Elino into a gallop. Elino's mane whipped her face as she leaned down low, balancing all her weight in the stirrups to let him run free beneath her. They reached Falidee in moments. "Billie!" Falidee gasped, pale.

His wide-eyed expression scared her. "What happened?"

"Your friend, Aliiren. He needs you."

She didn't need to know what happened. She just needed to get to him. "I'll need a guide to the temple."

"There's a devotee from his temple waiting for you."

The word devotee was only vaguely familiar, some temple person not yet skilled enough to be called a Protector. But the fact that they'd sent someone from the temple instead of a Gurra whipped her worry into frantic fear.

Billie urged Elino into a hard gallop. They left Falidee well behind. Billie guided Elino straight to the stables. An unfamiliar woman all in blue, including a blue veil that shadowed her face, waited beside an equally unfamiliar gray mare. The woman was Thedran, maybe, thick and with a straight, confident posture. She was armed with a short bow as well as a long, thin, elegant blade similar to what Aliiren carried.

Murina stood by Waliin, the next fastest horse to Elino, holding her reins. The shine of Waliin's perfectly groomed gray coat was so bright she looked silver, and she pranced, eager to run. She was saddled and ready.

Murina looked flushed and panicked.

Billie threw herself off of Elino.

"I hate that my last words about him were cruel," Murina said as Billie mounted Waliin.

"It's all right. You meant to help me," Billie reminded her as she secured her feet in the stirrups.

Murina's panic gave way to trembling and her voice wavered. "All they'll tell me is that he's badly hurt, and he needs you." She quickly passed the reins to Billie.

It wouldn't be for her healing. Anyone who could call themselves a healer in Ben Ariim would be better than her, and closer by.

Which meant that maybe Aliiren was beyond a healer's skill.

"I'll send word when I can." Billie couldn't promise Murina any more than that.

The woman hadn't finished mounting her scruffy gray horse before Billie took off for Ben Ariim. If needed she would promise a Gurra anything to guide her to Aliiren's temple.

It was just like Brian, only now she had no hope of helping him. But by the Gods she would be there to hold his hand. She would not fail him as she'd failed her family.

Waliin thought this was all in fun. She was young, and eager, and she liked going to Ben Ariim. She was fit, and the power in her body carried Billie at speeds that rivaled a falcon.

Billie didn't look back. She only looked forward, whispering prayers to no one and nothing, for she knew no God would hear her, never mind answer. She spoke anyway.

*Please let me be in time. Please let him live. Please.*

It was midday, and a hot wind blew in her face. Her shawl fell back but she didn't dare adjust it to protect herself from the sun. She needed both hands on the reins, to maintain her balance and to keep Waliin focused on reaching Ben Ariim as quickly as they could get there.

There was no one on the road. This time of day, it would have been unusual. Only the desperate, and the foolish, would be out working in this heat. The sacred sun was so fierce it dried her sweat before it could soak her hair. Waliin began to sweat too, and to labor. They would have to change pace.

No. No no no no …

But the horse could only do so much. Billie could only do so much.

Those excuses were like razor cuts all over her body. It was just like Brian …

There were people with horses walking slowly toward her near the horizon.

She would convince them to trade horses with her. It was a desperate idea, and she had no right to do that with Waliin, but Aliiren ...

She slowed Waliin into a trot, and then a fast walk as they neared the three veiled people and small group of horses. "Excuse me," Billie gasped. "Please. I need to reach Ben Ariim as quickly as possible. May I trade horses with you?"

Something was off.

Even in her desperation, she could sense it. One of them nodded, and the other two stood stiffly, as if she'd surprised them. That was natural when faced with a pale foreigner pleading to trade her unknown horse for a horse they may have raised from birth, with no guarantee that they would have a chance to trade the horses back.

That wasn't it.

There was something ... sharp ... about how those covered faces focused on her. They didn't look to each other at all to confer. She knew they could see well enough through those veils, though she couldn't see their faces at all. Wouldn't they talk to each other about it, make some sound, or at least ask her name?

The one that had nodded looked to the horizon from where she'd come. She could hear the devotee's horse galloping in the distance. Billie only glanced that way, her instincts telling her that danger was close.

They were about her height or a trace shorter, the right height for average Arrak men, but they weren't lean. The heaviness in their shoulders made her think of fighting men.

There was something predatory about the way the one closest to her reached for Waliin's reins.

Billie clucked her tongue and pulled the reins to back Waliin away and the veiled stranger dove forward to grab them. Waliin reared up on her hinds and it was all Billie could do to hang on.

The other men drew swords. Behind them, the horses sidestepped, and she got a clear view of a huge black horse.

She knew that horse.

She knew who these people were.

In an instant she knew she had two choices. Time seemed to slow for her, as it had when the man and his boys had come for her mother, her brother and her.

The man grabbed a rein.

Only one way now.

Billie kicked her feet out of the stirrups, gripped Waliin's mane with one hand to control her fall and flung herself off the horse. She hit the ground hard.

Time sped back up as she frantically drew her sword and dagger together. Waliin whirled and took off toward Murina's estate at a gallop while blades flashed toward Billie's body.

All she could think about was getting to Aliiren as she slashed and crossed blades. She flinched when fire from a cut that got past her frantic parries lit up along her skin. They were cussing now, not in Arrak but Thedran.

They seemed to be everywhere. She backed up with reckless speed, but they would soon encircle her and she'd be dead. So she picked one and charged.

"Look out!"

She knew that voice. It was the man on the horse that had been attacking Jasmine.

She bore his friend down. As she rolled off him she dragged her dagger across his face, unable to get the throat. He screamed. She dove for another one.

An arrow flew by her, so close she felt it yank her hair. The devotee! Billie punched her man with the pommel of her dagger and then slashed into him while he sunk a dagger into her shoulder. She screamed as it seared into her and yanked herself free of him, just in time to turn into the one coming in behind her.

He kicked her hard and she landed off the road onto rocks that scraped and cracked her ribs. Her gift flared to life.

She heard a sharp flit and flung herself aside. The arrow skipped off a rock right by where her waist had been.

The devotee was shooting arrows *at her.*

Billie scurried behind the rocks.

"You should have stayed in the Kilhells," the man she thought of as the grinning rider called to her. Approaching hoofbeats slowed as Billie moved to keep the rocks between her and the archer.

*Aliiren. I won't fail you. I …*

It was only then that she realized it was all a lie.

Aliiren didn't need her.

The devotee wasn't a devotee, at least not from Aliiren's temple.

They'd lured her here, when there would be no one on the road.

She laughed. She couldn't help it. She was terrified, hurt, outnumbered … but she'd found the people who'd hurt Jasmine. Or rather they'd found her.

Not that it mattered.

Very little mattered now.

She had no horse, but they had horses. She just had to get to a horse alive, and …

No. She had to kill the archer first. Then get to the horses.

It seemed impossible.

As she rested, thinking as fast as she could, bleeding, she came to the realization that she was dead. She just hadn't stopped breathing yet.

That would be all right. Maybe, in the next life, she could do the right things and not let her family down.

What would not be all right would be to allow that man, who'd fled on his horse, staring back at her with his dead man's grin and wild eyes, to live longer than her and maybe hunt down Jasmine and Aliiren like he'd hunted her.

One man she could kill.

One man would be enough.

Two would be better.

But she could die with one.

## Chapter Twenty-Eight

<><><><><><><><><><><><><><><><><><><><><><><><><><><><><><><><>

# Death

<><><><><><><><><><><><><><><><><><><><><><><><><><><><><><><><>

*The grazing lands, East of Ben Ariim*
*1st Labor Day of Wandering Month*

**B**illie remembered this feeling. Death was close, a would-be lover wooing her from the shadows. This time, she wasn't a virgin girl, trembling, while her little brother screamed in panic. This time she wasn't fighting an inhuman monstrosity, overcome by its speed and blinded by overwhelming forces that flowed from Gods. Her body sang with power. Her fear tasted like wine. She felt no desperation, no terror. Fear was a laughing, excited friend urging her to act and act now.

She had to argue with that friend to wait while she prepared to fight for her life and the lives of whomever these people would target once they were done with her. She could barely feel her hands. She looked to make sure she still gripped her sword, and a dagger. She squeezed the hilts of each, probably too hard, but better that than to drop a weapon. There was blood on her blade, blood on her hands, blood everywhere and the fight hadn't really started yet. She'd just had a taste. The terrible feast would begin in a matter of heartbeats.

They were moving. The sounds they made had the quality of mice scratching around barrels and crates in the quietest, darkest part of true night. Each of her breaths momentarily covered those tiny sounds. Her heartbeat rustled like velvet rubbing within her ears.

"If you throw away your weapons and come out, we'll make it quick." It was the man who'd ridden away, the man who'd called "look out!" before, when Jasmine was being attacked, and again when she threw herself off Waliin. "If you make us come for you, it's going to hurt more. It's going to take a long time. Come on, Kilhellion. You're brave. You're strong. And you're skilled. Maybe you're thinking, I can kill one, or two, like before.

"But we're ready for you this time. And we're just as determined to avenge our friends as you wanted to protect yours. You owe us your life." Those last words dripped with venom. He sounded like he really believed that. "None of *your* friends died. They were barely hurt. I lost my two best friends, Kilhellion. You *murdered* them."

*Murderer …*

But friends like his deserved no revenge, and like them, he had to be put down like a lion that had developed a taste for human children. She felt that truth deep down, but she said, "you're right."

"You're far from home." He sounded more confident now. That was probably a bad thing. "No one in Arrak Thedra wants you. As far as they're concerned, you're just a vicious animal." Not so long ago, that would have stung. Now, she had friends, and she had Roorah. She shifted, trying to move her weight over her feet. She turned so that only one shoulder was braced on stone. The footing under her was awkward, with the lay of the rocks going this way and that. Her right foot was set at a steep angle, and the only other place for it would pinch her boot between the larger rock and a smaller one set hard in the ground beside it. It wasn't great, but now she could move quickly if she needed to. "If you die, you'll go back to a place where you're loved. In a blink, you'll be someone's sweet babe without a worry to wrinkle your forehead. But I can tell you're going to be stubborn." The smile behind those words entered her mind, the rictus grin, filled with a nasty warmth that reminded her of the dead child held in the hellion's web.

Footsteps drummed toward her from around both sides of the rock. She saw a shadow—the archer—and charged.

The archer fired. Billie twisted her body as soon as she saw the release. The arrow missed, and then she was on the woman. Something slammed into them both and they all went down in a tangle. Billie had her dagger between her and the archer. Billie twisted, hard, then thrust her dagger by feel toward the archer's side while the man on her back grabbed Billie by the hair. His hand slipped free, holding Billie's shawl. Billie's dagger went in at a shallow angle, but the archer still screamed.

Something punched Billie—no, it was a dagger. She felt it penetrate, skid off a rib, puncture her lung. Her healing went mad. She didn't have much time left. The three of them rolled over and the one that had stabbed her tried to pin her.

He completely misjudged her sword. It was Kilhellion, shorter than Thedran swords, shaped like an elongated leaf so that both sides had curves.

That shape served a critical purpose.

She punched the blade, using the edge closest to the cross guard, into his throat and drew the entire length of the blade across his throat as hard and fast as she could. Veils parted, then flesh. He had leather over his throat, but she'd struck right above his throat guard under his jaw.

Blood poured out. He couldn't scream, but he gurgled. She threw him off and thrust instinctively toward the sky. She didn't hit the next one, but he threw himself back to avoid her blade. She reversed her blade down and sank it into the face of the archer, who was struggling to squirm free from underneath everyone.

Billie braced up using her blade, still stuck in the dead archer, and tackled the closest man before he could bring his long blade full into her. She still got cut, but she had him and he didn't know how to use his dagger close like she could hers. She blocked his arm at the elbow and drove her dagger into him.

And hit armor. She cursed and they struggled. He kept pricking her with his dagger, but she still had her arm inside his elbow. He couldn't quite sink it in, though he tried over and over to do it. They were locked together and the last one was coming up from behind her. Somehow she knew that he was grinning behind his veil. She tried to wrestle her opponent in the way so she could use him as a shield.

Blood gushed up from within her and Billie coughed, retched, and spewed blood into his face. He flinched back and she kicked hard into his knee. It gave with a sickening pop-crack. He screamed and collapsed back, dragging her with him. She felt woozy, and blood roared in her ears. Spots dappled her vision. She lurched to one side—he finally let go—and turned to the man behind her.

Steel flashed in the sun. His blade went into her bicep and she clenched, twisted. He lost his grip on the blade. She punched him as hard as she could, aiming for the nose. It glanced off his cheek. Something cracked. Her gift ran rampant through her body, hot and wild, but telltale bursts of heat didn't spark in her hand like they would have if her bones had broken.

He staggered too, and fell back. The man with the busted knee started to crawl. Billie tried to pull the sword from her arm but the blade was too long.

She coughed blood again. Her body made odd sucking and choking sounds, and everything looked like she was underwater. The daylight was smeared with large, dark patches.

The grinning rider—maybe he wasn't grinning anymore—ran toward the horses.

*You're not getting away. Not you. Not this time.*

She went to the friend he'd abandoned. He tried to crawl away. She kicked his hand when he swung his blade at her. The blade went spinning through the air. She chopped into him with her blade and he screamed and screamed, and then he stopped. His body made wet sounds while it died, kicking weakly. His soul would be gone by now, though. Dr. Val had taught her that.

It was a small comfort. Life, as blissful as it could be, was filled with suffering and there was no escaping that.

Billie stuck his hand through the guard of his friend's sword and managed to use his weight to pull the blade free of her body. Her left arm screamed in protest. Having the blade out felt worse than having it in. If she'd had time, she would have removed the blade slowly, letting her healing limit the bleeding and damage in its wake.

There was no time for that. The man, now mounted on his big black horse, was getting away.

She staggered to the archer, picked up the bow, and an arrow. Her injured bicep had no strength to it, but all she had to do was hold her left arm straight.

*I can do that much.*

She nocked the arrow, locked her elbow to hold her arm straight, and raised the bow. Too far. He was too far.

An unexpected, almost dreamy calm settled over her. A soft breeze blew a lock of hair from behind her ear to tickle her cheek.

Billie pulled with her good arm and aimed. The breeze picked up just a little. She held her breath, gauged the flight of the arrow within the breeze as she would when hunting a deer, and released.

The arrow flew but her fading sight couldn't track its course.

Nothing happened. Of course it didn't. She choked. She had to fight not to vomit as she coughed up splatters of blood.

But then the horse slowed. And the man began to lean.

Billie tried to run toward him. She had to finish him off before she died.

She choked again and coughed up more blood, spat it out, and limped along. The horse moved in a circle with him leaning over its neck, so overbalanced that any moment he would fall. But he wasn't falling.

Billie made kissing noises. The horse's ears perked, and it began to walk toward her. "Come on, come here," she wheezed, and made more kissing noises. "Good boy. You're a good boy, aren't you? Maybe not. Good girl."

The man finally fell, startling the horse. The horse gave a few kicks and then sidestepped away from him. Then, apologetically, the horse went back to him and sniffed.

Billie finally reached him. The arrow had gone into him just above the hip near the spine. Any lower, and she would have hit the horse. He moaned, laying on his side. She tried to catch her breath so her aim would be true, but coughing bent her double and more blood came up. She wasn't going to get any better.

"Wait," he groaned. "Wait. There's a helarin. You understand me? We made. A deal. You. And if we got you alive, she would help us. With Aliiren."

She had no idea what, or who, a helarin was. Some sort of hellion? Her skin prickled with gooseflesh. Did this have anything to do with the demon they'd killed?

Were hellions coming for her? For Aliiren? For Temric, and Edrion?

"I'll give you a name. Just ... don't kill me."

If this had anything to do with hellions, she didn't dare listen to one more word. Whatever he told her would be a lie at best, and at worst? It would be trap designed to endanger not just her friends, but all of Ben Ariim.

She hacked into him, half-blind, as near his head as she could manage. He let out a few cries, but it wasn't too bad. He died quickly after her first hit.

She wouldn't die quickly.

Billie sat in the heat. The sun, and her growing fever, made her feel like she was inside an oven. She stripped off her wool, used her dagger to cut it free where it tangled, and then sat bare to the sun save for a thin layer of linen underclothes. Sweat streamed in the shaded parts of her and dried instantly where the sun hammered into her. Blood soaked her clothes, and the yellow soil drank it up. A fly arrived, crawling happily over the dead man's head.

It was then that she felt something close, something vast. It sang to her a sweet song, far off in the distance. It promised freedom from pain, and a new beginning.

And then something brushed her cheek, as delicate and silken as Jasmine's skin. For a moment her pain eased, and she felt light …

A cough racked her, and she choked on blood. It was gone. But it would come back. She knew it.

Because it was Death.

She wasn't ready.

Not because she was afraid. Death was as sweet as she'd been taught.

Not because she had anything urgent she had to do.

She wasn't done fighting. Life might be cruel, but she honored Life with all her being, and she wouldn't let go of Life's gift easily.

Besides, it sounded like Aliiren and the others might be in danger. And Roorah needed her.

Billie closed her eyes and linked her nodes. Her body felt wet inside, sloshy, full of boiling water and searing crevasses. She took control of her vinus as best she could. It was like trying to gather hot water and spin with the streams as they poured out from between her fingers. But she managed to get a good flow of it to her lung.

Her punctured lung was a lake, and it shrank with every gasp. Her vinus swamped the hole. It wasn't that big of a hole, but Gods, it was big enough to kill her.

Her gift wanted to heal that hole. She'd spent a lot of time at the college knitting muscle and skin, but this … her lung was in constant motion, and she couldn't hold her breath long enough for it to matter. She worked on knitting anyway though she knew she'd fail.

Strangely, moment by moment it started to come more easily. Maybe it was because it was her own body, and not someone else's. Maybe because although her mind perceived something like sight, she could feel her way too. That sense of not-quite-touch made it damned easier to seal that hole than sewing or needlework, even though this was more delicate work than anything her mother had ever done.

Her fever was getting worse. She had to at least protect certain organs, especially her brain, as much as she could. She drew as much vinus as she dared back to her nodes, letting cuts bleed and bruises swell. And rather than allowing the vinus that worked on her worst injuries circle back to her nodes, she directed it to her skin where she hoped the fever would be carried away whenever a breeze came along.

Her skin felt like it was burning, not just from the fever, but the sun.

She'd never been this injured in her life. She was going to die. And yet, breath after choking, sloppy breath kept her going. The fever burned her, but she didn't go into a seizure. Any moment she could lose consciousness, and then it would be over. But somehow, woozily, swaying where she sat, she managed to stay conscious. The pain, though it made her clench her jaw and shudder and not want to move, helped keep her awake.

Finally, her breathing came more easily. It wasn't good. But it was easier. And the sucking, choking noises softened to wheezes, rasps and gurgles.

Billie felt over her skin. She had cuts everywhere. She should bandage them, but she didn't have the coordination to cut her shredded clothing into something useable. Besides, most of the wounds had stopped bleeding. What did bleed seeped instead of flowing freely.

When she could take a full breath, she braced herself up, got her legs under her, and stood. Her head buzzed, and she thought she would faint, but she managed, aside from taking a few staggered steps, to walk to the murderer's big black horse and take him by the reins. Then she gripped the stirrup. She didn't have the strength or balance to mount up, so she stood there, breathing, healing.

Healing.

Keeping her vinus under control and clinging to consciousness consumed her whole being while she took breath after agonized breath. By the time she'd opened her eyes again, that agony had grown, but perversely, she could breathe easier.

They hadn't wanted her to do this. The Champions. They wanted their questions answered. Would they be angry with her?

She didn't think so.

*I've done the work of a Champion. Not well, but this needed doing for the sake of humanity.*

It felt right, more right than healing, more right than anything she'd ever done since she'd killed her first man.

*I am a Champion.*

Her father's scoffing words—*you think you're a Champion or something?*—were distant now, and fragile as the first frost. And when she thought, *yes,* there was no answer from him. Surprisingly, instead, she heard Jasmine's voice in her mind.

*You should train at the Tower in Kal Ariim! You would pass the test. I know you would.*

The desert was so relentlessly hot and stark. It was nothing like home. But as she gazed at the clear blue sky, and the way it glowed against the land's warm colors, she didn't want to be anywhere else. The twisted trees, the silver grasses, the delicate flowers … it was the most beautiful place she'd ever seen. Death's sweet, tender kiss had awoken her from a muddy, sad dream to a world of vivid colors, lively birdsong, and the promise of hidden treasures.

Or maybe it was because for the very first time, she felt as if she owned her future. When Death had come for her, she'd seized her life and held on.

It was one thing to feel Death's touch and lose her dread of it. It was a wholly different thing to remember that she could fight, and survive, against evil. Fear that her family would resent her for stepping out of her place, fear of becoming arrogant, fear of trying to claim something she had no right to claim had held her back.

No more.

She'd seen a Champion with her own eyes now. He was magnificent, yes, and she quailed a bit at the idea that she could ever become someone with that much strength and confidence. Yet, he was human, as human as she was.

Jasmine believed she could do it. That helped. But as she drew breath after painful breath, with her enemies drawing flies around her, *she* felt it, as if she'd already passed the test and had been bladed. What had once been a fleeting childhood fancy, a silly girl playing at being a hero with her brother, now filled her body with joy that outshone her pain.

That glorious vision spurred her to gather what strength she had to do more than just stand and cling to a stirrup.

There was a canteen hanging from the saddle horn.

Billie drank a little water, then poured some over her head to help cool herself. The rivulets felt cold and silky on her skin. She pulled her shawl as best she could back onto her head.

Time to get to work.

*The Champion's Keep, Ben Ariim*
*1ˢᵗ Labor Day of Wandering Month*

THE GUARDS STOPPED HER AT BEN ARIIM'S EAST GATE. BILLIE LET THEM, focused on her breathing, which came well enough that she wasn't nearly so dizzy as before. Her string of horses, and the terrible baggage they carried, had attracted more than flies. She had a small mob of people following her. So far, no one had recognized any of the bodies, or didn't dare make a fuss about it in public, anyway. Thank the Gods. She knew, though her enemies deserved the deaths they got, that they still had family, friends, and lovers.

*I lost my two best friends, Kilhellion, he'd said. You murdered them.*

"What happened?" one of the guards demanded, while the other went to see if any of the ones that weren't very obviously dead might still be alive.

They weren't. She'd checked using her gift.

Would she have helped them stay alive if she'd detected a heartbeat?

She wasn't sure.

"Which way to the Champion's Keep?" It hurt to talk. It hurt to ride. Everything hurt, really.

"I'll escort her," the guard who'd checked on the bodies told his companion.

"Want to ride?" She'd found Waliin up the road and had added her to the line. Waliin wasn't happy about it, and so the guard would be doing both Billie and Waliin a favor if he said yes. He might keep Waliin from trying to get to the front, which annoyed the big black horse Billie rode. "That silver gray? She's causing me problems."

"I don't know how to ride," the guard admitted, which surprised her, but maybe it shouldn't have. "I can lead her," the guard added.

"Thank you."

They moved along in silence, gathering more people into the crowd that trailed behind them. It made her wonder if this was what a parade looked like. She'd heard about them in stories, but she she'd never actually seen one. The purpose was for public spectacle.

Well, this certainly was that.

Not that many people followed them all in all, but a few from each street they turned onto joined in, so by the time they reached the keep, she had what she thought made a very fine parade. Somewhere, someone was drumming, or was that distant thunder? She suspected she was hallucinating. She'd heard drums from time to time throughout her ride to Ben Ariim. It was possible that someone somewhere was playing them, but …

An especially sharp pain traveled up through her spine and she hissed. She turned her thoughts inward and tried to trace the pain to its source, but she felt her body start to lean and pulled her consciousness back so she could rebalance herself in the saddle. Her hands ached from gripping the saddle horn. Thankfully the horse had been trained to follow commands she was able to give through the stirrups and with her knees.

It wasn't until they'd reached the massive doors framing the short tunnel through the keep's walls that she remembered to warn her friends. "Is there any way to send word to Aliiren? He's a Light Protector." Aliiren had told her, but now she couldn't remember which Light temple he belonged to. South? Grass?

"In a moment," the guard said. He went past a pair of massive, open doors and through a short tunnel into a courtyard. She thought maybe she should dismount, but she wasn't sure she could without falling over.

Her parade had gathered around her by this point. "Who are they?" a Thedran woman asked.

"I don't know." Billie leaned forward and stood up in the stirrups experimentally to see if she could possibly get off the horse safely.

"Hey, Billie," Crellan called. She turned her head toward him, but no one was there. Dizziness rushed through her head and the drumming grew louder, joined by a noise like a waterfall. She closed her eyes and used vinus to keep herself from fainting.

*Crellan isn't in Ben Ariim. I'm definitely hallucinating.*

"Let me help you," a man offered.

"Please." His kindness surprised her, but she wasn't about to question it. It had been a very long ride through the heat, harassed by flies, her shredded, bloody clothes hanging off her, and every breath felt like she was being stabbed and breathing fire at the same time.

Billie stabilized her body's weakening hold on consciousness long enough to try to get one foot out of a stirrup. Someone else came up and pulled it off for her. She got her leg up over and then she had not just one person, but a pack of them helping her to the ground.

Suddenly everyone parted from around her and there was Sun Champion. He was dressed in layers of gray silk and leather that probably worked almost as well as his steel armor. How he could bear it in this heat, she had no idea. He wasn't even sweating.

"I brought you the criminal that attacked Jasmine," she said. "And some of his friends."

Sun Champion's eyes narrowed. He stared at her a moment, and then he went to each of the bodies in turn, looking at their faces if they had any left. Some other people came out of the keep while he looked. There was one in armor like Sun Champion had worn when she'd first met him. The other people looked like they had a good amount of fight to them too. And the guard came out with them. They were all looking at her and the bodies like they hadn't decided what to think. Mangy Dog took up a horse's reins, only half paying attention to what he was doing. When their gazes met, he stared at her with an expression of surprised respect.

Sun Champion came back to her. "What happened?"

"The one in blue lured me into the desert. The rest of them ambushed me."

"Just you?"

"Just me," she assured him. "No innocents got caught up in it."

He startled her by putting his hand on her face. She flinched back before she realized he was checking her fever. His hand felt cool, but not cold, so maybe that meant the fever wasn't that bad. She still felt wobbly, and now on top of everything else she was sick with thirst.

"You're a healer?"

Billie nodded.

"Trained?"

Billie nodded again. "Some. I didn't get far before I had to leave the college." Telling him that should have hurt, but it meant nothing to her now. All that mattered was that she'd made it to the keep.

The stone fortress didn't look very homey, and yet, she wanted nothing more than to stay here and work and train, even if she had to sleep on the floor.

"Let's get you into the keep." He gestured and the people who'd come out from the keep started gathering up the horses. Her parade stayed outside as Sun Champion put an arm across her back. It felt like he wanted to protect and support her if she needed it. The gesture helped her feel welcome, and safe.

The keep was smaller than she expected, considering the height and thickness of the wall. It was just two big buildings, one at either end of a large courtyard. All told, after Mangy Dog came in with the last of the horses and they closed the gate, there were fewer people in the keep than in her village. The keep almost felt empty. She wondered if most of the Champions were out in the city working. That had to be it. These few couldn't do all the great work Champions would have to do in a city as vast as Ben Ariim.

Or maybe there was another keep somewhere else.

*Was that Brian laughing? No, maybe it was Edrion.* "Edri?"

"Steady, there." Sun Champion led her into one of the buildings, the front room of which was a small hall with a kitchen at one end. He sat her down at the long table with its many chairs and benches in the center of the room, and then he began to ask questions. Where was she when the woman in blue approached her? What got Billie to follow her? Where did the ambush happen?

By the time she started to describe the fight itself, a healer had arrived. The healer couldn't use his vinus without making her fever worse, but he helped her by bleeding off as much of her fever as he could. Then he carefully washed her, salved her wounds, sutured her, and bandaged everything. After that, he mixed up and gave her what medicines he felt were right for her, including a soothing tea laced with honey.

By then it was dark outside, and Aliiren arrived.

He was panting and soaked with sweat. He must have run a long way. When he saw her he nearly collapsed with relief. She smiled, not because he was worried about her, but because she'd lived, and he was here.

"What happened?" Aliiren asked when he'd caught his breath enough to ask.

Billie felt like she'd been sitting forever, but she didn't have the strength to stand and take him in her arms.

For now, seeing him again was enough.

He'd asked her a question.

She could start at the beginning some other time. First, she had to finish telling her story to Sun Champion. "I was just getting to the part where the one I think might have been the leader—though no leader worth a day's meal would have left his friends like that—begged for his life," Billie explained. "He said something about a he—le? rin?"

"A helarin?" Aliiren and Sun Champion said, almost together.

The word made her shudder. "Yes. That's right. He said he would give me a name if I spared him. It sounded like something nefarious, so I killed him as quickly as I could."

Sun Champion didn't seem pleased with that. He'd encouraged her so far, saying things like well done, bravely done and all that, but now he frowned.

He looked to Aliiren, who was also frowning.

"Bad dog," Sun Champion told Billie.

Her face warmed, and it wasn't from fever. She was about to protest and explain her decision in more detail when she remembered what dogs were, or what she guessed they might be, to Champions.

But she'd agreed to nothing, had been offered nothing. As big as her dreams had been of training to be a Champion while she thought she was dying, she'd expected to have to fight for it. Having him assume that she would just *become* a dog, *had* become a dog, without even asking or explaining what that meant, felt strange.

Not that she would turn him down. But still.

"You're going to train her?" Aliiren asked, clearly shocked. He looked into her eyes, cocked his head, and silently seemed to ask—*is this what you want?*

"I haven't asked her yet."

Her hopes solidified into something more real, and more daunting than she'd expected. She hadn't expected to have the chance offered to her without asking for it.

Sun Champion straightened in his seat, but then seemed to think better of it and stood. He offered both of his hands to her. Uncertain, Billie took them. She started to stand up, but he gently told her, "You can sit for this."

*What is happening?*

Aliiren stood straighter, puffed out his chest, and lifted his chin.

He was proud of her. Aliiren was proud of her.

Mangy Dog's attention was as rapt upon her as a hawk on a rabbit as he stood. The scattering of other people in the room stood up.

Sun Champion's hands were cool and strong as they held hers firmly. "I have been learning about you, and about your deeds since you've come to Ben Ariim, as well as some of what came before." He exchanged a glance with Aliiren, which made her wonder what Aliiren had told him that day she'd been questioned by Sun Champion and Mangy Dog.

Her thoughts started to spin. She took a breath and focused on Sun Champion's golden eyes. She didn't want to miss any detail of this moment.

"I want to sponsor your training at the Champion Towers in Kal Ariim," he continued. "I would train you here myself, but I'm already training Mangy Dog, and the other Champions have dogs of their own to mind. Besides, they have proper training grounds and all the things you'll need to become a Champion in Kal Ariim. If you accept."

She wasn't sure she understood. "So, is a dog like a squire?"

That made him smile. "I can't promise it's the same as the Markan term. I only know how we train here in Arrak Thedra. We all share in the work, whether it's scrubbing dishes, or protecting the people of Ben Ariim from evil. There's a lot to learn besides fighting."

*Is this real?*

*This is happening.*

"If you need time to consider …" Sun Champion added.

She wanted to make sure she hadn't misheard, even if it made her look stupid. "You're going to ask the Champions in Kal Ariim if they'll have me."

"Oh, they'll have you," Sun Champion said with a smile. "In time, you will be adopted by a Champion and become their dog. Until then, you'll work with the rest of the pack in the keep."

"Dogs are trained to become Champions?" She looked to Mangy Dog, who'd worn a subtle smile but now hid it from her. She looked back to Sun Champion. "I'm to be trained to be a Champion." She wanted to make sure that she wasn't agreeing to something she didn't understand.

"Yes. You hardly need a blade that brings you back to life," Sun Champion said with a smile. "But if you pass your test, we'll gird one at your waist anyway."

Champions were legendary. They were unbeatable, heroic ... Sun Champion was clearly human, and yet at this moment he seemed more than human to her. She wasn't sure she could ever stand as an equal beside this man.

Not just him. Champions were men, and tall, strong men no less.

Then again, she was only a little shorter than Mangy Dog, and taller than just about everyone in the crowd outside. Here, she supposed, she might be strong enough. And, she was Kilhellion.

She was still Kilhellion.

"I'll do it." Test? Maybe she wouldn't pass their test. But she might.

No. She would. She'd pass their test and then ... Gods!

She laughed, and it hurt, and she started coughing but that only made her laugh harder. "Yes!" she laughed. "Yes." *Yes.*

She bowed her head as the weight of that possibility of greatness, and the potential for a devastating failure, settled on her like a heavy blanket. Sun Champion set her right hand over his, then set his left hand on the crown of her head. The weight felt good.

"The fight you had today is just the beginning," he told her. "It won't get any easier. But I don't think you're afraid of that."

"No. I'm not." She had purpose now. She had a future, a future that would be her very own. She would become a Champion, or she would die trying to become one.

## Chapter Twenty-Nine

<<<<<<<<<<<<<<<<<<<<<<<<<<<<<<<<<<<<<<<<<<<<<<<<<<<<<<<<<<<<<<<<<<<<<<<<

# Leaving Home

<<<<<<<<<<<<<<<<<<<<<<<<<<<<<<<<<<<<<<<<<<<<<<<<<<<<<<<<<<<<<<<<<<<<<<<<

*Ben Ariim*
*2nd Meet Day of Fall Month*

They waited for Jasmine.

Billie braced on her elbows at the long table in the center of the main hall within the Champion's Keep. She'd been there since breakfast. Temric crouched in front of much-reduced stacks of bags and crates. He wrote something on a paper placed on top of one of the crates, then picked up a different crate and carried it down a set of stairs to a storage room. The rooms where Billie and the others had stayed were also downstairs, nestled underground where she felt safe within the protection of the cool basalt that so effortlessly held the weight of the Champions' Keep. The green-toned sacred lights in the hall and her room reminded her of the soft light that filtered through oak leaves on a summer day.

Larani and Edrion giggled and chattered excitedly on a bench across from Billie. They'd packed and were ready to go. Aliiren sat beside Billie, his lone bag on the table, gazing at the soft autumnal light coming through the open door from the courtyard. Mangy Dog hummed to himself while mopping the last section of floor near the hearth. The Champions and the dogs had finished their chores and had gone to their rooms to prepare for the day. Bellies were full, and the hall was quiet.

Her friends had stayed with her during true night, much as they had spent true night at the keep when Sun Champion had asked her …

She couldn't remember exactly what he'd asked her. She just knew that she would train to become a Champion in Kal Ariim. And that Aliiren was there, and a drummer, and a healer. Or maybe the healer was from before. Was there a drummer?

That first true night at the keep hadn't been spent practicing writing and counting, or telling stories, or discussing their plans for the future like this recent one. She wasn't sure if Larani, Edrion, Jasmine and Temric had stayed at the keep back then so that the Champions could protect them, or if they'd stayed to help take care of her. Maybe a bit of both. Aliiren, though, had stayed to nurse her while she fought to stay alive. The fever hadn't been the worst part, though the way her body constantly switched between sweating and chills had been bad enough. It was the stab wound. Every breath had felt like someone was digging an elbow into a deep bruise.

Her friends made it all bearable. Temric, Edrion and Larani had taken turns watching over her, while Jasmine kept her clean, comfortable and entertained. But Aliiren stayed with her constantly, making tea, helping her get up when she needed to, and to settle back into her bed after. He'd brought her food, arranged neatly on a board, and took the boards away to the kitchen for her when she was done.

Jasmine returned to his pleasure garden that true dawn. By Somber Day, Billie decided that she was well enough to eat breakfast in the barracks main hall. Aliiren had washed Billie's hair, helped her dress into clean clothes, and shadowed her as she walked—mostly on her own—up the stairs and then back down afterward. By the end of the next true night she was well enough to manage with a lot less help.

Her progress was bittersweet. Aliiren, Temric and the Rill had to move to Aliiren's Light temple the following true dawn. Sun Champion insisted that they go. Apparently the keep was meant only for Champions and dogs, though rare and brief exceptions were allowed. Billie wished her friends could stay, but she understood. Larani and Edrion were especially restless by then, and though they tried to stay out of everyone's way, they were a distraction wherever they went.

Billie could fend for herself now, but she still hadn't completely healed. Even the battle with the hellion hadn't left her feeling so puny afterward. Her wounds still ached, especially the punctured lung, though she spent time before bed every night using her gift to soften the scars and break the adhesions that had formed around it. She did her best to hide her discomfort, but she suspected that the way she hunched over the table, leaning on her good arm, made it obvious.

She probably should have spent the same amount of time as what had already passed to get her strength back and full mobility in her injured arm. But the weather could turn any day. There had already been a few rainstorms, though nothing too serious. If they wanted to make it to Kal Ariim without getting bogged down in mud or getting caught in a dangerous storm, they had to go now.

She wondered if the message they received shortly after true dawn meant that Jasmine was coming with them. She wasn't sure how she felt about that. He'd been good to her. She cared about him. She just didn't know what his intentions were.

She hadn't known Jasmine long, but he'd become so much a part of her life, she didn't like the idea of being far away from him. She almost didn't care if he was manipulating her into liking him. He was kind, and sweet, and he made her laugh. Besides, if his feelings for her, Aliiren, and the others weren't genuine, would he really bother with them this much? She didn't think so.

Honestly, though she hadn't known any of these people for long, she loved them. These people felt more like family than her cousins back home.

But she wasn't as close as she'd been to her brother. That wound gaped wide, and always would. Sometimes it seemed like he couldn't really be gone. At those times she felt more or less as she always had. But then in the next moment she'd feel his loss as if it was new. The ache and guilt and pain made it hard to believe she had any right to a future.

This life she'd been given had been granted by the Gods, a life her mother had bled out of her womb in great pain. Billie owed so much to her, and the rest of her tribe. It made Billie feel sick to think about all the people in her tribe that now labored through their lives without the hope of the future that Brian's life had promised, or the comfort her gift might have brought them.

But she had to admit that Temric was a little bit right about it not being entirely her fault. Her family had chosen to disown her. They owned that part of the loss they now bore.

She still loved them, and always would. Her people were a testament and prayer in one breath about life's tenacity and beauty despite the harshness in the world.

*I'm still a part of that, disowned or not. I hope it's enough.*

*Enough for what? No one has the power to stand against every possible catastrophe. So maybe, I just have to be strong enough to … No. It's not strength that's needed. It's the will to do the hard things in life for the sake of others.*

*I can do that.*

Aliiren let out an impatient sigh. "Let me braid your hair," he said.

It took her a breath to realize he was talking to her. "What?"

"I'd like to braid your hair. Then we can secure your shawl, so that the wind doesn't blow it back and expose your skin to the sun. May I?"

He didn't realize what he'd suggested, at least in her culture. In his, it probably meant nothing. He just wanted to protect the skin that had so newly healed from all her wounds and the sunburn she'd gotten on the ride to Ben Ariim. She relaxed and tried to find a pocket in her mind to hide her disappointment. She'd known for a while now that she didn't mean anything to him in that way. Wishing for it wouldn't make it so. "I'd be honored."

He drew a comb from a small pocket on the outside of his bag. "Look straight ahead." And just like that, he started to tease out the tangles from the ends of her hair.

She sat stock still, back rigid, part of her still shocked by what was happening. Of course it didn't mean what it meant in the Kilhells. He hadn't just suddenly decided that they were lovers, and that he would devote himself to her, and she to him.

It still felt incredibly intimate to have him combing her hair until it was free of tangles. And then he began at the front, his fingers tenderly grazing her scalp, weaving the locks he made so that they all intertwined bit by bit together. He didn't twist the locks like they did in the Kilhells. Instead, he pulled the locks quite tight, though not tight enough to hurt. He finished it off with a single braid down her back. Then he took her shawl, folded it over on one side, and wrapped it around her head so the knot in the back circled her braid. He brought the ends forward over her shoulders. There was still plenty of length to cover her face when it was time to go out.

"That looks so beautiful!" Larani remarked.

Edrion made a sweeping motion with his hands from her to his chest. "La la!" he said with a grin.

"That does looks nice," Temric said, though it didn't look like he'd even glanced her way.

She drew her hand down one of the shawl's loose ends. "Thank you." She'd never felt this shy before.

"You're welcome." Aliiren kept his gaze lowered too.

Sun Champion came to the doorway from the courtyard. "The favorite, Jasmine, is here."

"Finally!" Temric stretched, then went to Sun Champion with his paper. They chatted—Temric's Thedran had much improved—while Temric pointed to some of his writing.

Billie shouldered her bags, as did the others. Temric would leave most of his crates behind until he found a place to live in Kal Ariim big enough to hold them all. For the ones he chose to take with him now, he had a large hand cart to pull. It looked heavy, so she promised silently to help him when he inevitably got tired.

As promised, Jasmine was waiting for them outside the keep with a new parasol, dressed all in red with golden brocade gores on his trousers and black brocade gores on the sleeves of his jacket. Silvery silk scarves hung from ties at his elbows and wrapped his waist. He was barefoot, as she was learning was usual for him, but he had rings on his toes and some sort of anklet that had strands of crystals and gold beads that covered the tops of his feet. The kohl around his eyes made them look incredibly large, and his hair hung in perfect coils, part of it drawn back into a crystal and gold pin.

He had a new sword at his waist. Unlike his other, it had no adornment, not even on the scabbard, but the hand guard and a basket of steel that protected his hand had twists in it. The spirals and edges along those strong bands of bright metal caught the sunlight as if they were jeweled.

The way he wore his blade was the only thing that was graceless about him. That awkwardness would change in time, with practice and a few adjustments to the frog that held the scabbard at an angle from the belt.

Jasmine had two strangers with him, a Sothroner and a Thedran. The leather armor and the profusion of weapons, including a bow and arrows, suggested that they were there to protect him.

Aliiren blinked when he saw the pleasurer. Maybe there was something unusual about Jasmine's clothes, though Billie couldn't say what. All clothing in Arrak Thedra seemed unusual to her.

"I wish I was going with you," Jasmine said roughly, and Billie's heart broke a little when he said it. "I can't. But I'll visit all of you as often as I can. I swear it." He went to Larani and Edrion first, and hugged them, and kissed them on the cheeks, and gave them each a little purse. He then went to Temric and gave him a long hug. From within his belt he drew out a small, leather-bound book no larger than the palm of his hand and gave it over.

Temric paged through it and his mouth fell open. He let out a short laugh. "Thank you!"

"You're welcome." Jasmine smiled up at Temric, then went to Billie. Though she dreaded the idea of a gift, at least this time she felt more prepared than before. She just hoped it wouldn't be too extravagant. He opened his arms, and Billie let him take her in.

Jasmine's hug was as sweet as the most sensuous embrace, so much so that she never wanted him to let her go, but he drew away and she had to release him. Then he pulled a scarf from his elbow. It had been doubled over and the ends pulled through the loop, so it came free with a single motion. He tied it at her elbow in the same fashion.

"What's this?" she asked, puzzled.

"It's an old tradition," Jasmine explained, "Friends and family would gift these to their loved ones on the eve of battle. They can serve as a bandage, or a tourniquet or something. Not that you're going into battle, at least not yet, but just in case. And these are gray, so they'll go with your Champion's things."

"They're silver, and she's not a Champion yet," Aliiren told him sternly as Jasmine tied a scarf at her other elbow, and then a long one over her tunic around her waist.

"I don't understand," Billie admitted. "Are they supposed to be gray?"

"Champions wear mostly gray," Jasmine told her. "At least in Arrak Thedra and the Sothron Empire. I don't know what they do where you're from."

The idea of Champions in the Kilhells seemed odd. "We don't have Champions. They were just … stories." Though she'd wanted it, and had been asked to train to become one, until Jasmine said that, it hadn't felt real. It still didn't feel entirely like this would be her life.

*What if I fail the test?*

Jasmine kissed her sweetly on the cheek, which made her blush, and then he kissed her on the mouth. Her whole body went hard and soft at the same time, and she gasped when he released her from the kiss. "There." He wore a pleased smile as he made sure the ends of her shawl draped more artfully than before. "That put a little color on your cheeks." And then he turned to Aliiren.

There was something intense, and tender, that made Jasmine and Aliiren's brief hug look more intimate than the kiss he'd given her. She fought the urge to look away when Jasmine caressed Aliiren's cheek and then kissed him on the same cheek. It wasn't jealousy. At least it didn't feel the same as jealousy. It was something that stung a bit deeper. "Be careful," he told Aliiren. "And keep our friends out of trouble if you can."

"I promise." Aliiren's lashes had lowered to shelter his eyes, and he seemed sad. She wished she could comfort him. Gods, he seemed so lonely.

Jasmine pulled up his sleeve to reveal a silk bracelet set with a brilliant light stone so pure and bright it was hard to look at. But she couldn't stop herself from trying, it was so beautiful. "Will you accept this? I know you can make them, but …"

"Jasmine," Aliiren whispered, his brows furrowing together in pain. She didn't know what was going on between them, but it made her heart ache.

"Please?"

Aliiren sighed and unbuckled the delicate silver buckle at Jasmine's wrist. He gave it to Jasmine, who fastened it on Aliiren's wrist with the bare minimum of skin contact. He then covered it with Aliiren's sleeve. As always, Aliiren was dressed all in different shades of blue, and the glow of that stone from beneath the fabric was as cold and bright as a star.

She was starting to realize that colors meant things in Arrak Thedra. She'd have to learn the meanings of those things, now that she lived here.

Except, she wouldn't actually be living here. Would Kal Ariim be just the same as Ben Ariim in all the good and bad ways? Temric had told her that it was vast, even larger than Ben Ariim. She feared she'd always be lost in it.

"Safe travels, my friends," Jasmine told them, his expression tight around his smile. "Keep each other safe." His eyes were bright.

She'd miss him, and would always wonder if he would be all right. "You stay safe too," Billie told him.

"I want all of you to write me. All of you." Jasmine looked pointedly at Billie, and then nodded as if he was agreeing for her.

Larani and Edrion hugged Jasmine again, and then Temric did, and finally Billie couldn't stand it and she hugged him again too. He held her with sensuous strength in his arms, and as always, he smelled good, like the best perfume with a hint of masculine musk.

"Goodbye," he called as they walked away together toward Ben Ariim's north gate, each of them burdened with their possessions. "Please write! And send word when you're safely in Kal Ariim!"

Temric let out a sigh as soon as Jasmine was out of sight. "That was harder than I expected. I hardly know him, and yet …" He shook his head. "It must be his training."

"Don't be so cold," Larani said in a telling-off tone. "He honestly likes us. I can tell."

"It's not like he's getting any money out of us," Edrion pointed out.

"Maybe he just feels obligated," Temric pointed out.

"He's a favorite." Billie could barely hear Aliiren's voice over the crowd as they moved onto a busier street than the one that ran along the front of the Champion's Keep.

"What does that mean?" she asked.

"It's a gift," Aliiren reminded her, though she didn't need the reminder. She nodded, encouraging him to continue. "Somewhat like your healing. From what I've read, he can create different kinds of spiritual bonds, depending on his intentions, and how open the other person is to the connection. His gift has even more of an effect because he's naturally beautiful, trusting, kind, sweet, and strong of will." He bowed his head. "It's common for people to fall in love with favorites very quickly."

Her heart twinged again. This time it really did feel like jealousy.

So the two of them might be in love?

Of all the people she'd met since she'd left the Kilhells, she'd never felt about anyone like she felt about Aliiren. She knew she was in danger of her heart being broken. But then, her heart had been broken so many times now, would she really feel it?

They would be on the road for days, and would reach Kal Ariim the morning before true night. They would camp together, sleeping near each other if not outright with each other under the same blankets. She was looking forward to all the time they'd spend together, but then what? Would they continue to see each other, or would Temric and Aliiren leave?

She'd committed to becoming a Champion. She couldn't go with them. For the first time, the consequences of her decision felt more like a burden than a welcome responsibility.

"Hey, Billie, you can put your bags in my cart," Temric said. "It's not hard to pull. I can take more."

She smiled. "I was going to tell you that I can take over pulling that cart when you get tired."

"That doesn't sound like a very good idea."

"It's good for me," she assured him. "Lazing around all day every day won't help me heal."

"I can help pull the cart," Aliiren said. "It's a long way to walk. And anyway, you have our tent and blankets in there. It's only fair that everyone takes turns. Except Billie."

Billie bristled, though she appreciated what he was trying to do. "I'm fine. I know how far I can push myself."

Aliiren gave her a look that could be understood in any language, then looked away.

By then their route to the gate was crowded enough that they had to spend all their time maneuvering along the streets without getting separated or bumping into people.

"Why is that Light stone so bright?" Edrion asked once they'd finally passed through the northeast gate. They were on the road with only a scattering of other people, all of whom were out of easy earshot as they walked, rode, or drove small carts pulled by mules or oxen or camels. Forever ago it would have seemed to her that the road was crowded and busy, but now, after walking the streets of Ben Ariim, the road seemed sparsely populated.

The north gate was apparently reserved for large caravans and important persons, while the northeast gate was slated for foot traffic or small groups. Theirs was a smaller road, but no less incredible with its smooth paving, garden walls and decorative light posts. Billie walked backward, gazing at the gates, wondering if she'd ever see such a magnificent place as this city ever again.

"It's because it's a diamond," Aliiren told Edrion.

"Really? Can I see it please?"

Billie had seen diamonds, had even held them in her hands, but the stone didn't tempt her. The city of Ben Ariim was far more precious. She tried to memorize her last sight of it.

Billie understood how arches worked, but it still shocked her how huge the one that dominated the northeast gate was. At the top reclined a pair of massive statues so large that even Roorah couldn't have carried them had they been flesh. They were human, a man and a woman, draped in clothes that even though they were carved, still managed to look delicate and translucent. They wore crowns from which draped strands of precious stones that gleamed in the sunlight. Their hair was obsidian, carved into Thedran coiled curls. They wore gold sandals. But the rest was marble streaked with gold and rose veins. They looked at each other with longing, and their hands clasped over the arch.

On either side of the gates two waterfalls cascaded into basins tiered like most of the other fountains in Ben Ariim, so that the topmost tier was the purest water for drinking. To the outside of the fountains giant date trees grew to nearly match the height of the wall. Someone had covered the ripening dates with silk bags to keep the insects and birds off them.

They were the first of a pair of long lines of date palms that followed the road. An emergency shelter was tucked between the fountains and the gates, in case someone was caught out during true night and the gates had already been closed.

There was so much about Ben Ariim that felt sacred. She'd never heard a hellion scream, never felt uneasy within the walls, never even felt nervous, not even that first night in Ben Ariim when they'd barely made it to the shelter. Which was madness, but it was true. Now that she was leaving Ben Ariim, it made her feel unaccountably sad to leave, just when she'd settled on the idea of fighting to be a part of this city and its people.

All around them were fields of sunflowers, crimson amaranth, blue flax, golden grain …. The colors, textures and patterns were muted, as a long, punishing summer had faded the once-bright colors into pastel harvest tones. The road curved through them, where it would eventually join up with the straight road that traveled directly between Ben Ariim and Kal Ariim to the north. Some of the fields were walled in, as she remembered when she'd traveled a different road not far from this one to Murina's estate. The outermost fence rose up at the horizon, whole trees rooted in thick stone with heavy netting strung between. Occasionally a breeze carried the scent of ripe fruit and the mellow sweetness of dry grain.

"When are you going to call Roorah?" Edrion asked.

"You are such a pest," Larani snipped affectionately, but then she chuckled and looked to Billie. "When *are* you going to call Roorah?"

"Is he safe to come with us?" Temric asked nervously.

"He'll be fine," Edrion said. "You'll see."

Billie wasn't so sure, but she didn't want to leave him without at least saying goodbye. Every time he came when she called with the curroket, she was surprised he answered. As she'd healed and prepared to leave for Kal Ariim, she'd only been able to call for him a handful of times.

Maybe he'd become wild.

Maybe that would be better for him.

And yet …

She loved his funny face, and how he put his head in her arms, and how he liked to follow her. As exciting as it was to ride him, she preferred to walk around with him, or lean on his belly while they lounged by the river. She'd taken a long nap with him by the river last week.

She missed sleeping with him in the stable, blanketed by his mane, or his tail. On especially cold nights he used to curl around her and covered her with both.

She liked the way he snuffled her hair, even when he made it a bit sticky. And she loved the way his eyes gentled when he saw her.

The rope they used for the netting on the outermost wall was thick, certainly thicker than she could break with her hands. The wall was tall, taller than Roorah could leap for certain, though she suspected he might be able to break through, even if the cross posts were as thick as her waist.

They went through a thick wooden gate, and then they were in the desert. By the time they'd joined up with the main road and started properly north toward Kal Ariim the sun was directly over their heads. But it still wasn't wild, at least not wild like it was to the east past the grazing lands where she'd taken Roorah that fateful day when she'd been attacked. The trees and clumps of grass were all tightly clipped by browsing goats and herds of antelope. To their left in the distance, the Jeweled River flowed slowly through reeds and silver-leaved willows, where huge white egrets and even bigger black herons waded among flotillas of napping river otters. If they'd wanted, they could just walk anywhere across the flat land with only an occasional ridge of dark basalt or mass of brush and grass to impede them. It gave her a good view of everything around them for a long, long distance.

She noticed something bright up ahead by the road, and pointed. "What's that?"

"What?" Temric asked.

"That shiny thing." She strained her eyes. "It's like a post, with … oh, it's another lamp post."

"How can you even …" Temric stopped in his tracks and set down the cart. "Billie, when you're writing, is it hard to see the letters?"

That was an odd question to ask now. "What do you mean?"

"Are the letters blurry?"

They had a long way to go, which meant, she supposed, that they'd have to take rests and would have a lot of time to go into detail about things that really didn't matter. "I guess it's like being drunk. But it's more like they fade and move around, and then if I squint, they're easier to see."

Larani and Edrion settled onto the ground and got out their canteens. "Blurry eyesight, drunkenness …" Larani mused. "That's a fair comparison."

Billie felt like she was missing some nuanced meaning of the word blurry. "It's frustrating. I don't know how you can read on and on like you do. Doesn't it bother your eyes?" And then she realized. "I guess with practice, you get used to it."

Temric exchanged a meaningful look with Aliiren.

"What?" she asked. Was this some other shortcoming about herself that everyone knew, but she didn't?

"I think you would learn faster, and find it less frustrating, if you had glasses," Temric said.

She had no idea what he was talking about. "There are glasses that help you read?"

"Yes," he said with a chuckle.

"So, you drink out of the glass, and it helps you read?"

This time Aliiren laughed softly, and she blushed.

"No, not those kind of glasses. Reading glasses," Temric said patiently.

She'd never heard of such a thing. It had to be some complex working of god power. "If there are such things, I wouldn't be able to afford them."

"I wouldn't think they would be," Temric mused. "Aliiren? Are they expensive?"

"Healers often assist people with vision problems," Aliiren said. "I'm surprised that they didn't do something at the healer's college for you."

"What are you saying?" She didn't like the idea that there was something else wrong with her, on top of everything else. "You're making no sense."

"I think your eyes are bad for reading."

"My eyes are perfect!" she protested. "The only one with better sight in my tribe …" And then she realized what she'd almost said.

Her father had better sight than her.

But she had no father. Not anymore

"I think you're far-sighted," Temric told her. "Which is not a bad thing. I mean, it's possible to see badly both at close and far distances. So you *do* have perfectly good vision, for seeing things far away." He squinted to look up the road. "Really, really good distance vision. But up close, I think you can't see as well as I can, or Aliiren."

"Or my mother," she realized, and it became clear how her mother could work so well with needlepoint and sewing and how she laid the colors on the loom in just the right places when she was weaving, and told Billie off because she never could do it correctly.

They hadn't said anything about it at the college, but then, she hadn't complained, and it wasn't like they'd assessed her for anything that specific. "I still don't understand how glasses would help me, unless they do the reading for me?" In which case, why were they forcing her to struggle to learn to read, if such a device existed and was something she might eventually afford?

"They don't read for you. They're lenses, that help your eyes focus at close distances."

Replace her precious lenses? "I'm not going to let anyone put glass inside my eyes!" The idea horrified her.

"No, no. You wear them on your face in front of your eyes," Edrion told her. "Like jewelry. Haven't you seen people wearing things on their faces, frames with glass pieces that are in front of their eyes? Usually, they wear them when they're looking at something small, or when they're reading. They wouldn't wear them all the time."

"Oh." She had seen that, but only a handful of times and she hadn't realized what she was looking at. "I think I understand." Or so she hoped. "That sounds expensive. I suppose I could earn them eventually." Which made her wonder how this training thing would work at the Tower, and how Champions made a living being heroes.

Murina had mentioned more than once that Champions lived in poverty. But then Murina's idea of poverty was quite different from Billie's. Billie's room at the keep was smaller than Murina's smallest tool shed, after all. And the armor that Champions wore was priceless. If she needed them to see, then maybe the keep would make sure she was able to acquire a glass, or a pair, to help her read.

"We'll see about it when we get to Kal Ariim," Temric said enigmatically, which meant he was probably thinking about giving her a gift.

She let out a frustrated sigh. Why did everyone want to keep giving her expensive gifts? "I still think it's a waste of time to teach me to read and write," Billie told him. "If I'm going to be a Champion, I won't need to read." It still seemed daunting, perhaps impossible that she might become a Champion, but she was walking, well, limping her way toward doing just that.

She could hardly wait to begin her training. The very idea made her want to dance.

"Being a Champion isn't just about being a ferocious fighter," Aliiren told her. "There's a lot more to it than that."

"But reading?" she protested.

"And counting," Temric added.

Her gut tensed. "I know. Because of money."

"You've been doing well," Temric said, taking a sip of water. It reminded her to have some water herself.

"Murina has been teaching me about money."

Temric nodded in approval. "I've noticed that you can reliably see coins in groups of four without counting them individually. I wouldn't be surprised if you could start to multiply soon."

Billie made a face. She'd been working on fives as well, but her mind rebelled whenever she tried to work with anything other than coins. Ones, singles, couples, pairs, twins and trios and all the other permutations of tight groups had always made sense long before she'd learned to count. The rest she could compare to sensible things like villages and cities and hunting parties. Unfortunately, that wasn't good enough in Arrak Thedra. A surprising amount of city life revolved around numbers. Large numbers.

"It'll be easier once you get glasses," Temric said. "I promise."

"You promise," she muttered under her breath, worried and annoyed. He was trying to help her. She just didn't want to have to do it. She knew she'd never be any good at it.

What if her being unable to read and count kept her from becoming a Champion? Gods, what if there was some sort of written exam, like Stayce had worried about, and failed, when she'd wanted to become the scribe's new apprentice?

"I'll help," Edrion promised.

"And so will I," Larani said. "And it won't be boring. We'll teach you to play card games. Then it'll be fun."

It wouldn't be, but she'd do anything to make them happy. And if it would help her become a Champion, well, she had no choice.

Aliiren took over pulling the cart for Temric after their rest. When they reached the lamp post, Billie walked off the road a short distance and pulled out her curroket. Roorah recognized its particular pitch and the rhythm of her swing, knew it was her and no one else when she used it. It could be used for other types of signals, she'd been told, but she hadn't learned those yet.

She climbed onto a rock so she was well off the ground. She checked the soundness of the long leather line. The wooden, wing-like part of the instrument was attached at its end. She carefully measured coils of the leather into the fist of her off hand. And then she started swinging the heavy, wooden wing on a short piece of line so that it spun round and around.

It was a fairly simple instrument to play as long as she maintained the correct rhythm. As she swung it in ever-widening circles around her, it began to hum, and then buzz louder and louder. Once she'd played out the line to its full length, the pitch and rhythm that was unique to Roorah's curroket, a hum roar hum roar hum, repeated over and over, so loud that her body quivered with it. It's resonance, though strange compared to the other sounds of nature, at the same time was as musical as a human voice.

She spun it until her arms and shoulders ached, and her breath came hard. Gradually she drew the line back in, until finally she was able to coil it back into her fist a short length at a time. Once she finished bringing it in, she wrapped the leather line around the wooden wing and put it away.

Now they had to wait. Everyone watched the horizon to the east for Roorah.

"How far can he hear that thing?" Larani asked.

"I don't know." Billie tried not to fret. She couldn't bear the thought of Roorah wandering around like a lost dog or pony, maybe looking for her, maybe believing she'd abandoned him. It would be different if he wanted to be alone. She'd miss him, but she wouldn't have this awful feeling that he missed her too, and grieved for her, and felt as if no one wanted him anymore. And who would pull the twigs from his tail, which was so long it dragged the ground, and from his mane that sometimes picked up thorns when he shook it out near needlebrush, and who would rasp his hind talons so they wouldn't get uncomfortably long? What if he got sick? What if he got hurt?

"Maybe I should go east," she fretted. "To Murina's estate, and call from there."

"I thought you said that it would be better if you called from here," Larani said.

"Murina said it would be better," Billie explained. "As part of our learning to work together. She said he'd always have her estate to go to, and that they'd take care of him as much as he'd let them, but that he and I … we have to learn how to do this."

"Then you should continue," Aliiren said gently.

He was right, but she was anxious, as anxious as she'd been when she'd left for Ruvall. This time she didn't believe for one moment that she would find a new life and love and happiness and fulfillment. This time, she knew what it felt like to fail, and not just a little failure. This time, she knew that failure meant so much more pain than a lecture and a beating. This time, she wasn't thinking about the fun she might have and the dreams she might fulfill. This time, she'd committed to doing something that truly mattered to her and to humanity with the experience of terrible failures to let her know that not every choice she made would be easy, or without cost.

*Will I be forced to leave Roorah behind?*

"All right," she said, more to herself than to them, and started walking north again. *He'll be all right. I have to trust him.*

*I have to fight to become a Champion, and this is part of that fight. I can do this.*

*We can do this. Roorah and I will be all right.*

The paving—bricks and stones set in a herringbone pattern—became increasingly covered with dirt and dust, until finally they ended, or were buried completely. Either way, the road had become a relatively flat stretch of dirt with stones lining the sides and parallel lines of stones down the center outlining a wide path where no one walked. "Why is the road divided like this?" she asked.

"The center is the royal road," Aliiren told her. "And we must always walk on the right of it."

"So, we'd be on the other side if we were going to Ben Ariim," she realized.

"Yes."

"Is it like the sacred streets in Ben Ariim?" she asked, remembering being chastised about that.

"No. There's no sacred design in a straight line," Aliiren said. "But it helps keep tradesmen moving between Ben Ariim and Kal Ariim from interfering with each other. Caravans stay to the outermost edge, while people on foot or in small groups stay closer to the center. The royal road between the two sides is for messengers and dignitaries on urgent business only."

Someone ahead of them on the road starting singing. It was strange and haunting, how he used his voice like the singing wild dogs she'd heard sometimes just after dusk at Murina's estate. But unlike the dogs, he used words. Sometimes he sang like a Thedran in between the musical howls and buzzing keening that sometimes harmonized in a way that sounded mystical. His voice could leap great intervals and then would fall away as the dogs sang. Was that Arrak singing?

Thedrans had a clear, sweet way of singing that was utterly beautiful but was very different from the passionate screams and cries of the Kilhells, full-throated and loud and full of heart. And this … this wild singing was also beautiful, and just as different as the singing and chanting in the Kilhells.

The music kept them company until Billie stopped, went off the road, and swung the curroket again.

She hadn't even begun to tire when she saw movement. And maybe it wasn't Roorah, maybe it was another desert horse, but her heart skipped to see it galloping. The long mane and tail streamed back, straw-colored like her Roorah, and the golden body with the dark nose and darkening of the legs …

It was him.

"Roorah!" She threw aside the curroket and started running toward him, running like a fool until her lungs began to burn and exhaustion stabbed through her side. Forced to slow, she half-trotted, half-limped onward until she felt the thunder in the ground from his weight.

And then he was there, circling her. She laughed, coughed, tasted blood but she didn't care.

He pushed his massive head into her arms, and she held him tight. "Roorah," she breathed. "Good boy, Roorah. Good boy." They were together. It had happened. Maybe it shouldn't have mattered, but it did, and now weirdly she felt hope that everything would be all right. "Good boy." She rubbed his face and swept tears from her eyes. He snuffled her shawl, but didn't try to pull it free, thank goodness, because her head probably would have come off with it thanks to how securely Aliiren had attached it. Billie walked along the length of him, feeling along his belly. Someone had clipped designs sacred to Life on his flank. In the center was her badger, teeth bared, body coiled and ready to leap into battle. She chuckled. This had to be Murina's idea.

She walked around the back of him and back to the front. He looked good. He was well-fed, no wounds, and his mane and tail weren't tangled. "Good boy," she praised. "Deba deba."

He went down on his knees first, then tucked his hind legs and settled onto the ground. She used his hind leg to step up, and tossed her bags onto him ahead of her. She made sure they didn't slide as she finished climbing onto him, and then settled on his back. She couldn't really ride him properly astride at the center of his back as she might a pony without a saddle. His back was too broad. But she could sit just behind the hump over his withers with one leg down and the other tucked. Mostly for security, she held onto his mane with one hand and held the straps on her bags with the other.

"Tuk tuk tuk."

He lurched up, front legs straightening first so she felt like she might slide off backward. Her bags, thankfully, didn't pull her off balance as she held them close. Then he leaned forward to get his hind legs under him. She settled back against his water hump, bags thankfully balanced behind her. Without her asking he carried her back toward the road. She directed him a bit by rubbing on one side or the other with her hands, but it was mostly for practice. She could tell he knew that she wanted to go to the road with the people. And not just any people. Her people. Maybe he could smell them on her, could smell Aliiren especially, from when he'd braided her hair.

"Are you sure that's the same desert horse?" Temric asked warily. "He looks bigger."

Billie chuckled. "It's him." With Roorah, she felt like she could do anything now. "It's definitely him." They'd grieved together, and now, together, they would become Champions.

## Chapter Thirty

<><><><><><><><><><><><><><><><><><><><><><><><><><><><><><><><><><><><><>

# On the Road

<><><><><><><><><><><><><><><><><><><><><><><><><><><><><><><><><><><><><>

*The Road Between Ben Ariim and Kal Ariim*
*2nd Meet Day of Fall Month, Meet Day*

Billie thought that riding the distance wouldn't bother her much, especially with the land so flat and with Roorah traveling at an easy gait. *Ha.* It exhausted her just holding on to her bags and keeping her own weight centered as he walked. There was no chance she'd be able to help Temric with his cart, but thankfully Aliiren, Rani and Edri traded off with Temric so he didn't have to pull it by himself. Edrion was very disappointed to learn that Roorah couldn't just carry the cart on his back without a special pack saddle. Despite his incredible size, Roorah's spine did need protection from heavy weights and the skin on his back, though thick, could develop bare spots or even lesions in short order.

By the time dusk came Billie had little thought of who she might lie down beside. She just wanted to sleep. She linked her nodes and checked through her body. Everything was still healing, slowly for her, quickly compared to someone with little or no gift. And of course everything hurt.

If Roorah had been a grass horse she would have worried that having no water and only the little bit of browse he nipped from the sparse offerings along the road would have made him sick, but he seemed perfectly fine. Once he settled, she checked through his body with her healing, confirming what his bright, inquisitive eyes and relaxed posture suggested. He wasn't thirsty, and he wasn't particularly hungry. Once her gift left his body, his tail switched across her body and all that coarse hair covered her. He was sheltering her, like he'd sheltered his former human companion, like, Murina had told her, he would shelter a foal or a member of a herd he'd claimed that had fallen ill. She shifted around, took out her cloak—thank the gods she hadn't sold it after all—and folded it to pad her legs and backside. Her body relaxed as she leaned against him. It was comfortable, and familiar, and he supported her wounded body. Her eyes drooped.

Larani and Edrion built a little fire fueled by dung and some twigs they'd wisely picked up along the way. Billie fell asleep listening to them talking and laughing softly with Aliiren and Temric. She even heard Aliiren chuckle once.

Or maybe that was a dream.

The next day she woke to the sleepy, thin calls of a lone bird. She was ravenous. It was still mostly dark, but a little light glowed at the horizon. In Ruvall, always sleeping inside the dorm behind a locked door, whether it was true night or not, she rarely heard morning birdcalls. And at sea as well as in Ben Ariim, the sea birds rarely seemed to vary in their cries. But here, in the quiet of the desert, she felt like she'd woken at hunting camp on Mount Cross, especially as the bird songs swelled into a cacophony of competing whistles, squeaks, creaks and purrs. The landscape was strange, but she recognized a few of the songs. There, a meadowlark. And there, sparrows traded sharp insults.

She eased her stiff body out from under Roorah's tail into still, icy air and stretched. Larani, Edrion and Temric had curled up together near Temric's hand cart under a combination of cloaks and patchwork blankets. Aliiren slept alone near the cold coals of the campfire, a worn wool blanket draped over his shoulders.

The morning cold made her nose run. She hadn't expected it to be this cold, cold enough to make mist of her breath, but it wasn't nearly as cold as it got in the Kilhells. To loosen up and make some use of herself, she took a walk, picking up dry dung as she went. Not far from them, another group had camped. They had a more comfortable arrangement with a cart at its center and a pair of mules. One mule dozed among his people, stretched out on his side, while the other mule napped upright beside the cart. The standing mule's ear switched in warning in Billie's direction, so she turned around and went back to her own camp.

There were a few tiny sparks in the ashes. Maybe Aliiren stayed up late and had fed the fire.

He looked cold. It would probably wake him, but ... She fetched her cloak and covered him. He made a soft noise, but then visibly relaxed. It made her smile, to see him at peace.

She had work to do.

She got the fire going, and heated water. By the time it started to boil, Aliiren was awake, though he hadn't done much beyond open his eyes. He just watched the fire burn quietly, apparently fascinated by the flames.

She realized, belatedly, that she had no chicory, and she had no idea how to make the tea that everyone in Arrak Thedra drank. She knew how to make chocolate—not as well as the chocolate shops obviously—but they hadn't brought any. It wouldn't be that different though, would it? She drew out a bundle wrapped in waxed paper and opened it. The scent of the tea was sweet and slightly bitter.

"If you add the tea now, it'll be bitter," Aliiren told her. "May I?"

She gave it over to him to tend.

"I boiled eggs last night," he told her. "We can have those for breakfast with some bread and mustard."

Billie nodded. Even now, having gotten somewhat used to it, the softness of his voice felt intimate, and she remembered too well the feeling of his hands as he'd braided her hair.

"It seems like every time I see you, you have bruises," Aliiren said.

She sighed. "I suppose."

"If you become a Champion, I fear that will get worse rather than better."

She hadn't thought about that. "Well, I'm used to it."

"It makes me sad to hear that."

It was a very odd thing to say, and she wasn't sure how to ask him about it. By the time she took a breath to try, Edrion groaned and sat up. "Holy Gods, it got cold last night." And then the rest of them woke, and they had breakfast with Larani, Edrion and Temric providing most of the chatter. She didn't mind. They made her laugh, which also made her cough, but it felt good.

Still, Aliiren's words kept coming back to her as they resumed their long walk to Kal Ariim. Had she become a healer in Ben Ariim, would she had lived a life without bruises? Did most people live lives without bruises and cuts? She remembered how pure Jasmine's skin had been. Aliiren had hardly any scars, and most of them were very fine, barely visible at all. Even Temric had few scars, just a scattering of very small ones on his arms and hands.

Maybe it should have bothered her, but instead she thought that she'd be far more suited to training to become a Champion than a healer. She thought, maybe, she might understand a Champion's life better.

And yet, what they'd all said about reading and counting the day before made her nervous. What would the training be like? How far could she get?

Would they even accept her? Sun Champion had given her a letter to give to them, and he seemed confident that they'd take her in, but still.

She'd gone to the healer's college full of excitement and hope, and her dreams had been stained by disdain and taunts and mockery. This would be better, she decided. Now she was prepared. Now, she knew that she'd have to fight for respect from the beginning. And this time, she expected that fighting would not get her into trouble. If it did, well, clearly Champion training would make no sense, and she might as well ...

What? Give up?

No. She had to give this everything she had. Not just because failing again would hurt.

It was, strangely, Sun Champion as much as her own desire to do something great that spurred her. He wouldn't have pressed her to do this if he thought she would fail. Which meant ...

When they stopped for a midday meal, she had to ask. "Do you ..." She looked to each of her friends in turn. "Do you think, honestly, I can become a Champion?"

"Absolutely," Temric said without hesitation. "I've never met anyone tougher than you."

"I wouldn't cross you," Edrion offered with a grin.

"You survived an ambush, four against one," Larani said. "And that's without the training." A quiet pride filled her as Billie realized that she understood what Larani meant when she said four on one.

"You're the bravest person I've ever met," Aliiren told her softly. "You'll succeed, if you really want it." His golden gaze lifted to meet hers. "Do you want it?"

That intense stare filled her with joy and a sense of power that she hadn't felt in a long time. "Oh yes." She'd been hesitant only because she feared failure. But now, with all of them so sure of her, she allowed herself to believe.

Aliiren closed his eyes, as if he didn't want to see her so excited about it. Was it because he knew something about Champions that she didn't? Or was it something else? She started to ask if he had anything against her becoming a Champion, but decided against it. Already, the others were looking at him like he was throwing water on their cooking fire. She would ask him later, in private.

His reticence did make her wonder, though, if she was reaching for something beyond her leap.

*No. I can do this.*

All she had to do was prove it.

✣

*Kal Ariim*
*2<sup>nd</sup> Labor Day of Fall Month*

WHERE THE WALLS OF BEN ARIIM HAD AN ENTRANCING GEOMETRY, KAL Ariim had taken that geometry and encrusted it with countless statues, waterfalls, sculptures and canals. And all the way around Kal Ariim, the fields had been planted with crops that formed blessings, making them appear like ornate rugs. Billie spent most of the approach to the city with her eyes wide, silent with astonishment.

Aside from telling Billie that she wasn't allowed to ride Roorah through the city and that she had to have a hand in his mane while leading him, the guards permitted them to enter without any trouble. Fortunately, Roorah seemed content to amble alongside her, his nose close to her shoulder, steaming her shawl and braided hair. To abide by the rules she held a fistful of his long mane in her left hand, which she braced on her shoulder because her wounded bicep, though healing well, hurt so much it felt like it was murdering her. Rani and Edri pulled the cart together with Billie's bags inside it, matching strides so Rani wouldn't step on Edri's heels.

Once they were within the walls, the shock of all that splendor grew even greater. Kal Ariim had roads laid out in blessings like Ben Ariim, but in addition every structure was imbued with the sacred. Even common buildings were carved deeply with blessings, the very tiles on the roofs printed with blessings. The profusion of temples all had tall, elaborate spires with delicate spiral staircases corkscrewing around the outside of them that may or may not have been built with the intention to allow a person to climb them. Each spire held multiple bells that rang the hours in a musical pattern, which was probably the only thing that kept the countless colorful birds in the trees and on buildings from perching there. Lamp posts stood everywhere, not just at intersections but spaced closely along the streets, while every alcove held at least one light, or was edged in smaller stones. The city sparkled even by day. She wondered how it would look at night.

Aliiren had an expression like he didn't approve, but he didn't say anything against anything, so maybe he was just tired. Still, she couldn't imagine why he didn't find all of this amazing.

Then again, he'd been here before. She remembered that now.

She didn't know if Roorah had been here before, or if he was used to crowds, but he stayed with her sweetly and didn't menace anyone. He preened whenever someone said something about him, which made her absolutely certain that he understood Thedran better than he let on.

"It's like a festival made love to Ben Ariim and had a huge family of beautiful neighborhoods," Edrion gushed.

Larani laughed. "You're so silly. But it is beautiful. I'm so glad we came here!"

"I thought Ben Ariim was impressive," Temric marveled.

"I believe the Champion Towers are this way," Aliiren said, and led the way. He made sure that when they walked on sacred streets, they all faced the correct way even before they set foot on the paving. "If you're caught going the wrong way, they'll arrest you," Aliiren warned. "So be careful and watch where you're going."

"Who will arrest us?" Temric asked, perturbed.

"There's an organized city guard, and all the private guards deliver miscreants to them," Aliiren explained. "It doesn't matter who catches you at it. You'll end up in the same jail, and you do not want to be incarcerated in this city. They don't tolerate mistakes, however innocently made. They have a strict code of laws, and ignorance will not excuse you from punishment."

"Like what kind of laws?" Larani asked nervously.

"Begging and gambling are allowed only in certain areas," Aliiren told her. "Brawls and duels that result in the injury of a bystander are severely punished. Animals and children may not be beaten under any circumstances. If food that you sell causes illness, you'll be fined or worse. Written contracts must be honored. And you must obey any lawful order given by a city guard or councilperson. That means that if you're caught doing a crime, and run, the running will add to your sentence."

"That's pretty strict," Edrion said soberly, while Billie thought about Aliiren's words. She'd have to be careful, but it sounded like it wouldn't be too hard to stay out of trouble.

"Those are only a tiny fraction of the laws."

Temric halted in the street. "Seriously?"

Aliiren edged to the side of the street, and they all followed him. He pointed to a wall with some sort of framed document on it. "There's a sign. No one is permitted to leave their carts unattended on this street. When it's posted like that, it's a law, and must not be disobeyed."

*I have to read to stay out of trouble?* "Oh gods," she breathed before she managed to get control of herself again.

For reasons that Billie didn't understand at the time, Stayce had desperately wanted to learn how to read and write. When Melissa chose Andrea instead of Stayce as an apprentice, their father had told Stayce that it was more important to speak to the living than read words of the dead anyway, an opinion that Billie had shared with him.

She'd never felt this desperate wish to read before.

"I'll help as much as I can," Temric assured Billie. "And I'm sure they'll teach you about the laws at the Towers. That only makes sense. Right?"

She hoped so, anyway.

Larani and Edrion exchanged a long look. "We're going to find some Rill," Larani said, "and learn more about the laws." She went to Billie and hugged her hard. Billie relaxed in her arms and hugged her back. "We'll come visit you at the Champion's—Champion Towers—and tell you what we learn. And you ..." She hugged Temric while Edrion hugged Billie. "Better tell her where you're staying, so we can find you."

"You are staying together, right?" Edrion asked Aliiren. "You and Temric?"

Aliiren nodded. "At first. I may decide to live at a nearby temple, depending on the situation."

She hadn't expected to part so soon from her new-found family. She had no idea if her training would allow her to see them, or for them to visit her. She'd already suspected that by the time she completed her training, they might all be gone, or so far apart they might never all meet again. But this ... this felt like everyone was already saying goodbye forever.

She schooled her expression. They'd been forced together by accident, not choice, and she doubted that any of them had any expectation of staying together any longer than they already had. The others had families, and friends, except maybe Aliiren, and he had his temple no matter what happened. They'd had lives without her, and they would go on living those lives without her.

At the same time, she believed fiercely with all her heart that no matter how far they traveled or how much time passed, she was one of them, and they would be a part of her until she died. Their friendships had been forged through adversity. She hadn't thought about it until now, but it was similar to what kept her village, and even her family, together. It didn't matter that much of that adversity was gone. She knew that if they were at all able, they would visit her, and she would do her best to be with them whenever she could. It wasn't the same as staying together, but she wouldn't be alone. Not anymore.

"Hey." Edrion set his hand on Billie's shoulder. "It's going to be all right. You'll see."

Captain Lily's words, spoken so long ago after the *Silver Parrot* had wrecked, came back to her all at once, whispered to her and her alone.

*Maybe you don't care about your life. Maybe you'd rather drown than face the possibility that your brother is already dead. Fine. There will be one less Kilhellion in the world. Only your family will miss you. But what about them?*

*They'll die with you.*

But he was wrong. They didn't die. They survived.

*We survived because we stayed together and took care of each other.*

She might not know much about Champions beyond stories, some of which might not be true, but she did know that they led dangerous lives. These people had already faced grave danger because of her. But she would never push them away, like the captain seemed to have expected her to do. They were her friends, her family now. They were in this life together.

There was one thing that stories about Champions made clear. They were alone. They decided alone, acted alone, and often died alone. Even if they had an army behind them, or a squire to help them, in the end they stood at the front alone, for they were the only ones who refused to run if things got too bad. It was who they were. The first to charge into danger, and the last ones standing between evil and good. If those stories were true, she suspected that her training would have less to do with winning, and more to do with doing the right thing at moments like these.

But that didn't mean that those Champions didn't have family, friends, even lovers. Those people were part of what Champions protected. Maybe those same people were part of what made Champions so devoted, and what kept Champions from hesitating when faced with world's most terrifying and daunting challenges.

This wouldn't be like going to Ruvall to train, after which she would have returned home to start her work. She wouldn't be acting as her friends' personal Champion. And Aliiren wouldn't be by her side, like she'd pretended that Brian would have been as a Mage fighting alongside Billie the Champion of Mt. Cross.

She had to learn to work alone, for anyone who needed her, regardless of how they felt about her, or how she felt about them. It felt strange, to think that she would devote her life to something other than the people she loved. Even as she claimed the people she loved as family, she had to think of the wider world as her tribe.

"Billie?" Aliiren inquired even more softly than usual.

She smiled for him. "I ... should go on alone," she decided. "I'll get a Gurra to guide me."

*Like before, like it always has been, it will be their choice to visit me when they want, but this path, a Champion's life ... I have to figure this out by myself.*

"Are you sure?" Temric said. "I'd love to see the Towers. Let's go together, all of us."

The more she thought about it, the more she knew that it was right for her to go there without her friends. "I'm sure." Her first hunt without help, the chieftain had shadowed her. Although he didn't help at all, his presence alone made it very different from her first hunt entirely by herself. Besides, what would the Champions think if she turned up with all of her friends? Looking through their eyes, she would suspect that her friends had dared her to try, rather than Billie deciding to do it on her own.

Everyone hugged her again, except Aliiren. He kept back, Temric standing expectantly a few paces away, while Larani and Edrion walked away, chatting cheerfully with each other.

"I'd like to speak with Aliiren, alone, if that's all right," Billie told Temric just as the two men turned to walk away as well.

Aliiren stopped and looked back at her, his eyes large with surprise.

"Of course. I'll just walk this way a couple of blocks," Temric told them, pointing down the street. He had a knowing look on his face, and a trace of a smirk. What was that about?

Aliiren crossed his arms and looked down and to the side.

She hadn't realized how awkward this would be. "I …." She felt like she was asking the wrong question, but pressed onward with a sigh. "Do you have something against my becoming a Champion?"

His gaze jerked up to her eyes and his lips parted. After a moment, he pressed his mouth into a line and shook his head.

"Are you sure? Because something's wrong. I'd like to think I know you at least that well."

A delicate blush colored his cheeks, and he looked away again, this time clasping his hands behind his back. "I shouldn't have said no. I'm sorry."

She was completely lost now. "I don't understand."

"It wasn't meant as a lie. I don't have anything against you becoming a Champion, not exactly. I think you will be one of the best this city has ever seen." His arms tensed and he shifted his weight. Thank goodness he wasn't looking at her face, because those words of praise meant more to her than everyone else's support put together. "My feelings are personal."

A warmth grew in her belly and the city's smoke-tinged air suddenly felt stifling.

"I don't want you to die," he said softly. "Not for this city. Not for some selfish, irresponsible piece of shit who wants to prove himself to a guild's petty tyrant." She'd never heard him curse before, and the word sounded both awkward and more emphatic coming from him. "Not here, where Kilhellions are thought of as something less-than, in the heat and the dust." His arms swept out and he looked around him, his eyes narrowed with pain, his face lined with emotions she hadn't known he'd held within him. "I see you surrounded by mountains and clear streams, with the other wild beings, living and fighting and loving as free as the wind."

Her heart pounded in her ears. "You want me to go back home?"

"No!" He spoke the word softly but with so much emphasis it felt like a shout. "No," he said again softly, and touched her hand.

She took his hand and held it tightly. His hand was hot, and strong, and gripped her back.

"No," he said, looking into her eyes. "I want you to be happy, Billie. That's all. I want you to be happy, and I'm afraid this city, this work … Are you *sure*? Because even if you learn to love this place, I'm afraid it won't love you back like you deserve."

She knew it wouldn't love her back. That didn't matter. But the question of whether she could learn to love Kal Ariim was new. "Well, if Kal Ariim doesn't want me, it isn't as if I'd have to stay in Kal Ariim once I became a Champion. Right?" She wasn't sure what her obligations to Kal Ariim would be, if any.

A muscle on his cheek twitched. "No. You wouldn't have to stay."

But Aliiren would stay, if not in Kal Ariim, then Ben Ariim.

He'd been honest with her. Obviously, it hadn't been easy for him to voice feelings that were less about living a life as a Light Protector and more about who he was as a man. It was a gift, a *real* gift, and she could think of only one way to thank him. "It doesn't matter if I'm wanted or not. I'll do what I have to, wherever I am," she reminded him. "Anyway, the people I love are here. I love you, Aliiren."

He yanked her into his arms. Reflexively she wrapped her arms around him and squeezed. The power in his body answered in kind, perfectly balanced with hers. His incense-laden scent suffused her being. Their combined strength bonded them in a way she'd never felt before, as if only Death could separate them. She tucked her head close against his, and he rocked her, the subtle sway of their bodies an echo of the trials they'd endured on the sea.

In his arms, she felt as if she could breathe again, and the heat didn't seem so bad. She would learn to love the desert, because Aliiren was of the desert, and she loved him fiercely.

They held each other close for a long time. He said goodbye so softly that she wasn't sure she heard it. He seemed to evaporate from within her arms. A heartbeat later she was looking at his back as he walked to meet Temric, who waited under a sign she couldn't read by a building at the end of the block.

Roorah let out a dissatisfied huff and took a step closer to Billie. She set a hand up on his shoulder. "It's all right," she assured him. "We're all right."

She stood there a long time, long after they'd vanished around a corner. The bright city seemed bleak now, and full of traps. Every bit of paper on a wall and every bronze plaque made her wonder what law she might be breaking. At the same time, she felt lighter and more free, more like the young woman she'd been when she left for Ruvall.

*I told him I loved him, and he hugged me.*

*I think he loves me too, even if it's not in the same way.*

"Come on, Roorah," she said in Arrak, and followed a person who looked like they knew where they were going. "Let's find a Gurra."

At least she still had Roorah with her.

But would she be able to keep him at the Towers?

## Chapter Thirty-One

<<<<<<<<<<<<<<<<<<<<<<<<<<<<<<<<<<<<<<<<<<<<<<<<<<<<<<<<

# Homecoming

<<<<<<<<<<<<<<<<<<<<<<<<<<<<<<<<<<<<<<<<<<<<<<<<<<<<<<<<

*The Champion Towers, Kal Ariim*
*2nd Labor Day of Fall Month*

Compared to the other buildings in this part of Kal Ariim, which had carvings of people and creatures all over them, including completely unrecognizable things that were crafted from half-forgotten dreams, or nightmares, the Champion Towers looked plain. A trim of blessings ran around the tops of the walls, and a broad band of blessings covered the base of the walls from the paving to a line higher than Roorah could touch with his nose while standing on his hind legs.

But in its own way, it was the most impressive building she'd seen in Kal Ariim so far.

"The Champion Towers," the Gurra informed her.

Thanks to Murina's lessons, Billie measured out enough small coins to pay him well with a confidence she'd never had before. "Thank you," she told him faintly. The Gurra nodded and ran off with his earnings.

A tower stood at each corner of the rectangular keep, and the walls between those towers were nearly as tall as the towers themselves. The massive stones—she couldn't imagine what could have possibly lifted them up so high—had such a tight fit that a hair couldn't have fit between them. It was almost as if the weight of each stone had mated it perfectly to the one beneath. There was a lone entrance, and it was as large as

Ben Ariim's north gate. Eerily, the doors were not stone, but steel bars, allowing her to see into a deep tunnel that went through those walls. On either side within the tunnel was a door, suggesting that there were rooms within the walls themselves. The view into the space beyond was blocked by a basalt wall with stones cut to form a beehive pattern. Light came in from either side of that wall, so she knew the tunnel didn't just end there.

Each bar on the doors were connected to the other bars by large steel blessings formed of bands and wires. Additionally, each bar was etched with blessings. She gripped one. It felt cool, strong. Her palm tingled. She couldn't channel faerus, so she knew that she wasn't sensing a blessing. It was just nerves. But she didn't need to channel faerus to sense the strength of the gate, and the power of the whole place. It had streets on all sides, an island surrounded by a moat of humanity that went about their business with no regard to this place. They were used to it being there.

They took it for granted, like every other wonder in Kal Ariim.

"Hello?" Her voice seemed to fall flat against the basalt wall. She waited, but no one came.

There had to be a bell or something to let someone know she was here.

Roorah snuffled the metal, then licked it experimentally while Billie went to the right of the gate to look for a small door like the one Aliiren had opened at the temple where the demon attack had happened. It would probably have its own blessing to keep hellions from using the bell to torment the Champions over true night.

Roorah started running a tusk along the bar, head bobbing. The bar rang as he rasped the long, curved ivory along the steel.

Despite her nervousness, she chuckled. "What are you doing?"

He hooked his talons around the base of a bar and tugged. The bars were set into a steel base as thick as her arm. It wasn't going to yield. At least she didn't think so.

He pushed his forehead into the gate, then rasped his other tusk against the bars.

"You're going to chip your tusk," she warned him, and went to the other side. There, among the blessings, she found a small door. She opened it, and inside she found a bar. She tugged, but it didn't shift, so she turned it, and it made a grating noise as it moved. The more she turned it, the tighter it got until she was forced to let go.

She barely got her hand out of the way in time as it spun. A bright ringing sound cut through the air somewhere beyond the end of the tunnel.

Roorah jerked back from the gate and puffed up, and then he growled. His mane stood up every which way. She had a hard time deciding if his fear was cute or terrifying.

"It's all right," she promised him. "Don't worry. It's just a bell."

He huffed, and his mane settled. His coat was still a bit fluffed up, though. Billie set her hand on his neck and patted him. "Good boy. Good Roorah."

He huffed again, but then his eyes gentled as she scratched along his neck. Sticky dirt clumped under her fingernails. He needed a bath. Maybe later they could find a place to go swimming. She wondered, a bit sourly, if there would be a law against him swimming in a canal.

A young man about Brian's age, short and fair with pale curls, came into the tunnel in front of the wall on the left side and stopped. She was a little surprised herself. It was the first time in a long time she couldn't roughly place someone's ancestry at a glance. Though he wasn't tall, he was heavy in the shoulders and legs and thick in the jaw. He wore little better than rags, clothes in a rough weave of cloth with holes and patches, stained with dirt and sweat and who knew what else. Murina's words came back to her yet again, about living in poverty. She didn't mind. It would feel natural to her, as living on the verge of being wiped out by a single storm had felt on Mt. Cross.

"The keep is closed to visitors. If you have business with a Champion, you'll have to go to the seneschal's hall across the street." He pointed behind her.

Billie looked over her shoulder. There were several doors along a long line of buildings that formed a sizable wall. "Which one?"

"Can't you r—" He stopped himself, but she knew what he was going to say. Her gut knotted and her face warmed. "Why are you here?"

"Sun Champion sent me. I'm supposed to train here." She hoped this wasn't going to be like Ruvall all over again. She held her growing disappointment tightly inside her. *In no way am I going to allow them to make me feel ashamed of who I am. Not anymore.*

His eyes widened and his lips parted. "*You're* the Kilhellion?"

"Do I look Sothron?" she countered, trying not to sound irritated.

"You're a woman?"

She had to admit it sounded unlikely to her too. "Last I checked, yes."

"Wait here." He went back the way he came.

She stroked Roorah, keeping him as content as she could while they stood in the sun. It was hot, as usual, but she wasn't sweating like she had in Ruvall. No, this was a dry heat, at the tail end of a long, seemingly endless summer, a heat that raked her throat with thirst and felt like a heavy weight on her shoulders.

Finally, a man with fair skin, gray hair and a short gray beard lumbered into view with the one from before close behind. The older man wore gray linens—simple work clothes without the gores and darts worn by Thedrans—armed with a single broadsword sheathed in plain steel. They both stopped in the same place as before. To her, he looked Markan. Maybe. She supposed it didn't matter.

The graybeard looked over not Billie, but Roorah. It wasn't until he'd had a long look at the desert horse that he finally looked her over. "Bad Dog?"

She wasn't sure she wanted to answer to that name, but she guessed it was part of the training. "Yes."

"I like the idea of Red Dog better. Or perhaps Blood Dog. I will think on it. The desert horse: does he have a name?" The gray man's—Champion's—voice was rough, and had a heavy Markan accent with the attendant, somewhat stilted formality that sounded a lot more natural and flowing when speaking Markan instead of Thedran.

"Roorah."

"This is the horse you saved?"

She knew a message had been sent ahead. She'd had no idea that the message had held so much about her. She wondered what else this person knew. "Yes. May I have your name?" she asked in Markan.

"Ironhand." He looked Roorah over again speculatively. "Roorah can come in for now," he told her, persisting in speaking Thedran, "but you need to keep him elsewhere if you're to train here."

Billie nodded, disappointed but not surprised. She'd expected as much, though the 'if' in his words now had her worried. "I have a friend who has a cousin with a place just north of Kal Ariim."

"How far from here?" Ironhand asked.

"I have yet to discover that," she answered, instinctively matching the more formal cadence of his Thedran.

"Hmm." He went to the gate and set his hand on a bar. One of the blessings near his hand made a scraping, squeaky noise, and then a clunk, though she didn't see anything move. He jerked up on something behind a blessing on his side and pulled toward himself. A large section of the gate hinged open from the middle. It had an irregular top hidden in part by blessings, and the bottom was uneven too, helping disguise its presence within the larger gate of which it was a part.

Billie stepped through, and Ironhand made way for Roorah when the desert horse followed her in. Roorah snuffled Ironhand, then snorted like he'd sniffed up something irritating. His tail switched.

"Be nice," Billie warned Roorah as he then stretched his neck to sniff at the other person, who'd tried to edge around her to shut the gate. She kept a hand on Roorah's neck, not that she could stop him if he decided to bite either of the men. Finally, Roorah allowed the younger man to pass, and he shut the gate.

"How long have you lived in Arrak Thedra?" Ironhand asked.

Time. She wondered if he would refuse to train her if she couldn't describe it except in the Kilhellion way. Fortunately, she knew what month they were in. "Not long. I left Ruvall just before a Sun festival, and I celebrated the next one in Ben Ariim." She'd stayed with Roorah at the estate in the desert for the Sun festival. At the time she didn't feel like celebrating anything. She'd picked at the buffet a bit, and had stayed the night with someone looking for a fling, but mostly she'd thought about her family and what they might be doing besides drumming and dancing around the bonfire within Torath's calendar stones. "And now it's autumn. So ... a year and ..." She silently recited the months after the Sun Month, tapping her fingers surreptitiously. "Three months?" Fall wouldn't be over for some time, so she was pretty sure she wasn't supposed to include it in her count. Or was she?

Gods, counting was so weird.

Ironhand nodded and started walking. At the end of the tunnel, they turned left, though it looked like turning right led to the same space.

It was a courtyard, like the keep in Ben Ariim had, but it was massive. There was a muddy pond, and pits, and ladders, and ramshackle sheds made of timber with gaps and wooden doors. There was a path all the way around the outer edge, and doors leading into various buildings. There weren't any people about. She smelled meat cooking, and spicy things.

In the courtyard's center was a large, round stone building with mostly open walls. Stairs led down to darkness underneath. Neighboring stairs led up to an area with no walls raised a person's height above the ground. A waist-high rail stood in place of walls. Stairs within that space led up to the rooftop, where there was another waist-high rail. In the middle of that rooftop space was a little tower and room at the top of the tower's roof to stand and survey the entire courtyard.

All around the courtyard open crates and barrels held wooden swords and daggers, blunted metal weapons, shields, balls, something that looked like a mummified severed hand ... was that real?

"The obstacle course," Ironhand told her after she'd had a chance to look around. "What do you think?"

"Looks like fun," she admitted. A lot more fun than trading bruises near the tree line with her parents and siblings while the ponies grazed in the meadow.

There was a rope bridge over the pond. She grinned, thinking about how much fun it would be to flip Brian off the bridge into the water.

Brian.

She couldn't let herself think about him too much. Not now, anyway.

Except … he would have loved this.

He would have cheered her on. With him as a Mage and her as a Champion, together, they could have defeated anything. Even a hellion.

He hadn't lived long enough for the two of them to find and live that dream.

Roorah ambled over to the pond. His lips pulled back after he sniffed the water, and he made a grimace that looked absolutely ferocious. But then he waded in and flopped over into water, and rolled onto his back. A tremendous wave rushed up the pond's banks as he rolled back onto his side. He let out a contented sigh.

"So tell me," Ironhand said abruptly, still watching Roorah. "Why do you want to become a Champion?"

His friend, dog, whatever person it was shadowing them now, made his way among the obstacles across the arena and disappeared through a doorway. They were alone now, and she hadn't given an answer.

She suspected that his question had a deep purpose. She dreaded the possibility that, like her father, he wondered if she cared more about being important than serving. "Not to become a hero. I don't think I will ever be that. But I will do everything I can to protect—" It struck her then, why she wanted this so much. She smiled. For the first time since she'd left home, things finally made sense.

Ironhand Champion smiled back at her and lifted his shaggy gray brows. She didn't think Champions got old enough to go gray. He would be someone to listen to, and learn from. "Is something funny?" he asked.

She took a breath, and a moment to put her giddy thoughts into sober words, but those words kept running around in circles like children playing a game with no actual rules. She grinned and decided that trying to speak seriously now would be a mistake anyway. "Have you ever set your mind on doing something for someone, been kicked in the teeth when you tried, and then realized it didn't matter? It wasn't so much that you wanted to help *them*, exactly. What matters is that someone was there when they needed it, no matter who they were, or whether they'd give thanks. In a way, it's easier without the thanks." She hoped that made sense. The words weren't quite right. It was just a feeling.

He just kept smiling.

She sighed. *Oh well.* "Well, that's why I want to train to become a Champion. Because it doesn't matter at the end of the day who I help, or how. Someone has to be there, to protect people. I'm willing, as long as I'm able." She doubted he would ever understand why she was smiling, or why this healed her heart the longer she thought about it. "I hope Champions don't have to be heroes, because no one will ever look up to me. I don't think I'd like it if they did. I would only disappoint them. But if I could be someone that people could ask for help knowing I am here for all of humanity—*that* I want to do. That's what I want to learn to become—someone who can help keep the worst things in the world from hurting people who have no one else to protect them. Can you teach that to me?"

"I'll help you become stronger, faster, smarter, and trickier. The rest is up to you."

That sounded fair. "When do we begin?"

"We already have," he said. "Are you ready?"

Her heart pounded as hard as the cliff drums she would never hear again.

*They will always be within me.*

Billie walked toward a barrel filled with practice weapons. Ironhand took up a slightly faster place. She laughed and sprinted for it, reaching, hoping …

And seized her future with both hands.

## Chapter Thirty-Two

◇◇◇◇◇◇◇◇◇◇◇◇◇◇◇◇◇◇◇◇◇◇◇◇◇◇◇◇◇◇◇◇◇◇◇◇◇◇◇◇◇◇◇◇◇◇◇◇◇◇

# The Helarin

◇◇◇◇◇◇◇◇◇◇◇◇◇◇◇◇◇◇◇◇◇◇◇◇◇◇◇◇◇◇◇◇◇◇◇◇◇◇◇◇◇◇◇◇◇◇◇◇◇◇

Sheriien's heart pounded in his chest as he waited in the helarin's tiny entry room. He'd never seen the helarin before. He was pretty sure that had been his good fortune. He remained rooted to the mat by the door, unwilling to set foot on the pristine, glossy black tile floor. A bench woven of twisted wood beckoned, but it looked like a trap, rather than something meant to offer him comfort. The three cushions on it didn't improve that impression. They were thick, square, made of fine linen with silk tops. The edges were embroidered with green and black flowers. They had deep, hungry, crimson throats and long tongues of red fading to purple and tipped in yellow. There was something unnaturally fascinating about those tongues.

He tore his gaze away. He'd only been in this room once before, when he'd made his promise.

*What do promises mean to a helarin?*

*I gave five drops of my blood, and I don't want to find out what would happen if I broke my promise.*

*I should have never made that promise.*

A short door beside the bench remained closed. He was grateful for that too.

The silence was unbearable.

He jumped inside his skin when the door handle clicked, and the brass latch within the handle, shaped like the flower's tongue, flipped. The door cracked open.

His throat was so dry, he wasn't sure he could speak. A voice inside him screamed for him to run, but he couldn't move. He was frozen, too scared even to tremble.

The darkness behind that crack was so deep, he would have sworn it was true night inside the room beyond. He didn't dare pray that the crack wouldn't widen. The Gods of Humanity would not hear him. He wondered, if They noticed him, if They would seek to destroy him.

The idea of praying to the Hellion Gods would have been insane.

*I'm not that far gone.*

"They reached Kal Ariim?" The voice was ambiguous as to gender, but sounded aged. He hoped the subtle edge of anger wasn't directed at him.

"Yes. All but the favorite."

"Did the Kilhellion and the others stay together?" The voice seemed satisfied with his first answer. He started to believe that he would survive this, assuming his next answer was also deemed acceptable.

He feared that it wouldn't be. He choked on his first attempt to speak. "They separated. The Kilhellion went to the Champion Towers. The Rill went to the market district and made friends with the Butterfly Clan. The Protector and the pale Sothroner went to the Mulberry Hospitality Home on Forgotten River Street." It had taken every bit of his wit and strength to do the work without being seen and without asking for help, even from a single Gurra. There was a moment when he was sure he'd lost track of the Rill entirely, but miraculously, he'd found them again.

"Did you put the envelopes where I asked you?"

"Yes."

"I'll send for you when I need you again. You may leave." The door shut with a click, the tongue-shaped latch flicking suggestively as it lifted and fell back into place.

He carefully turned on the mat and opened the outside door. The cloudy sky had darkened substantially since he'd stepped inside the helarin's lair. Rain was coming. He stepped out onto the correct flagstone and shut the door behind him.

He had no idea what he'd done, and he didn't want to know. Unfortunately, he suspected that he would not only find out, but he would be involved.

If the helarin didn't kill him, the Kilhellion probably would, just like she'd killed his brother.

He was too frightened to be angry at anyone for his brother's death. And he was too frightened to blame anyone but himself for being involved in this. Sheriien crossed his arms tightly over his chest against a gust of icy-cold wind. He'd only taken a few steps when it began to sprinkle, and then pour frigid rain that quickly soaked his clothes. He wished without hope that somehow it would wash him clean.

# Thank You!

There are few things that come to fruition through the work of one person alone. I want to give special thanks first to Rory for his imagination, inspiration, insight, and the initial ideas for the weird and beautiful world that Billie and her friends live on. Melissa, Janene, Sondra, Jacob, Linda, and Rick encouraged me and gave me insightful feedback on the early manifestations of what was originally called 'Mayhem'. They continued to support me on this final version, along with Shawna and Raven, and gave me so much fantastic feedback that I was able to get at the heart of this story.

This book wouldn't exist without my original mentor Mary Rosenblum, who sat me down after a devastating critique group session (my first ever) for the original first chapter of this book. She got me a tissue, and then patiently went over my first chapter sentence by sentence to help me see that it wasn't the story at fault, but the prose of an inexperienced writer. Her son later read the whole first draft, and helped me see what really mattered in this world to a reader.

Mary's passing left a huge hole in the Pacific NW writer and aviator communities. RIP, Mary.

I have to give special thanks to, and express my gratitude for, Norman E. Hartman, who was an integral part of that first writer's group. I had nearly given up on publishing the original book after years of near misses with agents and publishers. Sometime in the mid-1990's he stopped me in a hallway at a convention and asked me if my book had ever been published, because he wanted to read it. "I don't remember what you called it," he said, "but I remember a woman riding a skeleton horse across the ocean and ever since I wanted to find out what happened next."

Thank you too, dear reader. You're a part of this world now. The story continues in *To Free the Wind: Book Two of the True Dawn series*. Because I split up and expanded the book into a series, the rider on the skeleton horse is many books away, but she *will* make that ride to be with the man she loves. I'll write that scene better this time for Norm: science fiction author, friend, and my first 'wild' fan. RIP, Norm.